ALEX

In the Company of Snipers

Book 1

Irish Winters

COPYRIGHT

ALEX; In the Company of Snipers, 1

Cover design and author photo by Kelli Ann Morgan,
http://www.inspirecreativeservices.com

Interior book design by Bob Houston eBook Formatting

ISBN Paperback: 978-1-942895-03-9
ISBN eBook: 978-1-942895-04-6
Library of Congress Control Number: 2013956825

Irish Winters can be contacted at
http://www.irishwinters.com or irishwinters.blogspot.com

In the Company of Snipers

You can find Irish Winters on Facebook:
https://www.facebook.com/author.irishwinters

On Twitter: https://twitter.com/irishwinters1

For news on upcoming releases, sign up for Irish Winters' Newsletter at IrishWinters.com.

For more information about all my books, visit IrishWinters.com.

IN THE COMPANY OF SNIPERS

This series revolves around ex-Marine scout sniper, Alex Stewart, and his covert surveillance company, The TEAM, home-based out of Alexandria, Virginia. An obsessive patriot and workaholic, he created the company to give ex-military snipers like him a chance at returning to civilian life with a decent job.

This is not a serial with each book ending at a cliffhanger. I wouldn't do that to you. *In the Company of Snipers* is a collection of passionate love stories involving women and men who are tough enough to take on the world alone. Each is a stand-alone read, where in the course of an active TEAM operation, one agent comes face to face with his or her demons. The men and women I write about are all patriots and warriors, dealing with what they've lived through or the mistakes they've made

Spoiler alert: Every novel contains adult scenes including sexual situations (some explicit), language, and violence. I don't write sweet romance, so be forewarned.

At the end of each story, it's my hope that you, along with my heroes, will come to realize...

Love changes everything.

One

Kelsey

Kelsey sat down within the perfect cover of green pines and greener ferns. She had been walking for what—hours? Days? She wasn't sure. One minute walking through the forest seemed logical, but the next, she couldn't remember where she was going. Where was she? What happened? How long ago?

Nothing made sense. All she knew was she had to get away from—something. Whatever had initially propelled her into the woods, it must have been bad, or she wouldn't have this nagging feeling she had to keep moving. Maybe if she sat for a minute, she would remember?

Maybe not…

She pressed dirty fingers to her swollen cheek. Her head hurt the worst, but every muscle all the way down to her bones ached, too. Blood oozed from patches of scrapped skin she didn't know how she got in the first place. Sharp stabbing lights forced her eyes shut until it was too much effort to walk. She leaned against something solid. A wall. Why a wall was in the middle of the forest never crossed her mind. She had already slipped past the world where things made sense. It was hard to focus, much less think straight. Shock and slumber beckoned. The wall felt—safe.

From branches high overhead, a nosey chipmunk scolded, annoyed he had a new neighbor. The late afternoon sun shone down through layers of pine, casting a dusty beam of golden light as it fell. Insects buzzed. Kelsey closed her eyes to the gentle rhythm of nature. She relaxed. Simple thoughts flickered behind her eyelids. *Stay. Hold. Be still.*

She sighed in total surrender. *Okay. I can do that.*

Alex

No. It can't be. This is impossible.

Alex Stewart watched the Air Force reconnaissance footage, a black and white video feed that displayed a solitary man crouching outside a cave somewhere in eastern Afghanistan.

This wasn't supposed to happen.

The bearded man in the footage laughed into a satellite phone even as he kept nervous watch overhead. Smoking craters and debris pockmarked the winding road up to the cave, but stopped short. As the picture drew in, it became apparent the cave remained untouched. The surgical strike wasn't even close.

He lied to me. That bastard Rod Kensington lied.

Peering closer, Alex carved both hands through his hair, wanting to pull it out. Another video of smoking vehicles appeared on his computer screen. Darkly veiled women huddled around a prostrate man on the ground. Somber children stood nearby crying.

This must never happen again.

Alex burst out of his office. "Sit Room. Now," he bellowed to his team.

The few that were not out of the office on missions and operations scrambled to obey. The Situation Room was nothing more than a meeting room with video capability. On a good day, he held staff meetings, conducted intelligence briefings, and occasionally, they might have an uplink with a Department of Defense agency—Army, Navy, Air Force, or Marines. Today was not one of those good days. It was just Alex and his team. To make matters worse, one of his junior agents, Harley Mortimer, had been AWOL for weeks.

"You found Mortimer yet?" Alex lashed out at Mother, the first person in his line of fire. "Well?"

His genius admin assistant and self-proclaimed girl Friday shook her head. "Still don't know where he is. Zack went by his apartment again this morning. Ember ran down the GPS signal from his cell phone. Nothing. Guess he's MIA like last time."

"Then check again."

"Yes, Boss." Taking her place at the conference table, Mother didn't react to his rudeness.

He forced a deliberate breath. *Tone it down, Stewart. These people don't even know what happened yet.*

The room filled in silence. Three senior agents, four junior agents, and two genius info techies comprised his fledgling team. He needed more agents, and maybe he needed better men, but for now, they were all he had. His men were ex-military snipers, perfect for the work he needed done until today. Zack Lennox nodded grimly. He always was good at reading people.

Alex took another settling breath. *No need to preach to the choir. Settle down.*

Before the last person took his seat, he flipped the switch to lower the video screen. Stalking beneath it, he snapped a finger at the statuesque blonde seated at the computer console. "Roll it."

Don't take it out on her. She didn't do it.

Ember Davis, Mother's assistant, logged in, but, just as the feed came on-line, her screen went dark before the picture could materialize. Hurriedly, she worked the keyboard until it flickered back to life.

"Anyone want to tell me what happened out there?" Alex jerked his thumb at the screen. It blinked off again. He lowered his head and bit his lip to keep his anger in. Everything seemed to be working against him today.

Cool it, Stewart. Focus. Think.

"Sorry." Ember continued at the keyboard. The picture came to life.

"What happened out there?" He didn't mean his question to come out so accusing, so mean. But it did.

Silently, all eyes studied the overhead display. He watched their faces. Jaws dropped. Eyes widened. Mother, forever the drama queen, covered her mouth with both hands. Ember blinked wide green eyes. Murphy Finnegan growled without any attempt to use actual words. Zack pushed away from the table, contempt etched in his face at what he was viewing.

Good. Now you see what I see. Now you know how bad things can get when an agent fails.

Roy Hudson paled, if that was possible for a black man. He scrubbed his hand over his face. Only David Tao seemed unaffected, not like Alex was surprised. Even on a bad day, David would be calm. With his anger checked Alex blew out a slow deliberate breath. It was safe to proceed now. He was calm. These were good people. They weren't anything like Rod.

"What's wrong with this picture?"

No one responded. The thing about blowing your cool in the past is that people remember. His team had taken more than their fair share of tongue-lashings, all of them undeserved.

"I'll tell you what happened." He steadied his fingers to the table. "Our intel to the Air Force was wrong, and because of our wrong information, innocent people were hurt this morning. The target who I contracted to hit is still out there, and he is still killing American soldiers." Alex glared while everyone else avoided eye contact. Even Zack looked away. "This is not how we do business!"

Murphy Finnegan spoke up. He was the only one who dared. "Rod Kensington blew the op, not these folks here. Air Force OSI is looking for him right now."

"The Office of Security Investigations won't find him. I'll bet Kensington isn't even in the country anymore."

Murphy sighed. "You know these things happen. They're every bit as bad as friendly fire. It's a sad cost of war."

"Not in my company it isn't!" Alex let his cardinal rule sink in. His rage peaked again, threatening to override his common sense. Surgeons must never be wrong. They didn't have the luxury of making mistakes with other people's lives. Neither did he or his team.

Murphy gave up and focused on the pen in his hand.

Alex turned back to Mother. "Find Kensington. Track his GPS. Do whatever you need to do, but get him on a plane tonight. I need someone out there who can get the job done right."

She nodded obediently as if he had been polite. That simple reaction was the final straw. Abruptly, Alex stormed out the door. His anger won. Again.

"I might as well do it my damned self!"

The meeting only angered Alex more, and the calm with which his team took his abuse was beyond his comprehension. Once more, he had failed, made a fool of himself, and embarrassed them. If anything, he pitied them because they worked for him. Except for the errant Junior Agent Kensington, each of his agents gave back tenfold, while all Alex seemed able to return was hostility and impatience. Try as he might, his anger ruled. If he had worked for the man he had become, he would have quit a long time ago.

Out of control with no way to change, he cursed himself most of all. Even now, he wanted to upend his desk, throw a chair out the window, or hit something. Anything. He didn't. Instead, he seethed. *How do others do it? How could anyone lose their entire family and still function?* He didn't understand, and he didn't want to.

A thousand ways the guilt came back to him. *I should've been there.* As if he didn't know that? Four years without them was not living. A man can't have his family wrenched out of his life and not feel like the wretch he had become.

Every day was a trial, full of loneliness and one endurance test after another. It was torture.

Murphy would knock at the door soon, come in and talk about the weather, or something business related. That was another thing Alex couldn't believe he had done. Why did he, ex-Marine and current idiot, ever think he could start a business? *I'm a sniper. A soldier. Not a businessman. How stupid am I?* Anger fueled his already throbbing migraine.

The simple truth was that everything had fallen so easily and too quickly into place. He had even been bankrolled by the very prestigious Jed McCormack, an entrepreneur just up the road in Rosslyn, Virginia with friends in Congress and plenty of cash. Once Jed found out about Alex and his idea for The TEAM, he had put forth a magnanimous offer Alex couldn't refuse, and all because he had saved McCormack's son during the first Gulf War. Brady McCormack was a good Marine, a good soldier, and now a quadriplegic—but alive.

Jed's gratitude knew no bounds. It allowed Alex to own the building they resided in outright, lock, stock, and barrel. The ceilings high, the windows expansive, the modern building spoke of understated elegance. Polished aluminum-lined black marble countertops, and each agent's workspace boasted the same spacious design. His own executive office was more window than wall. But now he stood with his foot on that low windowsill and wondered why he ever thought he needed an office with a view.

He should be proud. Beautiful Alexandria, Virginia, sprawled to the Potomac below with people coming and going, friends meeting for lunch, tourists sightseeing, and families vacationing. He hated them all, but more than anything on this green earth, he hated himself. Four years ago was just yesterday, and the deaths of his wife and daughter just as painful now as then. Bitter rage ignited all over again.

I should've been there.

Dressed in the executive uniform of the day, charcoal suit, burgundy shirt, and black tie, he looked like any other captain of industry. Even the early gray at his temples belied his youth and added an air of distinction he didn't deserve. Salt and pepper he could live with. He just couldn't live without—them.

Two blonde-haired beauties materialized in his mind: Sara, the love of his life, and Abby, the child he would give anything to hold one more time. Their blue eyes still smiled, full of the happiness he missed every day. *How do people stop hurting? How do they recover and move on?* He didn't know. His hand reached out to touch their sweet faces. The cold window reminded him again. They were gone.

Cabin.

A single word bubbled up through the bitter caldron within his mind. Alex glanced at his watch. He felt for the people in that video clip. Those wailing women were the impetus to his decision to become a USMC scout sniper all those years ago. Collateral damage was not acceptable. Ever.

And now he would have to deal with an Air Force demand for mitigation, possibly litigation, and they were right. He would settle. The Air Force would expect redress, and no matter how much it cost, he would give it to them. It might be millions. He didn't care. They may never hire his company again. That much was sure. He owned a six-month-old business that already had a black mark against it. Again, he didn't care. It was those people a world away that would haunt him now. Kensington might have blown the op, but Alex took it personally.

Cabin.

The single word persisted. He pushed it aside. Like anything else in life, a man's word was his reputation, and now his sucked. His personal code was simple. Never late. Never wrong. Never miss. Anger smoldered hot and potent. He pressed two fingers to the temple that hurt the worst and cursed Rod Kensington as much as he cursed himself. *Never should've hired him. Kensington was nothing but a hired gun. Absolutely nothing but.*

Cabin.

He glanced at his watch. *What month is it anyway?* A quiet rap at his door interrupted his thoughts. He pushed the anger back where it belonged. Stowed it. Locked it up. Wished he could throw away the key.

"It's open."

"Need you to sign another contract, young man." Right on schedule, in came good old Murphy, as calm as Alex was volatile.

He had first met Murphy during a joint military operation when they were both still active duty. Murphy knew The TEAM inside out. He had been with Alex through the months of preliminary market research, of building a rock-solid business plan, and the nightmare of coming up with sufficient start-up capital. Thanks heavens for Jed. At least he had made that one problem go away, but thank heavens more for Murphy. It was the intangible benefits he brought with him that eased the burden of entrepreneurship. The old Army Ranger liked people. At this point in time, Alex did not. The truth was The TEAM could probably survive without him more than his right hand man.

He looked at his watch again. The silver and gold face declared the month of June. *Already? Seems like only yesterday...*

He blew out a deep sigh. "I'm taking a few days off, Murph. Soon as I talk with the Air Force, I'm heading west to do a little fishing."

Two

Alex

Alex took one last glance at his pickup, parked, locked, and left it behind at the Gas-N-Go, a combined service station and food mart. He had made arrangements with the owner years ago. The moment Dan Fletcher saw the truck, he would know Alex was in town. He might never see Alex, but Dan would keep an eye out for his friend's truck. That was one of the benefits of soldiering. Friends showed up in the darnedest places.

Calling his dogs, Whisper and Smoke to his side, he walked briskly into the trees, his mind already eight miles deep in the forest and sitting relaxed on his cabin steps with a cup of coffee in his hand. That's all he wanted, time to not have to keep up with all the balls he had set in motion. The drive across country had already restored some of his peace of mind. The solitude of this particular place ought to do the rest.

It might not make sense to others that he kept a cabin so far from where he lived, but it worked for him. Twenty-seven hundred miles between work and play made a decent buffer zone. Besides, this tract of twenty acres was the only thing his old man had ever given him. A son doesn't walk away from an inheritance like that.

He didn't know how his father came to own the land, and he didn't care. It was a decent chunk of property, so Alex had developed it with a cabin that was nothing more than two rooms and an indoor bathroom closet under a cedar shake roof. To keep things civil, he installed a septic tank and minimal indoor plumbing a couple years back. He had added a few amenities over the years: some dried food storage to supplement a successful day of fishing or hunting, and an outdoor shower that relied on gravity when he was ambitious enough to lug water.

Eight miles south of the two-lane highway, the tract of remote wilderness butted up against Forest Service land on the southwest side, and private property on the rest. The Forest Service kept easement rights to an old dirt road through his land, but Alex had never seen so much as another hunter, much less a ranger in all the times he had been there. The road came in handy to haul building supplies by ATV back then. The remote cabin was perfect for the remote man he had become. At least his old man got that one thing right.

He drew in a deep breath of the forest decay rising up from the ground, the sweet perfume of a much-needed retreat from the world. This was what he had driven across country for, the absolute surety he wouldn't have to see or talk to another human being for a while. He set a quick pace for himself and his canine companions.

Tossing a small branch into the thicket, he watched their fluffy backsides disappear. He wouldn't have them but for the mistake of listening a minute too long to his good friend, Max Randle, a top-notch Army canine handler. It turned out to be one of those good mistakes though. Before Alex knew it, Max passed away from cancer. Because of that one night's conversation, he left the dogs to Alex. They needed a good home. Max knew Alex would take good care of them. Somehow, Max must have known they would also take care of Alex.

Both were trained military dogs. Smoke was the shorter dog, a stubby version of a German shepherd called a Belgian Malinois, and by far the more obedient of the two. Whisper was another case all together. A pure black German shepherd, the dog was obedient enough, but he did a disappearing act sometimes, taking off by himself and showing up hours later. It had nothing to do with chasing female dogs; he had been neutered years ago. He seemed to be looking for something, like he was born restless. Alex chalked it up to the trauma of war. It was no big deal. After all, he was doing a disappearing act of his own.

With nothing but his compass to follow, the world slipped off his shoulders with every step. This trip he had packed light with only a few bottles of drinking water, fewer clothes and a small solar generator. He was tired of cold showers. He carried a thirty-aught-six rifle over his shoulder and his SIG P229 pistol in his pack. It never hurt to be prepared.

The dogs ran ahead, chasing squirrels and chipmunks as they explored deer trails and gopher holes. This was as much a vacation for them as him. Alex smiled when he caught up with them. Both dogs sat at attention beneath a low hanging pine bough. A black squirrel hung by his back legs, swaying back and forth as he let the dogs have a piece of his mind. It was a comical sight—sass and hope within a foot of each other.

Sunlight had faded by the time the cabin came into view. Hidden in the dark shade of Douglas Firs, its roof was covered in the accompanying moss that overtook everything in deep woods. Both dogs trotted off, but Alex paused to take in the welcome view. *Ah, home sweet home.* Maybe, rain willing, he would work on that rickety porch or patch the roof. Work as simple and mundane as that sounded like R&R.

Suddenly, his sniper's sixth sense pinged. Something wasn't right. But what? A bear? A cougar? He heard nothing, and the dogs hadn't raised any alarm. Caution tightened his stride. There sat Smoke, still as stone, his ears pitched forward at something on the porch. He glanced up at Alex, and then right back to the porch.

Someone's in my cabin. Alex pulled his pistol free of its thigh holster. *People have a lot of nerve these days.*

"What's up, Smokey?" He kept his voice low, approaching along the side of the log structure with caution. Glancing sideways and around, nothing revealed the source of his anxiety. The weathered porch creaked under his cautious step. He froze.

What the—?

There stood Whisper with his lips pulled back, his canines bared, and standing protectively over the splayed legs of—a what? A department store mannequin? A dead body? He couldn't believe what he saw. Those outstretched legs belonged to a young woman sprawled against his cabin door, her head bowed to her chest, her hands limp at her side, palms up. Covered with blackened patches of blood and bruises, she looked dead.

Whisper growled, for an instant threatening both master and canine companion.

"Knock it off." Alex brushed the dog out of his way, annoyed the mutt thought he could get away with that kind of behavior. There was no contest. This was no fresh kill, and Whisper wouldn't have won if it were. The dog whined once and backed away, relinquishing the porch to Alex, his tail tucked between his back legs.

Alex knelt beside the woman, feeling her neck for a pulse. It took a few seconds to locate, but a weak beat stuttered beneath his fingertips. Lifting the tangled mass of hair away from her face, he ducked closer to get a better look. Her eyes popped open.

"Don't hurt me," she moaned, shielding her face with her arm. "Please—"

"Who are you?" Instantly, he was angry she would say something like that, but she didn't answer. Her head lolled to her shoulder. He knelt closer, peering into her bloodied face. *Did she just die?*

"No," he ground out between clenched teeth. "You started this. You'd better not die on me now."

Whisper whined, crowding Alex while he eased the woman to her back. "Back off." He elbowed the dog. "Get out of here."

Whisper only stepped back two feet, turned a full circle, and came right back.

Alex pressed his ear to the woman's chest, holding his breath while he listened for a heartbeat. It was there and fairly steady considering how bad she looked and smelled. Sweat and dirt was not the welcome he had expected at his cabin. Neither was she. A ragged groan sounded deep in her throat. Okay. That was a good sign. Maybe she heard him. Maybe she actually listened and decided not to die.

He sat back on his legs and blew out a deep breath, his heart pounding at this abrupt about-face to what had been a relaxing afternoon walk. Glancing at the immediate forest around his cabin, he searched for a reason this mess of a woman would be here on his porch. There was nothing. No one. Just her.

He ruffled Whisper's thick black mane. "Sorry, tough guy, but you've got to give me some room to work, okay?"

Still trying to calm down, he checked her pulse again and smoothed his hands over her shoulders, down her arms, hips and thighs. It didn't look like she had anything major wrong with her, no broken legs or arms, but there was plenty of what looked like road-rash across her extremities and dried blood in her hair. As bad as she looked, he was afraid of a gunshot, but he found nothing. A concussion was a possibility, but it's not like he was a doctor. He had had some medical training in the Corps. A man didn't survive warfare without knowing how to tourniquet a bloody limb or plug a sucking chest wound, but this was different. This was a woman.

Damn. What the hell do I do now?

Whisper nestled his big black snout over Alex's shoulder like he was offering free advice with his whine.

"I know." Alex scratched the dog's nose. "You found her. Now what do we do with her? You got any bright ideas?"

Whisper slapped the porch once with his moose-sized paw.

"No. You can't keep her. She's not a toy," Alex muttered as he came to grips with this new development. Talking to his dog helped him normalize the shock he had just received, but he also found Whisper's reaction odd. Smoke had taken up residence at the bottom of the porch steps, but Whisper acted like he knew this woman. *Dogs. Go figure. They're as hard to figure out as women.*

"Well, let's get you off the porch and out of the weather, shall we?" Alex said to the woman. There weren't a lot of choices. The option to hike back to the road for help had expired with the fading afternoon sun. Besides, he wasn't convinced she was stable. She might die while he went for help. His cell phone wasn't any good either. No bars out this far in the sticks, not like it mattered until now. Like it or not, she was all his.

It took a minute to unlock the cabin door, and another to scoop her up and off the porch. She didn't resist, her head limp and her arms dangling while he angled her through the door and set her on the cot inside. She was barely an armful, light as a feather and cold to the touch. Grabbing a blanket from the back room where he stored his supplies, Alex covered her gently. She was a pitiful sight, her cheek bruised, one eye swollen and bloodied. Even now a bloody tear trailed over her cheek. He patted her cheek in an attempt to rouse her.

"Hey there. Can you hear me? Can you talk? How long have you been sitting here?"

Groaning, she rolled away.

"Guess not." He combed his fingers through his hair. Talking to an unconscious woman didn't make a lot of sense now that he thought about it. Still, it seemed the right thing to do. "Okay then. You stay here and rest. I'll bring some firewood in, see if we can get you warmed up."

Hurriedly, he lit the kerosene lamps, filled the small water tank from the nearby spring and put a kettle of water on to boil. He rummaged through what few supplies he had brought. If nothing else, they needed something to eat and drink. Lastly, he hauled in a few armfuls of firewood and cleared the chimney before he stoked the cast iron stove. In no time at all, a decent fire glowed inside the stove's belly. He bumped the stove door closed with his boot, turning back to his uninvited guest.

She hadn't moved. Alex took stock of his options, like there were any. Whoever she was, she looked to be in her mid to late twenties, maybe a hundred pounds soaking wet. Dark brown hair straggled down her back in a tangled mass that looked like it hadn't been washed in days. She was dirty, beat up, and the last thing he needed. Hell, she might die right there on his cot. In his cabin. During his vacation.

He stood with his arms crossed, watching her. Whoever she was, she was going to need help that required a lot of physical contact. This wasn't just changing a tire for some gal on the freeway, not just a thank-you-so-much-kind-sir type of assistance to a damsel in automotive distress. No, this would be personal and messy. He would have to be a nurse, and he just did not want to deal with her.

His training kicked in. At last, he decided. Wake her up. Get her moving, clean her up, feed her, and get her out of there. Maybe she'll snap out of it and be glad to be on her way. *Yeah, well, maybe I'm stupid, too. Who am I trying to kid? She's not going anywhere tonight.*

He snagged one of the few water bottles left in his pack and crouched beside her. "Come on. Here's some water. Wake up."

She groaned, slowly rolled to her back, and opened her one good eye. He waited, hoping she could at least sit up to drink. Not going to happen. She blinked rapidly like she couldn't focus. Begrudgingly, he knelt one knee to the floor and circled his hand beneath her neck just enough to lift her head to drink. The first few swallows ran down her neck, but this woman was thirsty. She grabbed his hand and all but sucked the bottle dry, leaning back with a sigh when finished. Her lips moved like she meant to say something, but the way she laid there panting and licking her lips told him plenty. He needed to break out his water purification system.

I should have thought of that sooner. Of course, she would be thirsty.

After a couple more groans, she pulled herself onto one elbow, glancing around the cabin like she was getting her bearings and having a hard time of it. Squinting up at Alex, her teeth chattered. "Th-th-anks."

He waved her gratitude off. "What are you doing out here? You're eight miles in the middle of nowhere."

"H-hurt my head. My head hurts." This was an encouraging development. She might not have answered his question, but at least she was talking.

He tried to sound concerned. "Looks like you fell. What happened?"

"Had to r-run." She rolled over and placed both feet flat on the floor, leaning forward like she intended to stand. Shaking so much the blanket slipped to the floor, a single tear squeezed out of her blackened eye when she bent to retrieve it.

"S-sorry. I sh-should g-go." She clutched her head in her hands, shaking it side to side.

"Hey, hold on. Hold on." Alex came to his senses. Guilt stabbed his dumb ass. "You're not going anywhere. Least not tonight."

Draping the blanket back around her shoulders, his hand covered hers. Cold and clammy, it was a sure indicator of how bad off she was. And how small. Her hand fit perfectly within his like it might have belonged there. He jerked away from her inadvertent touch, surprised at that stupid thought. It strengthened his resolve to get her on her way, but it also forced him to reconsider. Obviously she didn't want to be here either. She was in no condition to leave, and he wouldn't let her.

"Just sit there for a minute. Can you at least do that?" His words came out impatient and sharp. Even he noticed.

Of course, she did, too. Pulling the blanket under her chin, she leaned forward again. "N-no. I'm gonna g-go."

"No! I mean, no. You're not going anywhere tonight. It's late and it's cold, and … you're not going anywhere." Again he wished he could find his gentle voice. Everything out of his mouth sounded just plain mean. "Can you at least tell me your name?"

She buried her face in her hands. "K-Kelsey. I think it's Kelsey."

The tremble in her voice told Alex plenty. It was bad enough he had a strange woman to deal with. He didn't need her hysterical on top of everything else.

"Well, I'm Alex Stewart. This is my cabin." The tone of challenge out of his mouth surprised even him. He didn't mean to sound territorial like, "What the hell are you doing in my cabin?" He gritted his teeth as he accepted what he had to do.

"Let's get you washed and fed. You want something more to drink before we get started?" He blinked at his own words. Even when he thought he was being nice, they came out annoyed.

"N-no." She stared at the floor, frail, sick, and needy, the blanket clutched in one shaky hand, the metal bed rail in the other.

He retrieved a plastic washtub from his kitchen cupboard, filled it with warm water, and brought some supplies to the cot. A couple of old wooden crates served as end tables and footrests. He nudged one close to the cot with his foot and placed the washtub there, wishing she could do this next part by herself. As shaky as she was, he doubted it. The last thing he needed was to be picking her up again.

"Put your arm in this tub," he ordered brusquely.

She obeyed. Tears trickled down both cheeks now. Usually a woman in tears melted him, and this one was plainly frightened, but he was too annoyed to worry about it now. It was going to be a long night. He was hungry and tired and—*This is not how I planned my vacation.*

Smoke settled against the door with a disinterested thud. Whisper, on the other hand, sat close by, watching his new best friend with bright eyes.

Alex brushed the big dog aside with his knee. "Move it," he growled. "Go lay down."

The dog circled the cabin, but came right back to where he had been before, watching while Alex scooped a cup of the warm, soapy water and poured it down her arm. Instantly he regretted his words. Whisper didn't deserve the bad treatment he had just dished out any more than she did.

She shivered.

"Let me know if I'm hurting you." Right now, he just wanted to get this unpleasant task behind him and food on the table.

As he wrung the washcloth and commenced wiping the grime away, he saw imbedded gravel and dirt in the crusted-over patches on her hand and arm. This gentle cleaning had to cause some level of pain, but she didn't flinch or cry. Not so much as a whimper. He had to give her credit for not pitching a fuss even when he took hold of her arm, twisting it gently to make sure he cleaned it entirely. She trembled, but he ignored that response. Anyone in her condition would be shaking. *It's adrenaline, that's all.*

At last the softened scabs released most of the surface dirt and debris. By the time one arm and hand was clean and dried, Alex knew she needed real medical help. Unfortunately, he was it.

He tried small talk. "What did you do, fall off a motorcycle or something?"

"I don't think so," she said timidly, staring into the water.

Alex let it go at that. The problem was that one patch of bloody scabs only led to another, and they all needed to be cleaned and treated. His mind automatically catalogued every bruise, scrape, and cut as he worked. The damage was mostly confined to her hands, arms, shoulders, legs, and back. Apparently she had tucked her face into her chest when she fell. In doing so, she must have also taken a hard knock to the back of her head. As more of her skin came into view, he detected other marks as well, little round scars, like chicken-pox maybe. Maybe not.

"I need to clean your back." Might as well get the worst part over and done with.

Wordlessly, she dropped the blanket off her shoulders and looked away.

The second he lifted the back of her torn shirt, she jumped. Threads of it stuck. He winced as fresh blood trickled from her scab-encrusted shoulder blades. Empathy brought the same feeling to his shoulders. He had been here before, once due to a stunt on his Harley motorcycle and again due to that rope swing over the river when he was a know-it-all kid. He looked closer, not believing what else he saw. *Oh, hell...*

He tugged the shirt off, leaving nothing above her waist but her bra. Those shoulders had taken the brunt of something else long before the road rash. He bristled. Ugly scars marked her skin. Some were too pink to be very old. He knew cigarette burns when he saw them. That explained the other marks on her arms, too.

Compassion glimmered. This woman might have fallen off a bike or out of a car a couple of days ago, but someone had been hurting her long before that. His conscience pricked him. In a flash, his demeanor softened, and he wanted to kick himself. His irritation vanished in a rush of sympathy—and shame.

Damn. This gal needs help.

The truth had finally broken through his hard head. This poor woman needed more than just help. She needed somebody to care. Kelsey hadn't asked to be here anymore than she had asked for the abuse he saw heaped on her back. For all Alex's complaining and feeling sorry for himself, he wasn't much better. *Poor kid.*

Just as quickly, recrimination followed. *I'm such an ass.*

"Listen. I'm going to put some antiseptic ointment on these scrapes." At last, he found his gentle voice. "It will deaden the pain. Then we'll get you changed into something clean. I've got a pair of spare sweats in the back, if you don't mind me helping you out of these dirty clothes."

She didn't agree or disagree. It looked like she could barely hang onto the edge of the cot; she was trembling so hard. Alex covered her with the blanket as he removed her cutoffs. By the time he was through, she sat shivering in nothing but her underwear, looking like a survivor plucked from a natural disaster—or from a man who beat his wife.

Alex moved more efficiently now. In no time at all, he cleaned and spread ointment, making sure to keep her covered as he went. Her legs were the least damaged. On closer inspection, he noticed gravel imbedded there as well. The nearest gravel road was eight miles back. He cleaned and analyzed, then cleaned some more. If she had fallen or been pushed out of a car on that road, she had certainly walked a long way.

Her words came back to him. "I had to run." From who? Or what?

He looked up from two skinned knees. "We're almost done. Can you hang on for just a couple more minutes?"

Again, she didn't answer.

With unexpected patience, Alex turned his limited nursing expertise to her battered face. He began awkwardly, wrapping a towel around her neck so he wouldn't get the blanket wet. That's when he truly realized the intimacy involved in the care and washing of another human being, especially one as vulnerable as this woman.

She squeezed her eyes tight when he moved in close. With a quiet gasp, she held her breath. Suddenly, he was back in an Iraqi village, trying to help a little girl who had been injured when an insurgent's improvised bomb exploded in her village. Kelsey had that same look. As much as she needed help, she was scared. Of him.

"Hey. It's okay. I'm just going to clean your face." He wanted to reassure her, but it was too late. He had already made too much of a negative impression.

Alex blew out a long, slow breath. The more he handled her, the more he realized his hands were too large and too rough for this kind of work. He was a pipe wrench performing delicate surgery on a china cup.

His sweet wife's admonition on the night of his daughter's birth came back to him. "Sweetheart, she's not going to break."

His heart stuttered. Sara? He hadn't thought of that night in years. Why now?

As he smoothed the cloth over Kelsey's forehead and cheeks, he was close enough to notice the long eyelashes beneath a puffy eyelid. Squeezing a dribble of water against the sealed eyelid, the dried blood softened enough to be wiped away. He did everything with extra gentleness now, but she still trembled.

"Am I hurting you?" he asked softly.

"No." Her one word answer came out squeaky, fast, and sad. Again, he felt ashamed. This poor woman was primed to fight or flee—from him. Not a response he was proud of. The last thing she needed was another monster in her life.

"I'll fix some soup when we're done. Do you think you can eat?"

She sniffed, her one clean hand to her nose.

Very gently, he stretched a butterfly band-aid across her split cheekbone and placed another band-aid over the cut above her swollen eye, just beside the arch of a delicate brow.

Her petite nose sported a smattering of brown freckles and shouldn't have been as full of dried blood and dirt as it was. As angry as he was at the person who had hurt this petite woman, he was angrier with himself. He had acted badly today.

It was too much for her. She pushed his hand away and took a deep breath through her mouth. "Do-do you have a tissue?"

"You bet." He scrambled for a paper towel, and then thought better of it and dampened it with cool water before he handed it to her. She was shaking so hard she could barely blow her nose, but he saw the blood.

He braced a hand to her shoulder. "I'm almost done. Let me check your lip, and we'll call it good." By now, Alex was nose to nose with her. He held a damp cloth to a lip that was swollen and split. He had been in enough brawls to know this kind of wound well. He just hadn't seen it on such a delicate face before.

"Ouch," she said softly when he smoothed a layer of ointment over her lips.

"Sorry." He tried to be more careful. "Did someone hit you or something? Did you fall?"

"I sat down..." She glanced toward the door. "Out there."

"Right. You were on my porch. Is that all you remember?"

"A bear." She nodded toward Whisper. "A big bear."

"That was just my dog," he offered her a glass of salt water to rinse her mouth. "He won't hurt you. Here. Swish this around and spit it out." He held the washbasin so she could spit the blood from her mouth. That's when he saw her teeth were bloodied as well. Probably loose, too.

"Thank you," she whispered, wiping her mouth.

"Hey, don't worry about it. Looks like you've been through a pretty hard time."

She was in rough shape, but at least she was halfway clean. She still wouldn't look at him though.

"You had enough for one night?"

"Yes." She shivered, pulling the blanket tighter around her shoulders.

"Good. Let's get you into some clean clothes. Come on. I'll help you up."

She rose shaky from the cot, balancing with both hands on his shoulders while he eased her into a pair of his old grey sweats. They were way too large, but at least they were clean and warm. They would do for tonight. That's when he saw the bloody patch on her hip. There was one more scrape to wash and treat.

"Looks like we missed one. Lie back down and let me treat your hip. Then you'll be done."

"No." She pushed him away. At least she tried to push him away. In the process, she plopped gracelessly onto the cot, off balance and exhausted. "I don't want you to."

"Come on. It'll heal faster if it's clean." This time, his concern was genuine. "I promise. I won't hurt you."

"No-o." Another tear squeezed from her puffy eye. "Please. I just don't want to."

He knew that look. "It's okay. I won't do anything you don't want. Maybe tomorrow."

She still didn't look at him, her gaze fixed on the floor planks.

Well, I deserved that. Why should she look me in the eye? What was I thinking? She just needed help. That's all. It's not like she had broken in and stolen anything.

Dinner was quick and hot, just a cup of noodle soup and crackers, but putting something in her stomach did the trick, along with a few Advil. She had no more than emptied her cup of soup when her eyes drooped, and she slumped to the pillow.

Alex was straightening the kitchen area when he noticed Whisper had made himself comfortable on the cot. Kelsey held the big dog like a teddy bear, her arm wrapped around his neck, her face buried in his fluffy black mane. That's when Alex heard it—the saddest sound he had heard in a long time as this stranger wept into his dog's neck. Her stifled sobs filled Alex's ears as quickly as it filled the cabin. Sympathy lanced the hard-as-nails crust over his heart. He wanted to hug her himself and tell her everything would be okay, but Kelsey was already in good hands, or paws rather.

Whisper laid his muzzle across her neck, his sharp black eyes focused on Alex as if telling him, "It's okay. I found her first, and I've got her now. She's mine."

Alex let the dog stay. Kelsey needed a security blanket tonight. By the looks of it, Whisper sensed it, too.

Three

Alex

Alex sat on the floor, watching his patient sleep. Kelsey was restless. She moaned out a name, but he couldn't decipher the mumble. There was no doubt in his mind she suffered from dehydration and exposure. The poor woman had to be hurting more then she had shown, but it was also clear someone had used her face as a punching bag within the last week and abused her long before that. He hadn't seen any defensive wounds on her arms or hands. Why hadn't she fought back?

She would be a pretty little thing if she didn't look like she had just been through a war. Although she had avoided looking at him most of the evening, he knew there were dark brown eyes beneath those long lashes and swollen eyelids. He could also tell she didn't care what happened to her. True, she had let him scrub her wounds until she was semi-clean and sore, and she had said thanks, but he didn't get the feeling she meant it. Her whole attitude was more like 'do what you want' instead of 'please, help me.' Alex recognized the look. He could write a book on hopelessness.

His mind worked through different scenarios of the trouble she might be in: prostitution, gangs, or drugs, but Kelsey didn't seem the type. No. There was a genteel quality to her that spoke more of sadness than anything else.

A sudden burst of wind kicked up against the cabin, slamming the screen door back and forth on its hinges. She jumped in her sleep; her hand to her mouth as if she might cry. She didn't. Instead she let out a small groan that was instantly lost in the sound of rain drumming loud and hard against the windows. Alex stood over her. How did a woman like her get into so much trouble?

He couldn't solve that puzzle, so he secured the door and planned his next day's chores instead. First thing in the morning, he planned to hike back to the gas station, call the sheriff, and let the authorities take over. While he waited for the sheriff to show he could rig a shower so she could get that hip of hers cleaned, maybe wash her hair, too. Being clean always improved a person's outlook.

He took out his cell phone and snapped a couple pictures of her battered face for evidence, berating himself for not thinking of that earlier when she had looked a whole lot worse. That would have been the smart thing, but no, he was too caught up in feeling sorry for himself then. Guilt poked at him. He should have handled finding her a whole lot better.

An inexplicable wave of tenderness inundated him. His unwelcome houseguest was sound asleep. For tonight, she was safe and warm, guarded by two working dogs and one grouchy ex-Marine. He tucked the blanket under her chin. She didn't move, but something stirred inside of him. He brushed a strand of dirty hair off her clean face. Realization flooded a part of his heart he thought had long ago died.

She needed him.

By morning, the sun shone bright through the high trees. Kelsey was still sound asleep when he got up, and Alex felt better about going for help this morning. She wasn't as close to death's door as he had thought. When he cracked the door to his bedroom, she still lay on her side, with one hand on Whisper. The dog had moved to the floor beside her. He didn't budge when Alex quietly gathered his boots. With his muzzle on his chin, Whisper watched his master intently.

Alex scribbled a note on an old scrap of paper so Kelsey would know that he had gone for help and would be back soon. He left the last of his bottles of water and the Advil on his counter. She would need them the minute she opened her eyes. He paused to listen to her breathing, slow and steady with no whimper or congestion. A little food and water had gone a long way. A little soap hadn't hurt either. Overall, she had a few bumps and some nasty scrape, but last night could have turned out a whole lot worse.

He opened the cabin door and whispered to the dogs, "Out." After they took care of their business and rousted a few chipmunks from last year's woodpile, he ushered them quietly back into the cabin. "Stay."

Once again, Whisper took up his post at Kelsey's side. Crazy dog. There was definitely something going on between him and this woman, although most of it was probably in Whisper's hard head. Kelsey would be in good company until he got back, and that's all that mattered. Slinging his backpack over one shoulder, he shut the door quietly and locked it from the outside, just in case. He didn't need any more surprises. Neither did she.

As he hiked back to the service station, he discovered last night's storm had caused quite a bit of damage. Trees were torn up, branches scattered everywhere, and when he crossed the road to the gas station, he noticed the power lines were down as well. Mother Nature had left a trail of destruction. To top it off, local phone service was out.

Fortunately, the clerk at the station had shown up to check his business for storm damage. He was in the middle of clearing fallen branches and shingles out of the parking lot when Alex stepped out of the trees. According to the clerk, it would take a month of Sundays before utilities this far out in the woods were back online.

Alex listened to the man ramble. It was then he noticed the flyer taped inside the store window. Kelsey's sad eyes stared back at him from behind the glass.

"What's her story?" He nodded toward the picture, downplaying his interest.

The man shook his head. "She's a mean one by the sounds of it. Got an Amber Alert on her two little boys, too."

"Why's that?" Alex asked evenly.

"Guess she up and run off. Left her husband. Poor man's been looking for her over a week now."

He studied the flyer. Kelsey Durrant. According to the paper, she was five feet tall, long brown hair, brown-eyed and twenty-six years old. Known to have psychotic breaks. Left home with her two young sons in a 1978 blue Ford Fairmont. The active Amber Alert taped alongside Kelsey's picture showed two little boys, Tommy and Jackie, ages two and four respectively. Their last known location was listed as their apartment in Lakewood, Washington. No description of what she or her boys were wearing was included.

"Yeah," the talkative clerk continued, "Channel Five had a press conference a couple days ago for the poor fellow. He was all tore up and crying. It's a shame is what it is. A guy thinks he's marrying the girl of his dreams, and he ends up with some lunatic, you know what I mean?"

Alex hesitated. His gut told him different. There was more to her than the flyer disclosed. His plan to contact the authorities didn't feel like the right thing to do anymore. Instead, he talked the clerk into opening the store for a couple items— antiseptic ointment, sterile gauze, a travel-sized bottle of baby shampoo, a hairbrush, and a small ladies T-shirt. He topped off his pack with a pound of bacon, a dozen eggs, and a loaf of bread.

"Looks like your lady friend musta forgot to bring her beauty supplies," the nosy clerk commented at the cash register.

"Dan Fletcher still own this place?" Alex changed the subject. Nobody needed to know he had that missing woman safe and sound in his cabin.

The clerk's eyes brightened. "You know Dan? Sure, he still owns this place. I reckon he'll be in later to see how much damage the storm did."

"Tell him Alex stopped by, will you?"

"That your truck out there?"

Alex nodded.

"Well, I'll be. Dan's always talking 'bout you. Sure glad I got the chance to meet one of the guys he served with." He extended a hand for Alex to shake. "I'm Pete Sanders by the way."

"Nice to meet you, Pete." Alex returned the handshake. "Tell Dan thanks letting me park here for a couple days."

"Sure. No problem. Lots of guys leave their rigs here."

"Keep the change." Alex handed over several twenties. "Something extra for opening the store for me. I appreciate it."

Pete waved the money off. "Sorry, but your money ain't no good around here. Dan wouldn't take it, and neither will I."

"He still as hard-headed as he used to be?" Alex chuckled as he stuffed the bills back into his pocket.

"He's a good man." Pete nodded. "You take care."

"You, too." Alex nodded as he placed his purchases inside his backpack, the eggs on top, and headed back to the cabin. He checked the bars on his cell phone. Fortunately, the cell tower must have survived the storm unscathed. That was a welcome break, but instead of contacting the local authorities like he planned, Alex called his right-hand man. The forest made for a good office.

"You miss us already?" Murphy was his usual cheerful self.

"Need you to run a background check, Murph."

"What? You working a case out there in the Cascades, are you?"

Alex ignored the friendly banter. "I'm sending a couple pictures. See what you can find on a missing woman in the Tacoma and Seattle area. Name is Kelsey Durrant."

Murphy stowed the chitchat. "Send me what you got."

Alex sent the pictures he had taken while Kelsey slept. If nothing else, he wanted to know exactly who she was before he handed her over to the locals. He owed her that much for being a jerk.

The forest smelled extra good this morning after the nighttime rain. It was alive with the rowdy chatter of birds, squirrels, and chipmunks. A Western Jay fluttered away in a flurry of deep indigo, squawking like the murderer it was, the pink kernel of another bird's baby hanging from its beak. Alex watched the parent birds attack the fleeing predator, while it dodged branches to escape. As beautiful as life was, it was still cruel.

His phone rang on his hip holster. "Stewart."

"Exactly how'd you run into this gal?" It was Murphy again, concern heavy behind his question. "You've only been gone four days, and three of them had to be on the road. What'd you do? Pick up a hitchhiker?"

"Special delivery, Murph. Found her on my porch last night. Why?"

"Well, I'll tell you why, son. There's a missing person report all right, but there's an Amber Alert in the tri-state area for her two boys, too. I'm sending pictures to your phone now."

"Already know that. Tell me what's not on the Amber Alert."

"She got the boys with her?"

"No."

"She say where they are?" Murphy's grandfatherly interrogation sparked Alex's anger.

"For hell's sake, look at the picture I sent. She can't remember her own name."

"Now hold on, son—"

"No. You hold on. I asked for information, not an inquisition."

"You're right. I'm just thinking of those little fellows." Murphy calmed.

"And I've got a woman who can't stand on her own two feet. I spent he whole night doctoring her. Now what else do you have?" Alex kicked the ground as he walked. He didn't mean to come across harsh, but this vacation just kept getting better and better.

"Okay," Murphy continued. "She's got a sister, Louise Timpson, who lives in Pendleton, Oregon. She's the one who filed the missing person reports on Kelsey and her boys."

"What about her husband?" Alex already suspected the answer.

"Name's Nick Durrant. I'm sending his photo now. You would have thought he would be the one to file the missing person report on his wife and kids now, wouldn't you? Mother pulled a TV newscast from two days ago. Guess Durrant held a press conference and asked for help in locating his missing wife and kids. He said she wasn't stable, that he was afraid for his boys' safety. According to him, she suffers psychotic breaks and has threatened to kill them in the past." Murphy's voice filled with disgust. "You should've seen it. This guy's lying through his teeth."

Alex opened the picture of Nick Durrant. A weaselly-looking man with greasy, blond hair, a wispy excuse for a goatee, and thin lips stared back at him. "What else?"

"Well, okay, so Mother contacted Louise Timpson. According to her, Durrant is the dangerous one. She thinks he's been beating Kelsey since they got married. Timpson said her sister hasn't been the same since."

"Why don't women leave jerks like him? What else?"

"Mother located Durrant's employment, financial, and police records. The man's a two-bit thief. Hasn't worked a steady job in his life. The one thing he does have is a healthy rap sheet, mostly car prowls, shoplifting, petty thievery, and stuff like that. Plus, I've got two reports of animal cruelty. Thought you'd want to know that. A couple neighbors claim he shot their dogs. Plus there's a whole list of emergency room visits on her. She's had a broken nose, broken fingers, broken left arm, as well as repeated spiral fractures."

"Let me guess. She fell down the stairs?"

"You know what you're looking at, don't you?" Murphy was clearly concerned.

"Yeah. A bastard who beats his wife. She's a tiny little thing."

"Never could figure out guys like that," Murphy said quietly.

"Me either." Frustration curled Alex's fist as he walked. He couldn't decide who he was angrier with, Kelsey or her deadbeat husband.

"This guy's dangerous. Best thing for you to do is—"

"What else?" Alex didn't want free advice.

"Okay, well, so she married this Durrant guy four years ago. She taught school before that. There's only been one police complaint against him, and she didn't file it. Guess one of her neighbors heard screaming one night. When the police investigated, Durrant opened the door with a crying baby in his arms. Said the little guy had an earache."

"Was she there?"

"The police report didn't indicate one way or the other."

Alex trudged through the trees, absorbing the information. He had never experienced abuse himself, and he didn't understand it. The solution seemed clear to him. If a bully hits you, hit them back. End of story. Of course, that might be harder for a little gal like Kelsey. He hiked, silently considering all the ways she could have defended herself. There had to be more to the story, a piece to this puzzle he wasn't seeing.

"You still there?"

"Yes," Alex muttered, his mind picturing Kelsey with an iron skillet in her hand, defending herself, maybe exacting a little domestic revenge, too.

"If those little boys aren't with her, I'd say he's already killed them," Murphy said somberly.

"Got that same feeling."

"Just so you know, Mother couldn't find anything on those two little fellows besides their birth certificates and health department vaccinations. It's like they disappeared. Neither of them went to the emergency room, not once. Just sent the pictures."

Alex blew out a huge sigh as he opened Murphy's text. It was a better picture than the Amber Alert photo. Two little boys smiled back at him, their hair cut with bangs across their foreheads. He noticed the similarity to their mother. They were miniatures of Kelsey, small-boned and brown-eyed. That old familiar pain stabbed at him with its irrational mantra. *I should've been there.*

"Listen, Murph. Contact the Washington State authorities. Let them know I've got her. The pictures I sent should be enough evidence to prove she's not what Durrant claims. Maybe they can focus on finding those two boys. They're welcome to come check on her if they want."

"Okay. Will do."

"But ask them to keep this quiet. The less Durrant knows about his wife's location, the better off she'll be. I'll bring her in as soon as she's able to travel. I'll stay in touch."

"She hurt bad?"

"Nothing broke, if that's what you're asking, but he's a mean SOB."

"What you gonna do?"

"Let her sleep. She's not going anywhere."

Murphy chuckled across the distance. "Never figured you for such a soft touch."

"Me neither," Alex grumped as he answered. "I should've stayed at work."

"Before you hang up, Mother's got Durrant's GPS coordinates."

"Where is he?"

"Look around. He's right at your location."

Alex snapped his phone shut. So. Durrant was out here in the woods. A GPS coordinate like that meant he was close, but Alex didn't spot any movement in the immediate vicinity. Normally he would have tracked the man down, but his first thought was to get back to Kelsey. She was alone. As he hurried, he analyzed what Murphy had said. She might be in rough shape, but she was safe. The real problem now was where those two little boys were and why was Durrant out here? Alex's gut clenched. There was only one conclusion. Kelsey was unfinished business. Durrant was hunting.

But Alex was mad at Kelsey, too. This was all her fault. She should've left the bastard—not waited until he killed her children. If more women did what they were supposed to do, there would be a lot less child abuse in the world today. The more Alex thought about it, the angrier he got. Yes, there were always two sides to the story, but the black and white of it was pretty straightforward in his mind. He had learned that lesson early in life. No matter what, never lie down and take a beating from a bully. Always fight, even if you're knocked down and have to crawl back up.

His self-righteous thoughts vanished the second he opened the cabin door. Kelsey was gone. So were the dogs. An icy chill slithered down his spine. He dropped his pack just inside the door, stepped back onto the porch, and whistled. Instantly, Smoke peered around the corner of the cabin, his head cocked and a curious look on his silver face.

"There you are." Alex leaned over the rickety porch rail. There stood Kelsey against the cabin with both dogs at her feet. By the looks of her muddied knees, she had been down to the creek. Running away? Washing her hair? It didn't matter. As soon as she saw him, she lowered her eyes. He figured he had startled her. She shook like a leaf. Again. Still. Whatever. He didn't know if he cared anymore.

"Need a hand?" He suppressed his aggravation.

"No," she said quickly.

"You're going to fall if you keep standing there." The words were no more out of his mouth than her knees buckled. Alex jumped the rail to catch her, but then the fight was on.

"Let me go!" She squirmed against his grip while he hoisted her over his shoulder. She kicked, landing her knee hard into his solar plexus, all the while twisting to escape his hands on her back and backside. "Don't hurt me."

"I'm not hurting you." He cocked his head to avoid her flying elbow. Just as quickly, she yanked a handful of his hair so hard that it knocked him off balance. He staggered, trying to maintain a hold so they didn't fall, but it was like holding a wild cat with all claws in attack mode. He fell backwards with her tight in his arms while he hit the floor, falling against his backpack.

Was this the same woman he hadn't thought would make it through the night? She sure had enough fight in her now.

"Hey. Knock if off." Wincing, he opened one eye, hoping to dodge another elbow in his face. She had landed square in his lap, for a moment the wind knocked out of her, too. The feel of her panting and out of breath in his arms heightened that annoying protective feeling he had been fighting. He leaned his cheek to her shoulder blade, as much to calm her and hopefully to avoid any more flying limbs.

"It's okay," he said softly, listening to her heart pound fast and hard. She stilled. He loosened his hold, but still kept her restrained on his lap.

She relaxed, blowing out big breaths through her open mouth. "I, I got, I got really scared."

"I know," he said quietly, "but you're safe here. No one's going to hurt you anymore."

He felt the tension drain from her body. Her shoulders slumped.

"It's okay," he muttered over and over, smoothing his hands up and down her arms, hoping to settle her nerves while he calmed his own heart rate. The feel of her in his arms awakened his common sense. There was no way this woman could defend herself against an adult male. There wasn't enough of her to pack a solid punch.

She tipped her head back against his shoulder, still breathing plenty hard. "Where am I?"

"You're in my cabin," he explained. "I'm Alex Stewart. Do you remember how you got here?"

"No." She shook her head, still trembling so much he didn't want to let her go just yet. "All I remember is waking up. The dogs kept following me. Everywhere."

He moved her into a sideways position on his lap. Once he had her turned, she burrowed into his neck like a frightened little girl, her hand clutching his collar while she panted beneath his chin.

"I'm lost," she cried. "I don't know where I am. I don't know—who I am."

"Shush now," he whispered, rocking back and forth even as he recognized that crunching sound at his back. Eggs were no longer on the breakfast menu. "It's okay now, baby." That tender endearment came unbidden to his lips. For some reason it felt right. She made no effort to move. Neither did he.

"Thank you," she whispered breathlessly.

He cupped her cheek, pressing her face into the crook of his neck, and still feeling her breath against his skin in fast, shallow huffs. Her wet hair smelled dirty, but he didn't care. She needed a safe place, and for all his bluff and bluster, this was as good as any.

"I see you tried to wash your hair at the creek."

She nodded against him. "I fell. The dogs scared me."

"Who? These old mutts?" He snagged Whisper by the scruff of his neck. "They won't hurt you. I think this one kinda likes you. Whisper, say hi."

She nodded again, her hand outstretched to the dog's eager nose. He licked her hand, then stepped a big paw onto her knee as he moved in to bless her with a sloppy kiss.

"Off," Alex commanded softly. "Leave the lady alone."

Kelsey relaxed. Her slender body molded to his. She gave up the fight, her gaunt backside noticeable against his hips.

"Are you going to be okay now?" he asked, peering down at her face.

"Yes," she said softly, covering her black eye with her hand.

He scrambled off the floor, still keeping a grip on her in case she fell. As strong as she had seemed a minute ago, she swayed now, unsteady on her feet. It had to be the adrenaline that had lent her strength to fight back. Poor thing. It wasn't much of a fight. He settled her onto the cot, pulling the blanket over her shoulders.

"Why don't you catch your breath while I fix breakfast?" He calmed down, too. "I know you're hungry."

"No, I..." She glanced around the room nervously. "I should go."

"Where?"

Her lower jaw trembled. "I... don't know."

He waved toward the door. "No one's stopping you, but you'll feel better if you eat first. Then decide."

"Well." She bit her lip in indecision, still watching the door. "Okay."

Stooping, he snagged his backpack off the floor. "Bacon and toast okay? I think the eggs are already scrambled," he teased.

A shadow flitted across her face. "I'm sorry."

"No big deal." He emptied the contents of the backpack on his kitchen counter, carefully separating the gooey, broken eggs from everything else. Fortunately, the clerk had bagged them separately, which contained the mess. He pulled the bacon and the mashed loaf of bread out along with everything else. Before long, coffee percolated on the stove while bacon sizzled on his old cast-iron griddle. The sun peaked through the curtain behind Kelsey. She seemed calmer. Watchful eyes stared at him around the curtain of her wet hair.

Alex stopped what he was doing to counter her stare. "Are you feeling any better?"

And just like that, she looked away.

"You're going to have to talk to me sooner or later. It's not like there's a lot of room to avoid each other in this little shack."

She seemed intent on trying.

"Okay, later's fine. Well, just so you know what's going on, I hiked out here with my dogs yesterday afternoon. I thought I was taking a break from work for awhile, that maybe I would get some fishing in or work on the roof of this old cabin. But when I got here, there's this half-dead woman on my porch." Alex smiled, hoping she would look his way. "I'm sorry I was such a jerk to you last night." *That's putting it mildly.*

"You were?" Her brows furrowed.

"Yes," he admitted. "I guess you could say I have anger issues." He grunted at his very obvious understatement. If she only knew...

She took a deep breath and smiled. Just like that, the sun came out. He had to look twice. Beneath the shell of this battered woman glowed a definite light.

"Good morning." He raised his cup of coffee to her.

"Hi." Her voice was so soft he strained to listen.

"Breakfast is ready. Don't get up. I'll bring you a plate." He buttered a slice of the seriously wrinkled toast and poured another cup of coffee. "Cream and sugar, ma'am?"

"Yes, please." She smiled again when she took the coffee cup out of his hand, and again that warm feeling oozed into the room, like frosting on cinnamon rolls.

He moved the crate next to the cot for a makeshift table. "Hope you don't mind just toast and bacon this morning. It isn't much, but it'll fill you up."

She was a different person when she smiled. At least they were on talking terms, and maybe after breakfast, he could get her to talk. Relieved, he reached over her shoulder to pull the curtain aside.

"Don't." She jerked away from him. Her cup flew out of her hands. Coffee went everywhere.

Alex froze.

"I'm sorry. I'm..." She clutched the blanket to her like it offered protection, her eyes on the floor.

"Hey, calm down." He placed a hand on her shoulder to reassure her, but terror shuddered off her. "I'm only opening the curtain. It's okay."

"But I'm sorry. I..." she whined. "I didn't mean to spill, to drop—"

The level of her anguish far outdid the simple problem of spilled coffee on a plywood floor. Alex watched her curl her knees to her chest and hide beneath the blanket. This woman was scared to death, their brief encounter finished. He had hurt her feelings. Again.

Four

Alex

What the hell was I thinking?

Alex took a deep breath as he stood, slapped some bacon and toast together, and headed out the door. She didn't want him around, and, to be honest, he didn't want to be around her either. All that sympathy he had felt earlier was nothing but stupid imagination. Sleeping outside might just be better than having to deal with a crazy woman inside.

But after what Murphy had told him that morning, there was something else he needed to do. Alex fed and watered the dogs, then got down to business. He took Whisper back inside to guard Kelsey. He had hoped to tell her he would be hiking for a while, but she was already sound asleep, the blanket pulled up to her neck, tears glistening on her eyelashes. At least she had eaten her breakfast. *Good. That'll help.*

Even as angry as he was, Alex paused to look down at her. She looked sad. Whisper had already settled down under the cot with a thump and a grunt. His dog had decided he was Kelsey's protector.

Alex quietly removed his rifle from the top of the high kitchen cupboard and headed out with Smoke to find the source of that GPS signal. When he had hiked back to the gas station earlier, he hadn't come across any tracks besides his own. Now he widened his search and was more observant. Instead of the direct route, he headed east, thinking Durrant might still be close. Nothing. He followed a couple of deer trails through his parcel of land. Still nothing. It wasn't until Alex was almost back to the highway in the northern most part of the adjoining parcel of land that he came across fresh boot tracks.

They meandered. Before long, he knew where the man had relieved himself on the deer trail as well as where he had taken a smoke break. Alex tracked the man all the way back to the asphalt road where a rusted out diesel sat idling on the shoulder—directly across the road from where his own truck was parked. Disconcerted, Alex stepped back into the shade of the big trees, looking for the driver. If it was Durrant, he had to be close. Alex crouched to be sure he hadn't allowed the man to slip behind him. It was then that he noticed someone slouched at the wheel.

It was almost noon, and the sun was high in the sky. Alex approached the truck cautiously from the side. It was Durrant. Alex snapped several quick pictures with his cell phone of Kelsey's supposedly distraught husband, sprawled across the driver's seat with his mouth wide open, and a Winchester thirty-thirty propped across his legs. The four empty beer cans and potato chip bag scattered on the floor of the truck confirmed what Alex suspected. The police needed to see this. Nick Durrant didn't look like a desperate man searching for his missing wife and sons.

Tracking Durrant gave Alex further insight into Kelsey's husband. The man hadn't scouted more than a mile from his truck, about where Alex had been when Murphy gave him the GPS coordinates earlier. That told Alex Durrant was lazy.

After all these days, he assumed she would still be close to the road where, most likely, she must have jumped or been thrown from a moving vehicle, judging by her wounds. Second, Durrant didn't have a clue how to track, much less how to conceal himself while he did. But most of all, Alex knew that a man searching for his wife didn't need a deer rifle.

Alex hurried back to the cabin. He would give Kelsey some space for a day or two, but then they had better come up with a plan to get her back to civilization. Her old man was too close for comfort.

Alex phoned Murphy as he hiked.

"Afternoon, Alex." Murphy's familiar voice sounded as steady as ever. "How's your guest?"

"I just sent three pictures. Forward them to the Washington State Attorney General."

"Whatcha got?"

"Proof," Alex growled. "Durrant's not the victim he claims."

"Well, let's see what you've sent." Murphy stilled as he opened Alex's text. "Danged if you're not right."

"He's hunting her."

"I see that. I'll have Ember clean up these shots and send them right away. How is she?"

"Better."

"And how are you, son?"

"Fine. Send the pictures. I'll be in touch." Alex snapped his cell phone shut.

By the time he got back to the cabin, it was mid-afternoon. The sun cast a yellowish light through the trees. He leaned his rifle against the cabin wall of the porch and went inside to check on Kelsey. She was still asleep, and by the looks of the place, that's all she had done since he had left. He waved Whisper outside with him.

There wasn't enough daylight left to do much in the way of roof repairs. The noise would wake Kelsey anyway, so Alex cleared the storm debris and hauled more firewood. He stacked it against the tree opposite his cabin, planning to chop more in the next day or so. It never hurt to have a good supply of firewood, and he enjoyed the hard work. After he covered it with a tarp, he changed his mind about the evening menu and decided to go fishing. He had hunted turkey and grouse on his property before, but the season for them was later in the year. Deer, too. Tonight's meal would be pan-fried or grilled in a fish basket, his favorite. His mouth watered just thinking about it.

As he headed up the porch steps to retrieve his fishing pole, the door opened in his face. Kelsey stood there as surprised as he was, her hands gripping the doorframe. She looked like it took all her strength just to stay upright. Alex stepped back, not wanting to frighten her again.

"I wanted to..." She didn't make eye contact. "I just want to say thanks for breakfast."

"Don't worry about it." He held the door while she turned back to the cot. "Are you feeling any better?"

She covered the swollen side of her face with her hand. "I'm just thirsty and tired."

Alex opened another bottle of water and handed it to her. "Here. Help yourself. I can get more from the creek and run it through my purification system. Do you need anything before I go?" He rummaged around the kitchen to locate the fish basket. It was there somewhere.

Kelsey shook her head. "No. I'm okay. Really."

"You sure? Advil? Anything?"

"I could help with dinner, or something."

"Right now, I'm looking for the fish basket. It's a wire mesh contraption that ... Here it is." He pulled it out of the back of the lower cupboard and raised it in his hand. A good pass over the flames would scorch the dust off of it, and it would be good as new.

Her brows furrowed. She was a different person this afternoon. "You catch fish with that? Are they really small?"

Her naiveté made him smile. For a split second he was tempted to string her along, let her think exactly that. One glance into her trusting face, and he couldn't do it. "I think I'll use my fishing pole for that. This basket is to grill whatever I catch."

"Oh. That makes sense. I guess." She nodded as if she was trying to figure things out.

"Do you like to eat fish?" he asked. *Hope so, cuz that's what we're having for dinner.*

"I think so." There it was again, that thoughtful look on her face. She blushed when she noticed he was watching. Her shoulders scrunched like she was embarrassed. "I really don't remember, but food is good."

That simple statement made him smile. *Yes. Food is definitely good. She must be hungry.*

"Listen. I don't think you're up to much right now. You take it easy and rest. We'll be back before you know it. How about if I leave Whisper here while I'm gone?" He grabbed his fishing pole from behind the door and called the dog inside. "Whisper. Guard."

"He's a guard dog?" she asked timidly.

"Yes, but he's just here to keep you company. I won't be long." Alex left with Smoke trotting alongside. He glanced back at his cabin before he ducked into the trees. Overall, the day hadn't turned out too bad. He knew where Durrant was—and wasn't. Kelsey no longer looked like she was at death's door, and dinner, hopefully, would be roasted instead of boiled. Best of all, he was going fishing.

After the fiasco over the spilled coffee earlier, this had ended up being not too bad a day at all.

Kelsey

Fishing didn't take long.

Kelsey cocked her head to listen. That Alex Stewart guy was already back with his other dog. An irrational sense of panic filled her, but she couldn't understand why she felt like she needed to run, so she did nothing. There was no place to hide anyway. He was outside the front door, talking quietly to his dog. She was trapped.

I should have left while he was gone.

That solution posed another problem. Run to where? She didn't know where she was, much less where she should go. Taking in a deep breath, she focused on the fact that he had been kind, that he even fixed breakfast. And when he had held her this morning, he didn't hurt her. *So why am I frightened now?* Nothing made sense, not the awful shape her body was in or the fact she couldn't remember what had happened.

She decided not to run. A man with two dogs couldn't be that bad, could he? Besides, he was going to feed her again. Her stomach rumbled at the thought. She pushed her anxiety away and focused on the positive things that had happened. Like breakfast.

Kelsey didn't want him to think she was willing to sleep all day, so she washed the few breakfast dishes then took a couple of paper towels and washed herself, too. Her hip was the most painful, so she took care to clean the huge scrape there. But twisting her body to see how bad it was took her breath. Not only was the hip covered with a big raw patch of skin, but her backside and thighs were literally black and blue all over.

She lifted her sweatshirt, checking herself front to back. More scrapes and bruises met her eye. *No wonder I feel so bad.* The dishwater had stung her sore fingers when she did dishes, but her hip needed more than just sudsy water and a paper towel. Glancing around, she detected a tube of antiseptic ointment on the counter, along with medical gauze. She used both, thankful again for that guy with two dogs.

Her anxiety diminished a little more. She was safe, mostly clean, and she was going to eat pretty soon. Running her tongue over her tender lip, she wondered about that fish basket. *Do I like fish? It sounds kind of familiar.* The prospect of eating instigated another thought. *What else is there to eat around this place?* She rummaged through the cupboards until she came across several packets of instant rice side dishes. The fish she wasn't sure about, but she liked rice with broccoli. Removing a medium-sized saucepan from the same cupboard, she added the correct amount of water and added the rice. There. They would have rice and fish for dinner.

The outside noises subsided, and she smelled the fragrance of a campfire. Whatever that guy was up to, he was quiet. While she waited on the rice to cook, she took stock of her surroundings. The inside walls of the cabin were unfinished plywood, the solitary kitchen cabinet not much better. A green camp stove sat on the counter while the rickety wooden table where she had found the ointment was shoved up against the wall by her cot. Obviously it served as a cutting board because long knife marks hashed its top. The floor needed sweeping. Both windows were grimy, nearly too dirty for the shaded forest light to get through. Even the makeshift curtain was nothing more than an old sheet hung over a wooden dowel balanced on two big nails pounded into the wall. Everything was rustic times ten. Maybe a hundred.

Oddly, the ordinariness of the simple room calmed her. This guy's idea of dishes consisted of a couple mismatched coffee mugs, two chipped bowls, plastic plates, a blackened fry pan, a large stockpot, and that saucepan she had found. A Dutch oven looked like it hadn't been used in years. It was rusty. The pans were as black as the tin percolator on the camp stove. *He must not know how to use a scrub pad.*

A backpack lay slumped behind the door alongside a pair of beat up, dirty hiking boots. Cobwebs draped all the high corners. This place needed spring housecleaning in the worst way.

Her nose twitched. Kelsey caught a whiff of something tasty on the air. Dinner. She checked the rice. *I'm hungry. Time to eat.*

She gathered her courage and ventured outside. Whisper trotted alongside, bumping into her like he needed to keep in touch. A rifle and a fishing pole leaned against the porch railing, tucked into the corner so they wouldn't fall. The man stood with his arms crossed, gazing into the flames.

She hadn't taken the time to really look at him yet, so she did now. He was definitely good-looking, broad-shouldered, dark-haired, and trim. A strong jaw marked his profile. The way he stood with his head high and shoulders back gave him an air of authority, but the baseball cap perched brim backwards on his head made him seem too young for any kind of serious responsibility. Even in her tired state, she had to admit the blue-checkered flannel shirt and jeans fit him well. He appeared lost in thought, just like the silver dog sitting to his right. Both stared at the fire. She giggled.

"I didn't hear you." He looked up, startled. "What's so funny?"

"I'm sorry." Kelsey covered the left side of her face to hide her bruises. "I didn't mean to laugh. It's just that you and your dog have the exact same expressions on your faces."

"Well, we are meat eaters, aren't we, Smoke?" He nodded to her. "Did you remember if you like fish or not?"

"I think so." She licked her lower lip. Four fish complete with heads, fins and tails sizzled inside the fish basket. "They smell good."

"They do, don't they?" He sniffed the air. "Trout don't take long to cook. They'll be done in a minute."

"I made rice," she blurted out. Her stomach growled again, embarrassing her.

"You did?" That made him smile. "Good. It's nice to see you on your feet again."

"Sorry. All I've done today is sleep." Kelsey stayed on the top porch step where she could keep an eye on this guy.

"Sleep is a good thing." His voice sounded kind enough. "Besides, you needed the rest. How's that eye?"

There was no way to hide the mess on her face. "It's sore," she muttered, covering it so he didn't have to look at it. "I feel like I'm wearing a Halloween mask."

"Don't worry. The swelling will go down in a couple days. There's no need to hide it either. How do you feel otherwise?"

Slowly, she lowered her hand. "Like I've been run over by a truck or something. I seem to have forgotten a lot of things, too, like what I'm doing here?"

He maintained the distance between them. "By the looks of it, you took quite a fall in the past few days. Are you telling me you can't remember anything?"

"Well, I remember some things, like running. I must be a klutz though because it looks like I fell down a lot." She glanced around the porch, still expecting something to jump out at her. It was hard to relax. Once more she needed to confirm there was no danger here, just a friendly stranger who seemed content to stay far away from her. That was fine with her, as long as he fed her again. Breakfast was a long time ago.

He nodded at her to continue, so she did.

"I'm really sorry I wasn't very nice to you this morning." Her next words burst out in a rush. "I didn't know who you were, you know, and you picked me up, and you scared me. I mean, here I'm trying to figure out why these dogs are following me, and then you show up, and you're talking to me like we're supposed to know each other. Do I even know you?"

His handsome smile turned mischievous. "You don't remember last night at all, do you?"

"Last night?" Worry crinkled her forehead. *Oh, oh. What did he do to me?*

He smiled wider. Those blue eyes sparkled. That didn't ease her misgivings, not one bit.

"At first, I thought you were dead. To make a long story short, I cleaned you up, fed you, and put you to bed. You're telling me you don't remember any of that?"

She shook her head. "I guess I don't know much."

"Do you remember what I told you this morning?"

"I think so." She squirmed. It seemed like a long time ago, and it didn't end so well. "You told me about your dogs, and you made breakfast, and then I kinda freaked out."

"Yes, you did." His voice turned tender. "Why?"

"It just scared me, and … I don't know." She felt lost all of a sudden. The truth was he had scared her, and she didn't know why except that she was entirely at this man's mercy. That didn't seem like a good thing, no matter how nice he was.

He shrugged like it was no big deal. "Let's start over then. I'm Alex Stewart."

"Nice to meet you. I'm, umm, Kelsey." Her brain failed to provide her last name. *Everyone has a last name, don't they? He did.*

"Nice to meet you." He nodded to her in friendly acknowledgement. "I came here for a vacation with my dogs. The silver one keeping track of tonight's dinner is Smoke. You've already met Whisper. He's already decided you're his, so I suspect he'll keep following you around. Hope you don't mind. Anyway, don't worry about your memory. It'll come back sooner or later. You're welcome to stay as long as you want."

Whisper leaned into her side like he needed to remind her he was there.

"Hi, Whisper," she said, her hand on his wide forehead. "You're a good boy, aren't you?"

"Whisper, down," Alex scolded, but Kelsey grabbed the big mutt before he had time to obey.

"No," she said. "It's okay. I'm not scared of him." The heat of embarrassment blossomed up her neck, so she snuggled Whisper for an extra long time. Her words made it sound like she was scared of Alex. *Should I be?* She didn't have time to worry about that because his previous words had sunk in. "Did you say you cleaned me up, and put me to bed?"

Kelsey pulled at her pant leg. That explained the bandages and the greasy ointment on the rest of her. It also explained the baggy sweatpants and shirt she was wearing. She might not remember much, but she was pretty sure she had better taste than this. So this stranger, this Alex Stewart guy, had washed her, spread ointment on a large portion of her naked body, changed her clothes, and put her to bed like a child? She cringed. She couldn't remember any of it, yet he acted like it was no big deal. Part of her wanted to cry, while the rest of her was just plain embarrassed. What else did he do?

If Alex noticed her discomfort, he didn't let on. "Yep. Got you cleaned up and fed. Just like I'm going to do now." He lifted the fish basket up with a bemused smile in his eyes. "Dinner's ready. Let's eat."

Five

Alex

"Are you going to eat that?"

Alex could not keep the smile off his face. Four fish were not enough. To say Kelsey ate dinner was an understatement. Devoured was more like it, and now she eyed his plate.

"Are you still hungry?"

She licked her bottom lip. "Maybe."

He slid the last trout out of the basket and onto her plate. "Be careful of the bones."

"It's really good," she mumbled, her mouth already half full of fish.

The question of whether she liked fish was put to rest. They had already gone through a second pan of rice also. She chased the last kernel of rice across her plate with her fork. It did not get away. This woman was feeling better. A lot better.

Despite her black eye and bruises, she had a very pleasant face tonight. She wiped her mouth and fingers with a paper towel and tucked the towel into the elastic on her sweat pants. That made him smile. Those pants were way too big—for now. The way she was eating, they wouldn't be too big for long.

"Whew." She scrunched her shoulders when she caught him looking. "I like fish."

"I see that," he smirked. "You like rice too."

"I do." She nodded, a mischievous light in her eye. "Sorry, but I was really hungry. All I need now is a piece of chocolate."

"I almost forgot." He jumped up and went quickly into the cabin for his backpack, returning with a couple of mini-chocolate bars. He offered one to her. "I always bring a couple of these when I'm hiking."

She took the closest. "Thanks. I was just kidding, but this is a nice treat."

"Will one be enough?" he teased. She wasn't really kidding. He knew a hungry woman when he saw one.

"Yes." She ripped the end of the wrapper with her teeth and expertly removed the bar. At the first bite, she closed her eye, savoring the morsel as she slowly chewed. "Mmm. I like chocolate too."

"You are feeling better, aren't you?" Listening to her moan over a piece of chocolate made him smile. Kelsey was definitely going to live.

"Don't you feel like you just need a teeny piece of chocolate after you eat?" She finished the chocolate with a satisfied smack of her lips.

"Nope. That's a girl thing." He sat on the steps with her. "Us guys just need meat, huh, Whisper?"

The big dog had made himself comfortable right between them. They sat in silence as the fire crackled and popped. She sighed, and even that little sound made him smile. Daylight still shone at the tops of the giant pines, but shadows deepened in the forest. Smoke tendrils from the campfire smelled good, Alex had food in his stomach, and he was feeling pretty mellow. It was a comfortable moment, but he could tell she was becoming nervous again. She fidgeted with her napkin and wiped her puffy eye.

"Since I can't tell you a whole lot about me, maybe you could tell me something about you?" She glanced at him sideways.

Alex leaned back on his elbows, stretched his legs down the steps and contemplated an answer. Her anxiety was back. It seemed to come and go. Food obviously made it go. *Mental note to self—catch more fish tomorrow.*

"What you really mean is: who the hell am I?"

"Maybe." She ducked with a shy smile.

"Okay, so you already know my name and my dogs' names. What else would be interesting?"

"Maybe like where you live when you're not at your cabin?"

"That's easy. Alexandria, Virginia."

"Is that very far away?"

He smirked at her innocent question. Even the best answers didn't mean much to an amnesiac.

"It's a couple thousand miles that way." He pointed east. "I try to get out here every June to do a little fishing. My old man left me this land a long time ago. This time, I got a little sidetracked."

"Sorry." She blushed again. "Guess that's my fault."

"Nah." He waved it off. "Just glad I was here to help." He couldn't believe the lie that just rolled off his lips, but it sounded true. He acknowledged it. He was glad he had helped her.

"Where is here?"

"Well, we are in Washington State—"

"That much I know. It's funny. I do remember some things, like I know I live in Washington. I just don't know … where."

"The official post office address for this place is Spanaway."

"I guess that's helpful once I remember where Spanaway is." She giggled very quietly. "I'm sorry. It's not funny. I mean, look at me. I'm all beat up, and I look like heck, and you're trying to help. It's just that..." She scrunched her shoulders again. "I don't know, it just feels good to laugh, you know? For some reason, it feels really good."

Alex sobered at the knowledge he possessed, and she did not. There was a reason laughing felt good to Kelsey. Her laugh had a sweet, musical quality. She should do it more often.

He debated telling her about the Amber Alert and her own endangered status, but it felt too soon. Too cruel. How do you tell a woman who is just getting on her feet that her husband is trying to kill her? That he may already have attempted murder? How do you knock her back down? He couldn't do it. Not yet. Maybe tomorrow...

"So tell me more. What's in Alexandria, Virginia?"

Her question jolted him back to safer topics. "Work. Started a business. Needed a break."

"Cool. So you're a savvy businessman then?"

Alex snorted at her very kind description of himself. Here he was sprawled out in dirty jeans with an old flannel shirt. He had a baseball cap on his head and probably had hat hair for sure, plus he hadn't showered yet today. Savvy was the last thing he was. "Let's just say I started a business. Right now, it seems to be running me."

"Why's that?"

"It's a long story." He watched the fire. "Thought I had a good idea awhile back. Even got a surprise benefactor to ante up the cash to get it off the ground."

"It's successful then?"

"The demand's greater than I anticipated." He shrugged as the gloomy predicament of his business invaded his thoughts. Success should make a man feel a whole lot better than he felt. That it didn't was a puzzle he couldn't figure out. The old adage that money wasn't everything annoyed him, like he didn't already know that? That lesson had been stamped indelibly into his heart exactly four years ago when he had lost—them.

"Cool. So you're making lots of money, and you're successful. That's supposed to be a good thing, isn't it?" Her face lit up with her cheerful summarization of his life.

"I guess." He stared at the dying embers, not wanting to share anymore.

"But it's not?"

"Let's just say it's not what I expected." Alex stood and stretched before he tossed a couple more logs in the fire pit. He settled back on the steps by Whisper, hoping she would stop asking questions. She didn't.

"What? You don't like to work or something?"

He noticed no recrimination in her voice, amazement maybe, but no judgment. She just wanted to know.

"Just didn't think I'd get stuck behind a desk all day." He suppressed his impatience. "Maybe when I get a few things figured out, I'll be able to spend more time with my agents. That's what I'd rather do."

"Agents? Like insurance agents? Secret agents?" Kelsey fidgeted with her broken fingernails as she listened. "What kind of business did you start anyway?"

Again, Alex deliberated how much he should tell her, so he gave her the simplified version. "I'm an ex-Marine. Once I left the Corps, I didn't fit in civilian life. Most people don't realize how hard it is for a guy to leave the service, especially in my line of work. Anyway, a lot of good men are coming back from overseas. I needed something to do, and they needed work, so I started a covert surveillance business."

She studied him intently. "What's covert surveillance?"

He studied her, not sure how much information her brain could process right now. She seemed to have some capacity for remembering. He just didn't want to overload her the first moment she felt halfway decent.

"It's not a big deal," he muttered. "We do undercover work. Most of it's just a game of watch and report, kind of like the work private investigators do. For instance, think about the drug trade in Afghanistan. I've got a contract on my desk for two agents to do surveillance over there. All the State Department wants is to understand how heroin is impacting that country."

"Okay. That's interesting."

"And we're all ex-military snipers."

Kelsey blinked hard. "Snipers? You're a sniper?"

"Do you know what a sniper is?"

She nodded rapidly. "You shoot people."

He couldn't help the smirk on his face. "Not always. We were all in special ops. I've got two vets from the Vietnam era and a couple from Afghanistan and Iraq. I haven't hired a Navy SEAL yet, but it could happen. We're trained professionals, and we try real hard not to shoot people. We do good work."

She gulped, but he wasn't sure if she understood what he had just told her or not.

"Not what you were expecting?"

"No, it's just that I..." Kelsey stared at her fingers.

"A lot of folks don't understand guys like me. You're probably thinking you're out in the woods with Hannibal Lecter, huh?" The moment he used that descriptor he wanted to call it back. *Damn it, Stewart. Think before you speak. Just once. Think. After all she's been through....*

"No." She spit the word out. "I was trying to say that you're a very nice man, and you've been taking care of me, and feeding me. Besides, you have two dogs that love me. I don't think a murderer would be as nice as you are. I don't think..." She paused, looking directly at him. "I'm not afraid of you. I was this morning, but ... I'm not now. You've helped me. A lot. And, umm, you keep feeding me."

He grinned. Food did seem to be an integral part of the conversation. "Sorry. I shouldn't have teased."

"I feel safe with you," she declared, "and you aren't creeping me out with that scary question either. I never thought you were like Hannibal Lecter. Sheesh. What a question."

For some odd reason, his stupid heart flipped at her scolding. Kelsey was comfortable to be around tonight. Even as beat up as she was, she trusted him. Glancing out of the corners of his eyes, he felt drawn to her. There was something familiar he couldn't place, like he had known her a long time ago.

"It's odd though," she stretched her fingers in front of her. "I can remember someone like Hannibal Lecter, but not my last name."

"You'll remember. Don't worry." That familiar pang of recognition poked him again.

"So, anyway." She changed the subject as she ruffled Whisper's mane. "Tell me about your dogs. They're beautiful. Where'd you get them?"

"A friend left them to me in his will."

"His will?"

"Yes. Max was an old Army canine handler. He used to adopt the dogs he worked with when he got the chance. One night, he showed me how smart they are. Little did I know it was a job interview. Long story short—Max got cancer last year, died and left me his dogs."

"They're such good boys." She stroked the sleeping black mutt beside her. "Max gave you a special gift, didn't he?"

"Guess so." Alex smacked Smoke on the butt as the dog strolled by. Smoke was instantly ready to play. "They're good company. Smoke's the clown. Whisper's the thinker." Alex wrestled with Smoke a couple minutes longer. Whisper was just as ready to join in, but Alex gave them a quick command, and they settled down.

"Sounds like you live a very interesting life."

Yep. That was him all right, interesting to the bone.

Kelsey grimaced as she fingered the back of her head. "Ouch. Would you mind if I warm a pan of water when we go in, so I can wash my hair? It's really gross." She made another funny face, and again, his heart kicked into overdrive. He hadn't felt like this in a long time.

"Let me do that for you." He offered his arm as they stood to go into the cabin. It was not a big deal. He had done this a thousand times with women of all ages. It was just the polite thing to do, but when Kelsey said, "Thanks," and took hold of his arm right at the bend of his elbow, it was an entirely new feeling. He looked down at her, still so battered that she could only see out of one eye, but he felt like he was looking at a woman of royalty. There was a quality about her he couldn't see or touch, yet it was there. She glanced up at him, blinking shyly like she didn't want him to look at her. He couldn't stop.

Opening the door, he stepped back so she could enter first. He brushed the nonsensical feeling away, retrieved his rifle from its resting place and went into the cabin behind her. After he replaced his weapon on the high kitchen cupboard top, he filled a large pan with water, and set it on the camp stove to heat. She sat waiting on the cot while he set up a makeshift washbasin on the counter for her use.

"You're quite the gentleman, aren't you?" she asked shyly.

"Nah." His cheeks warmed at her unexpected compliment. "I picked up a clean shirt and some shampoo for you when I was out this morning, and a hairbrush, too. Let me know if you need anything else."

Alex headed for the door, intending to clean up around the fire and take the dogs for a quick walk. He didn't get far. As soon as he glanced back, he knew she would need help. She stood gripping the counter for support. The last thing he needed was for her to get a cracked skull on top of everything else.

"On second thought, how about if we do it this way instead?" He stepped back to her side and moved everything to the table. Leaning the only chair in the place against the table's edge, he made a small flourish with both hands toward the improvised beauty salon. "You sit here. I'll tip the chair back and wash your hair for you. Last chance offer, ma'am."

"Do you call all women ma'am, Mr. Stewart?" she asked timidly.

"Only ladies." He winked, and she blushed again. "Please call me Alex."

Kelsey turned away from him, a shadow darkening her face. "No, it's okay. I'll figure something out."

"Come on now. It will only take a couple minutes. We'll be done before you know it."

"Well." She glanced at him and then the chair, biting her lower lip in uncertainty. "If you really don't mind."

"Not at all." He held the chair while she made herself comfortable. Within minutes, he had her tilted back and was pouring warm water over her head and into the washbasin. He poured a small bit of the baby shampoo onto his hands, and then worked the shampoo through her long dirty hair. Instantly it transformed into fudge-colored silk. Alex felt Kelsey relax when he massaged her scalp. With a sigh, her nervousness faded, and just as quickly, he relaxed, too. The clumps of dried blood and dirt dissolved. Very gently, he traced the cut at the back of her head with his fingertips. Jagged, nearly two inches long, it sat just above her neck. Overall, she was lucky she hadn't gone into shock considering all she had been through.

"I'm not hurting you, am I? You've got a good-sized cut back here."

"No, it feels good." She sounded sleepy. "So tell me more. Are you married? Any kids, or are those dogs your kids?"

It was an innocent question that he had certainly answered enough in the past. Why it affected him differently tonight, he didn't know. Something about Kelsey made him want to explain. "Three times. Once for love. Twice for nothing. One daughter."

She didn't respond, so he focused on rinsing her hair thoroughly. He lathered her head again, determined to keep his mouth shut, but then he thought maybe talking about his daughter might help her remember. He couldn't get the pictures he had seen of Tommy and Jackie out of his mind.

"Her name was Abby."

He squeezed the suds through her hair and concentrated on working it around her face so he didn't get soap in her eyes. With his hands full of suds and chocolate silk the cabin transformed into a time machine. Before he knew it, he was lost in recollections of his perfect daughter. The smell of baby shampoo took him to a different place and time when little feet pounded down the hall to his and Sara's bedroom in the early morning hours, when any garden spiders that might have wandered into his house were deaf from little girl screams of, "Pider, Daddy. Pider!"

Once more, Alex smelled his child's sweet breath in his nose and felt the softness of baby kisses on his cheek. He always called them butterfly kisses. Her little-girl hugs were the magic balm that took away every care in his tough military life. Abby was sunshine and joy, everything good in his miserable life. He could almost hear her squeal, "Daddy!" She had loved him. He adored her. It felt like yesterday.

Another memory demanded revelation, so he shared it. "She was so tiny when she was born. The minute the nurse handed her to me, that little girl snagged my shirt like she was gonna punch me for pulling her away from her nice, warm mama."

"And?" Kelsey asked, and Alex couldn't refuse her any more than he could stem the tide of love for his daughter that had swelled inside.

"I spoiled her. Honest. If she wanted a sucker, I got her a sucker. If she wanted a kitten, we got her a kitten. That little girl..." He sighed. "Here I'm supposed to be leading men into battle, and she could turn me into breakfast mush."

"I can see that side of you."

"You should've seen me trying to give her a bath the first night we brought her home. Sara was tired. I thought I was hurting Abby. It was like bathing a fish. Heck, I didn't know babies don't like water on their faces."

Alex stilled as he played with Kelsey's hair the same way he used to play with Abby's, his fingers full of chocolate loops, tangles, and bubbles. Leaning relaxed against the table, he didn't want the moment to stop.

"She got bossy when she turned two. So she's standing in the bathtub telling me she's in charge of the bubble bath. She was so dang cute." He poured another cup of rinse water carefully over Kelsey's head. "She kept hollering, 'Me do it. Me can do it.'"

"I'll bet you had tons of bubbles that day."

"Tons." Once again, his blonde angel peered up at him through the mounds of frothy bubbles with the same Popsicle grin on her bright, shining face. Memories of Abby flooded through him. They filled his heart with peace, and for a moment, he was happy. But, just like that, regret sucker punched him—hard. His voice cracked. He pulled away from the table, stood straight, and faced the empty hole that was his real life. "That was a long time ago."

"What happened?" Her question was so innocent.

The words stuck in his throat. "They died. Car accident. Four years ago."

"Oh Alex. I'm so sorry."

"Forget it." He cursed himself for letting his guard down. He should've quit while he was ahead.

"I'm sorry. I shouldn't have asked."

The magic of the night popped like just another bubble in his hand. With a jolt, Alex was back in his cabin, helping a strange woman. That's all. Sara and Abby were gone, and tomorrow Kelsey would be in police protection and out of his life. Self-disgust chased the peaceful feeling away. He was his own worst enemy. *What was I thinking?*

He felt the tear slide out of his eye and brusquely wiped it against his shoulder. Once again, he was caught in the riptide of guilt and regret. He had said too much. It was past time to shut up. He noticed she had grown quiet, too. Had he hurt her feelings again?

"How you doing?" He hated the tremble in his voice.

Kelsey didn't answer, so he leaned over to see how much damage he had caused. Tears coursed down her cheeks. She buried her face in her hands. Within minutes, Alex rinsed her hair, wrapped the towel around her head, and had her sitting upright.

He cursed his stupidity. This was the last thing he needed. The second he put his arm around her, she pushed off the chair and into his arms, buried her face against him, and wept. Surprised, he held her gently at first, then a little tighter. She shuddered, and he couldn't help himself. He scooped her into his arms and sat on the chair with her on his lap.

"Hey now, what's this about?" His voice was soft and tender as he tipped her chin up to see her better. "What's going on?"

She wiped the towel across her face, struggling to pull herself together. "I'm sorry. It's just that I got this feeling all of a sudden that I have children. I know I do. I mean, I think I'm a mom, only I can't remember," she whined. "I can't see their faces. I don't know their names. I just can't remember anything."

Well, Alex noted dourly, he had achieved what he wanted. He had sparked a memory. Turning her face into his shoulder, he wiped his eyes again without her noticing.

"You'll remember," he whispered hoarsely. "You have a concussion right now and maybe a little amnesia, but it's all going to come back to you. You'll see." He kissed the side of her head where the towel was wrapped. "A good mother never forgets her kids. I'll bet you're the best mom ever. Give yourself time."

Kelsey looked up at him, her brown eyes brimming with tears. She had noticed his watery eyes. With the tenderest hand, she caressed the clenched jaw that barricaded his pain. "What's the matter?"

Her touch was light and soft, so warm and caring that he leaned into it. No woman had touched him like this in years. As much as he wanted to tell her nothing was the matter, he knew something deep inside had broken open. Her gentle touch resonated to his core. For the first time since he had been notified of his family's death while he was in Fallujah, thoughts of Sara and Abby hadn't morphed into out of control anger. No monster screamed that their deaths were his fault, or that he should have been there. He could still breathe. His head didn't pound with guilt. The burden he had attended to so faithfully and for so long evaporated under her hand.

"Guess I just miss my little girl." His voice caught at that profound understatement.

"You poor thing. I'm so sorry." She smoothed her hand against his whiskered cheek.

He choked with shame at those words, spoken so kindly by the very woman he had cursed. He repented instantly. "I'm so sorry for the way I treated you last night. I was wrong. I've been so wrong about so many things."

"For what?" she asked kindly. "You couldn't hurt anyone."

He couldn't speak. Here she was offering mercy to the beast he was, to another man who didn't deserve it. He shivered as the truth roared over him. There was no way she could've hurt anyone. If anything, she was as much a victim as her sons. That's how Kelsey got tangled up with the likes of Durrant. She trusted too easily, and she believed people were good—just like she was doing now.

"You're a good man," she said softly. "I know. I can tell."

I'm not, but I have been. I can be. I will be.

She pulled his clenched fist to her lips and placed a small kiss on his knuckle, like she might have done for one of her little boys. His heart swelled. He wanted to run and hide. For the first time in years, his emotions of choice weren't anger or self-loathing. He blew out a shuddering breath. He felt— blessed?

She was a gentle armful. Her soft hand on his shoulder called out to the man he used to be, the gentle man, the guardian and protector, the fixer of all things mechanical, the killer of spiders, and the protector from all bad dreams. The fragrance of her just-washed hair seemed to work a magical spell in his dumpy two-room cabin. Sharing a few more stories about Abby and Sara felt natural, especially the way Kelsey listened. She smoothed the worry lines at the corner of his eye with the tip of her thumb while he held her safe and secure in his arms. It happened without notice. The anger whooshed out of his soul, and the world was once again a pretty good place to be.

The miracle of the evening amazed him. He caught himself rocking back and forth, not sure who was comforting whom. It didn't matter. It was nothing more than a parent's automatic comfort response, and right now, they both needed it. If only for tonight, they were no longer strangers thrown together by the chaos of chance. No. He saw Kelsey and himself clearly now. They were two people who had loved with all their hearts and souls—and lost.

Only now, they weren't alone.

Six

Alex

He shouldn't have looked. He should've marched right by the cot and minded his own business, but no. Alex paused to check on his guest on his way out the door, and then he couldn't step away.

Kelsey had fallen asleep on her left side last night, the bruises and black eye hidden against her pillow. She had brushed her damp hair and woven it into a loose braid that had come undone during the night. This morning, it spilled a crimped stream of shiny cocoa around her face, over her shoulders, and across the pillow. With the blanket pulled up to her chin and her lips pinched in a pout, she looked child-like, angelic, and downright perfect. Whatever magical power she wielded held him fast and made him weak. He couldn't force his eyes away.

The sight of her spiked that protective feeling again. Alex shook his head to clear his head, but the warmth of the moment spiraled through his chest like a bottle rocket with a different kind of spark. He squelched the desire to hold her again.

Knock it off, Stewart. She just needs a little help. That's all.

"Whisper. Stay," he commanded hoarsely, although the dog hadn't so much as lifted his head from his place beneath the cot anyway. All he did was blink his big, black eyes as if to say, "Duh."

Alex's hands shook as he shouldered his rifle and shut the cabin door quietly behind him. He couldn't think straight with Kelsey around. Even with her sound asleep, he felt an inexplicable attraction, and she hadn't done a thing to encourage it. Heck, she wasn't even his type. She wasn't blonde like Sara. She didn't resemble blonde replacement wife number two who looked like Sara, and neither was she manipulative and domineering like blonde wife number three. Heck, Kelsey wasn't even single. She was a stranger whom he didn't really know. The moment that thought entered his mind, he knew better. Kelsey felt more like everything.

So he left. He needed to know for sure she was safe, but hiking also cleared his head, and he really needed to hike. The only problem was, as he checked the deer blinds in the area and walked the trails, Kelsey stayed in his mind. So did Sara.

Sara was his first true love, and he missed her deeply. His memories of her had faded since her death until he had forgotten the nuances and details of her kiss, her smile, and their life together. This morning she didn't seem so far away. He remembered everything.

She was the daughter of another military man, an Army brat who had fallen for a Marine. That was the only shortcoming Alex could name, and that was only because she married down when she had fallen for him. It also meant she was accustomed to the way things worked in military families. The woman's role was oftentimes mother, father, plumber, coach, and any other job that came along while her man was deployed. Sara shouldered that role as quickly as he shouldered his gear when he left on assignments. It was just the way it was.

The last time they had kissed was the morning he had to leave for an overseas operation. He had promised to build a broom closet for her kitchen and a tree house for Abby when he got back. She had kissed him hard then, like she would never let him go. The closet and tree house never got built. Even with those sad memories, a peaceful sensation settled over Alex. Here he was walking the farthest perimeter of his property to protect Kelsey, and of all things, the spirit of his dead wife walked with him. Alex smiled. Sara would've liked Kelsey.

As he was about to turn back, he caught a movement out of the corner of his eye. About a hundred yards away in a stand of sun-deprived hemlocks, Durrant stood puffing on a cigarette, the same baseball cap as yesterday pulled low over his face. Alex crouched low and leveled his rangefinder for a better look. Durrant was deeper in the forest today, not safe by his truck. That could mean trouble.

The blond-haired man appeared gaunt and nervous, a drug addict kind of nervous, like he needed a fix. The Winchester thirty-thirty hung off Durrant's back along with an aluminum canteen. He wasn't hunting though. It looked more like he was taking a smoke break, like he had all the time in the world.

Alex studied him. Durrant didn't look like any kind of a skilled hunter, but looks weren't everything. He flicked his cigarette butt into the trees and stood scratching his nose. For a moment, Alex thought he might have been seen, but no.

Durrant brought his rifle to his shoulder and fired high into a tree, chuckled like he had actually hit something, and reloaded. Needles and twigs fell to their death. He swung around and fired again, this time with his rifle at his hip, and once more without taking time to aim properly. More branches dropped dead. Some bark chips expired. Tired of shooting at nothing, he headed north, back toward the asphalt road.

Alex watched him go. His assessment of Durrant's hunting skills was once again confirmed. A fool with a gun, that's all this guy was. He didn't have a clue. That fact alone eased much of the concerns Alex felt. Durrant wasn't so much a skilled predator as he was a bully. Alex knew the type. Durrant was the sneaky man who won his fights by a stab in the back instead of a direct one-on-one confrontation. He was the typical woman beater—a coward.

When Alex got back to the cabin, the first thing he did was check on Kelsey. He didn't step into the cabin though. No. He glanced in just enough to wave Whisper out. She was still asleep, which was a good thing. The more she rested, the faster she would get back on her feet. Besides, he didn't need to see her all sleepy-eyed, her hair tousled first thing in the morning, not the way he was feeling. Absolutely not. That's the last thing he needed, to see her yawn and stretch under the covers, or to hear the soft sounds she made as she woke. *Hell, no.*

Instead, he leaned his rifle into the same porch corner as before and gathered a few branches for a fire. Campfire smoke always smelled good, and besides, he needed to keep his mind off the beautiful lady sleeping inside his cabin like she belonged there. He noted with chagrin last night would have been a whole lot different if he hadn't gotten the bright idea to go down memory lane, or to help her wash her hair for that matter. That's the problem with doing a good deed. It always came back to bite.

His mind wandered. All that gorgeous hair of hers had felt like liquid comfort running through his fingers. It was the same feeling a man gets when a woman wraps her arms around him because he's the absolute and only one she loves, the one she wants to build her world around. Everyone knows a man can't build a world. Only a woman has that wondrous ability. Alex knew that much for sure. He had tried two times and failed.

He lost himself staring at the flames. Kelsey had felt so fragile last night, as if she could've easily been broken or just as easily loved. He knew his thoughts were foolish. This woman had a world of grief. She was plenty broken. What would she be like when she got her memories back? For that matter, did she have any memories worth remembering? Did she smile very often? Did her musical voice giggle in real life? He doubted it. The weight of what he knew burdened him. She deserved so much more.

Instantly another question posed itself. What kind of a man could hurt a little thing like her? The fire crackled and popped as Alex's mind wandered back to the stand of hemlocks. It would've been an easy shot. No one would've known. He shook the dark thought from his head. He didn't work like that. No. Let the authorities take care of Durrant.

He would take care of Kelsey.

Kelsey

"Mommy."

The sweet boy wrapped his whole hand around her index finger as he pulled her into the dark light of nighttime. A million stars glistened like new fallen snow in an arc across the heavens.

"Pretty, Mommy. Pretty." The smiling child squealed, his little hand so warm and good in hers. It felt like it belonged there. Kelsey knelt to pick him up. She longed to hold his wriggly body. He smiled with sparkling eyes framed by chocolate-colored hair.

"Up, Mommy. Up."

She knelt, but with a puff of cold air, he was gone. Her arms gathered nothing. Once more, she stood alone on weathered planks. No stars glittered overhead. Darkness engulfed her. She sank to her knees and then to her elbows as the porch disintegrated, swallowing her into more darkness. The wooden planks were gone. No hand reached out for rescue. No one knew she was there. No one cared.

Jerking upright, Kelsey woke with the scream in her throat, her heart pounding like a runaway train. *Where am I? Whose cabin? Where...*

Reality edged out the nightmare. She remembered. *Alex. I'm in his cabin. I'm safe.*

There was no magic arc of stars, no childish look of love, and no darlin'g boy. Sinking back against the pillow, she wiped the sweat from her face. Whatever had happened to her, it was bad. She felt the whiplash of it in every bone, joint, muscle, but mostly, in her heart. The nagging sensation of motherhood lingered. Did she really have children? If she did, where were they? Did they miss her? Who was taking care of them? Were they boys? Were they girls?

She pulled the cover tight under her chin and stretched the last of the nightmare away. The smell of coffee on the stove created a homey feeling, or maybe that homey feeling came from Alex. Thoughts of him easily intruded. He was handsome, strong, and kind. When he had put his arms around her last night, she'd felt unusually safe, as if that was something to luxuriate in and never let go. She wouldn't have minded sitting with him a little longer. He had done so much to help her, a total stranger.

Whisper yawned, stretching to his feet. She rolled over on her side to see him better, and that's all the invitation he needed. He took her forearm into his big mouth, his way of telling her he trusted her. Before she knew it, both monster front paws were in her lap. Soon, she was nose to nose with the gorgeous black dog that thought he was a poodle.

"You're just a big teddy bear, aren't you?" Scratching behind his droopy ear, Kelsey pressed her forehead against his furry face. He growled in his typical German shepherd speak, as if telling her he agreed one hundred percent.

"Hey." Alex stood at the cabin door, a smirky smile on his tanned face. She saw the tease in those blue eyes. "Are you lazy louts ever getting up?"

"I, ah, I, ah..." She ended up not saying anything at all.

"Nice T-shirt by the way. Looks good on you." He winked.

A warm flush blazed up her neck and over her cheeks. She was wearing that pink shirt with the words "Gas-N-Go" emblazoned in gold lettering across her chest. She laughed. She must look like a walking ad, only with a trick or treat kind of scary face. "Very funny. How about I fix breakfast today?"

"You're too late. It's on the fire. I just came in for the coffee." He grabbed an old hot pad as he picked up the coffee pot. "Sugar and cream?"

She eased herself off the cot, surprised he remembered. "Yes, please."

"Grab a couple more ibuprofen if you're stiff."

"Thanks, Mr. Stewart. I mean, Alex." Kelsey stepped out on the porch with him and sat gingerly on the top step. "I have a favor to ask. After breakfast, could you..."

She couldn't speak. He stood too close, his blue eyes so gentle it took her breath away. Here she was ugly in a really gross way and about to eat the breakfast that he, a very kind and handsome man, had fixed for her. She could barely breathe.

"Did you need something?" he asked softly, a bemused twinkle in his eye. "Can I help you get that hip cleaned up?"

"Umm, no." She had to be ten shades of burgundy, red, and scarlet all mixed together by now, not to mention she sounded like a total imbecile. "I took care of that, but I need help putting ointment on my back. I can't reach it."

"Sure." He ambled over to the fire pit where he had a frying pan balanced on three rocks. Smoke and Whisper watched attentively from a respectable distance while Alex returned with a plate of breakfast and a cup of coffee for her. "That's easy. I thought you were going to ask something hard the way you were hemming and hawing."

"I hate asking for help," she said softly. At this proximity, Kelsey was very aware of his breathing, the way he held his fork and the way he sipped his coffee. Even the closely trimmed hairline above his collar somehow spiked her libido.

She looked away to break the spell. *Wow. I must've really hit my head hard. No man can look this good.*

"We'll take care of it after we eat." He had settled on the bottom step with his plate and coffee while Whisper and Smoke watched breakfast disappear.

"Thanks."

Besides his good looks, this man had an air of authority about him. He wasn't like anyone she had ever known. Was he? Even without her memory, she was pretty sure she had never met a man like him before.

It seemed he inhaled his breakfast. Before she was half finished, he was ready to doctor her again. She set her plate aside. He smoothed the ointment over the scrapes on her arms first, and then, very neatly, he rolled the way too long and very baggy pant legs up to her thighs so he could doctor her knees. He slathered the ointment gently over her scabbed skin.

"I look like a pasty white zombie." She watched him at his task, embarrassed and thankful—and then embarrassed all over again when his strong fingers stroked her sun-deprived calves.

"Nah. I wouldn't say a zombie." He smiled up at her from his kneeling position.

Her heart thudded like a crazy bass drum in the proverbial high school band. She blinked at those wells of blue mischief. Something passed between them she couldn't quite interpret, and just like that, he moved quickly to kneel behind her on the porch.

"If you lift the back of your shirt, I'll finish the job."

Kelsey blushed as she pulled her shirt up, but it stuck. Her damaged skin had oozed and dried during the night.

"Ouch. Sorry. It's kinda stuck," she murmured, embarrassed she was so much trouble. "Never mind."

"Take it easy. Let me get it." He tugged gently until the shirt was free. "There, now let's get you bandaged so this doesn't happen again." With careful, long strokes, he spread the soothing ointment over her back and shoulders.

She closed her eyes and relaxed. The scrapes didn't seem to hurt when he touched them like that.

He slathered more ointment along her spine and around her sides. Without thinking, she moved into the warmth of his hand. Abruptly, he stopped the tender massage and went into the cabin. Within seconds, he returned with the gauze. Very gently, he bandaged her back, taping the corners before he eased her shirt down.

"There." His voice sounded odd, restrained somehow like maybe he didn't care for her reaction. "I've got a spare shirt if you need one."

"Thanks." Kelsey turned to look at him, but he had already gone back inside the cabin. She noticed the distance between them. She finished her coffee, but he didn't return to the porch. Instead, he refilled the indoor water tank, making one trip after another with the heavy bucket. She watched as he worked. *Who are you, Alex Stewart?*

After the water tank was filled, he pulled a battered aluminum ladder from underneath the cabin and a bundle of wooden shingles. When Kelsey took her dishes inside, she noticed a black men's T-shirt folded on the counter. *I'm certainly wearing a lot of his clothes.*

She changed quickly, setting her pink shirt in the sink to soak. Putting his shirt on only added to her confusion. It was clean and folded, but it still smelled of him. She held the front collar to her nose and breathed it in. She shivered. Yes. She liked it very much.

The rest of the day passed quickly. Her headache faded, and with it, the flashing lights that had plagued her vision. Kelsey washed her cut-offs and hung them over the porch rail to dry. The blouse she had worn when she first arrived was damaged beyond repair, so she tore it into strips and used one of those strips for a hair tie.

Alex kept busy with roof repairs. He was up on the ladder most of the afternoon, so with two big dogs for company, she explored the camp and the creek. It was a very peaceful setting. She spent the afternoon picking a pan full of plump blackberries from an overgrown bush behind the cabin. Fortunately, there was a bag of pancake mix in the kitchen cabinet, so she improvised and baked a Dutch oven cobbler over the embers in the fire pit. It wasn't much, but it felt good contributing something for a change.

When he came off the roof, she served him a heaping bowl of the sizzling treat, and then she waited. He had been so quiet all day, preoccupied and remote. She half expected him to tell her that he had work to do; he didn't have time for such nonsense. He didn't. Instead, he blinked at the piping hot dessert like he had never seen blackberry cobbler before in his life.

"You made this?" he asked, his voice tight.

She held her breath, wondering why on earth this simple homemade treat felt like she had committed a sin all of a sudden. It was just—dessert. Irrational fear clutched her throat. She wanted to run, the suspense more than she could stand. *What if he doesn't like blackberries? What if he blames me for using his supplies? What if—*

"Thanks." He turned to her with an unrecognizable shadow in his eye. "You're very thoughtful."

And just like that, her fear evaporated. It wasn't a shadow in his eye. It was gratitude. The cobbler was a good idea after all. She blurted out her confession anyway, not exactly sure why she always thought she had to apologize. "I used some of your dried milk and pancake mix."

He pulled the only chair in the place to the table and sat down, took a forkful of the syrupy, berry-filled cake, and then another. She brought him a glass of water to wash it down, pleased with herself for the first time in—heck, she didn't know how long. The important thing was he liked it. She could tell. He closed his eyes like he was savoring every last morsel.

Alex paused, his fork suspended between his mouth and the second helping of dessert. He gave her a look she couldn't decipher. "You didn't need to do this."

"Yes, I did." Cheerfully, she squeezed his shoulder, her fingers lingering on the flannel. He felt warm from the sun, his muscles strong and hard. It was a small gesture, just a simple thing any friend would do, but it was the first time she had touched him like that.

He looked up at her. Loneliness flitted like a shadow across his face. Realization dawned. *He's just as lost as I am.*

"I'm glad you like it," she whispered, unsure which she meant, the cobbler or her hand on his shoulder.

"Join me?" he invited.

"I'd love to."

She grabbed the other chipped bowl, and together they enjoyed their first dessert together.

Alex

He took extra care replacing the few missing cedar shakes from the cabin roof, but who was he kidding? He was on the roof because it gave him a bird's eye view of her without being seen. Doctoring Kelsey this morning had taken on a whole new dimension. One look into her trusting eyes and he knew he had better put some distance between them. The warmth of her skin had changed his idea of medical attention to attention of a different kind. He didn't want to just smooth ointment on her legs and back anymore. Even scabbed and torn, her skin had glowed under his touch, and he liked it, but too many feelings begged for release. He just was not going down that road again. One true love in his life was enough, and two divorces more than plenty. No more heartache. Not now. Not ever.

So he buried himself in the remedy that had served him in times past, work and distance, all the while keeping careful track as Kelsey wandered below with his dogs at her heels. She picked blackberries, another pleasing sight. After the first few handfuls in her pan disappeared thanks to Whisper's lip-smacking company, she had to carry the pan everywhere she went.

She never grumbled at the big mutt though, even when he had munched all the low hanging fruit, leaving only the hardest-to-reach berries for her. In fact, she talked to him like he was a little boy and understood. She hummed some jingle Alex couldn't place. It didn't matter. Anything that rolled off her lips sounded good. Even from the rooftop, she was pleasant company.

A couple days of sleep, food, and rest had an astounding impact on her. In just one day his watchfulness had changed from worry about her health to watching her for an entirely different reason. Scarred, bruised or not, a beautiful woman was emerging from the battered husk he had found on his porch, and it wasn't just physical. Kelsey had a way about her that invited everything in, him and his dogs included, like she already loved the world and everyone in it.

He growled to himself at the thing that was happening. He was losing his mind, heart, and soul to her. He could feel it. So he fixed the rickety roof on his rickety cabin like he had nothing better to do, and he watched the most beautiful woman in the world dance with Whisper and Smoke.

Seven

Alex

"Looks like you've had a good day."

Alex kept his head down. He had to. It was either that or act like a fool again, and he had done enough of that. He forced himself to concentrate on the wood in his hands instead of staring at Kelsey. His knife glinted in the firelight as notch after notch of the soft pine dropped to the ground between his boots. He had a plan for this piece of wood. He hoped.

"I actually contributed something today, huh?" she teased.

He ignored her cheerful jab. "So, how's your head? You remember anything yet?"

Kelsey's fingers combed through her long hair, pulling it over the left side of her head, still trying to hide the bruised part of her face. "Once in a while I get the oddest feelings, but that's all."

Alex blew on his carving, sending a small cloud of dust and shavings into the air. "Amnesia's a tricky thing."

"It's like being in limbo," she muttered as she watched from her perch on the other side of the fire pit.

Alex noticed both dogs lay near Kelsey with Whisper bumped up against the log she sat on, his velvet fur dusty with wood shavings and dirt. His dogs had already succumbed to her charms. He was next. The chunk of wood in his hand proved it.

"I'd really like to remember my children. It's like they're right here in my head, but I can't quite reach them. Do you think they're safe? I mean, if I do have children, why am I out here without them?"

He heard the plaintive tone in Kelsey's question. Deep within her mother's heart, she knew something was wrong, and yet she didn't know anything at all. Once again he deliberated telling her everything he knew. Maybe it was time. His heart thudded. Maybe not. Maybe tomorrow...

She had stopped playing with her hair and scratched Whisper's belly while she talked. He gave a lazy growl of thanks in return. Alex bit his lower lip watching her hands move easily over the big mutt's body, pausing to scratch his ears, her fingers moving comfortably through his fur and ending up scratching his belly again. Of all the stupid things, he envied his dog.

He blew out a slow breath. She wasn't the weak one here. She wasn't the coward either. He cleared his throat and swallowed hard. Maybe it was time. She deserved to know everything he knew. Maybe one piece of information would spark a memory, and everything would all come back to her. And that's why he hadn't had the heart to tell her anything. *How do I do to her what was done to me? How do I take everything from her? Right now she's happy. It's a lie, but she's happy. How do I tear her world apart? How do I tell her the truth?*

He blew out a deep sigh. The time had come. There was no choice. It had to be done.

"I can fill in a couple of those blank spots if you'd like," he offered.

"You can?" She traded her log across the way for a log closer to him, her eyes bright in the fire's glow.

The minute she moved, he nicked his thumb. He grimaced, hoping she hadn't seen the effect she had on him. His heart pumped hard, like some high school jock. He forced his eyes back to the work at hand, his head full of conflicting emotions.

"Well, let's take it slow. Why do you think you're so far from town?" He hesitated. This was hard.

Kelsey looked at her torn fingernails. "I've been trying to figure it out. I mean, look at me. It's not like I don't know someone beat me up. Someone must really hate me."

She genuinely did not understand how close she had come to death.

"I'm not trying to scare you. You're safe here with the dogs and me, but someone did hurt you."

"What else do you know?" She edged closer, her eyes full of questions. "Have you been keeping something from me?

Bull's-eye. His heart leapt in his throat, and he nicked his thumb again. This time he wiped the blood on his pant leg because the knife went deep. She had just read him like a book. "I don't want to scare you, but yes. I had my team back east do some checking around."

"And?"

"And your name is Kelsey Durrant. You're married to a man named Nick Durrant." He waited to see if anything registered. There was no sense dumping everything on her all at once.

"Kelsey Durrant?" she asked. "My last name's Durrant? Hmm. And I'm married to Nick Durrant? Do you know what he looks like? Is he nice? Is he..." She paused as the reality of this new puzzle piece dawned on her. "Did he, I mean, is he the one who..."

Alex watched the light in her eyes fade as she fingered the corner of her recently opened black eye. She shivered.

"Did he do this to me?"

"Yes. I believe he did."

She clutched her arms like a little girl needing a sweater. "Okay, so what else?"

He hesitated knocking any more dominoes of information down on top of her. "Your sister reported you missing ten days ago. That timeline matches most of your injuries. I'm still not sure how you got your black eye though. That and your cut lip seem more recent."

"I've been missing ten days?" She looked surprised. "That's a long time."

Again, he waited as she processed that single fact.

"But I've only been here two days. Right?"

"That's right. You were here the afternoon I got in, the day before yesterday."

"So where have I been? Where was I before I got here?"

"I don't know. You were pretty out of it when I found you," he said gently. "I thought I'd found a dead body."

The bleakness in her eyes chilled him.

"But what did I eat? That's a long time to go without food or water."

"I don't think you did eat. That's why you were in such rough condition that first night. You probably stumbled across a creek or something along the way and found some water to drink. There are plenty of bogs and marshes in this part of the forest. That's the only reason you made it as far as you did."

She glanced toward the creek. "I'm pretty lucky that you showed up."

He nodded. The enormity of her situation still astounded him. *No, I'm the lucky one.*

"You said my sister reported me?"

"Yes."

"What's her name?"

"Louise Timpson."

Kelsey looked at him for a full minute before she spoke. "Are you telling me the truth?"

"None of this sounds familiar, does it?" He didn't think it would.

"No."

Her lip trembled, and he was done talking. This conversation was going nowhere fast, and he couldn't bear to hurt her anymore. The rest of it could wait.

"Why can't I remember?"

He stilled, the anguish in her question the last thing he needed to hear.

"What else do you know?" She wiped a tear out of her eye and once more moved closer. She needed comfort, and he wanted to give it, but he had nothing good to offer.

"Come on," she insisted. "Just because I can't remember anything right now doesn't mean I shouldn't know who I used to be, does it? Maybe if you tell me, it'll come back. It could, couldn't it?"

He sighed as his knife dug deeper into the notched piece of wood in his hand. "You lived in an apartment in

Lakewood. You used to be a schoolteacher, and you've been to the emergency room a lot."

"Why? What's wrong with me? Am I sick? Am I dying?"

"No, you're not sick." He glanced at her, hoping that simple answer would suffice, but then he couldn't look away. He saw it in her eyes. She trusted him to help her again. The only problem was this wasn't just ointment and band-aids he had to offer. This was heartbreak.

"You've had quite a few broken bones and spiral fractures over the past few years," he said somberly. "Do you understand what a spiral fracture is?"

"No."

He faltered. If he were smart, he would distance himself right this very minute and be done with her. Too bad he never was that kind of smart.

"Come here. I'll show you."

Kelsey moved beside him. He took hold of her right forearm, instantly reminded how delicate she was, and how warm.

"A spiral fracture occurs if your arm is twisted like this." He took hold of her wrist and elbow and barely twisted his hands in opposite directions. "The twisting motion causes too much torque. The bone fractures because both ends are turning in different directions, but it's not a clean break. Your arm's been broken like this a couple times." He rubbed his fingers along the length of her forearm. He might have been trailing a path of sparks. The energy off this woman amazed him. Did she feel it, too? He couldn't tell, but neither could he breathe.

"Feel this spot right here."

She pressed her fingers where he had traced. "I feel it. It's a bump."

"Yes. It's where your bone was broken, and then twisted again before it had a chance to heal." He released her arm before he made a fool of himself and pulled her onto his lap again. She already sat too close. The misery in her eyes compelled him to care more than he knew he should. She was damaged goods, another man's wife. He had no business thinking about her, much less caring for her the way he did. Even though every male instinct urged him to keep her safe, he couldn't. She wasn't his to protect—or keep.

"Your husband's out of work most of the time. He's got a police record," he muttered.

"For hurting me?" she asked timidly.

"He should be shot for hurting you!" The words blurted out of his big mouth before he had time to think. He stifled his emotions. "No. His record's just petty thievery, shooting dogs, and other stuff the police actually caught him doing."

"You mean they haven't actually caught him hurting me?"

Alex bit his lip. Her husband's police record was the last thing she needed to worry about. He bowed his head to the work in his hand again, mentally cursing himself for leading her down this ugly path that was her life. Wood shavings flicked out of his hand with every twist of the knife. He didn't stop carving until he felt her hand on his arm.

"Thank you for helping me," she said quietly.

"Yeah, well..." Particles of pine dropped steadily to the ground.

"Is that why you take off every morning? Are you looking for him?"

He let out a big sigh. "Your husband's still hunting for you."

"How do you know?"

"I've seen him. He hasn't come close to the cabin yet, but he's packing a rifle. We need to get you back to town."

She glanced sideways into the dark forest, her voice small and quiet. "Am I right? Do I have children?"

"Two boys," he whispered.

"How long have you known?"

"Since the morning after you got here."

"But you didn't tell me?"

"No." Alex shook his head. "You were so beat up, and I, I couldn't."

"What are their names?" The longing in her voice shredded his heart.

"Tommy and Jackie."

"Are they safe?"

"I don't know."

He held his breath as she studied him, her eyes full of frustration. Neither the names of her sister or her sons had raised so much as an eyebrow.

"If that Nick guy hurt me like this..." She looked at Alex, the horrible question unasked. "It's awful not to remember your children, isn't it?"

Her words struck a startling chord in his heart. For some reason, every conversation with this woman bared the tenderest part of his soul, leaving him exposed, vulnerable, and thinking too much. Until now, thoughts of his daughter had only meant pain, but Kelsey's question made him wonder. What would his life be like today without all those memories? Yes, he had to give Abby back much too soon, but

he'd had her for six incredible years that were priceless
beyond compare. Without realizing it, he brushed his
knuckles to his cheek as butterfly kisses reached through the
years. The memory of Abby's smiling blue eyes came back to
him. She loved him–still.

Kelsey sat watching, her eyes shining with trust. He saw
her clearly now. There wasn't any part of her not tuned to
him. Maybe it was just that they were alone, far from
civilization and dependent on each other. Maybe it was just
the horrible circumstances of her situation. Whatever the
reason, they had become human radar transmitters and
receivers, each picking up the slightest nuance, wish, and
hope from the other without any effort at all.

His heart thudded loudly in his ears. Even now, the tip of
her tongue on her healing lip excited nerve endings he hadn't
felt in years. He wasn't dead after all. No. The light in her
eyes drew him in like a too-willing moth to the certain death
of a beguiling flame. He changed the subject to break her
tender gaze. Somehow in their short time together, she had
become much too dear. He didn't want to lose her, too.

"We hike out tomorrow," he said gruffly. "Can you do
it?"

"I can." She glanced into the trees. He read her body
language loud and clear. She was scared.

"Listen to me. Whisper and Smoke are highly trained
working dogs, plus I'm armed. We'll get you out of here safe
and sound, okay?"

She concentrated on the shiny fur of the beast snoring
beside her. Whisper's feet twitched in his sleep. "This is a
highly trained attack dog?" Her eyes sparkled with
unexpected mischief.

"Yeah, well..." Alex relaxed. Her gentle jab diffused the tension he felt. "He does have his moments, don't you, old hound?"

Whisper looked up with one bleary eye and went right back to sleep.

"You're a bit of a smartass, you know that?"

She shrugged. "I guess. Everything was getting so serious. Besides, the cobbler's all gone."

He smirked at her implication that he had eaten the entire dessert by himself. "How's the road rash?"

"Mostly I just need Advil now."

"Muscle aches?"

"No, for my head."

"Headaches?" Without thinking, he smoothed her hair back over her ear. He paused, as his fingers cupped the edge of her jaw. An arc of electricity drew his eyes to hers. Again, he noticed the depth to those brown wells of mischief and the wide-open innocence of a kind woman. She broke the spell.

"I have a pretty crappy life. Bet you wished you'd never found me."

"No," he declared, his voice husky. "I'm glad I found you. You've just had more than your share of trouble."

She leaned into his hand with a sigh, her eyes closed.

"Don't be scared," he whispered.

"I'm not," she said softly. "I'm not scared at all."

He trailed his hand down her jaw and pinched her chin gently when he remembered she was the wife of another man. The pinch was an innocent act of endearment that covered his true feelings. If he kissed her once, everything would be worse. Dusting the shavings off his jeans, he got to his feet and tossed the chunk of wood he had been carving into her lap.

"I've had a long day," he announced. "I'm going to bed."

His feet were on the porch before he glanced back to gauge her reaction to the gift he had given. It was still a rough piece of pine, but now a German shepherd with a droopy ear peered from the wood. He had carved the grain around the dog's face into feathers, like Whisper was in any way her guardian angel. She didn't have to say a word. The light in her eyes told him everything. He let her sit alone by the fire for just another minute.

"You coming in?" He retrieved his rifle from its corner of the porch and stood waiting at the door, not willing to let her linger outside without him.

She smiled.

His heart stuttered loud and clear. Yeah. It was happening. He cared. A lot.

Eight

Alex

The next morning, Alex was up before the crack of dawn. With his backpack slung over one shoulder and his rifle on the other, he was anxious to get away from the cabin and have this final task finished once and for all. As an extra precaution, he had also strapped his thigh holster on this morning and secured his pistol where it belonged. He worried about Kelsey though. She was better, he just hoped she was strong enough for a long hike.

Focusing on her safety pushed his other thoughts away. They lingered just the same. Last night, he had tossed and turned. Try as he might, he could not get his brain to shut up and let him sleep. No. All night long, it reminded him of the genteel lady in the next room of his ramshackle man-cave. His ears followed every little creak of that beat up old cot she slept on, every sigh that left her lips. He had even heard her quiet whisper of good night to his dogs. That was sweet, but when he heard the cot squeak, he knew Whisper had climbed up onto the cot with her. For some stupid reason, Alex wanted to push the mutt back to the floor where he belonged. She would have her arms around his silly dog's neck, and Whisper would have his chin across her chest, and—

For hell's sake, Stewart. Knock it off.

Kelsey seemed to understand the seriousness of the day. She was up, dressed, and ready to go at first light. She wore her cut-off jeans again and the pink T-shirt. Alex loaned her one of his flannel shirts to ward off the morning chill. She looked good in flannel, more so because it was his. He smirked. She would look good in anything.

When they set out, Alex let both dogs run. Whisper and Smoke were a lot like children. They scampered ahead for a couple minutes but always came back to see where their slower companions were. Whisper was comical at every squirrel or chipmunk hole he encountered. He hunched himself up into a tight spring with his front paws against his chest while he nearly stood on his back legs. Then the big mutt dived straight into the hole like a furry submarine. He snuffed so hard it looked like he might vacuum the rodent out of its hole with his big, old nose. Kelsey's laugh at the goofy dog's antics made Alex smile. It was a pleasant start to the day. He pushed the inevitable good-bye out of his mind.

After a good romp, he called the dogs back and gave them the command to guard. Something wasn't right. The sixth sense of a sniper was keen in his head this morning. The rule was simple. *If you ever get a creepy sensation you're being watched, you probably are.*

"We need to keep moving."

She obeyed without question. The wind blew lightly in their faces, which wasn't good. It meant the dogs wouldn't scent anyone behind them. He didn't think Durrant was savvy in the woods, but anything was possible, even with a half-wit. The early morning breeze created a huge blind spot in the playing field. As they stepped up their pace, she tired faster. At last, he selected a fallen tree to rest behind.

"Get down." He pulled her down with him as he crouched against the tree. There was a hard tone in his voice this morning. He meant business. "Whisper. Smoke. Guard."

Instantly, both dogs sat alongside Kelsey, but she protested. "No, it's okay. I don't need to rest yet. I can go farther." Despite her words, she held her side. "How far do you think we've walked?"

"Two. Maybe three miles." He glanced around the area, watching and listening for the slightest deviation in the natural landscape, the glint of a rifle barrel, the odor of cigarettes, anything. He couldn't shake the apprehension he felt.

"Here." He offered her a bottle of water.

"Thanks." She took a sip and replaced the lid. "You're awfully quiet."

"Just cautious," he said. Then he noticed she rubbed her left foot. The light canvas shoe didn't fit quite right. In a second, he had the shoe off. One of the long bones on the top of her foot jutted upward in a pointed bump, obviously an old break. With all her other injuries, he hadn't thought to examine her feet.

"When were you going to tell me about this?" The words snapped out of him.

Her face blanched white, and he wanted to call his rudeness back. "Sorry. How long have you had this break?" he asked more gently.

"It doesn't hurt. Really. It's just a little sore," she apologized. "It rubs on my shoe."

Silently, he berated himself. He should've noticed this a lot sooner. It was his fault, not hers. She slid the shoe back over her foot just as something crashed through the brush.

The dogs heard it, too. Both scrambled around the log as Alex jumped to his feet and peeled the rifle off his shoulder. He instantly relaxed. It was just a doe, grunting as she trotted quickly past their resting position. Something must have spooked her. Whisper and Smoke watched her go. His cell phone vibrated at his belt as the deer continued west.

"Stewart." He turned away from Kelsey as he took the call.

"Alex," Murphy said quietly. Right away, Alex knew this was not a good news call. "Just heard from the Pierce County Sheriff. Thought you should know."

"And?"

"They found the Durrant boys last night, at least what's left of them."

"Where?"

"Henderson Bay. Sonofabitch drowned them in her car."

"Positive ID?"

"Yes." Murphy sounded sad. "Plenty of evidence, too. ME puts time of death ten days ago."

"Witnesses?"

"A couple teenage girls. They were on the beach. Saw a blond guy in a wet suit who matched Durrant's description. He came out of the water, changed into some clothes, smoked a joint, and just stood there like he was looking at something in the water. They're the ones who called the sheriff's department."

Alex steeled his face to mask his feelings. Kelsey needed to get back to civilization before he dropped this bombshell.

"Where is he?" He hissed.

"Where are you?" Murphy's voice hardened with concern.

"Answer the question."

Alex listened as Murphy muttered an order for Mother to check Durrant's GPS signal. In a second, he was back on the line.

"He's right on top of you, son."

He snapped the phone shut without another word. He turned and studied the landscape. Nothing moved in any direction, but he knew better. He cursed to himself. How was that lazy sonofabitch all of a sudden so close to them? Tommy and Jackie's smiling faces filled his mind. He choked at what he was about to do to their sweet mother.

"You ever shoot a gun?" He turned to Kelsey, maintaining his best drill sergeant voice.

"I don't think so," she whispered. "Why?"

He unsnapped his pistol from his thigh holster and held it out to her. "Take this."

She shook her head. "Ah, no."

"I said take it," he snapped.

With shaking fingers, she accepted the gun, but it was apparent she didn't know how to handle it.

"Please don't hit me," she whispered anxiously.

That plea jolted him back to her reality. "Kelsey," he said in surprised anguish. "Why do you think I would ever hit you?"

She scrunched her shoulders like a little girl. "I don't know, but … you're so mad."

He blew out a big breath of frustration as he re-thought how to train this frightened woman in less than five minutes. "I'd never hit you," he murmured, "and I'm not mad at you. I just need you to be safe."

"Why?" she asked timidly. By now she was shaking like a leaf. She glanced around the forest. "Is he here?"

"He's close," Alex said grimly. "I don't want you hurt again."

"Okay." She held the gun in two fingers, her arm extended like she was holding something dirty and didn't want to touch it.

"Don't hold it like that," he groused as he pulled her to his side and took her hand in his. The second their bodies touched he felt the familiar arc of electricity. Her hip molded perfectly against his, even more so when he wrapped his arm around her and took her trembling hands in his. He focused on gun basics, trying to ignore the effect she had on his male body. This had better be a quick lesson or he was in trouble.

"It's a nine-millimeter. It won't hurt you if you handle it right. Now listen. To shoot, hold it straight in front of you like this, fingers alongside, but not on the trigger. That's good. Now cup your left hand under your right. Good. See this lever right here?" He pointed to the safety. She shivered, and it was all he could do to not set the gun aside and comfort her in all ways possible. His instincts screamed, "Hold her. She needs you." He couldn't.

"Push it down. The red dot means the safety is off. Think of it this way, when the safety is off, the gun is red hot, ready to fire."

"Okay," she whispered. "Red means fire."

"Then do it," he ordered sternly. "Push it down."

She flicked the safety off with her thumb, but her hands were shaking so hard he knew he was going about this all wrong. Whisper and Smoke stood watching the lesson with bright, black eyes, and for a moment he considered sending them to search out Durrant and whoever else might be hiding in the trees. He didn't. He needed them to stick with Kelsey, just in case the unthinkable happened. All the worst-case scenarios plagued him. *What if Durrant had company with him today? What if Durrant was better than he thought? What if the dumb bastard just plain got off a lucky shot?*

"Okay, now. Pull the slide back, all the way." He showed her where to grasp the top of the gun in order to rack the slide. "Good. That puts a round in the chamber. A round is a bullet. You're ready to shoot, okay?"

"Not really," she murmured.

He closed his eyes and breathed in the warmth and scent of her. Ahh. Everything about this gentle soul reached straight to his groin, but holding her like this messed with his head and he needed to be sharp. He took a step back, removed the weapon from her still-shaking hands, returned it to safety, and stuck it back in his holster. This was his stupidest idea ever. There was no way this woman could kill another person. She was a lamb caught between two wolves.

"You have to be able to take care of yourself," he stressed angrily. "What if something happens to me? What if I have to leave, and you're alone?"

"But I don't want you to leave me," she whispered.

That lovely truth fell soft and sweet between them. Alex stared at what she had just said. Damn it anyway, she had taken the words straight out of his heart. He didn't want her to leave him either. No, he wanted to hear her laugh again, and maybe tell his goofy dogs good night. Heck – he wanted her to tell him good night, and not from the other room either.

The last of his resolve evaporated. He pulled her into his side with a trembling sigh. She stilled against him. All he felt was the hammering of her heart as she rested her head on his chest, her hands gentle on his ribs. He wrapped his arms around her and sighed. This was what he wanted. Even in this moment when she was still a murderer's wife, he knew she belonged with him.

"I won't leave you, Kelsey," he said quietly as he cupped the back of her head. "Don't be scared. I'm here."

She didn't have to answer. The way her body conformed to his told him everything. They stood quietly for a few minutes before he untangled his arms and stepped back, trying to regain his composure. "We have to get going."

For a while, they hiked a little quicker, and the dogs stayed close. It was slower going than Alex preferred, but they moved steadily toward the road.

"How's your foot?"

"It's fine," Kelsey answered breathlessly. "It doesn't hurt. Honest."

"Let me know if you need to rest." He glimpsed a movement to their right, but it was quite a ways off. Could Durrant have someone else helping him?

They hiked steadily for another hour until a low branch caught her foot, and Kelsey stumbled. Alex caught her by the elbow. "You'd make a pretty good soldier," he said quietly.

"I think the pink shirt gives me the real military look," she teased.

Alex cocked an eyebrow and smiled. He couldn't help it. The lady was out of breath, in danger, and still she cracked a joke.

"Last rest stop." He selected a fallen log for them to crouch beside. "Here. Carry this." He handed her the pistol again. This time, she took it with the tiniest shred of confidence.

"I hope I don't have to use it." She set it gingerly on the ground beside her, the safety still on.

"Me, too." He retrieved his range finder from his backpack for another look at their surroundings. If Durrant was in the forest today, he was acting like a real hunter, and that was cause for concern. Alex couldn't detect anything or anyone until both dogs gave a small whine of alert, their ears pitched forward as they faced back toward the cabin. *Where the hell are you, you bastard?*

He scanned in the direction the dogs faced. Finally, he caught a glint of gunmetal. There he was. Durrant lay flat to the ground beneath a low growth of dense pine branches, nearly one hundred percent concealed in the shadowy boughs. The man still carried his thirty-thirty only now it balanced on a tripod and sported a high-powered scope. And it was aimed directly at Alex.

He studied the assassin, two predators finally eye to eye. Durrant's concealment was actually an excellent sniper hide. Alex gauged the distance. Six hundred yards give or take a foot or two. The scope brought Durrant close. Too close. Silently, Alex traded his rangefinder for his rifle, and secured it into his shoulder. *Two can play this game. How about I put a round right down that fancy scope of yours and straight into your head, you sonofabitch?*

The shot was easy. Durrant didn't stand a chance. Kelsey wouldn't know until the man who hunted her was dead. Alex pressed his finger to the trigger, applied just the right amount of pressure, and—

"Ouch!" She jumped up from the log. "Something bit me." She twisted around to look at her backside.

"Get down!" Alex jumped up to cover her. He almost had hold of her when he heard the far off crack of a center-fire round expelled from its chamber. With blinding heat, the bullet rifled through his left shoulder, exiting just beneath his collarbone and pushing him forward. He gasped. A startling spray of blood splashed across her shocked face as he collapsed onto her. He fell to his hands and knees, his forehead pressed into the dirt. It happened so fast. The dogs erupted in lethal fury as they charged back into the trees. He tried to call them back, but Whisper and Smoke were past the point of hearing.

"Kelsey," he groaned. "Rrrr-uuu-nnn!

Nine

Kelsey

She didn't run.

Kelsey stared dumbfounded back into the trees, her eyes locked across the distance with a face from her past. Nick had scrambled out from under the branches, his rifle in his shoulder, and ready to fire again. She waited for the shot. It never came, or if it did, she never heard it. In between the rifle shot and Alex's cry, every repressed memory poured back into her mind like a noisy flood in an eight-ounce cup.

He had taken her for a ride in his diesel, supposedly to retrieve the boys from his mother's. That's when he told her. She felt the stinging pain of Nick's fist on her cheekbone as if it had just happened all over again. It felt so real that she touched her cheek, half expecting bruised skin and blood beneath her fingertips. She saw his top lip curled with sadistic pleasure when he'd said he had drowned her babies, how he had to tape their mouths so he didn't have to hear them cry. They weren't at his mother's. By the time Nick started telling her his lies, her boys were already gone.

He killed my boys.

She saw the sweat at his throat and the leer on his face. His eyes had glittered like a deranged animal, and she had fought back. She had dug her nails into his cheek, all her fury unleashed, but it wasn't enough. He slammed her face into the dashboard, so she made the only choice she could. She pulled the handle on the truck door and flung herself out— away from him forever.

He killed my boys.

The shock of asphalt against her knees grated again. Her shoulders, arms, and elbows burned where they had been shredded. She remembered her three-point landing and the bittersweet thought that her dead son's hero, Spiderman, would have been proud. But Nick had turned that smelly diesel truck around, grinding the gears as he faced her again. He would have run her down if she had stayed. So she ran into the forest and unknowingly to Alex.

He killed my boys.

She clutched Alex's pistol as her history assaulted her all over again. As quickly as she remembered, she knew exactly what she was going to do. Yes, she might share this monster's name, but she was also the woman he had beaten. Most importantly, she was Tommy and Jackie's mother. She would gladly have died for them, and now—she would kill for them.

He killed my boys!

She watched in a trance. The dogs roared over Nick like a throw rug tossed in the wind. His rifle flew over his head when Whisper hit him. Nick tried to deflect the big dog's teeth with his arms, but he never stood a chance against the trained predator. He fell backwards in a flurry of black fury that was quickly joined by silver, Smoke's saliva frothed jaws clamped alongside Whisper's on their quarry's neck. Within seconds, Nick was subdued, crying, and whining. The dogs stood hunched over him, their jaws locked, eyeing Kelsey for their next command.

She walked the distance to her ex-husband in a slow-motion dream. The pistol felt good in the palm of her hand, like it was nothing more than an extension of her fingers and her will. Alex was right. *It's not going to hurt you if you handle it right.*

She stood over Nick. He seemed smaller than she remembered. She felt like she was a long ways off, as if she looked down at him from a very great height. *Imagine that. Nick Durrant's nothing but a mean, pitiful little man.*

She dropped her knee onto her husband's scrawny chest, the weapon concealed at her side. She fully intended to handle it right.

"Whisper. Smoke. Off." She used the words Alex used. The next step was easy because Nick never could keep his mouth shut.

"You bitch!" He started to push her off, but as quick as that, she shoved the gun barrel between his crooked teeth and over his tongue. The smell of his breath struck her nose with its stink. Yeah, this was the man she had married, all sweat, beer, and cigarette stench.

"You killed my boys," she screamed so hard she spit in his face.

He gagged, his eyes wide with terror. Whisper and Smoke stood focused and ready to help. She pushed the gun in deeper. A trail of blood drizzled out of the side of his mouth as he tried to mumble words she didn't care to hear.

"You murdered them." In a bizarre, detached kind of feeling, she heard the shriek of a monster blast from her throat. It sounded demonic and strong, not hers at all. Between it and the thundering in her head, she gave into rage. She wasn't timid, mousey little Kelsey anymore. Not today.

No. She was the powerful one. Finally, she was strong enough to scare Nick Durrant for a change.

He tried to talk, but could only choke and gag—until something clicked in her hand. His eyes blinked wild and crazy then. His hands almost grabbed the gun, but terror kept his palms wide with submission, waving like stupid little flags at the side of his face like he would back up if he could. The bizarre pleasure of the moment did not escape her. It felt good to watch him squirming for his life.

She lowered her nose to his. Once again, the monster screamed out of her, "You killed my boys."

The noise in her head drowned out her conscience and, along with it, the waiting dogs at her side. All she knew was Nick was going to die right here and now. She was the one. Yes. She, Mrs. Nick Durrant, was going to blow his head apart like a melon and watch it splatter into a million chunks. Then she was going to shoot him again—and again—and again!

The sweet faces of her dead sons came into her mind. Sparkling brown eyes smiled back at her with all their love. *My boys suffered.* She pushed the gun until Nick threw up in his mouth. Tears rolled down his face and neck. He writhed beneath her, but she knew what was really going on. Right about now he would start begging forgiveness. He would whine and cry, promise to never hit her again. What did he think? She was fool enough to believe him? The roar of insanity filled her mind. *No. Not today. Never, ever again.*

Another voice pierced the churning maelstrom. It was calm and deadly serious in the way of true strength. She recognized the virtue in its tone, but just as quickly ignored it. *No. I have work to do.*

The voice persisted.

Kelsey glared over her shoulder, searching the trees for its source. She gasped to see Alex standing just yards away. Sweat and dirt covered his face. Blood saturated his shirt. For a split second, blue eyes penetrated the thunderstorm in her head. She saw his lips move, but it was too hard to listen. She turned back to finish the job.

"I hate you," she screamed at Nick. She froze. Her plan was flawed. Why should he get to die so easily when her sons had suffered? Maybe there was a better way to do this. Maybe if she tilted this gun up just a little bit, the bullet wouldn't go straight through right away. No. Maybe it would ping around inside his skull for a while.

Kelsey pushed down on the handle of the gun, which pushed the end of the barrel up into Nick's palette. She wanted pain and a slow agonizing death—just like drowning. That's what she wanted. *Yeah. This will work.*

"How's it feel?" she growled. Her hair flung over the two of them like a shroud, a death shroud. She liked that thought. She also liked that his eyes bugged out of his red face, but the annoying voice spoiled the moment.

"What. Do. You. Want?" she screamed without turning around. It was Alex. She knew what he wanted. The answer was no.

"Kelsey." His calm penetrated to her core. He couldn't have hit her harder if he had used his fist. She froze. Time stopped. Kelsey glanced over her shoulder to see him more clearly.

"Sweetheart." His voice was softer this time, more air than strength, but it still commanded. "You're... not... him."

She heard. She just couldn't stop. She had to do this one thing for Tommy, for Jackie. *Don't make me stop. Not now. Don't you understand?*

"Kelsey." He sank to his knees, his eyes still riveted to hers as he swayed back and forth. With a soft groan, he fell face first into the dirt.

"Alex."

Just like that, the fog of madness dissipated. Her brain stopped churning. In a second, she scrambled back to him and pulled him onto her lap.

He whispered to his dogs. "Hold."

Whisper and Smoke latched onto the child-killer's throat while Nick vomited and cried.

"You're hurt. You're shot." She leaned into Alex's face. In a rush of tears and anguish, she blurted out what he already knew. "He killed my boys, Alex. He killed my boys."

"I know, honey. I know." He wiped a bloody thumb across her chin, but his strength was gone. His hand dropped into hers.

She pulled his shirt open. Blood oozed from an ugly hole under his left collarbone. In a minute, she wiggled out of the pink T-shirt, ripped it in half, and pressed one piece against his shoulder and another at the hole in his back. He groaned while she cried.

"We need to get you out of here."

The blood kept coming. Within seconds, the pink fabric was drenched in red, and she was scared. "I don't know what else to do. There's so much blood. What should I do?"

But instead of telling her what to do, Alex looked at her bra.

"In another place and time—" He tried to joke, but his voice was too weak, his face too gray. Blood trickled down his neck. "My phone. Press one..."

Kelsey fumbled his cell phone out of the holster on his belt and speed dialed his office. It was a roundabout way to go, but it worked.

"Alex?" A man answered on the first ring.

"He's hurt," she cried out. "He's been shot. He's hurt."

"Kelsey? Alex is shot?" the man asked. "Is he alive?"

"Yes, but he's bleeding, and I can't stop it, and I don't know what to do."

"Calm down," he said firmly. She heard him turn to talk with someone else before he came back on the line. "Help is on its way. Are you hurt?"

"No, I'm just..." She looked down at the man in her lap. "But he's dying," she whined. "He's dying. I don't know what to do. Please. Help me."

"Listen. My name is Murphy. Talk to me. Where's he shot, honey?"

"In his back. It came out the front of his shoulder. There's a lot of blood," she explained quickly.

"They'll be there in five minutes. Five minutes, I promise. You just stay with him and keep talking to me, you hear me?" Murphy sounded scared, but she couldn't hold the phone and Alex, too. He had passed out, and she was scared he would die right there under the trees. She gathered him into her arms and dropped the phone.

Memories poured over her. She cried. With death so close, the sweet faces of her boys came to her mind. She saw them crying for her while dark cold water swirled around them. Tommy never liked water in his face, and now... and now...

She choked. The thought of their final moments suffocated her. They had suffered. Alex groaned against her neck. They had cried for their mama. His blood trickled down her elbow. He was dying in her arms. Everything was mixed together as Kelsey prayed for Tommy, Jackie, and Alex. Somehow, they were all connected. She hadn't saved her boys, and now, she couldn't save him. Like his blood in the dirt, everything good was spilling away from her.

Alex

Where the hell am I?

Alex pulled the nasal cannula off his face. The monitor next to his bed beeped with stats of oxygen saturation, blood pressure, heart rate, plus a dozen other things he didn't care about. *Shit. I'm in a hospital.*

An IV line hung from the metal tree by the bed. Its line snaked around the rail and taped to the back of his hand. Several more tubes circled out of his chest. *Those have to go.*

But the worst indignity of all, he was catheterized and he knew it. *That definitely has to go. No bag of pee hanging off my bed.*

He ached, but not too bad, all things considered. He had felt a lot worse. *Some vacation.* Fragments of the last few days edged their way back into his head. *Kelsey. That bastard husband of hers shot me. Damn. She knows.*

His groggy mind relived the bullet's impact and the look in Kelsey's startled eyes. The frightening image of her rage came back to him. Thankfully, she listened and remembered who she was, that she really didn't want to kill her worthless husband. She had ripped her pink shirt off to staunch his bleeding. He thought it funny all recollection stopped there. He smiled. That was actually a pretty good place to stop being held in the arms of a half-naked angel. A man couldn't ask for a better way to die.

The room was quiet except for the sounds of the hospital machines and his steady breathing. Sometimes it's nice to just listen to your own breathing. This was a good day. He wanted to sit up. Heck, he wanted to check the hell out of this place, but it had taken too much effort just figuring out where he was.

Gradually, his head cleared. He noticed Kelsey sound asleep in the chair beside him, her head resting on her folded arms on the edge of his bed. He smoothed his hand over her cheek. She sighed as a small smile pinched her lips. Another memory surfaced through the meds. *She prayed for me.* That kind act humbled him. Nobody'd prayed for him in years unless it was for him to die. He remembered something else. She glowed?

She looked peaceful, her hair tied back in a ponytail. Somewhere along the line, she had borrowed a nurse's gray shirt. Scrubs. That's what they're called. He traced his thumb along the line of her jaw, but she didn't stir. He wished he could pull her into his arms. He knew he would sleep a lot better then. They both would. He closed his eyes.

And hoped she would stay.

Ten

Alex

People still surprised him.

Everyone turned out for the funeral of Tommy and Jackie Durrant. The tragic story had a powerful effect on the town where Kelsey lived. In an instant, they took the long-suffering mother into their hearts. They wanted her to know they cared. Too late maybe, but they cared.

Alex walked through the cemetery dressed in his grey suit, white shirt, and black tie and his black trench coat pulled over the sling on his arm. It was funeral attire, somber dress for a somber day. Murphy had overnight expressed it.

The police had informed Alex that Durrant's confession corroborated what they already knew. His only motive for murdering his children was that he was sick and tired of two bloodsuckers in his life and their ungrateful mother. He claimed Tommy and Jackie weren't his. After that outrageous statement, the medical examiner ran DNA testing. The boys were Durrant's all right. Kelsey wasn't what he had claimed, but he was a murderer and not a very bright one at that. He had left a trail of evidence the police had no trouble following.

Alex saw Kelsey, a slender wisp of a woman in a simple black dress at the graveside with the minister. For the first time, he noticed her long legs. The road rash on them was concealed beneath black stockings ending in low black heels. She stood staring at the docile minister in front of her, her expression as vacant as his. No soft, sweet laughter graced her face. She looked lost, the biblical leper everyone looked at and talked about, but nobody really knew. The only things missing were the stones.

Alex couldn't get to her side fast enough. The minister asked everyone to take their places for prayer, so Alex halted where he stood, just a few yards behind her. The minister gave Kelsey his blessing. The righteous man told the grieving mother how Tommy and Jackie were in a better place. She should be thankful their earthly journey was completed because now she had two little angels in heaven watching over her. He challenged her to live in such a manner that she would be fit to join them someday.

Alex heard her whimper. His own heart screamed, *"Bullshit. There's no better place than with their mother."*

With a closing prayer in her behalf, the graveside ceremony concluded. A crowd of well-wishers, do-gooders, and a couple local news reporters engulfed her, their murmurs of understanding and compassion a quiet buzz of hot air. She stood just beyond his reach, her eyes locked on the small oak box that now held the two little brothers for eternity. An elderly couple turned to introduce themselves, but Alex adeptly passed them by, his eyes only for Kelsey.

She trembled, her hands to her mouth.

One more step.

She shook as the reality of the day depleted what little resolve she had brought with her.

Yet another step, and he took her gently by the elbow. Kelsey turned to him with a blank look that registered no recognition. "What am I supposed to do now?" she asked, her voice eerily calm.

He pulled her against him, not caring if it hurt his shoulder or not. "Whatever you need to do, honey."

"I don't know." Dazed brown eyes returned to the casket. "I don't just leave them here alone. Do I?"

He didn't speak. She had spoken his sentiments exactly, only four years later.

Kelsey took a step toward the oak box, her hand outstretched. "I can't just go. I mean, how will they ... where will I..."

"Where's your sister, honey? Where's Louise?" Alex panned the audience. The woman he thought might be her sister was still engrossed in a serious conversation with the minister.

"Am I supposed to walk away? Is that what I should do?"

The incredulity in her voice stabbed his heart. He couldn't answer. *Yes, Sweetheart. Now you're supposed to go on living, as if you still have a reason to. Walk away. Leave them behind. They have to stay. You have to go. The sun will come up tomorrow like nothing happened here. Everyone will get on with their lives while you forever wish that you lay in the grave, too.*

"Alex?" She clutched his sleeve, insistent that he respond. "Tell me. Am I supposed to leave, too?

"Yes." There, he said it. The awful truth was spoken. "But I'm right here with you, Kelsey. You're not alone."

"But, I can't." She leaned her forehead into his shirt, her hands clutching the lapels of his coat as she unraveled. "I should've been there. I should've been there."

All he could do was stand and keep her from falling. Louise was at his elbow, but Kelsey was past consolation. He guided her to a nearby chair, hoping to make it before she collapsed. Within the silken curtain of her hair, she sat with her face buried in her hands, her pain whining out of her in an escalating crescendo.

"He … he wouldn't let … he wouldn't let me go with them."

The local television cameraman leaned in for a close shot, but one scorching look from Alex and the man wilted. Alex shielded Kelsey with his coat and a curse. He pulled her to her feet, escorted her through the crowd, and into the rear seat of her sister's rental car. He tossed his coat into the front seat and slammed the door behind them, cursing all stupid people everywhere who just wanted to see this fragile woman's suffering.

Kelsey collapsed, half on the seat, half on the floor of the car, hiccupping sobs that wouldn't stop. "I should've been there."

"Come here." Alex pulled her off the floor and onto his lap. The day was taking its toll on him, too. Too many memories had come back to life. Hot tears drenched his freshly pressed shirt. He didn't care. His heart ached for this tender woman hugged up to him. He let her cry, wishing there was some way to help.

"You're stronger than you know," he whispered into her hair. Instantly, he wanted to call his words back. *I sound just like the minister.*

"No. I'm not." She burst into more tears. He didn't speak again. All he could do was hold her, let her cry, and wipe his own face. At last, the storm subsided.

"I ... I don't know ... how you did it," she murmured weakly against him.

"Did what, sweetheart?"

"I don't know how you survived after ... Sara and Abby. I don't know how you did it."

"What makes you think I did?" He gently massaged the back of her neck.

"But you did. You're successful. You're ... you're—" Tears took over again.

"One day at a time, Kelsey. That's all. Just take one day at a time."

A happier memory broke through the sadness.

"We—I had a birthday party for Tommy last November," she whispered, biting her knuckles as the story unfolded. "He was so excited. I made brownies. He got chocolate frosting all over his face and in his hair and even in his armpits. He looked like a little chocolate boy."

Alex choked. He had seen their pictures. The boys were smaller versions of their pretty mother. He gathered her hair over her shoulder in a ponytail and continued the massage down her back. She was thin and gaunt under her simple sheath dress, her backbone sharp beneath his fingers. She had lost weight. Skin, bones, and grief, the woman felt like she was staged to fade away.

"Tommy was so happy when he was born. He came out of me smiling like he was glad to see me, or something." She buried her face in his shirt. "I want him back."

He stifled his emotion. *I want Abby and Sara, too.* A memory of lovelier times surfaced, the day his daughter was born. Abby had come into the world eager to see everything. She had craned her little neck like she couldn't afford to miss a single sight, and she was born hungry, ready to eat. Even as a newborn, she had latched onto Sara and nursed like it was going out of style. It was one of the most precious pictures in his heart, his lovely wife with his newborn daughter at her breast.

His pain was in lock step with Kelsey's. It was as if those in that golden casket out on the lawn were his boys. This tragedy had become a welding link. He didn't know how, but Sara and Abby's deaths were intertwined with Tommy and Jackie's.

Kelsey sniffed. "Last Christmas I gave Jackie a red and green dump truck. It was just plastic. It was just from the dollar store, but he used to take it to bed with him." She brushed another stream of tears away. "He would sleep with his truck like it was a teddy bear."

She relaxed, her cheek pressed against his chest. Alex cleared his throat, blew out a big sigh and shared one of his favorite memories. "When Abby was three, she decided she was Snow White." His mouth went dry telling that sweet story. "She wore her princess dress for three weeks straight. Sara and I had to call her Snow White, Your Majesty, or Your Highness. She wouldn't answer to Abby. So we did. We called her Snow White for as long as she wanted." He bit his lip. *I'd call her Snow White forever if it brought her back.*

"You're a good father." Kelsey sighed.

He breathed in the clean smell of her hair. The feel of her in his arms comforted him. For a moment, tragedy relinquished its chokehold.

"You're still hurt." She noticed the sling.

"Nah, I'm fine."

This was nothing, but she had to check his shoulder, and he didn't really mind. She loosened his tie and the top buttons on his dress shirt. His heart jumped at that simple personal touch, and when she made him lean forward so she could check his back, too. There was nothing there to see except the hospital bandage. It didn't matter. She needed something else to think about, and he liked the sensation of her fingers on his skin.

Life almost felt normal. Her hair fell across his face. The fragrance of her perfume filled his nose. He closed his eyes, wanting the nearness of her to last longer than it would. Her softhearted murmurings were an unexpected balm in the middle of an incredibly crappy day. Here she was the one needing comfort, but instead, she comforted him. That was so like Kelsey. All those suppressed tender feelings resurfaced with a heated rush. He wanted more time, more memories, and more Kelsey.

When she was through, he kissed her forehead instead of her lips, and changed the subject. "How long is your sister staying?"

"I don't know."

Alex sighed. Louise had probably told her. She just didn't remember. Kelsey eased back into his arms, and there they stayed until the crowd left. With his arms around her, he was at peace with the world.

At last Louise and her husband Phil ceased socializing and joined them. Alex excused himself. They said their quiet goodbyes, and he watched them drive away to their hotel. Kelsey's dark eyes never left his from where she sat in the back seat. He stood until their car was out of sight before he folded his coat over his arm and walked back to his truck. The hard part was done.

Now the hardest part, the living without any reason to live part, began.

Kelsey

Down. Down. Down.

Black nothingness pushed her deeper in a descending current she couldn't escape. A woman's hysterical shrieks sounded from far away. They scared Kelsey as she searched the murky water. It sounded like that woman was being killed. Or worse.

Several objects swept along in the current with her—a big black dog with a crooked ear, her old blue car, and a tin percolator. A smiling little boy appeared in the dark water. He looked so sweet, but what was he doing all the way down here? Panic clawed up her throat as he slipped beyond her reach. There was no choice. She was scared, but she had to save him.

The water changed to trees and bushes. The boy was gone. Kelsey wasn't swimming anymore. Instead, she was running. She ran and then she ran faster, but she couldn't run fast enough, and—

N-o-o-o-o!

Kelsey clutched her mouth shut, the only way to silence the terrible sound that filled her hotel room. The screams were hers. They died in her throat, and just as quickly, the dream let go. In a moment, there was nothing left but the sweat on her body and the pain in her heart. She shuddered under the bed sheets. Nightmares ate her alive, while exhaustion had become a relentless companion. It stalked her. She wiped her nose on her sleeve, still panting for enough air. Each day was a repeat of the last until she lost track of time. Nothing mattered.

She ached for little boy smiles and grumbles, those grubby little bodies against hers, but they were gone. At every turn, regret and guilt suffocated her. There was nothing, not even two strong arms to hold her, or someone kind enough to remind her she might be stronger than she thought.

Alex. How was his shoulder? Did he think of her? Did he miss her? She missed him. The last time she remembered being happy was with him at his cabin. How cruel was life that her happiest recent memory occurred when she couldn't remember her babies? What kind of a mother was she?

The day he was shot came back to her. The emergency room doctor had examined Kelsey while others performed emergency surgery on Alex. In the doctor's opinion, her amnesia was temporary, the result of a concussion, most likely induced from the fall out of Nick's truck, or the blows to her head when he hit her, or the shock of her boys' deaths. He couldn't identify the exact cause. There were so many possibilities.

He called it retrograde amnesia, said she might have a few more headaches, but she was past the worst of it. She needed to protect against head injuries in the future. Wear a helmet. Avoid dangerous sports. Seek counseling. Then he gave her a tube of analgesic salve for the skin abrasions, but said they were healing nicely. She was a lucky woman to have treated them so effectively. Things could've been worse. He released Kelsey and told her to go home and rest. She never filled the pain prescription he offered.

Instead, she stayed in the waiting room until Alex was out of surgery, and then in his room while he slept those first couple of days. Only when Louise and her husband, Phil, arrived did Kelsey leave. Decisions had to be made. She spent the next days with her sister, letting Louise make most of the funeral decisions. Louise was good at handling those kinds of things, and Kelsey didn't have the strength to argue with her domineering sister even when Louise insisted one casket was expensive enough. The thought of her boys together offered a shred of consolation. They would be together.

When the medical examiner released the boys' bodies, Louise and Kelsey scheduled the funeral. That day was hard, but the days that followed were harder. Alex tracked her down before he drove back to Virginia. He held her close when he whispered his sad good-bye in her ear. She had felt his strong heart beating against hers and cried in his arms. *"Please stay. Please don't go. Don't leave me."*

She knew better. His life was not here. He had to go.

So, she let him.

Last of all, Louise and Phil went back to their comfortable country home in Pendleton, Oregon. They had a farm to manage, fields to cut, hay to bale. They had a life.

Kelsey tossed the sheets aside, and pulled herself to the side of the bed. Dizziness from that quick movement took her breath. Goose bumps covered her arms and legs. She was cold all the time now, like the grave her boys lay in. Her heart ached for Tommy and Jackie. She missed Whisper and Smoke, but most of all, she missed Alex. He had saved her, and then anchored her to sanity at a time when grief had ripped her apart.

One by one, she had lost everyone.

She was nothing—again.

Alex

"Morning, Boss."

"Morning, Mother. Where's the final report on the Iran op?" Alex rounded the customer service desk where his two techies, Mother and Ember, sat engrossed at their computer monitors. As usual, Mother was her perky, annoying, and nosey self.

"I put it in the middle of your desk where you'd be sure to see it first thing this morning. The debriefing is your eleven AM appointment. Do you want all the agents to attend?"

"Just Lennox. That will be all."

"So how was your vacation?" She leaned over the counter as if he actually ever once in his life paused to chat. "Did I hear you met someone interesting in Washington? How's your arm? Anything you'd like to talk about now that you're—"

"I said that will be all." He cut her off and kept walking. She was the last person he would share his private life with. Might as well put it in the newspaper.

Alex opened his office door, half expecting to find a desk overflowing with work. It wasn't. Murphy had taken care of everything. Alex had stayed in Washington two extra days after the funeral. At first, he told himself he needed a couple more days rest, but the real reason was he didn't want to leave Kelsey. His arm ached and the sling was an annoyance, but what bothered him most was he hadn't been able to reach her by phone.

"Hey there young man." Murphy settled into one of the leather chairs opposite Alex. "Good to have you back. How's the shoulder?"

"Shoulder's fine. Lennox isn't in yet?" Alex arched a brow at his trusted second in command, intent on making his injury a non-event.

"He's flying in from Iran this morning. Mother has him scheduled to de-brief this afternoon, doesn't she?"

"Yes. One o'clock. You mean Lennox filed his final report before he's home?" Alex was surprised.

"Told you he was good. You might want to go easy on him though. You know, jet lag and all."

"His reports have all been spot on. I'm not sure I even need the debrief. Why don't you hire ten more just like him?"

"Now that you mention it, I do have four interviews lined up with some youngsters you might want to meet. I figured they'll work in the Seattle office if you like 'em."

"The last time I checked, we didn't have a Seattle office."

"A year goes by pretty fast. If we train them here, they'll be ready when it opens, and they'll be darn good to boot."

"We'll discuss where they work later. Get them on board first."

Alex turned his attention to Zack's written report, but as usual, Murphy wasn't done with the morning's pleasantries. Alex dropped the report to his desk as he eyed his friend. A

Vietnam vet, Murphy had served in the Army as long as they had allowed, but he might have put his foot in his mouth one too many times in support of his troops over Army politics. He cared about his people, and he liked small talk. Alex let him chat.

"How was the funeral?"

"Tough. Her sister's taking her to Pendleton for a while. They're flying out tomorrow."

"What an awful thing that was. How's Kelsey holding up?"

"She's had four years of hell being Mrs. Durrant, that's for sure." Alex rubbed the tension out of his eyes.

"But you'll keep in touch with her, won't you?"

"For a while." Alex was guarded in his answer, even with Murphy. His personal life was a closed book. Murphy might know about Sara and Abby, but that didn't make him privy to his feelings for Kelsey.

"Too bad you couldn't bring her home with you. Washington's a long way off for any kind of a meaningful relationship."

"We don't have a relationship." Alex scowled as he picked the report up again.

"Oh? From what the nurse at the hospital told me, that little gal spent every day in your room. You might not know that since you were sleeping most of the time, but Kelsey stayed with you until her sister came to town and dragged her away."

"There wasn't much reason for her to go to her apartment, was there?" That bit of information was news to Alex. He had vaguely remembered Kelsey in his room, but thought he had dreamt it.

"Whatever you say." Murphy rose to leave, but the twinkle in his eyes bugged Alex.

"Besides, she's a mess. She needs her sister." The report was flat on his desk again.

"You called her yet? I mean just to see how she's doing and all?" Murphy stopped at the doorway, his head cocked as he waited on an answer.

"Called her last night to let her know I was home."

Murphy still waited.

"I told her I'd call. It's the least I could do," Alex snapped.

"And?"

"And she was out."

"Well, it's three hours earlier on the west coast. You might want to—"

"Don't you have work to do?" The report was back in Alex's hand, and his temper was up. "Because I've got plenty I can offload to your desk if you've got time to stand around and bullshit."

Murphy outright chuckled. He headed out the door, completely unaffected by Alex's temper. "Okay, okay. She sounded like a pretty little thing, that's all. I only got to talk to her that one time, but I'm dang glad she called. Let me know how she's doing, will ya?"

Alex waited until the door closed. *Yeah, right.*

He read the Iran Op report from front to back before he called her again. He had hoped the three-hour time difference meant she was asleep in her hotel room. It was early enough, but the phone just rang in his ear, so Alex called the front desk. That's when he discovered Louise and her husband had already gone home. The room was registered for another week to a Kelsey Durrant. Alex left his name and cell phone number with the message for Kelsey to contact him as soon as she got in.

"You'll make sure she gets this message?" he asked pointedly.

"Yes, sir. I will personally hand deliver it if you'd like." The clerk at the hotel desk was cheery and helpful.

Alex hung up with more questions in his mind. Where was Kelsey so early in the morning? It was only six AM Pacific Time. Why wasn't she still asleep? But mostly—why didn't he stay? What was so important he had to rush back to work? Since he had gotten home, all he wanted to do was turn around and go back. The rest of the day became a waiting game. Even the successful return of Zack from Iran wasn't enough to squelch the niggling fear creeping into Alex's every thought.

"Good job." He tossed the Iran Op report to his desk after hearing what Zack had to say. No need to belabor the details with such a thorough agent. They discussed politics, future operations, and general opinions. Alex was pleased.

"Thanks Boss." Zack was fresh and ready to work, not the dragged out, jet-lagged agent he should've been after a twenty-hour flight from the Mideast. A top-notch scout sniper, he had held the record for distance and accuracy in his Marine Expeditionary Unit before Alex lured him away from the Corps.

"This job agrees with you, doesn't it?" Alex studied his junior agent's enthusiasm.

"Hell yeah." Zack pushed back, his hands crossed behind his head in a comfortable position. "I'm glad every single day you convinced me to leave the Marines."

"Don't tell them. So what's next?"

"I figured I'd hit the weight room when we're done here, unless you've got another job for me." Zack looked expectantly to his boss.

"Now that you mention it, I've got three more contracts I need to assign. The first one's with the Bureau of Land Management out west. The other two are the usual ones with the Army—one in Pakistan and the other in northeast Afghanistan. I'd like you to take the Afghanistan op if you're up to it. You'll work with their special operations people."

"Army Rangers? Great. I can travel tomorrow." Zack's hands were on his knees. As always, he was ready to go.

"You're a kiss ass, Lennox."

"Call it what you want. I'm traveling, I make good money, and I like what I'm doing. Best of all, I don't always have to shoot anybody in this job."

Alex would enjoy working an op with this kid if he could ever get away from all the deskwork. Zack was sharp, diligent, and more than just a little bit cocky, all good traits by his standards. "Take a break. Roy's due in from Mexico tomorrow. The BLM contract isn't time sensitive, but the others are. How about you and I work Afghanistan in a couple weeks and let Roy handle Pakistan?"

"Sounds good to me."

"It will be a long operation, maybe a couple months." Alex warned.

"No problem." Zack reached across the table to shake hands. "Just keep me busy. That's all I'm asking."

"I can do that," Alex replied. "Would you send Mother in on your way out?"

"Sure thing."

Zack was gone less than a minute before Mother poked her head in the door. "Whatcha need, Boss?"

"Have a seat." Alex motioned to the chair beside his desk. "I've got a couple questions."

Mother sat within arm's reach of her boss, eager and ready to help as always. A genius at anything computer related, she was also secretary, administrative assistant, project coordinator, and a wealth of other duties as assigned – or unassigned. Basically an all-around-girl-Friday type, she took it upon herself to do what needed to be done. Alex relied on her despite the fact she could be just as *helpful* in everyone's personal lives as well. That nosey attribute, along with her head of silvery hair, earned her the nickname of Mother. The dubious moniker stuck. The problem was she liked it.

"How's Ember working out?" Alex got right to the point.

"Good. We're getting along fine. She's a lot like me. She's smart as a whip and—why? What's up, Boss?"

Mother's quizzical expression evoked caution lights in the back of Alex's mind. In her brilliant, probing way she was always on the lookout for personal information.

"She doesn't seem like an admin type."

"She's a hottie, huh?" Mother beamed.

While her description was right on, Alex wasn't going to admit anything. He had hired his latest techie based solely on Mother's recommendation, sight unseen. When a statuesque, blonde bombshell showed up for her first day of work instead of the techno nerd he had expected, he had his doubts. Ember looked like she belonged in a chorus line in Vegas instead of behind the keyboard in a consultant office. At least, that's how she looked the first day. The real problem surfaced the next day when her hair was blue, but in her quirky way, she was every bit as good as Mother at her job. Maybe better.

"I want to make sure she's a good fit for this office. Are you keeping her busy? Is she keeping up?"

"Yes. Today she's writing a security program to keep hackers out of our system. We've still got a couple problems in that area. Later we're going to tackle an archival program, so you can have any report you'll ever need right at your fingertips. Then, there's the encrypted protocol—"

Alex waved her answer off. "Fine."

"Don't you want to know about the new video surveil—"

"No." He tried to interrupt her litany of self-aggrandizing accomplishments and to-do-lists. Most of the time, he didn't know what she was talking about anyway.

"Or the new idea I had for the satellite reconnaissance—"

Alex glared. Sometimes there was no way to shut Mother up—or off. He was sorry he had asked.

"Okay." She huffed, her lip in a childish pout. "Whatever."

"I need the phone number for Louise and Phil Timpson in Pendleton, Oregon."

She smiled her annoying I-know-something-you-don't-know smile that peeved Alex to death.

"What?" He was irritated now.

"Oh, nothing. I'll be right back with that number, or did you want me to place the call for you?" She paused at the door, her eyebrows arched at her seemingly helpful suggestion.

"Just get me the number." If she weren't such a genius, he would fire her just for being so smug all the time.

As soon as the door closed, he dialed Kelsey again. Still no answer. With the phone ringing in his ear, he remembered their good-bye. She had cried. He had to push her gently away before he uttered the words he shouldn't. In the end, all he had whispered was, "Good-bye. See you around."

Her sad eyes were forever burned into his memory.

Why didn't I stay?

Eleven

Kelsey

Another day. Another park bench. The same old heartache.

Kelsey smoothed her hair off her face as she walked back to where her boys lay. It felt like a dream, but she knew it wasn't. She could almost hear them giggling from their casket, just like they used to when they would hide under their covers at bedtime. Silly boys didn't realize then that blankets and sheets might have looked solid, but their happy little noggins still rose like two round dinosaur eggs beneath the cotton and fleece. Tommy's delighted anticipation at being discovered by his mom had always been too much for him to contain. He had chuckled gleefully when she had asked, *"Where did my little guys go?"*

Unable to disguise their exuberance, they had flung back the blanket with rowdy squeals.

"Surprise." Jackie had shouted amidst Tommy's exuberant chortle, and she had gathered them like teddy bears, and tickled them until they collapsed in a mound of motherly, childish love.

Yes. She could almost hear them laughing sometimes. Maybe today they would throw back that in-between layer of sod and green, and invite their mom to join them under the covers one last time.

Today was lawn-mowing day. A crew of cemetery maintenance workers strolled the grassy rows between reverently placed granite and stone, removing old flowers and forgotten Memorial Day vases. They clipped and pruned, too busy to notice the wraith-like woman who walked by. She knelt in the grass where Tommy and Jackie's heads rested only feet below. Once again, their smiling faces beckoned, and sadly, she knew those joyful expressions were only imagination.

She was losing her mind.

Alex

Senior Agent Roy Hudson was not to be taken lightly. A Vietnam vet like Murphy, he had called Alex to advise the Mexican operation with the Drug Enforcement Agency was completed earlier than expected. He was on his way home.

"That makes two final reports today," Alex replied. "You and Lennox keep this up, and maybe I don't need to hire any more agents."

"What? That Lennox kid beat me again?" Roy's booming voice was full of mock anger at the junior agent. "I suppose he's already halfway around the world on another assignment, isn't he? You give him another operation already, Boss?"

Alex chuckled. "It's good to hear from you, Roy. When will you be back?"

"Flight arrives six PM tonight."

"Well, good. I've scanned your report. Looking forward to the debrief. How about tomorrow at eleven?"

"Sure. Hey, you thirsty? How about a fifth of tequila?"

"Your place or mine?" Alex chuckled. Leave it to Roy to think of everything.

Just then, Mother popped her head into Alex's office with a knowing smirk. "Hey, Boss. There's a woman on line two. Says she's Kelsey's sister. You want me to take a message for you? She sounds real worried."

Alex shook his head as he finished his conversation. "Listen, Roy. I have another call. See you in the morning. Fly safe."

As soon as Mother closed his door, he took the call.

"Stewart."

"Is this Mr. Alexander Stewart?"

Alex recognized the west coast accent. "Yes, Louise. How are you doing?"

"Thank goodness." Louise sighed effusively through the phone. "I'm fine, but I lost your business card. You're not an easy man to track down, you know. Land sakes. Thought I'd never catch up with you."

"Is Kelsey with you?"

"No, she isn't. Do you remember how I said I was bringing her home with me? Well, I have a room all cleaned up and ready for her just like I told you, but that little sister of mine can be one stubborn woman. I couldn't get her to leave. No sir, she dug her heels in at the last minute, said she wasn't leaving her boys, and what was I to do?"

Alex listened as Louise rambled. "Where is she?"

"That's why I'm calling. I've been trying to reach her at the hotel since I left day before yesterday. Only I'm not getting any answer. I called a couple of her neighbors, you know, those nice folks who were at the funeral that day? Only they haven't seen her, so I know she hasn't gone back to her apartment. I'm getting worried, especially if you haven't been able to get hold of her either. Have you?"

"No. I haven't," Alex said thoughtfully. "Let me make a few calls. I'll get right back to you."

"I'd sure appreciate it. Thank you."

"I'll be in touch."

Alex hung up on Kelsey's talkative sister. He made two calls, the first one to the police department. They had been more than helpful during the days before the Durrant boys' funeral. Within minutes, he had verified Kelsey's location. She was exactly where he had suspected she would be. The other call was to his travel agent. He called Louise back to tell her his plan. If all went well, he would be back in the office tomorrow morning in time for the debriefing with Roy.

Murphy was just coming back from lunch as Alex rounded the corner to leave.

"I'm leaving early. See you tomorrow."

Strolling past granite markers, stone angels, and an occasional floral wreath, Alex had to admit this cemetery was a restful place. The shade from the oak trees planted years ago covered most of the landscape in peaceful repose. Park benches had been strategically placed. The grass was lush and freshly trimmed. Yes, it was almost a place where one could sit, linger, and think for a minute. But it wasn't his baby buried here, and the only time he had ever lingered in a place like this was with a gun in his hand. He kept moving.

As he had listened to Louise, his feeling of urgency had grown. After he landed at the SEA-TAC airport, he grabbed a rental car and made the drive to the cemetery in under an hour. It was two weeks since the funeral. Louise had said she and Phil went home two days ago. What happened to Kelsey since then? He had asked the police to check the cemetery, hoping she didn't have the same idea he'd had four years ago. They found her easily. Two officers still watched the grieving mother from their patrol car. Thankfully, she didn't have a weapon.

Draped in the privacy curtain of her hair, Kelsey stroked the grass over the grave. With her shoulders slumped, she looked like she was talking. Alex dashed a tear off his eye. He knew how fast grief could turn into depression, and just a hop, skip, and a jump to mental illness. Yes, he knew all about the steps of recovery. A person was supposed to transition through denial, fear, anger, and a bunch of other emotions until eventually, they would end up back at normal. Only it didn't work that way.

Grief was a tough master. Too often, people didn't know how to ask for help, and others didn't know how to give it. He had never asked. Even today, he would deny he ever needed it, and as far as transitioning through all those psychobabble steps of bullshit, the only one he had ever made it to was anger. There he stayed, raging against God and man until the only way out was at the end of his gun. He didn't know how he had survived—or if he had.

An involuntary shudder shook him at the memory of that cold steel in his mouth. The sensation came back like it was yesterday. He had planned it so well. He knew the physics. One shot, one last breath, and peace at last. He had even closed his eyes, ready to be done with it when, out of the blue, a little girl across the street somewhere squealed, "Daddy!" His heart had lied and said it was her. Abby. Whatever. The dark moment passed. He never thought of suicide again.

Alex crouched beside Kelsey in the fading afternoon light. "Kelsey?"

She didn't seem to hear him. Now that he was closer, it was easy to see her hair was uncombed, her clothes looked slept in, and the only color on her face was the dark circles under her eyes. She had the same look as when he had first found her. Kelsey was lost again. He circled her slender waist with his arm. She would never make it alone. Alex pulled her gently off the grass.

Kelsey was a wooden statue, come to life at his hand. Her stiffness gone, she slumped against him, her voice far away and flat. "Alex."

"I know, baby. I know." He scooped her into his arms, and carried her like a child to the closest park bench. For a long time, he just held her on his lap and rocked back and forth. The police drove away.

Alex whispered into her hair. "I know how you feel. I didn't want to live then either."

She whimpered, her head against his shoulder, her hands a dead weight in her lap.

"It's not the load that breaks us down, sweetheart. It's how we learn to carry it." Alex knew she didn't understand right now, but eventually, she would. "You're coming with me."

He set her on her feet and led her from the cemetery. She didn't resist. After placing her safely in the front seat of his rental, he drove to her apartment.

When Kelsey unlocked her front door, he saw why she hadn't been there. Sparsely furnished and dirty with empty beer cans and fast food wrappers scattered around, it was a depressing dump. Obviously, Durrant had spent his last days there when he wasn't out hunting his wife. And just as obvious, the man was a pig.

A small cardboard box of toys stood in the corner by a broken down couch, and a baby blanket lay on the floor where it had been stepped on. Kelsey went to that blanket and held it to her nose, breathing in the smell of her dead baby boy. A strangled sob choked out of her. Alex turned away. The smell of Abby's breath came to his nose, even in this dreary place. This was too painful to watch. Kelsey was running on empty at so many levels, and maybe he was, too.

"Where've you been staying?" His voice cracked.

But once again she stood in a daze, her answer distant and vague. "Around."

Alex guessed the cemetery or maybe a park bench. Wherever she had been, she hadn't been home, showered, or had anything to eat in days. He recognized the agenda. She wanted to die.

"Let's get you packed and out of here."

Obediently, she went to one of the two bedrooms. Alex followed. A bloody handprint on the light switch caught his eye. Her handprint. He cringed. *Poor thing. What she must have suffered.*

There was no dresser, only a couple cardboard boxes that didn't hold much. He left her to pack while he loaded the boys' few things into the back of his rental. Somehow, it was all going to the east coast.

There were no photographs anywhere, only a couple of crayon drawings on the refrigerator door. One might've been a picture of a green and red truck. It brightly proclaimed *Jackie* in red crayon at the top of the page. The other was a bunch of scribbles in a rainbow of colors with an adult's handwriting that declared it belonged to *Tommy.* Kelsey had beautiful penmanship. Alex folded the drawings and placed them in his inner suit pocket.

The truly telling story lay in the black puddle of blood on the dirty kitchen floor. She whimpered when she saw it, her knuckles to her teeth. Alex watched her fall apart.

"He wouldn't let me go. He said it was just him and Tommy and Jackie. He said—he said—" She fell to her knees, trying to wipe the dried mess with her bare hands. "He said he would bring them back in time for their naps. He promised."

Alex knelt beside her, thinking again how he had misjudged her. None of this was her doing. She was no more able to defend herself against the monster in her life than her boys.

"I wanted to go, too." She pressed her face against the dirty linoleum.

So that's what happened. The only way Durrant could get the boys away from her was to beat her senseless. Alex pulled her off the floor and settled her onto the couch. He returned to the kitchen to get a drink of water. At least the glasses in the cupboard were clean. She must've washed them before hell broke loose. He returned to her side with the water and two Advil from his pocket. "Here. Take these and drink this."

Dazed, she obeyed.

He took the glass from her when she was done drinking, half afraid she might use it to hurt herself. He would have. "Stay here," he commanded her again, but there was no need. She had retrieved the baby blanket by then, her face buried in its stained, yellow fabric.

Once more, he returned to the kitchen, pulling a couple fingerprint lift cards from his jacket pocket. In his line of work, he never knew when they would be needed. Then, as carefully as if they were Abby's, he salvaged every tiny fingerprint smudge he could find. He scoured the lower refrigerator door and the legs of the cheap kitchen table. He hunted the two bedrooms, bathroom, and the living room for any trace the little boys had left behind on walls, windows, or doors. These were treasures, and Kelsey would want them some day. Satisfied he had gotten the best, he returned to the couch. She stared into space, the baby blanket carefully folded on her lap.

He pulled her gently off the couch, his arm around her too-thin waist for support. "You up for a visit to Virginia?"

At last, his words registered. She stopped dead in her tracks. "No."

"You're coming home with me," he coaxed, his arm firmly directing her toward the door.

She balked. "No. I can't."

But he wasn't leaving without her. "Yes. You can. Just for a week or so. Just 'til you're stronger."

"No. My boys are here and—" She crumpled to the floor. "I'm not leaving them."

This was the first time he had heard sharpness in her voice, but it was also the first time Alex knew without a doubt how much he cared for her. "Your boys don't want you sleeping on park benches." He ran a thumb over her quivering lip. "Think about it. They'll always love you no matter where you are."

She sat rooted in indecision, her voice a whisper. "But I left them once. Look what happened."

"You didn't leave them, honey. They were stolen from you," he whispered tenderly. Alex held out his hand. Nothing else needed to be said.

She looked up from her valley of death. With a whimper, she placed her hand in his. Alex pulled her into his arms, and shut the door to her hellish past. He placed her in the front seat of his rental car and fastened her seat belt. She cried halfway to the airport before she fell asleep, still clinging to Tommy's baby blanket, and her head propped against the window.

Alex took her with him to Alexandria, Virginia. They rode first class under a starry sky, riding a westerly jet stream. The lights in the cabin were dimmed for the late night flight, and the attendants were extra kind and thoughtful. They brought a warm meal, probably Kelsey's first in days, Alex suspected. He plied her with a sip of wine, but she refused, so he covered her with the airline blanket instead. She cried herself to sleep.

This may not have been the best decision, but one thing was sure.

He cared.

Twelve

Alex

Boring can be good.

Alex sighed as he pulled into his driveway. His home wasn't much, just a one story, three-bedroom, older brick home set in an established neighborhood of Alexandria, Virginia. Modest by any standards, tall oaks lined the comfortable, winding street. Most of his neighbors had lived there all their lives. Dull and boring had served him well.

It wasn't always that way. He and Sara had bought the house with the intent to move Abby into a nicer school and neighborhood, a family-friendly area where she could build a lifetime of friends. Alex didn't want his little girl to live the life of a Navy brat, moved from port to port. He took it upon himself to be the one inconvenienced and did the traveling instead. His family was his only port, his safe harbor. Life had a different plan.

The home itself was built in the compact utilitarian style of the early 1940's. It boasted a glassed-in foyer at the front entry with a built-in bench and coat closet, a place for winter boots and shoes beneath the bench. Amber glass French doors opened into a living room furnished with bookshelves, a dark leather overstuffed set, and an old-fashioned stone fireplace.

Gradually, it became a solitary man's place to sleep, eat, and not much more. No pictures adorned the walls. The drapes were dark and drawn all the time. He had installed a gun safe in the bookshelf years ago. Eventually, he set up a woodworking shop in the basement, and at least once a year, he worked down there. The last thing he had built was a doghouse for two.

It was early morning by the time they arrived on the east coast. Kelsey sat dazed on the seat of his truck next to him. Within minutes, he moved her into one of his two spare bedrooms, made up the bed with clean sheets and blankets, and stored her meager belongings in the closet. He knew he had pushed her to make this decision, but he wasn't going to second-guess himself now. The important thing was she would be safe. That's what mattered.

"What do you think?" He stood quietly at the doorway to her new bedroom.

She was pale and exhausted, her eyes and cheeks dry for now. "It's nice."

"This is just a two-week vacation. That's all. You say the word, and I'll take you right back to Washington."

He studied her apprehension, second-guessing despite himself. As much as he wanted to gather her in his arms and calm her fears, now was not the time.

"Make yourself at home. Bath towels are in the hall closet. There's not much food in the house, so I'll leave some money on the kitchen table if you need anything."

"No. I couldn't. I—" Brown eyes darted down the hall.

"There's a neighborhood grocery store two blocks down the street. You get whatever you need. Mr. Shablonski owns the place. He'll treat you real good. I might be home late so don't wait up."

"Okay." She acquiesced quickly, but then she heard what he had really said. "You're leaving?"

He heard the real question in her voice. *You're leaving me?*

"Yes, ma'am. I'm going back to work. You get some rest. The dogs are in their kennel out back, so it's not like you're alone here. Just open the gate and let 'em inside. They would love to see you again. Their leashes are hanging next to the back door if you feel like a walk."

She hugged herself like she was cold.

"I left my business card on the kitchen table. Call if you need anything."

Alex stopped at his front door before he left. She still stood forlorn in the hall, looking into the bedroom, but not yet entering. He stifled the urge to pick her up and put her to bed like the lost soul she was.

"Will you be all right?" he asked tenderly.

"Yes," she whispered without meeting his eyes.

It's odd how the glow from a sixty-watt bulb at eleven PM can change the way a house looks. It made his plain little tract house look like a home. Alex unlocked the front door, hoping the noisy click of the deadbolt didn't wake Kelsey. He needn't have worried. She sat on the couch with a book, waiting for him. His nose twitched. The house smelled like—dinner?

"I didn't expect you to still be up." He dropped his briefcase next to the door and loosened his tie.

She looked up from the book in her hand with a worried glance. "It's kind of late. Would you like something to eat?"

"Sure. What's on the menu?"

"Lasagna?" She phrased her answer in a question. Was she afraid he wouldn't approve of her menu choice?

"Sounds good to me." The instant he replied, she visibly relaxed, but that single reaction told him volumes about her past life, back in the days when she probably couldn't do anything right.

He pulled the holster off his shoulder and stowed his weapon in the gun safe. By then, she had returned from the kitchen with a plate of lasagna, two slices of Parmesan toast, and several kalamata olives on the side.

"Don't wait on me," he protested, but she had already set the tray on the coffee table and turned back to the kitchen. "I mean it, Kelsey. I'm perfectly capable—"

He heard the refrigerator door close and the clink of a glass against a bottle.

"And I can get my own beer, too."

She returned with a frosty glass over a bottle of beer, and a napkin with eating utensils rolled inside. He scowled. "You don't have to do all this."

"I know." She sat back on the couch with her book. "I didn't know what kind of beer you like so I looked in your garbage can. I also bought some coffee and creamer for tomorrow. I left the receipt on your table."

He looked at the food spread on the coffee table as he opened the first two buttons of his dress shirt and sank into the easy chair. The kindness of her actions warmed him. "No one's waited on me in years.""

"I'm just repaying you for everything you've done for me." She paged through her book as if she had lost her place.

"How about I take you to dinner tomorrow night?"

Kelsey looked up, a shadow darkening her face. "I don't think so. I mean, there'll be leftovers, and you work late, and..."

She seemed to be looking for excuses, so he dropped it. "Okay. Well, this is good. Thanks," he said between mouthfuls. "I mean it. This is really good."

"Food tastes better when someone else fixes it." Her voice was quiet, not shy so much as uncertain, and maybe a little afraid.

He wiped his mouth with the napkin. "Did you already eat?"

She nodded, offering a tiny smile.

In that instant, he knew exactly why he had made such an outrageous decision to move a bereaved woman all the way across country. Even her half smile lit up his dingy little house.

"What did you do today?"

"Well, I slept most of the day, kinda like I did at your cabin," she answered softly.

"Ha. Guess I have that effect on women."

She ignored his teasing comment. "And then me and the dogs went for a walk. I stopped at the grocery store so I could fix dinner. You're right. Mr. Shablonski is really nice. Do you want more?"

"Yes, but I'll get—"

"No. You stay there. It's easier for me to get up."

Before he knew it, she was back with another serving of lasagna and toast, only this time she also brought a plate with two chocolate chip cookies. "I didn't know if you like cookies, but I made some."

"You shouldn't have done this just for me," he insisted.

"I didn't. I made them for the people at your office. They'd like homemade cookies, wouldn't they?"

Her question caught him by surprise. "Heck, I don't know. I don't take treats to the office."

"Really?" She looked around like she didn't know what to say next. "My kindergarten class always liked them."

"I do feel like I work with kindergarteners some days."

"I didn't mean that." She blushed at his inference. "It's just that I needed something to do so I baked, and then I cooked. What did you do today?"

"Signed contracts. De-briefed agents. You know. The usual." He finished the last mouthful of lasagna and leaned back into his chair with a satisfied sigh. "Thanks. That was real good."

"Your work sounds important." She watched attentively from the couch, her book long forgotten.

"I talked with your sister today." He gathered his dishes as he studied her response.

She turned a beautiful shade of pink. "I need to call her."

"It's okay. I told her you were visiting a friend on the east coast. I think she was good with that explanation." Alex deposited his dishes in the kitchen sink and stood with his hands braced against the front room doorway. "Now she knows where you are and that you're okay."

"Louise is a good sister." Kelsey's eyes dropped.

"And she's worried about you. Anyway, I want you to consider this your home for as long as you decide to stay. Use the phone, drink the beer, eat the food, do whatever you want." He sat at the edge of his easy chair again, his hands on his knees. "So what are you reading?"

She patted the book beside her. "Just something I found on your bookshelf. It looked interesting, but I can't seem to focus enough to read it right now."

Kelsey had a quiet sadness to her voice. She had done a lot more today than he did when he was dealing with his depression. That she wasn't curled up in bed and crying her eyes out was surprise enough. The dinner and cookies told him this woman was tougher than he expected. There was still a side to her that he didn't know.

"The books are leftover from my college days. I need to spring house clean one of these days and send them to the dump."

"Don't do that." Kelsey's eyes lit up when he said that. "I'd never throw a book out."

"Salvation Army then?" He pushed the idea of discarding the books as far as he could, just to see another spark of enthusiasm on her face.

"How about if I just dust them?"

Her words made him smile. "You're a bookworm."

"By the looks of it, you used to be, too. You've got a lot of stuff on George Washington and Abraham Lincoln. Jefferson, too."

"It's been awhile." He changed the subject again. "So how are you really doing? Are you going to be okay here?"

She blinked, her voice tight and sad. "I'm going to bed."

He stood the minute she did. "Do you need any more blankets? Anything?"

"No." She headed down the hall. "I'm fine."

"Don't leave." The words came out before he knew what he had said. "I just got home. It's nice talking with someone besides the people at the office."

But she was already at her door by then, her eyes full of tears.

"I'm sorry," he said.

She nodded and closed her door behind her. Alex listened to the silence in the house. He wondered if he had pushed her too hard. She seemed just as lost here as she was in Washington. The only difference was she was safe now.

He hoped that mattered to her as much as it did to him.

Kelsey's Flashback

"But I don't wanna." Jackie took a stubborn, four-year-old stance with two hands on his hips, his lip stuck out like a small ledge on his determined face. "I kin still see the sun. Look it."

Kelsey took the same stance out of sheer enjoyment at his temper tantrum. He and two-year-old Tommy had played all day in the warm May sunshine, but as tired as he was, Jackie was not ready to give up one second sooner than he had to. They needed to be in bed before Nick returned, so she cocked an ear for the rattle of the diesel at the curb. Satisfied he was still gone, she turned back to her son.

"Okay, little man. How about if we compromise?"

"I don't wanna *comp-a-mize*." He stomped his foot earnestly, his hands on his hips and as stern a stare as he could muster. "I wanna play."

She loved it when he thought he was being tough. Her laugh lit up the dreary apartment. "Ha. You come here, mister. If you promise to go right to sleep when I say it's bedtime, I'll let you stay up a little longer. That's what they call a compromise."

"Oh. I get it." His chocolate-colored eyes sparkled. "Wanna play camping? We kin build a tent. Tommy kin help."

Tommy watched the high stakes bargaining from his corner of the broken down sofa. He was as calm as Jackie was energetic, and clearly ready for bed. He could've passed for Jackie's twin if he had been two years older. She smiled at her second baby boy who sucked his pacifier with a dreamy stare. She had tried to wean him off the pacifier, but he had doggedly resisted. *Well, good. You can keep that plug as long as you need. Tomorrow everything changes.*

"Mama." Jackie's stern face jolted her back to the moment. "I is talking to you."

She laughed again. He looked so serious. "I hear you. What if we build a tent in the middle of your bed? We could use my sheet and make it extra big for your truck."

"That's a really good idea."

Kelsey listened for the heavy sound of the diesel one more time. So far, so good. There should be enough time to play a little longer. "Okay then, let me change Tommy and get him into his pajamas—"

"Do we hafta go to sleep?" he asked with sudden suspicion.

"No, you don't, but this way if Tommy goes to sleep, he'll already be in bed. Does that sound like a good plan?"

"It's a good comp-a ... comp-a-mize." His face filled with total satisfaction as he pronounced that terrifically big word.

She smoothed the cloth diaper on the couch as she changed Tommy. Even the silly diaper in her hand made her thoughtful tonight. Nick always used to complain about the expense of disposable diapers, so, to please him she had resorted to cloth. Only then, he had complained about the cost of detergent and utility bills. Well, tomorrow that would end.

Tomorrow. Tomorrow. She felt like singing. Almost.

The truth was there was no pleasing Nick. Period. When they had first married, she thought she could change him. Lately, he spent more time at his mother's apartment than at home. He said it was because she had a television. That was Kelsey's fault, too. If she hadn't gotten pregnant, none of this would've happened. They wouldn't have to live in a rundown apartment, they could afford a TV, and he would be happier.

Yeah, right. The truth was that Nick had never held a steady job in their four years of marriage, and he had never been a happy man. That was the real problem. Everything was her fault or someone else's. Lately, his moods had grown darker and meaner, but the day he came home drunk and raised his hand against Jackie, she saw Nick for what he really was—a bully. There was no hope. He would never change. The blinders fell off her eyes.

When Nick left for his mother's instead of looking for work, Kelsey set the ball in motion. She shivered. All that tremendous decision-making had happened just this morning. A shiver of fear tap-danced across her shoulders. This was the most dangerous thing she had ever done, but the mother bear in her had surfaced with a power she hadn't known she possessed. No one was going to hurt her boys. No one. Still, she was scared when she sneaked to the phone by the hardware store, called her sister, and planned her little family's escape. But she did it. Louise bought the bus tickets on-line. Kelsey and her sons just had to show up at the bus station tomorrow morning, climb aboard, and change their lives forever.

Tomorrow. The word had never terrified and thrilled her so much. *What if—*

She banished the thought. *No. It would work out. Somehow. It had to. Think positive. Tomorrow. Tomorrow. It's only what? Twelve hours away?*

She hugged Tommy to soothe her nervous anxiety. With a lip-smacking, pacifier-sucking slurp, he pushed his face into her blouse while she carried him to bed. She wished she still nursed. There was nothing she loved more than the warmth of her baby boy in her arms, his blankie fisted against his plump baby cheeks while he nursed to his heart's content. His droopy eyes closed in slumber before she made it into the boys' room.

"Aw-w. How we gonna make a tent now?" Jackie's lip protruded again as he jumped up and down on his bed. "Tommy's a sleeping."

"I'll have to work one of my mommy miracles. Just you wait and see. Now stop jumping." Kelsey laid the sleeping baby at the foot of the single bunk bed. She listened again for the diesel. Still nothing. Still good.

"Now let's raise our tent, okay? Here it goes." Kelsey stretched the double-sized sheet from her bed across the boys' bed and tucked it loosely around the edges. Then she used the free yardstick she had gotten from the hardware store for the tent's center pole. She actually smiled. The next homemade tent they made together would be a couple hundred miles away, and no one would be angry when he saw it.

Jackie's eyes lit up with wonder. "Wow. You did it."

"Okay now, where are you going to park your truck?"

He scrambled under his bed until he pulled his plastic red and green truck out with a big grin. "In the middle. It's safe in the middle."

She cocked her head at his answer. "Safe?"

"In case the tent falls down."

"Hey, you little rascal." She tickled his ribs as he wriggled away from her. "My tents don't fall down."

"Daddy might make it fall down. He might hurt my truck." The simple joy of a homemade sheet tent disappeared. "I don't want him to hit you no more. Not never."

Kelsey ducked her head under the tent as she pulled her son into her arms and changed the subject. The lump in her throat hurt. "Let's read a story."

Jackie patted her cheek with grubby fingers in a tender gesture of a son's love. "Daddy's naughty." he whispered. "He hurts you."

Baby of mine, he's never going to hurt me again. She brushed the sudden tear out of her eye and hugged him tighter. "Don't worry. Mama's going to be fine." She hiked the leaning yardstick up straighter to distract her son. "I know. Let's read about Herman the flying dinosaur. Do you remember his little brother's name? Was it George?"

He flopped onto his back, giggling. "Brothers can't be called George. Everybody knows that."

"Then what was it?" She tickled his sock-covered feet.

He rolled away from her. "Sammy. And he had a magic purple rock."

"And the magic rock turned him into a giraffe?"

"It made him fly." He chuckled with boyish enthusiasm that he might know more than his mother. "And he and Herman flyed to the moon," he crowed.

She snuggled the happy child in her arms. She had covered for their father's lies and drinking long enough. Tomorrow and every day after would be about living the truth for a change, and nothing but bedtime stories and imaginary circus tents. She would get a job. They might be poor, but they would be happy.

"I love you so much." He squeezed her in an extra tight hug. "And I gonna marry you when I grow up. I gonna find a magic rock, too. You and me can fly to the moon."

"Just like Herman and Sammy?"

"Ah, huh." Jackie rolled to his stomach to play with his truck.

Kelsey paused. Once they were safely on the bus, she would tell Jackie about Aunt Louise's big farm in the middle of absolutely nowhere. Together they would watch the pines of the Pacific Northwest transform into the desert and sagebrush of eastern Oregon. She planned to tell them stories about cowboys and cattle drives, rodeos and stagecoach robbers. She might even buy them cowboy hats. They would make darlin'g little cowboys.

They were welcome to stay at her sister's place indefinitely, but eventually she might find her own place. Phil, her brother-in-law, was as kind as the day was long. Raised in Pendleton, he had farmed all his life. He would love having the boys in his home for as long as Kelsey could tolerate her sister. That would be the challenge. Louise meant well, but she tended to think she knew everything on every subject under the sun. That made her bossy. Phil seemed able to tolerate it; Kelsey could not.

The first thing she planned to do though was to see if there was a woman's shelter in Pendleton. She needed someone not family related with whom she could talk with about the changes in her life. And who knows? Maybe this fall she could go back to teaching kindergarten. The world was full of working mothers. She and her boys would be fine.

A surge of determination flooded her. There were a lot of maybes in her future and tomorrow would be scary, but every day after that would be better. Purple rock or not, the best part of her life was only a day away.

A diesel engine rattled at the curb. Her throat went dry.

Playtime was done.

Thirteen

Kelsey

Remembering hurt.

With one arm around Whisper's neck, Kelsey sat on the edge of the Potomac missing her boys with her whole heart. There were other good times, but this one stood apart from the others. It had been the perfect night. Now it would forever stand as her last memory. She had come so close to saving them.

But what had pushed Nick over the edge that morning? What started the fight she couldn't win? She had never seen it coming. There were no accusations or warnings this time, no lies or bragging. He had just snapped. When she came to on the kitchen floor, the apartment was empty. Her boys were gone.

As Kelsey thought about it now, she suspected Nick's mother, Ethel Durrant had something to do with it. Ethel never cared for her son much less her grandsons, and the woman despised her most of all. Ethel lived for things that came in pints and fifths, not baby bottles. A mean alcoholic, she badgered and nagged to get what she wanted, but murder? Yes. Even murder. Kelsey'd heard the story of how Ethel had bludgeoned Nick's father over the head while he was passed out drunk, robbed him blind, and took off for parts unknown with her son. Nick never saw his father after that. Yes. Nick had certainly learned from the best.

I should've left him then.

Nick hadn't always been mean. There were times when she and he had been happy. Yes, her getting pregnant didn't help, but for a while it seemed Nick loved his new family. She kept the house clean, and while they weren't rich, they had enough. So what if they didn't have a television? They played cards, walked to the corner gas station for an ice cream cone once in awhile, and they made do with what they had. It was Tommy's birth that seemed to change everything, that and Ethel's continual digging and nagging. Her eternal berating must have worn Nick down. And then he snapped.

Kelsey calmed as she combed her fingers through Whisper's velvet fur. Alex had it right when he had carved this dog as a guardian angel. Whisper surely stayed close. He allowed her to use him as a pillow, teddy bear, and a wailing wall. Even now this gentle beast stood steadfast, watching the boats on the Potomac while she finished her latest melt down.

Smoke was only an arm's length away, but it was Whisper who sat nearly on top of Kelsey like he required her touch, too. She wondered what trauma he carried behind those intelligent, black eyes. He had been a military working dog. Was he hurt somewhere deep inside his canine psyche? Had he seen too much death like she had? Did he need her as much as she needed him? It seemed like it. He settled with a grunt onto her legs, his muzzle to his paws as he turned himself into a comfortable blanket.

"You think you're a poodle." She stroked his face from the top of his black nose to his one droopy ear.

He sighed as if in answer.

She took a deep breath. She was healing. She could feel it. Little by little, the truth Alex had taught her was becoming her reality. She was learning how to carry her awful burden. Want to or not, she was going to live.

But night times were harder.

Kelsey woke with a start. *Not again.* What on earth would Alex think if he had to listen to this racket one more night? In frustration, she pulled the pillow over her face, hoping it would smother the scream that wouldn't stop. *What's happening to me? I'm going crazy.* She pressed it firmly over her mouth until the panic attack subsided. That's all it was, another panic attack. It had to be. The nightmare faded as usual, but not until she had rent the night with the shrieks of a crazy woman. He must be thinking he's brought a lunatic into his home. At this rate, he would pack her off to Washington before the two weeks were over.

The nightmare always started and ended the same. She was playing with her two boys, the feeling peaceful and sweet, almost heaven on earth. Sometimes she was just telling them a story or baking cookies with them. Other times, it was nothing more than the feeling of them warm and alive in her arms. It always ended the same. A truck door slammed. She stood drenched in blood as her children sank in dark water. The panic of not being able to reach them strangled her every time. The terror in their eyes stabbed her. Gut wrenching screams crawled up from her heart until they made their way out of her mouth like some horrific siren she couldn't shut off. Every single night, her boys died all over again.

Am I going insane?

She pushed herself off the bed and to the window, staring at the streetlight on the corner. With her heart racing a thousand miles a minute, it felt like she was falling apart. Only the pressure of the window against her forehead offered cool solace. *I can't go on like this. I need help.*

A gentle knock at her door startled her. How long had he been there? She didn't know, the noise in her mind too loud.

"Are you okay?" he called kindly to her. "Is there anything I can do?"

"Yes, ah, I'm fine. Everything's okay." Her voice quavered. Kelsey wanted to die from embarrassment. She was an awful houseguest, crying, needy and stark-raving crazy.

"You're sure?"

She envisioned the worry in his blue eyes, and yet, she repaid him with nothing but screams every night.

"I'm fine. I'm fine." She panted, her forehead pressed against the cool glass of the windowpane. Maybe it was time to leave. Maybe she would call her sister first thing in the morning. Louise would help, just like before. It was always a double-edged sword asking for anything from Louise, but she would always help simply because she knew better.

At last Kelsey's heart resumed a semi-normal rhythm. Her prayer came fervent and sad. *Please God. If you want me to stay, help me get through tomorrow. Just one more day.*

"Room service."

"What?" The bed creaked as she rolled herself to the edge of it.

"Are you still in there? Do you know what day this is?" Alex sounded too chipper for such an early hour, especially since she had kept him up half the night.

Of course I'm here. Where else would I be? She pulled her robe over her shoulders and opened the door. "What day is it?"

"This will help." He pushed a cup of coffee in her hand as he steered her to the kitchen table where a plate of breakfast and a glass of orange juice waited for her.

"I have to go to the kitchen for room service?"

He grimaced as he pointed at her coffee. "That was room service. This," he pointed at her plate, "is an old family recipe. It's how I impress folks around here."

She stared at the breakfast sandwich on her plate and took a seat. "You impress people with an egg sandwich?"

"Yes, ma'am. Now eat. We don't have all day. When you're done eating, go take a shower."

"You're very bossy this morning." She took a bite of her sandwich and gulped it down with a swallow of juice. It was actually good.

"I'm bossy all the time. You should know that by now. Eat."

Alex stood at the open back door watching his dogs. Instead of his usual business suit, he was dressed in navy jeans with a matching golf shirt tucked in at his narrow waist. Broad shouldered, always immaculately groomed, the man knew how to dress. For the first time, she noticed how his jeans hung off his hips, and how angular those hips were to begin with. He had long legs. She shook her head to scatter her errant thoughts, but he had turned and watched her. She blushed. He had caught her looking.

"You know, now that I think about it, I've never seen you this early in the morning. Don't tell me you're one of those grumpy morning types," he teased.

"I am if you're one of those annoying type A personalities."

Instantly, a smile flashed across his face. "Think about it, Kelsey. I work 'til midnight most nights. What kind of personality do you think I have?"

As quick as a wink, she was lost in those blue eyes. Her brain stalled in low gear. *Say something. Anything.*

"Why are you still home?" She stuffed another bite of sandwich into her mouth.

"Because we have places to go and people to meet. Now get your butt moving." With that he was out the door to feed the dogs.

It didn't take her long to finish breakfast, shower, and get ready to go. Her limited wardrobe made choosing her attire for the day simple. She decided on her navy blue capris with a simple white blouse. As they exited the front door, Kelsey remembered what day it was. An American flag flapped proudly from the flagpole in Alex's front yard.

"Oh." She smiled to see the flag. "It's July Fourth."

"See? I knew you'd remember. Now come on. We're catching the metro."

"The what?"

"The metro. It's like the subway in New York, only safer."

Alex set a quick pace, which she matched easily. The morning was bright, and the warm Virginia sun felt pleasant on her shoulders. Before she knew it, they had walked the few blocks to the metro station. The weather was warm, but pleasant.

Alex purchased two fare cards from the vending machine, and ushered her through the ticket gate to the platform. She stood amazed at the busyness around her, people rushing off and onto trains, one train coming and another departing. It was confusing until Alex leaned into her and explained the schedule and the different routes. And then it got worse. She couldn't think with him standing so close. The whiff of soap and his aftershave in her nose made her light-headed and dizzy. He might as well have been explaining a tangle of blue, green, and yellow spaghetti as the different train line routes.

"Does that make sense?" he asked, like she had any idea what he was talking about.

"No," she admitted as she snagged her own metro schedule. "I need to study this. Then, I'll let you know."

"Good idea." His eyes lit up like she had just impressed him or something.

Thankfully, the blue line train roared into view, and he ushered her onboard. That simple action calmed her, but the touch of his hand at the small of her back set off a tremor in her legs. When she sat, she gripped her knees to stop the shaking, and hoped he hadn't noticed. She seemed to be falling apart for an entirely different reason this morning. She smirked to herself. *What was in that sandwich?*

"We have a dozen or so stops before we get off, so sit back and enjoy the ride." He seemed so at ease. She took a deep breath, prepared to absorb herself in the sights along the metro track, but then he put his arm across the back of their seat. The hair on his arm brushed against hers. He didn't seem to notice, but tucked against him with his arm almost around her, she could scarcely breathe.

His cell phone chirped. He tensed as he withdrew his arm and pulled the phone off its hip holster.

"Stewart." He listened for all of two seconds. "No, I said Lennox, not Hudson. Two weeks, not four. Write it down next time." He stowed the phone brusquely back into its holster without so much as a good-bye to whoever had just called.

"Trouble at work?" she asked timidly.

"No more than usual." Instantly, his smile reappeared. "I thought you'd like another option to walking or riding the bus. The metro will take you anywhere in the DC area."

She looked up at him, and wondered what it would feel like to lean into him, but the journey ended before she got the nerve. Before long they were off the metro and had explored the beautiful Smithsonian Information Center, the castle as Alex called it. They lunched at the National Museum of American History, and walked through some of the museum's numerous halls and exhibits when his cell rang again.

His eyes darkened. He turned away, but she heard restrained aggravation on his side of the conversation. "I told you once. No. Read the fine print. Eight percent sucks. Their offer's no good." Without another word, he snapped the phone shut, his lips pursed in thought. He looked like he was a million miles away.

"You're a busy man." Kelsey eyed him. Whatever the phone calls were about, they had effectively dampened an otherwise happy day.

Alex ran a hand through his hair. He turned to her with a frustrated glint in his eyes, but it passed quickly and he resumed his cheerful tour guide persona.

"Come on. You'll like this." He led her to a display case in the Exhibit of American Stories.

"The ruby red slippers." She recognized the shoes made famous when a little girl from Kansas defeated the Wicked Witch of the West in the childhood favorite *The Wizard of Oz.* "How cool."

"I thought you'd like it." He beamed like a little boy. "You know, the whole no-place-like-home thing." Intense blue eyes studied her.

"That's very thoughtful," she said.

He looked away. She thought she had made him uncomfortable, but that single insight made her smile. This was a very different side to this man called Alex Stewart, one she hadn't seen until now.

Before long they had seen not only the original flag stitched by Betsy Ross, but also George Washington's sword, the chairs Robert E. Lee and Ulysses S. Grant sat in during the Civil War surrender ceremony at the Appomattox Court House, as well as a Huey Helicopter from the Vietnam War. By late afternoon, her feet were tired, but she had enjoyed herself. They walked westward to the World War II Monument. When they got there, she took her shoes off and sat on the concrete edge of the huge reflecting pool.

"Ah. This feels good." She leaned back on her palms, basking in the summer afternoon sun with her head back and her feet dangling in the pool. "You're a good tour guide."

"I've just lived here longer than you," he replied quietly. He leaned back, too, his eyes hidden and unreadable behind his Oakley sunglasses. With the National Mall stretched behind them to the east and the Vietnam Memorial to the west, crowds of tourists were everywhere.

"I'm sorry I woke you last night." Kelsey didn't look at him as she apologized.

"Don't worry about it. That old house has heard its fair share of bad dreams."

"Do you still have nightmares?"

"Not for a few years now, but you're not the only one. Sorry if you thought you were something special."

"No, not special." She stared at the noisy crowd around the pool. *Not special at all.*

"You know, Whisper would sleep with you if you'd like." He said it so quietly that she had to look twice. "That is if you don't mind sleeping with a big ol' hairy dog in your room."

She gulped, her eyes full of tears at his gentle suggestion. Alex knew. He understood. She felt like a little girl who had just been offered a big fluffy teddy bear to keep the boogey man away.

"Whisper kinda likes you, you know." He turned to look at her, but his dark glasses only reflected her face back at her.

"Thanks." She bit her lip and blinked hard. They fell anyway.

"Ready to see some more sights?" he asked softly.

All she could do was nod. He pulled her to her feet and off they went again. This time Alex hailed a cab. She sat glued to her window while he took her on a whirlwind tour of the city. They circled the Capitol building as well as the Senate and House Office Buildings, the National Archives, the Library of Congress, and dozens of other hugely prestigious buildings that appeared to be monuments unto themselves. All the while, he explained the history and other interesting trivia that went along with each site. As night fell, they were once again on foot, just west of Arlington National Cemetery. He seemed to have an indomitable source of energy.

"One of these weekends, we'll tour inside the Capitol," he announced as he walked. "Maybe Arlington, too, but right now we're going to the best place in the city to watch fireworks."

"The best place, huh?" She couldn't keep the smirk out of her voice. He sounded so sure.

"You'll see."

She caught the boyish excitement on his face. How had she missed this side of him? He was charming.

"Come on, slow poke." He nodded uphill. "Almost there."

The fireworks show was imminent when they reached their final destination. Apparently, everyone else in the city knew the best place to watch fireworks, too. Crowds of revelers swarmed the expansive lawn around the thirty-two foot high memorial of the Pacific Battle of Iwo Jima. She stared up at the mighty bronze statue of five Marines and one Navy corpsman as they had raised the American flag during that historic battle. Unfurled and flapping in the breeze, the beautiful stars and stripes stirred her heart as quickly as it filled her eyes. As Kelsey read the words of the monument, she noticed the somber look on Alex's face.

**"In honor and in memory of the men of
the United States Marine Corps who have**

given their lives to their country since November 10, 1775."

"I don't need fireworks," she declared. "This is awesome."

"It is, isn't it?" He looked so pleased with himself, but just then his cell phone rang. He turned away to answer it, but she heard the blatant hostility in his voice.

"What do you want now?" He paused. "Yes, yes, three percent. Write it like that then—No. Make it April. Wait. No. June." He took another step away, his hand brushing through his hair again. "Then tell 'em no."

She walked away and around the huge monument to give him space while he ranted. When she glanced back at him, he was still deep in conversation with someone who obviously didn't have a life since they were working on a federal holiday. It had to be someone from his office. What kind of a slave driver was he?

Within minutes he was back at her side, his good humor nearly restored.

"Sorry," he muttered. "Work."

"You have people working today?" she asked, hoping the amazement in her voice didn't come across rude.

He grimaced in exasperation. "Not really. One of my techies creates video games on the side. She uses the office computer equipment sometimes. It's got more bits or bites or something like that."

"So she's working on the job while she's..." She didn't know what to say next.

"Yes." His jaw clenched and Kelsey could tell this was a sore subject for him. "She's a busybody is what she is. Can't leave well enough alone."

These phone calls revealed an entirely different side to Alex. She questioned what she really knew about him as they circled the monument in silence.

"Iwo Jima was one bloody battle." He peered up at the faces of those men like he knew them. The first burst of fireworks arched across the dark ceiling overhead. Voices all around oooh'd and ahhh'd, but in the brightening crescendo of falling stars, she noticed he brushed something out of his eyes. Another volley of shooting sparks splashed through the night. Kelsey studied his profile against the lighted sky. She saw pride mixed with sadness on his face. The phone calls forgotten, she wanted to take his handsome face in her hands and do something to make him smile again.

"I didn't know the Marine Corps has been around so long." She wanted to get his attention off his sad thoughts.

"Since the Revolutionary War. Of course it's changed a lot since then." His voice was husky as he stepped back from the monument. Kelsey looked at it one more time before she followed him away from the crowd and walked uphill again.

"Mount Suribachi. That's the dormant volcano on the southern end of Iwo where those men raised the flag that day. The statue is actually designed after the actual photograph that was taken." He gave her another history lesson as they walked.

"Were those men killed there?"

"No. Not that day anyway. Three of them died out there, but the others came home. Nearly seven thousand men died taking Iwo though, almost a tenth of the American force that was sent. Another twenty thousand were injured, most of them on the first two days of battle," he said somberly.

"That's a lot of death and suffering in just a couple days." Kelsey walked beside him. "I can't imagine what it must've been like for all their poor mothers."

"I'm sorry." He cupped her shoulder with his hand. "I shouldn't be talking about this."

"No, it's okay." She walked in silence. They had been just talking about boys dying, but she hadn't fallen apart. It really was happening. She was learning to live again.

"It was one of those times when uncommon valor really was a common virtue." Alex's voice was extra low. "Seems those are rare things these days."

It happened without notice. He slipped his hand around hers. Her breath caught. *My goodness, he's held my hand before. What's the big deal?* But this was different. This wasn't a friend comforting a grieving woman or a stranger helping an amnesiac through a hard time. No. This was Alex reaching for Kelsey. This was a man reaching for a woman. For some reason, he sought her hand tonight.

A splash of false meteorites tumbled overhead, lighting the sky in sparks and embers as they descended back to earth. He looked heavenward. Again she caught his profile, the way his chin jutted sharp and strong, the square line of his jaw. His nose was straight, but flared as he inhaled the drift of gunpowder from all the revelry in the crowd. Kelsey gulped. She had never seen him like this before.

"Had enough for one day?" He caught her gaze.

She blushed. While his question begged an answer, all she saw was the scintillating waves of warmth around them.

"No," she said softly, her eyes still hooked to his while brilliant red and green flashed above them. Every whorl of his fingerprints, every crease of his palm burned hot and pleasant against her hand, somehow resonating the heated display in the sky. "This is wonderful."

"It is, isn't it?"

His gaze was a magnet she couldn't pull away from. She swallowed hard, not knowing what she had just described, the monument, the fireworks, or him.

"Your choice of rides home, ma'am. What'll it be? Metro or cab? Rosslyn station's only a couple of blocks away. It's still quite a walk, but—"

"Metro," she said a little too quickly, and then lowered her eyes. "That is, if it's okay with you."

"Then let's get walking." They trudged across the grounds and back to the sidewalk, her hand still tight in his.

"It was my grandfather." Alex nodded back toward the bronze monument. "He was one of those twenty thousand. Gramps was a good man, but he drank himself to death. They didn't call it post traumatic stress back then."

"That's why this place is important to you." She noticed he had adjusted his stride to match hers.

"Yes. They don't make guys like him anymore."

"Do you come from a military family?" Even as they walked, the answer was obvious. Straight posture, head held high, and eyes forward as if he never doubted where he was going.

"Gramps was a Marine. My father, Navy. So, yeah, I guess it runs in the blood."

"Do you have any brothers or sisters?"

"No. Mom passed when I was nine. Dad sent me to live with his parents."

"Where was he?"

"Who knows? He didn't stay in touch. Besides, I was just a pain-in-the-neck kid."

"I'm sorry. That must've been hard for you."

"No. He was a mean old bastard. We're both better off." There was no recrimination in his words, just fact.

"So this was the grandfather who raised you then, the one injured at Iwo Jima?"

"Yes. Patrick Bradley Stewart. Gram was Patricia Rose Southerland Stewart. Pat and Patty. Both good people. You'd have liked them." The way he said those words struck a chord with her. There was no doubt she would have liked them because she liked him.

"Is your grandmother still alive?"

"She passed four years ago."

"Oh, Alex. That's—" She gasped. She couldn't finish the thought.

"Losing Sara and Abby was hard for Gram." His voice tightened.

"I'm sorry." She wished she could call her words back. Instead, she squeezed his hand and he squeezed hers in return. "Where's your father now?"

"Don't know. Don't care. He left me the land that I built my cabin on, but I haven't heard a word from him since." He didn't slow his pace for a second as he related the history of his family. Before she knew it, they arrived at Rosslyn Station and just in time. Their train had arrived. She felt his hand at the small of her back guiding her onboard. For some insane reason, her heart fluttered at his touch again. *What is going on with me?*

She hoped the train would be too crowded, that maybe they would have to stand, maybe jostling against each other as the train whisked along the track. It wasn't. There were seats aplenty. Then she wished the train would corner a little sharper so she could lean into him, or better yet, so he could lean into her. Either way would be nice. She sighed in disappointment. The metro was the smoothest train ride she had ever ridden.

"Our stop's just ahead. Metro will get us close, but it's late so I'll call a cab. Sound good?" He leaned in for her answer. "Or would you rather walk some more?"

With her voice lost somewhere in her heart, Kelsey squeaked out a puny, "Yes."

He smiled, his eyes dark and teasing, and for a moment she felt as if she had answered a completely different yes or no question. She blushed at her carnal thoughts. Not for one minute in her past life had her mind wandered the way it did tonight. Never.

"What? Say again?" He cocked his head and leaned in close enough for a—kiss.

With his body tilted toward hers, Kelsey had a sudden impulse to wrap her arms around his neck and nibble that ear. Instead she breathed another timid, "Yes."

He smirked. "Then we walk."

The train pulled into their station and once again, he politely escorted her off the platform, his hand warm on her back as they jostled through the holiday crowd. Just as quickly as they passed through the exit turnstile, he reclaimed her hand for the short walk to his house. Fireworks and sparklers flashed around the neighborhood as revelers continued their Independence Day celebrations, but Kelsey didn't see or hear them. Every tingling nerve in her body tracked, analyzed, and somehow drew energy from the man walking proudly beside her.

Too soon they stood at his front door while he unlocked the deadbolt. Again, his hand rested comfortably at the small of her back as he ushered her into his house. That simple act of chivalry made her feel special. She wanted to look up at him, but didn't, afraid her eyes would reveal too many feelings she didn't know how to deal with.

"Well, there you have it, ma'am, your first tour of Washington DC. What'd you think?" He plugged his cell phone into the charger on the table and sat on the opposite end of the couch from her.

Kelsey sat in a tired heap. She kicked her shoes off and massaged sore feet. "It's an awesome city. It was very kind of you to take a whole day just to do that for me."

"I do have an ulterior motive." His eyes were extra blue tonight. "I have to go out of town for the next couple weeks, maybe longer. I didn't want to leave before I showed you around. Will you be okay while I'm gone?"

With her mind all a twitter, she wondered what he was really asking. *Do you want me to stay? Should I cancel my travel plans? Would you like to come with me?* She shrugged her foolish thoughts away. "I'll be fine. I've been alone before. Besides, I've been thinking of taking some on-line courses to get my teaching certificate back."

He studied her before he spoke again. "That's a good plan, Kelsey, but I don't have a computer here at home. How will you do that?"

She shrugged. For some reason it was important to let him know she was more than just a hysterical woman in the middle of the night. "The library has computers. It's not far. Besides, I can take the bus. I'm also going to apply for a student loan, and if I decide to stay in Virginia, I'll need my own place. I can't impose on you forever."

"Did you realize it's been two weeks?"

Startled, she had to think for a minute. "Wow. You're right."

"It went fast, didn't it?" Again, that smirk played at the corner of his mouth. That mouth. His tongue skimmed his bottom lip and she wondered what that mouth might taste like.

"By the sounds of it, you don't want to go back to Washington." His voice low, he pulled his knee onto the couch as he turned to face her.

Kelsey shook her head, her feelings a confused jumble. If he had asked that question last night, she would have been ready to go. Today – not so much. "You'll need someone to take care of your dogs while you're gone, won't you? I could stay a little longer –"

"Kelsey." He meant for her to look at him so she did. Instantly her brain disengaged, her heart stopped beating, and time screeched to a breathless halt. She felt off balance, on the verge of falling off the couch and straight into his arms. "I want you to stay as long as you want. Finish your schooling. Then you can make a better decision to stay or leave."

She only heard his first three words. *I want you.*

"I'll take good care of the dogs," she whispered.

"I know."

His voice was so soft.

"I have to go to bed," she said.

"So do I."

Hmmm. Bedroom soft.

"When, ah, are you leaving tomorrow?" She forced herself to focus on his words instead of his lips and those incredible blue eyes. Right now everything he said sounded like an invitation she very much wanted to accept.

"I'll be gone by the time you wake."

By the way, my answer is—yes.

"Good night then."

"Good night, Kelsey."

Such sweet words. Are my feet touching the ground?

"Will you call or... or anything? I mean, what if something happens to one of the dogs?"

"I'll call, but I'm not worried about the dogs."

She forced herself to look away.

"Good night, Alex."

"Good night, Kelsey."

His voice sounded calm, strong and deep and—*oh, my gosh.* She grabbed her shoes, and all but ran down the hall. With seconds to spare, she locked her bedroom door behind her, her heart thumping as if something entirely different and very wonderful had just happened.

What is going on with me? For heaven's sake, I'm a fool.

She flopped breathlessly onto the bed breathless.

First I'm sick out of my mind. I'm screaming. Having nightmares. Now I'm what? Delirious? Stupid?

Her introspection followed by a flurry of other questions. *Did he mean to take my hand tonight? And if he did, did he mean it that way, or was he just being nice? Did he know he touched my arm while we were on the metro? Did he mean to say good night the way he said it, or was it just* good night*?*

She lay awake long after she turned the light off, feeling like a foolish schoolgirl with a crush on the home-team quarterback. Her mind rattled more questions. *Did he mean he was worried about me more than the dogs? Was he really worried or just being nice? But he said he would keep in touch. What is wrong with me?*

Her prayer from the night before came back to her. She had gotten exactly what she had asked for.

Fourteen

Kelsey

The house was extra empty.

Hollow. Kelsey sipped her coffee alone at the kitchen
table. It was Monday, a travel day for Alex, but just another
day for her. He had been so quiet when he left this morning
that she had slept right through it, which was probably a good
thing. Who knows what dumb thing she might have said if
she had been awake? She realized she didn't know where he
was traveling to or why. How strange that the prospect of him
being gone for a couple weeks made her feel more alone than
his outrageous work schedule. At least before, she had known
he would be home every night, and he was always happy to
see her. Wasn't he?

She finished her coffee and washed the single cup before
she placed it back in the cupboard. She meant what she had
said last night, so her first accomplishment of the day was to
call an on-line university. The woman she spoke with was
very helpful. By the end of the call, she knew exactly what
classes she needed and had also completed a student loan
application. She hung up feeling proud of herself like she
used to. Wouldn't Alex be surprised if he came home to find
her recertified and moved into her own place? She needed her
own space. Didn't she?

Kelsey had little time to think about her plans or troubles. At nine o'clock the doorbell rang. Within minutes, the living room was full of boxes of everything and anything a person would need to set up a home computer. She was no more finished with that delivery, when a furniture truck backed into the driveway, and she was asked to accept delivery of a solid walnut roll-top desk. The deliveryman handed her the paperwork to sign and a card that simply read: *I've been meaning to set up a home office. Would you mind? Alex.*

"Our instructions are to move this desk into the southwest corner bedroom and make sure we situate it exactly where the lady of the house tells us. Are you the lady of the house?" The deliveryman stood waiting for an answer while his partner rolled an overloaded hand-truck up the walk.

She started to shake her head, but the implication made her smile. "Well, I guess that's me right now, only I'm not the lady of the house, only—never mind. I don't think it will fit in that room because it's full of—" She opened the door to the other spare bedroom to find it empty. The furniture had been cleared and the floor recently scrubbed. When had Alex done all of this? Last night?

The deliverymen set the desk where she would be able to see out the window while she worked. Just when she thought the day couldn't hold any more surprises, the doorbell rang again. There stood a man from the computer store. "I'm here to set up your computer, ma'am. I understand you're taking some on-line classes?"

Dumbfounded, Kelsey showed him to the computer boxes and the rapidly improving home office.

"Excellent choice, ma'am. This is some of the best hardware out there. I'll have this set up and working in no time. If I do say so myself, I think you'll be very happy with this equipment."

Before he had finished installing hardware, software, and everything else she could possibly need, the doorbell rang again. This time it was a repairman from the telephone company, come to install a second phone line. His instructions were the same. *Install the line in the southeast corner bedroom and do exactly what the lady of the house desires.*

Kelsey sat in the living room with a foolish smile on her face while the servicemen traipsed back and forth until their work was finished. She was thankful Alex was out of town because he would surely have read her mind. Last night she had told him one little piece of information, and now all this.

At last the servicemen left, their work accomplished. The phone rang and her heart was instantly hopeful it might be Alex. She had so much to say, but it wasn't him. It was just the bank advising her student loan was approved, and she could commence taking courses. The low-interest repayment schedule would not become effective until she was gainfully employed. Would there be anything else?

Kelsey placed the phone back into its cradle. She didn't know what to think or how to feel. Should she go? Should she stay? Should she walk the dogs or knuckle down to class work? Should she cry? Should she laugh? With a silly twirl in the middle of the boring dark living room, she let her emotions take over while she laughed and cried at the same time.

On an impulse, she picked up the phone to call Alex, but just as quickly dropped it back in its cradle. *No. Control yourself. Think. Stick to the plan. Get your teaching job back.*

Don't do anything stupid. Move out. Get your own place. Be smart for a change.

And then she fired up the computer.

I hate math.

The phone woke Kelsey. She had fallen asleep on the keyboard, puzzling through an on-line secondary math class, not her favorite subject.

"Good morning." It was Alex speaking over a lot of noise. "You there?"

"Yes. I'm here. How are you?"

"Doing good." His deep baritone voice competed with a great deal of racket in the background. "Meant to call you sooner. How's the new office?"

"You shouldn't have done all that. It's too much." She shouted to be heard, her answer lost in the continuous noise of wherever he was. "Where are you? It sounds like you're in a war."

"Afghanistan." He shouted as well. "Hang on."

"Are you okay?" Her consternation grew as the noise level of his call prevented further dialogue. All she could do was listen. The phone sounded like it was dropped, dragged, and tossed. At last, the noise diminished, and his voice came through strong, clear, and very good.

"Sorry about that. I didn't expect the whole squadron of helos to land so close to our tent. I'm okay. How are you?"

"I'm good, but why are you in Afghanistan? You're not in the military anymore."

"We're helping the Army with a couple projects. It's good to hear your voice."

She smiled. Despite the miles between them, he sounded like he was in the next room. "I've been working on math all day."

"Why do you need math?"

"Because the Virginia school board only accepts some of my credentials. It's not a big deal. I have to take a few classes in secondary math, that's all."

"For kindergarten?" He sounded surprised.

"Kindergarten teachers have to be smart, too."

"But how are you, really? Are you okay?"

Again, his deep voice struck a chord. She couldn't help the foolish smile that blossomed all over her face. "I'm good. The dogs are fine and—"

"I don't care about the dogs." The impatience in his voice surprised her. Immediately, it softened. "I'd rather hear about you."

Her heart fluttered. "I'm doing fine. I'm busy with school and the dogs and—"

"You're not thinking of moving out, are you?"

Did she hear a tone of worry in that man's sexy voice? Kelsey paused, not sure what she planned anymore. "I really should do that one of these days—"

"Do me a favor. Don't move out until I get back. It's only two more weeks. Can you promise you won't leave until I get back?"

"You've already been gone four weeks. I really don't want to move, but—"

"Listen. I know it's been longer than I expected, but we're clearing out a couple pockets of insurgents. They don't exactly follow a schedule. Can you wait a little longer? For me?"

Again she hesitated. For heaven's sake, this wasn't a marriage proposal, and it was only two more weeks. Its not like she was ready to move out anyway. It's just that, it's just that—what? She didn't know what she meant any more.

"Okay," she said softly.

"What? I can't hear you. What?" The loud chop of helicopter blades cut his side of the conversation into blocks of unintelligible garble. Click. The line went dead.

Kelsey stared at the phone in her hand, not sure if he had heard her or not. One minute she felt blue eyes looking into her soul, and just like that, he was gone. She raised the phone back to her ear. The words rolled easily off her tongue.

"Yes, Alex. I will wait for you."

She placed the phone back on its cradle with thoughts of Alex swirling through her head. He wasn't home and she decided, why not? Kelsey stood up from her computer and stretched as she thought about what she was going to do next. It felt like a breech of trust, but somehow, she didn't think he would mind. So she did it.

She opened his bedroom door and stepped over the threshold. A queen-sized bed stood between two single windows. Dark curtains kept the world out so well, she had to turn the light on. Judging by the dust on the folded pleats, those curtains hadn't been opened in a very long time.

Summoning a shred more courage, Kelsey tiptoed around his bed. The chenille bedspread was old-fashioned and worn, but she could tell the corners were square beneath the spread, the two standard-sized pillows tucked just as neatly at the headboard. Alex was military through and through. She wondered if Sara had bought the spread. Probably. The room resembled everything else in the house, as if his life had stopped years ago. She knew the feeling.

As she continued her invasion of his privacy, Kelsey turned her attention to his dresser. There were only two items on the dusty surface. A small wooden tray held a silver and gold watch, a pair of gold cuff links, a few tie clips of flags and other military insignia, and some shirt buttons. Kelsey noticed the metro ticket stub dated July fourth still in the tray. It touched her that he hadn't thrown it away.

Next to the tray stood a picture of the Alex Stewart family, one of those generic department store types. She examined it closely. They looked like a very happy family. Alex had worn a tan shirt with blue slacks, most likely part of his military uniform. Sara was dressed in a simple blue dress with capped sleeves. She looked happy with Abby on her lap, her husband's arm draped casually around them both. The family resemblance was obvious. Abby had his blue eyes but Sara's white- blonde hair. Abby's face was lit with the innocent smile of Daddy's little girl, her top two teeth missing.

Alex was a lucky man. Contentment glowed from his handsome face. His hair was darker and his eyes less guarded, and his wide-open smile made him look even younger. Happier. A stab of remorse whispered. Kelsey didn't have a single picture of her dysfunctional family, much less a nice portrait like this. Even if she could've afforded one, too many bruises would've shown. It was never an option in her universe.

She wondered what a normal family life with Alex might've been like. What kind of father was he? What kind of husband? Judging by the look on Sara's face, Kelsey knew. A twinge of foolish jealousy pricked her heart. Once upon a time Sara had everything.

Carefully Kelsey replaced the portrait in the exact same dust-free line where she had found it. She sat on the edge of his bed, feeling foolish at her schoolgirl feelings as she bounced the mattress once, then twice. The springs within creaked. Guilt poked at her conscience. What difference did it make if she investigated his room or not? He was thousands of miles away, and yet – she could almost picture him sitting with her. He would be kind, maybe wondering and maybe hopeful. With a sigh, she leaned back onto the bed, her heart pounding as she felt the nubby chenille against the back of her arms. She didn't want him sitting next to her on the edge of the bed. No. She wanted him climbing all over her body, ripping her clothes off, covering her mouth with—

STOP!

Kelsey snapped to attention. She gulped as another thought surfaced. This was where he had made love with his wife. The thought rattled her. She shouldn't be here. This was a private place. Intimate. She was nothing, but an uninvited interloper. Jumping off the bed, she straightened the bedspread until it was exactly as he had left it. No imprint of her body must remain. He must never know she had betrayed his trust.

On her way out the door, another picture caught her eye, only this was a crayon drawing taped to the closed closet door on what looked like his side of the bed. It pulled her across the room. With trembling fingers she examined the childish figures marked in bright crayon colors. A big stick mommy with straight yellow hair stood beside a smaller stick daddy with spiky brown hair. In between them stood a little stick girl with the same yellow hair as her mother's. She smiled with bright red crayon lips and vivid blue eyes, the same as her daddy's, while her spaghetti arms were stretched to reach her mommy and daddy's hands. A string of multi-colored flowers and green stalks of grass lined the bottom of the page, while a grinning sun streamed long, yellow sunshine over the happy family. The paper was faded and covered with wrinkles as if it had been crushed into a ball, but then smoothed flat again. The happy words across the top of the page said it all. *My Family.*

Her mouth went dry. Jackie had drawn this exact kind of family picture at the Durrant kitchen table not too long ago. He had concentrated so hard that his tongue stuck out until the last flower was colored in his favorite colors. Red and yellow. He had even drawn his truck in the portrait. Tears blurred the lovely image as Kelsey touched the waxy outline of a dead little girl's face. She could almost smell the crayons and construction paper. The image of Jackie's proud smile when he displayed his finished masterpiece on their refrigerator door just so his daddy could see it flashed into her mind. Nick. The awful irony sliced her heart to shreds all over again. Jackie had loved his father like any son would. He wanted to make sure his daddy saw his artwork. But Nick—

What was I thinking?

She couldn't get out of Alex's room fast enough. The devastation of all she had lost swept over her like wildfire. Curling up on her bed with her arms wrapped around her knees, she cried, like that could in any way keep the pain at bay. It couldn't. *What on earth am I doing in Alexandria? How could I have left my boys behind and so far away?* A torrent of tears blinded her. She didn't belong here. She didn't belong anywhere.

Smiling eyes of crayon blue from down the hall chided her. Abby had lived the perfect childhood loved by both of her parents, but in the end, she was the same as Tommy and Jackie. Loved and lost. Kelsey thought of Abby's very unhappy father. She stilled as she remembered the tender light in his eyes the night before he left, and the sound of his voice when he called, "Can you wait a little longer? For me?"

The thought calmed her. He was the difference between her family and Sara's. He had truly loved his wife and child. He still did. Everything in this sad, depressing home testified to that.

Alex. Kelsey took a deep breath and exhaled slowly as her emotions returned to normal. Abby and Sara were gone. Tommy and Jackie were gone. But she and Alex were still here. They weren't so different. Want to or not, they still had to live.

She set her feet to the floor and resolutely returned to the brand new home office with its state-of-the-art computer and very expensive roll-top desk. Alex had given her another gift she didn't deserve. The least she could do was accomplish what she intended.

Whisper interrupted her plans with a yelp from his kennel. Without a backward glance, Kelsey snapped the laptop closed and snagged the dog leashes off the hook by the back door. In a minute, she locked the house and deserted her schoolwork for the day. She opened the kennel and let her two best friends loose to rampage around the backyard for a couple minutes. In two weeks Alex would be home. She would do what he asked. She would wait for him.

And then she'd leave.

"Kelsey. It's me, Alex."

"Are you coming home yet?" Kelsey's heart fluttered at the sound of his voice. He called the minute his plane touched down. By then his original operation had been extended into a comfortable two-month zone of solitude and healing for her. She did feel stronger, but she would be happy to see him again, too.

"Just landed. I'm at the airport. I need to stop by my office first, but how about a date tonight?"

She choked, her throat suddenly too dry to swallow. "A date? Us? I mean, us? A date?"

"Now don't get all excited. Just thought I'd see if you'd help with a project of mine. We wouldn't even have to leave the house."

She coughed again. Not leaving the house and date in the same sentence played crazy tricks on her libido. "What kind of project are you talking about?"

"It's a woodworking project. I do a couple things for the children's cancer ward over at one of the DC hospitals every

Christmas. Would you mind lending a hand? That's all I'm asking."

Kelsey smiled more and more these days. She felt swept along in the wake of a man with more life in him than most people. "That sounds okay. I guess I can do that."

"I'll be home at four. Do you want me to grab something for dinner?"

"I've got two rib-eyes waiting to be grilled."

"Good answer. See you soon."

Fifteen

Kelsey

He's home.

She didn't know how to act by the time he pulled his truck into the driveway. As much as she wanted to run to him, she wanted to hide from him. All afternoon she had talked herself out of any excitement at seeing him again. She used logic and scolding, common sense and religious fortitude, but then she applied fresh lipstick and checked her makeup just in case.

The doorknob turned. He stood in the doorway, tall, deeply tanned, handsome, and incredibly close. An odd rush of fear took her breath even as she realized how much she craved his crooked smile. His eyes seemed bluer than she remembered, and he had been to a barber on the way home. The manly smell of aftershave filled the small front room. The black polo tucked into tan cargo pants emphasized his athletic waist and hips. His broad shoulders looked broader. Her breath hitched as her eyes drank him in.

Her first impulse was an out-of-control run to him, bowl him over, and kiss-the-stuffing-out-of-him kind of a feeling. She didn't. She waited, frozen as another feeling from her past suffocated her with dread. *He's home.* Those words had once meant terror. Her mouth went dry and her heart pounded as fear and desire collided. This was when it happened, the accusations, the arguments, and the lies. She stood waiting for Alex to make the first move. Then she would know if she should run.

"Hello." He seemed restrained also, too calm and composed compared to the level of her anticipation. He stood at the door, his eyes taking her in from head to toe in one scorching glance. He saw through her, she was sure of it. With panic stifling all reasonable thought, she felt more vulnerable than ever. Only small talk saved the day.

"How was your flight?" She held her breath.

"Good. How was your day?"

"I've been busy as usual." She strived for a matter-of-fact tone to her voice, no fear and no nervousness. That might set him off. "Dinner is already on the table. Are you hungry?"

"Yes, ma'am."

Her silly heart skipped a beat. *He called me ma'am.* For some reason, when he called her that, it heard sweetheart and darlin'g instead. She relaxed and took a deep breath. "Let's eat."

Confusion bounced around in her head as Kelsey headed for the kitchen. Alex followed, just a step behind. She wondered if she slowed her gait, would he place his hand at the small of her back again? Instead she strode purposefully, as if the only thing she wanted to do right now was food service related. The table was already set for two. Quickly, she served the rib-eyes along with baked potatoes, green beans, and a spinach salad. A chocolate pudding cake waited in the refrigerator for the cream already whipped to perfect peaks. His steak was more rare than medium, just the way he liked it. Despite all her excitement only a moment ago, now she moved like a waitress at a fast food joint with a customer.

"I have a bottle of wine somewhere if you'd like—" He was half out of his seat, half smiling. Still watching.

"No, thank you. I'd just fall asleep." Even she heard the no-nonsense tone in her voice. It was her old coping mechanism, but now she didn't know how to turn it off. *What is wrong with me?*

"Looks like you've had good weather." He had to be hungry after a day of travel, but for some reason he just pushed his food around the plate.

"Yes. We've had a couple rain showers yesterday, but nothing else."

Scolding herself for getting excited about nothing, she focused on washing the few dishes in the sink instead of the deep tan on his face and arms. It made the hair on his arms almost blonde, and she wondered if arm hair could be bleached from the sun, and whatever, she really didn't care because it looked good on him. The tan on his face made his eyes a deeper blue. She inhaled the smell of him from across the small kitchen, the manly odor of wind, soap, and him.

"Aren't you going to eat?" he asked quietly.

Embarrassed, Kelsey looked up from the dishwater. He looked unhappy.

"I already ate," she lied even as he looked at the second table setting.

"I see." He pushed back from the table, his food barely touched. "You're probably too busy to help with the hospital project then."

"No, but I have dessert if you'd like. I made—"

"Thanks anyway." He turned to the basement door. "I'll be downstairs."

"I said I'll help and I will." Kelsey went to her room and changed into one of her older, more tattered outfits.

She joined him back in the kitchen. Somehow the evening had turned from a welcome home party to a game of uncomfortable strategy. Move here, counter move there. He stood at the basement door waiting, his eyes analyzing as usual. The last time he did that, he had bought an entire home office just so she could take a few college courses. Maybe that's what he was waiting for?

"Would you like to see your new office?" she offered, still very much in control of her emotions.

"No. I wouldn't." Alex opened the door and flipped the basement light switch, his eyes hooded and dark. "Workshop's downstairs."

She followed him as they descended the basement steps, but Alex was quiet. He waved at the cutout wooden pieces laid out on the table as he busied himself at the workbench. "These are for the kids in the cancer ward over at Washington Central."

Kelsey stood at the far end of the table, surveying the organized room. A sturdy bench lined the entire far wall with an array of tools attached to the pegboard above it. A shelf to the right housed other equipment that looked like drills or saws while a box full of wood scraps sat on the floor beside the shelf. Long fluorescent work lights hung from the low ceiling. In the middle of the room stood a long worktable with twenty-five individual stacks of wooden pieces lined up like table settings. It was easy to see he had an assembly line in mind.

Without looking at her, Alex tossed a pack of sandpaper across the table. "First, we sand. Then we glue."

She smiled, but he didn't notice. He was already focused on the first stack, his eyes hooded and dark.

"There's a chair if you'd rather sit." He pointed to an old office chair in the corner, again without making eye contact.

"Okay." Kelsey pulled it to the table and sat opposite Alex. This frosty attitude from Alex was her fault. She knew it. She just didn't know how to change it. As she examined the puzzle pieces in front of her, she determined they were precut with tabs so they would fit together without nails or screws.

"It's a cradle." She looked at his tight-lipped face. "You make cradles?"

"Yes."

She picked up the piece of sandpaper and ran it along the edge of what looked like a headboard.

"Not like that." Instantly the temperature in the room plummeted. She nearly jumped out of her skin he came so quickly to her side. Brusquely he took the sandpaper out of her hand and smoothed it across the wooden piece in a firm, smooth motion. "Sand in the direction of the grain. Always. Like this."

"Oh. Sorry. Okay." She gulped, glancing timidly up at him as he demonstrated what he expected. Flustered as much by his cold shoulder as his close proximity, she could barely breathe. Where was that nice man who had taken her on a whirlwind tour of DC only a couple months ago? She didn't recognize him.

Confusion rattled her nerves. How could someone so kind also be so cold? The smell of him filled her nose. Hmm.

Absence does make the heart grow fonder, she thought, and the olfactory senses as well. She closed her eyes to breathe him in and to calm herself. Hmm. That guy is still here. Somewhere.

He walked back to the other side of the table. Without another word, they sanded and glued. Alex was the epitome of a workaholic. Since he had planned to complete the cradles that night, that's exactly what they did. She finished eight by the time he finished seventeen. Okay, so she was slow, but she enjoyed the work if not the silence. It was late when they finished sanding, but he gave her a succinct demonstration how to glue the pieces together anyway. As she glued, he followed with a set of braces for each cradle.

"Are you going to paint them?" Kelsey asked when he braced the final cradle.

"Yes."

"What colors?" She pushed her hair back over her shoulder and out of her face.

"White."

"Just white?" She wished he would look at her again.

"Just white." Alex sighed and adjusted a knob on the final brace until it was snug.

"What if I made doll blankets for each of them? Would you mind? It wouldn't take much time. I could crochet twenty-five different colored blankets. It might be fun." She was going to say, "That way I could teach you how to crochet," but she didn't. What little nerve she had started the evening with had long since fled. Kelsey wondered why she had wasted her time with make-up and mascara. She didn't need to look good for this kind of an endurance test.

"Whatever you want." He gave her a sideways glance that didn't really see her. Alex was excellent at the cold shoulder. Kelsey shivered. Those tender blue eyes could also be ice.

"When do you need them?"

He tightened the final wood clamp an extra long time. "Christmas Eve."

"Good. Okay, then I'll start tomorrow." He was making her nervous.

"Fine." Alex gathered the sandpaper and stowed the glue bottles. Without another word or glance, he gestured toward the basement steps.

"Okay." She dusted her hands and headed up the stairs behind him. "You're easy to work with."

"Yeah, right." He sounded gruff and tired.

"You probably have jet lag."

"Yes."

"Are you too tired for a bowl of ice cream?"

This was her last chance effort. The twenty-five cradles might be done, but this whole night had turned into one, big disaster. Right now, moving back to Washington state seemed like a good idea. Just as the thought materialized, Alex reached around her to turn off the basement light. It was no big deal, except all that muscle training from her life with Nick Durrant was still alive and well. Kelsey ducked, yelping like a kicked puppy with no place to hide. In less than a second, she was out of control and ready to fall down the stairs. Hot tears sprang to her eyes. She grabbed the handrail for support before she did something stupid, like scream.

Alex froze. He stood over her looking down, and that didn't help. A black wave of claustrophobia swarmed her. *I have to get out of here.* Instead, she clenched the handrail tighter, her voice small and squeaky. "I'm going to get over that someday."

He didn't move.

"It's just that..." She looked up and into blue eyes.

The ice had melted.

"He used to... and I..." she mumbled. Kelsey didn't mean for her words to come out so lame, but he had been gone a long time. While she had no reason to be afraid of him, she was very afraid of —everything.

"Talk to me." His voice had thawed, too. "I'll listen."

"No." The tears spilled over. She looked up again. He looked sad. With a huge breathy sigh, she licked her lips and relented. "Oh-kay."

The second he offered his hand, her heart lurched. Panic shook her from head to toe. Here she was standing on the same precipice all over again. To trust or not to trust. To believe or not to believe. Nothing in her history could help her take this tiny step forward. She wished he had never come home. *Please, if I give you my hand, don't hurt me.*

Kelsey cringed and placed just her fingertips at the edge of his. Surely that was enough. He could kiss them or break them. It was the now-or-never, the live-or-die moment she knew would eventually come. No matter what happened next, from this telling moment on she would never be the same.

He blinked hard and fast as he pulled her gently up the last steps and into the kitchen. Alex pulled out a kitchen chair for her, waited until she sat down, and cleared the last of the dinner dishes from the table. "Sit down. I'll make us some coffee," he said calmly.

She composed herself as much as possible, but she couldn't stop shaking. Before he turned around from the coffee maker, she balanced her chin on her fist hoping to hold her head still. She had to get a grip.

"How'd you meet him anyway?" he asked quietly.

She blew out a big breath before she could begin, still trying to calm herself for what she knew was ahead. "At school where I taught kindergarten."

"He was a teacher?" Alex brought two cups to the table.

"No. Maintenance crew. One day when I took my class out to recess, he was watching me, and then he showed up at my apartment with flowers." She shook her head at that stupid recollection. She had actually been excited for the attention. "I was so dumb."

"Here you go. Cream and sugar included, ma'am." He poured the coffee and sat across from her, watching intently. "Why do you say you were dumb?"

Kelsey clutched her cup instead of looking at him. *How do you tell the man you want to impress that you were socially inept?* She bit her lip. *Might as well just spit it out. Then he'll gladly help you pack.*

"Because I'd never dated much. I had my books and my kindergarten kids, and I thought I was happy. I'd never been with a man before and—" Tears welled up. It was embarrassing admitting what a social misfit she had been, how backwards, and what a fool. "Anyway, I thought why not? He was kind of cute. It was just one dinner. What could go wrong, right?"

This story did not have a happy ending. She deliberated walking away, but gritted her teeth instead. Someone needed to know what she had lived through.

"What happened?" His eyes looked so kind, maybe even forgiving. That did it. The closet door to her self-loathing was wide open now.

"At first, he was fun to be with." She gulped. "I mean he didn't always have money, so I paid for movies and stuff like that, but he was fun. He made me laugh. He was always showing up with presents and flowers and stuff." Those things had all been stolen. *How could I have missed all the signs?*

Abruptly he pushed away from the table. She thought maybe she had disgusted him, but he returned with a box of tissues. She took several, blew her nose, and mopped her face. "Thanks."

He didn't answer, just watched and listened.

"It seemed like a fairytale. He wanted to marry me, and he bought me a ring." Yeah, right. A full carat diamond ring that had turned her finger green. "I believed everything until it was too late."

"You don't have to tell me anymore if you don't want to." His voice sounded sincere, but she couldn't stop.

"No, it's just that I was already pregnant." She focused on the soggy tissues in her hand. Her guilt reminded her for the millionth time that none of this would have happened if she had been a *good girl* and gotten married *before* having sex. But guilt was as much help now as it was then. She brushed her negative judgment aside.

He reached his hand across the table, but she didn't take it.

"I had morning sickness. At first he was happy when Jackie was born. I was happy. We weren't rich, but we were doing okay. But when I got pregnant again..." Her voice trailed away. Everything was her fault. She had spoiled her happy family. "He changed. He stayed at his mom's more and more. Everything I did made him angry. It was hard to be sick all the time.

The day came back with vivid clarity. "He punched me. He said the boys weren't even his and, and he punched me." Her fingers went automatically to her cheekbone. She thought he had literally knocked her head off it had hurt so much.

Alex groaned and offered his hand again. She ignored him. This way he couldn't pull his hand away in revulsion. Besides, if she never held it, she could never lose it.

"He cried afterwards. He said he was sorry, and he would never do anything like that again. He kept apologizing, and I thought it was my fault. You know?" By now the tissue was shredded.

"I'm sorry."

"Me, too," she whispered. "I had to stop teaching. I was sick all the time anyway."

"It's okay." His hand lay warm and gentle on hers on the table. She hadn't noticed when he had done that. Kelsey thought she heard another tone in his voice, or maybe it was her guilt raising its ugly head again. *You deserved exactly what you got. You should've known.*

"I wasn't always like this." She glared at him, her sorrow turning into anger. "I went to college. I loved my job. I was good at it, you know? I had a nice apartment. It wasn't big, but it was nice. Did you even know that?"

"Yes, I do know that about you."

She stared at him. Was he lying, too? How could he know? The gentle squeeze of his fingers seemed to bridge the gap. All she saw was a friend and her strongest, heck, her only protector. He pulled the sodden mass of tissues from her fingers and replaced it with another batch, his gentle hands never losing hold of hers in the process. She glared at those blue eyes that had only moments before been cold and unfeeling. Whatever was happening between them, she wanted it out in the open, all the poison and anger, all of it. Now.

"You know, people think women like me are stupid because we stay," she explained, "but it's not easy to leave. It's like I changed over night. One day I'm doing pretty good. I've got a job, and I'm happy, but the next day, I'm ugly and all beat up. It's hard to get away. I couldn't believe anyone could hurt me like he did. I'd never been in a fight, not even once. Ever. I didn't know how to slap anyone." Her words rushed out in a squeaky crescendo through the tissues.

Alex cringed, and Kelsey caught herself just in time. There was no need to explain what he already knew. He had seen her at her worst.

"I always thought it was my fault." She stared as she remembered. "But the day he almost hit Jackie, I knew it wasn't me. It was him. There was something broken inside of him that I couldn't fix. I had to get my boys away. I couldn't save him, but I could save them. Louise bought bus tickets for us, only he found out." Kelsey bit her lip, blinking hard. What was she doing? This was a stupid idea. Angrily, she pushed away from the table. Her chair clattered to the floor behind her.

"You know what? I can't do this anymore. I deserved what I got. I asked for it, okay? Is that what you're thinking, because you're right. What was I thinking?" She bolted to the sink, shaking so hard she wanted to throw up.

"You're the victim here." His quiet statement hit a tender chord in her heart. "No one blames you. No one."

"I blame me." She wiped tears that couldn't be held back. "Do you know what I hate the worst?"

"Yourself." He was as calm as she was agitated.

"Yes. I hate me. I hate that I was such a coward." She thumped her forehead hard into the overhead kitchen cupboard. Hot tears drenched her face, but the pain against her forehead felt deserved. The truth was she had stayed with Nick because she hoped she could change him. He'd had such a pitiful childhood that she had blinded herself to the animal he truly was. Hearing her sad story out loud only made her more aware of how foolish she was. She hit her forehead harder and harder. Dishes rattled. "It's my fault. I should've killed him."

"Well, then can I teach you to shoot a gun?" His question stopped her self-abuse.

"W-what?"

She wiped her face with another fistful of tissues before she turned to face him. His invitation sounded like he would help her kill the man who had murdered her sons, but when she looked at Alex, his face was filled with tenderness. A creeping awareness tickled the back of her mind. No. This man wasn't going to help her commit murder.

"Think about it. It might be nice to get some of your power back. It's not like we have to blow anyone's brains out, but we could put some more tools in your arsenal. You'll feel better knowing you can protect yourself." He was so matter-of-fact, his eyes searching hers like an intense probing spotlight looking for what? She had nothing to offer, nothing but sins she would never be able to atone for.

"But I did want to blow his brains out."

"No, Kelsey." Alex shook his head slowly. "I know you. You wouldn't kill anyone. Besides, the best thing you can learn is how to defend yourself. Lots of women are expert marksmen. You're smart. You might be surprised."

She recognized the truth in his words. Alex was right. She couldn't hit another person much less kill them. The false heat of her anger dissipated in the warmth of his eyes.

"Do you remember the day I got shot?" he asked quietly.

"Yes," she whispered. She couldn't look away.

"You never even racked the slide."

"I never what?"

"Remember the gun I gave you? It's a semi-automatic. It was still on safety. You have to switch the safety off and rack the slide before a round enters the chamber. You couldn't have killed anyone even if you'd tried."

"How do you know? You were dying."

"The sheriff told me that's how he found my gun. He kept it for evidence."

"But I thought I could."

"Like I said. I know you," he said gently. "You don't have a mean bone in your body."

She blew out a huge sigh of relief. The knowledge that she had almost killed Nick, even though he was a murderer, had tormented her. But now she wanted to know.

"Why are you doing all of this?"

He shrugged. "It's easy to be nice to the nice."

"No, I mean it. You've saved my life over and over again. Why? What do you get out of all this besides someone to walk your dogs?"

There was a quiet tease in his voice. "If I remember correctly, you saved my life, too."

"No." She shook her head to emphasize her words. "This isn't just a payback. You've taken care of me for months. What's really going on between us?"

Alex hesitated, his gaze soft and tender. "I'm a selfish man. Before you came into my life, this house was just a mattress in the bedroom and a refrigerator in the kitchen. Oh yeah, and two dogs out back in the kennel. Now it's a home."

She studied him carefully, trying to make sense of his words.

"I need to know you're safe, Kelsey. I can't take that for granted this time. I need to be sure."

She stilled as the confusion in her head dissipated.

"And I like coming home to you. At least I did. Not sure what happened this afternoon. Guess I was expecting a different welcome than you were."

"I'm sorry. I..." Somehow she had to make him understand.

"You're afraid of me. You've been through hell. I get it. I'll back off." He leaned back in his chair, but that simple gesture of distancing himself from her said it all. She had misread his intentions every step of the way.

"No." She panicked, the foolish game of avoidance clear in her mind. Yes, she was afraid, but not of him.

"And I'm sorry I pushed you into coming all the way across country. That was arrogant of me to think I know what's best for you. If you'd rather be in Washington, I'll take you back first thing in the morning." He brushed a hand through his hair, the look on his face confused and maybe a little exasperated, too. He was such a handsome man when he wasn't giving her the cold shoulder.

"No."

"It's okay. You don't have to explain."

"No!"

Alex shut his mouth, a bemused twinkle in his eye.

"Yes, I was afraid, but not of you. I mean, I was afraid of what you'd think of me if I—"

"What is it you want, Kelsey?"

A shiver spiraled down her spine and back up again. What she thought or wanted hadn't mattered in a long time. His quiet question elicited an electric charge that wriggled all the way down to her toes. *What do I want?*

Something intense and hot stirred in her belly for the first time in forever. She saw him clearly now. Alex was a man in love. Just like that, she knew what she wanted.

"I want you."

Sixteen

Kelsey

Too close. He's way too close.

Kelsey clutched the counter's edge as anxiety ratcheted up her throat. She wanted to throw up she was so scared. With those three words barely out of her mouth, Alex was across the room, and leaning over her where she stood with all her sins dripping off her face. Part of her wanted to scream, the other cry, while yet another wanted to run and hide. Instead of taking hold of her though, instead of grabbing her by the hair and slapping, choking, or shaking her, he simply braced a hand at each side.

Courage stirred for the first time in months. *Hold. Wait. Be still.*

He leaned his face into her hair, his own breathing as ragged as hers. Fight or flight. She wanted to run. She was caught. No, not caught— trapped. No, not even trapped— maybe just surrounded? With her heart hammering in every vein and artery, thinking was impossible. His warm breath brushed her cheek. She cringed, her head turned into her shoulder and her neck exposed. *Oh my God, he's too close.*

Courage whispered to her again. *Listen. Just hear him out.*

"And I want you, Kelsey. I've wanted you since the first time I held you that night in the cabin." He breathed against her cheek before he kissed it tenderly. As he trailed a warm, moist path to her mouth, every kiss and nibble sparked a reaction that robbed her strength. Her skin tingled beneath those simple contacts, each touch coaxing and deliberate, leaving a line of heat in its wake. He seemed to be asking permission all along the way.

She squeezed her eyes as the prickly roughness of his whiskers and the intoxicating taste of coffee on his mouth descended for his first taste. His lips so gentle on hers were the most persuasive sensation she had ever felt. A clenching pool of heat pulsed deep in her stomach, a livewire of achy, trembling need that demanded relief. He tasted her lips with his tongue, and then the tip of her tongue.

Her stupid heart screamed *YES. A thousand times YES.*

But irrational guilt stopped her cold. *Not yet. It's too soon. Waaaaayyyy too soon.*

Courage intervened again. *You're okay. He won't hurt you. Keep breathing.*

Alex whispered against her ear. "The honest truth is I don't want to lose you. I need to know you're safe, because I love you."

His lips hot against her ear, she shivered as he kissed a tender path down her jaw again. A rush of heat swarmed up her legs, over her clenched stomach on its way through her chest. It felt like it exploded through the top of her head. A bolt of lightning could not have burned hotter. Without touching anything but her lips, he had claimed her right then and there. She was his. She knew it, and she wanted to give him anything and everything he asked.

Still pressed against the counter, she felt sure he could hear the wild staccato hammering in her heart. She wondered if she leaned into him, would he catch her? If she fell, would she find herself in his arms? If she fainted, would he—

"I'm late for work." With those unexpected words, Alex straightened and walked out the door without a backward glance.

What the—?

Kelsey slid down the counter, every ounce of strength evaporated. She landed on her butt with a graceless thump, his kiss gone too quickly from her face. The wonderful warmth of the moment went out the door with him, leaving her alone? Unhappy? Empty? And definitely unbalanced.

Her tongue tasted where his lips had just been. Her chin still felt the rub of his stubble. The lingering scent of sawdust and spice filled her nose. She shivered, still tasting, still feeling, and finally breathing. Like a fool, she had stood there without so much as a return hug. She hadn't even returned his kiss. *Am I insane?*

Kelsey scrambled to her feet. She knew what she wanted and she wasn't afraid. Well, okay, so maybe she was, but he needed to know, and she needed to tell him. She threw open the back door, intending to run if she had to. She just didn't think she would nearly run him over.

Alex stood in the pale glow of the back porch light, his arms folded as he leaned against his truck in the carport. She couldn't see the blue of his eyes, only the quiet worry on his face. Another strike of lightning sizzled. White-hot lightning. Hot enough to melt two people together if they weren't careful. She had no intentions of being careful, not any more.

"You're here." Kelsey blurted out the first dumb words in her overheated mind.

"Yes. I am."

Alex

What was I thinking?

He had just made an ass of himself, turned tail, and run for the first time in his life. It was too soon, and she too fragile. She hadn't even responded, other than to tremble all the way to her toes. The only thing he had gotten for his stupid adolescent move was the feeling she couldn't breath with him in her face. After finally doing something right in his life, after giving her shelter from the storm, he had mugged her like some cheap pick-up in a bar, like he had only helped her in the first place for a final roll in the hay.

I'm such an idiot.

Worry followed recrimination. *What if I've hurt her? What if she wants to leave?*

He knew the truth. Between the two of them, he was the real sinner. He had intentionally visited evil on wicked men, but her? She was an innocent woman who had honestly believed in the goodness of others even when they didn't deserve it, and it had cost her dearly. That's why he had run. Was he just another snake in her life? Were his feelings for her in any way noble? The moment her lips had touched his, he knew she deserved a better man. He carved a hand through his hair, exasperated that he had acted no better than a horny teenage boy.

The back door burst open, flung wide on its hinges, and there she was, blinking with surprise, and the pale porch light glowing behind her. "You're here?"

He almost told her, "I'll leave if you'd rather," but he settled for, "I am," instead.

Alex watched her cross the short distance between them, wondering if this was in any way a good idea. She looked more full of doubt than anger. That was the difference between her and other, more aggressive women. Any other gal would be in his face reading him the riot act, and she would be right. He deserved it. But Kelsey had no over-inflated self-esteem. Just hope. And yet...

He couldn't take his eyes off her. Every step this woman took shouted courage, and his foolish heart wanted her to take another. She faltered, bit her lower lip, and he thought for sure she would run back to the safety of the house, but then she took one more. And another.

At last she stood in front of him, visibly shaking and her eyes wide with intrepidation. His heart caught in his throat. The light in those glistening chocolate browns drew him in. The man he saw reflected there was a better man, maybe even worthy of this woman's love. Maybe.

He reached for her with shaky hands, but she had other plans.

"I've wanted to do this for a while now." She leaned up on tiptoes, her own shaking fingers splayed across his biceps for balance. Her timid kiss began as gentle as a sigh, so soft as to be nearly unfelt, like the brush of a trembling feather over his lips.

He closed his eyes, and let the energy begin. Instantly, his heart spiked off the charts with the sexual charge she didn't even know she possessed. He wanted to take her in his arms, rip her clothes off, and make wild, savage love—but he didn't.

He was the cautious one now. Nothing he did or wanted to do must remind her of the past. He stilled his desire and let her take the lead. This was her show. She was in charge. This had to be what she wanted and how she wanted. This was about her. Only her. If she wanted him, he would truly be surprised.

The softness of her kisses became more insistent. Her nervous hands prowled around his neck and over the top buttons to his shirt. She so did not have a clue what she was doing, how every touch left burning handprints, how every breath offered life. The knowledge that she was unskilled in the art of lovemaking only added fuel to the fire already raging. He leaned against the truck when Kelsey clutched the sides of his head, her kiss deepening. Her mouth demanded more and he complied, trying to control the burning ache his body had become. Every muscle yearned to encapsulate her, to fill her, and never let her go.

She pressed the length of her body to his. At last he felt the soft swell of her breasts against his chest. Groaning with need, he stooped to accommodate her height, his hands resting lightly on her hips. Boldly, she accepted the invitation and wrapped her arms around him, offering the delightful meal of her mouth, and he thought he had died and gone to heaven. He had never tasted sweeter. Another rush of warmth swelled over him, and he groaned, crushing her where he had wanted her for months – against his heart.

But he needed to be sure. Easing out of her arms, he set her down just as quickly as he had picked her up, and pushed her gently back a step. With his voice husky with emotion, he took her face in his hands. "You need to think about this, Kelsey. Be sure. Once we go down this road, you and me..."

His words of caution came too late. The sultry smile of a woman in love gazed back at him. Desire stormed his last shred of caution. He pulled her back up where she belonged, where she covered his face with another onslaught of tender nibbles and kisses. Overcome, Alex picked her up and carried her through the back door, past the kitchen table, and down the hall to his bedroom. Angling her into the dark, he felt Kelsey tugging at his shirt, feeling her way to more and more skin. He thought he would explode. With a haphazard dance of undressing themselves and each other, they crashed onto his bed, tasting each other's bodies with a hunger that would not wait.

Kelsey

As the first tiny ray of sunlight glimmered its way into his darkly curtained bedroom, it found the two lovers still wrapped around each other. Kelsey lay tucked against Alex, her back to his chest as she woke and his leg sprawled comfortably over both of hers. When at last she stretched, he responded with his breath in the nape of her neck. Kelsey gasped at the feel of his naked male body against hers. It felt so right.

She caressed the hairy arm that enfolded her, kissing his knuckles while she sized up her hand in his. His was big and calloused, so much a man's hand. Even his long fingers were rough, the cuticles ragged around closely trimmed nails. Her smaller hand fit neatly within. A clutch of fear stole her breath as the shifting paradigm in her life reminded her of a different hand. Panic squeezed her eyes tight, but all she had to do was barely move to feel Alex behind her. The memory fled.

There was no reason to fear. During their midnight tumble, he had expressed his love so tenderly that she had cried, and immediately he had stopped everything.

"Did I hurt you?" he had asked in alarm, but all she could do was shake her head. "I'm sorry. We can stop if you want. Tell me what's wrong."

He had smoothed her hair off her face, and kissed her gently. That made her cry even more. *What a novel idea—a man who cares if he hurts me.*

When she could finally speak, she had sounded like Minnie Mouse. "It's just that I'm happy and I love you so much."

"Ah, Kelsey." The love in his eyes said it all. "What did I ever do to deserve you?"

And that's where she had fallen asleep last night, held tight in the arms of the man who treated her like the most precious thing on earth.

This morning she had time to think. In her old life, she would sneak out of bed as early as possible to escape any close encounters of the uncomfortable kind. Today was different. Her body felt sore, but in a pleasant, well-used kind of way that made her smile instead of cringe. Where Alex had touched, she tingled. He had taken his time, doing things with her body that made her—want to. His hands smoothing over her breasts and abdomen had excited. He hadn't kissed her with a mouth tasting like cigarettes and tooth decay. And he smelled heavenly. Whatever he had splashed on when he shaved, she intended to make sure he had another bottle.

As he stretched against her now, she relished the feel of his hard body against the bare softness of hers. He grunted, his hand wandering down her ribcage, lingering for a fraction of a second at her waist before he cupped her bare bottom. She shivered, daring herself to bump into his hand.

"Now you know," he breathed into her tangled, messy morning hair. "I can't be held responsible if you keep doing that."

So she bumped him again, and that's all it took. With an unexpected growl of energy, he rolled her onto her back, covering her from head to toe with his body. A kiss to her forehead, and she was shy, not willing to meet his eyes. Her breath caught. *What have I done?*

Smoothing a hand down the side of her cheek, he peered into her face, trying to get her to look at him. "Good morning, brown eyes."

She smiled, the tremor of fear quickly replaced with anticipation. The smiling glint in his eyes only heightened the heated sensation in her stomach. She ran a tentative finger along his whiskered jaw. Every part of this man was deeply tanned and muscled. Whatever he had done to get so physically in shape while he was gone, it agreed with her.

"Hi." She wished she sounded incredibly sexy like Marilyn Monroe or Madonna or some other on-screen vixen, but all she heard was squeaky Minnie Mouse again.

"Hmm, you're much quieter this morning," he teased, and instantly the searing heat of a blush covered her face, neck, and, well, everything. Yes. Last night she had certainly been a little noisier. Okay, so she had been pushy. He hadn't minded, but she was embarrassed now. Common sense had flown out the window then, and in came something definitely, wow, so unlike her. But now?

"Ah, huh." She knew it the minute she opened her mouth, whatever came out would be dumb. She was right, but all those feelings splashing around in her muddled head made for so much confusion. Here she lay naked under the most handsome man in the world, and he eyed her like a delectable morsel. To make matters worse, her body betrayed her at every turn, arching toward his touch, flushing at his words, and pleasing him of its own accord. The heady sensation of him sprawled over her brought forth thoughts she had never entertained before. Even the stupid smile on her face was revealing, as if any part of her wasn't.

"Are you a morning person?" He nuzzled under her chin, his breath hot and heavy. She tipped her head back to allow him more access to her body. The heat in her belly clenched tighter as his tongue played across her breasts in little circles of tingling sensation.

"May-be." She blinked at the hunger in his voice. Right now she would be a morning, afternoon, evening, or an all-night-long person if he wanted.

"There's one way to find out," he teased.

How could six simple words sound so hot? With soft nibbles and kisses he made his way over her chin to settle on her mouth, his lips and tongue gently insistent while his hands and fingers wandered to her other willing body parts. And they were so-o-o willing.

Where she had been accustomed to pain, now she shuddered with tremors of pleasure under his gentle persuasion. Where she had experienced harshness, he whispered enticing words that sparked shivers of anticipation. She pulled him close as he pushed into her. It came so naturally. Surprised by the depth of wanting every part of him, she wrapped her legs around him. And it was happening again. *How does he do this to me?*

"Ah, ah, oh Alex," she cried, her nails digging into his shoulders like she couldn't get enough of him. A quivering wave of fireworks exploded deep inside again and the pleasure of it pushed her higher. She arched upward, suspended for a breathtaking moment in space and time, weightless, and totally absorbed by this man. There was nothing, but him. His arms. His legs. His breath. Him. All past memories evaporated in the cleansing, burning embrace.

He groaned as he held her tight in a final push. They clung to each other just as they had the first time. A fleeting thought of death tugged, but at last, she knew better. If she died now, she would die a very satisfied woman.

Panting, he collapsed on top of her, his weight pressing her into the mattress. Again, the tears she didn't want him to see flowed. She squeezed him tight, hoping he would stay right where he was until she got herself under control. He didn't.

Alex rolled to her side, propping his head on his hand to see her better. She heard the concern in his voice as he wiped the trail of tears off the side of her face.

"Are you okay?" He kissed her soggy cheek.

The tears wouldn't give her a break, and her voice wasn't any help either so she nodded.

A sexy smile tugged at his lips. "That's all I need to know."

Finally brave enough, she said, "I've never felt anything like that before."

For some reason that made him grin. "Good."

He wrapped her in the comfort of his body then pulled the sheet up to cover them both. She was content just breathing in the smell of him, and listening to his strong heartbeat. For the first time in all her limited experience, sex felt good. Instantly she upgraded her choice of words to great, but even that didn't feel right. No. Exquisite. These two times with Alex were exquisite, like first-time-ever moments. And the best part, she wasn't afraid. She hoped he felt as good as she did, because she felt really good.

He kissed the top of her head. "I love you."

She sighed along with him. "Me, too."

Alex

When Alex finally left his boring little cracker box house, it was two mornings later and he had upgraded his opinion of his house to home again. The twenty-five cradles didn't get painted, and he had missed more consecutive days of work than he had missed in his entire career, but he didn't care. His over-the-top work compulsion had at last taken a back seat to a very delightful lady.

By then they had spent forty-eight hours in lovemaking and play the likes of which he could not remember. They had explored each other's bodies, minds, and anything else that got in their way. While their first encounter was ruled by nothing but passion and heat, the next encounters were more deliberate and romantic, even a little enlightening.

She seemed like a woman out of a time warp, so timid one moment but rowdy the next; one minute shy, the next over the top curious. And that's why he had needed two more days off. All her explorations turned her on as much as him. *Eventually*, they made it into the shower. *Eventually,* he had ordered the pizza, which they ate in his bed along with a bottle of wine he had saved forever. And *eventually*—they got out of bed.

They only made it to his front room. Kelsey spread a mattress of blankets and pillows in front of the old fireplace that hadn't been used in years. "I thought you were mad at me when you came home from Afghanistan," she admitted as they lounged together on the makeshift bed. She lay comfortably on his chest, propped up on one elbow and tracing little circles on his chest.

He smoothed his hand over her hair. She had so much of it. Even now it fell like a silky cascade of tangles through his fingers. "I was playing it cool."

"Me, too. It's funny. I wanted to run to you and away at the same time."

"I didn't help much, did I?"

"And I was afraid."

"Never be afraid of me, okay?"

"Mostly, I was afraid what you'd think of me. It's so soon after..." She let her words trail away.

Alex sighed deeply. "It's called survivor's guilt, Kelsey. You're going to live with it the rest of your life. Get used to it."

"Do you have it?"

He nodded.

"Sometimes, I just want to be alone."

"I can be a mean bastard."

"You're never mean," she protested.

"Oh, yes." He of all people knew better. "I am. It's a rut I can't pull myself out of sometimes."

She kissed his chin, her fingers trailing through his hair while she studied his face. "I think of that last day, and I want everyone to leave me alone."

"That's because a part of you still wants to die." He kissed her forehead. "I've got news for you. You're here now, and I'm never going to let you."

She stifled a small chuckle.

"Are you laughing at me?"

"No," she smiled. "Well, maybe. You just sounded so cute when you said that."

With a playful growl, he rolled her over. Of course she ended up beneath him, pinned with her arms over her head, and still giggling. He secured her wrists with one hand and ran the other down her ribcage to the hem of her T-shirt, which was really one of his USMC shirts anyway. With a quick flick of the shirt, he bared her belly and gazed down at her perfect navel just above the line of her panties.

"Hold still." He placed his lips just below her navel. She tensed, her breaths shallow and fast. Pausing for effect, he drew in a big breath, and blew a big sloppy raspberry into her tightened abdomen. Goose bumps covered her from head to toe. This woman was highly responsive to his touch, and he loved touching.

"Alex. No." She laughed and wriggled, but he held her fast as he launched another lip smacking raspberry all over her tummy. The more noise he made, the harder she laughed until the raspberries turned to fervent kisses. He pushed the shirt up under her chin and bared her breasts. They were so small. The unlikely possibility that she had ever caught his eye on the street humbled him. He had been looking for the wrong woman all these years.

"You love it when you laugh." He smoothed a hand over each breast as he studied them with reverence. This woman was beautiful at so many levels.

"It's my best asset, huh?" Her eyes glistened with lustful mischief.

He looked down at her bare body with an evil smirk. "Ah, no, but it's definitely in the top three."

She arched against him, her head thrown back with another delicious giggle. "I feel like dessert."

He covered her mouth with his as emotions took over. Words escaped him. Kelsey was so much more than dessert. She was an oasis in a parched desert, meat and potatoes in a concentration camp, and oxygen in the middle of chemical warfare. She was everything he had rejected for so many years, now come back to him tenfold. The enormity of her innocence and love humbled him. When the kiss ended, he held her tenderly with his face in her chest, this gift he so did not deserve.

"What's the matter?" she asked, her hands on his cheeks even as she lay half naked beneath him.

"Nothing," he whispered hoarsely. "I'm just loving you."

She wrapped her arms around his head, and he felt her kiss on the top of his head. Her sigh told him everything.

She was happy, too.

"Toast?" Kelsey asked as she poured him a cup of coffee to go.

"No, ma'am. Just coffee. Black."

"I already know how you like your coffee." Kelsey's eyes twinkled. "I know a lot about you, Mr. Stewart."

"And I know a lot about you." Alex came up behind her at the kitchen counter, gathered her hair into a ponytail, and nuzzled the nape of her bare neck just above her robe's collar. She leaned back into his chest. "If you keep this up, I'll never get to work."

Accepting the challenge, she set the coffee pot down, turned and wrapped her arms around him. Her eyes were melted chocolate drops he couldn't resist. Here he was trying to make a living, but she was so wonderful to love and too difficult to resist. Kelsey was contagious. Everything about her took his breath away. With all the willpower he could muster – and it wasn't much—Alex kissed her one last time before he lifted her onto the countertop and out of his reach. He shook his head to clear his thinking.

"I really do have to go to work. I've been gone two months and a couple days."

"But they were good days," she smiled shyly.

"Oh, yes."

Still, he couldn't take his eyes off her. She was a different woman this morning, a very beautiful woman in love and love made her glow. He smirked. All the sex wasn't so bad for her either. She never looked so gorgeous sitting there in her bathrobe without a shadow of makeup on. Alex recalled the day when he had first seen her glow, the day he was shot. Now he was sure it wasn't delirium. There was a definite light within this woman.

She smiled sweetly from her perch. "How about T-bones and baked potatoes for dinner?"

"Works for me. I'll let you know when I'll be home." He picked up his suit jacket from the back of the kitchen chair, grabbed his cup and headed toward the door. Like a fool in love, he glanced back. Big mistake.

She still sat on the counter, her feet crossed at the ankles, her hands braced beside her while the morning sun poured though the window behind her. Once again the rest of the world fell away. Somehow his kitchen had turned into a shrine with this lovely woman he adored. His heart lurched. Other body parts noticed her, too. He wanted her. Again. Still.

"Bye." She smiled and gave him a small good-bye wave. "Love you."

There was no leaving now. With a rush he was back, his face buried against her chest. "What are you doing to me, woman? I have to get to work."

"Then go." She clutched his head and giggled delightedly. "I'm not stopping you."

"But I can't. I'm under some kind of spell or something." With his blood on fire, he parted her bathrobe to taste her neck and her shoulders and—

"Then poof." She pushed him away. "I release you. Go forth and get thyself to work."

He grabbed her hands and met her eyes, every fiber of his being on fire from the sparks he saw there. Her beautiful smile was an overflowing pitcher this morning, and all that love poured over him, bathing him in sweetness and healing the likes he had never known. It was as if a dam had broken, the door at last unlocked, and the magical power of this woman released. Somehow the *damn* in him was broken, too, and he had become the lucky recipient of her love. He shuddered to think what she had made before, but knew it was never love.

"What the hell." He pulled her over his shoulder like a sack of potatoes. She giggled all the way back to their bedroom as he walked with one hand patting her backside. "I can always go to work.

Seventeen

Alex

"G'morning, Boss." Mother beamed with that tell-me-all-about-it glitter in her eye. "My, my, don't you look chipper?"

As usual, Alex ignored his nosey technician. Murphy and Roy looked up from Murphy's office as he passed by.

"Well, well, well. Look who decided to show up for work," Murphy exclaimed.

Alex kept on walking. "You two got work to do?"

Roy rolled his eyes. "Heck, we were beginning to wonder if you remembered you worked here. It's been nice and quiet the last couple of months. We were getting used to that."

"I need to know where we stand on the latest Army contract as well as the new Department of Justice offer." Alex looked around at the empty desks. "Where is everyone?"

"If you'd come to work once in awhile, son, you'd know weapon proficiency is this morning. Everyone's at the range. Ember's with them." Murphy was still smiling. "You'll like these new kids. They're sharp."

"Good. Tell me when they're back."

Zack nodded to Alex from his desk, his phone to his ear and already engrossed in the business of the day. Alex didn't slow down until he reached his office. After closing his door, he contacted a local furniture store. It was time. Tonight when he bedded his beautiful lady, it wouldn't be on an old, out of style, scroungy mattress and old linens. The thought of her in his bed made him smile. She belonged there.

He followed that phone order with a call to a high-end lingerie store. It had been a long time since he had shopped for nightgowns, but Kelsey would look beautiful in gift-wrap. That's all lingerie was in his mind, gift-wrap to be undone and tossed to the floor. Even that picture made him smile. Playtime. Making love with Kelsey was fun.

Her innocence enamored him. Out of respect to her, he had removed his family picture from his dresser bedroom, but Kelsey had caught him in the act. She never missed a beat, but asked if he had any other pictures she could frame. Even Abby's childish artwork now had a place of honor on his mantle, alongside a picture of Jackie and Tommy. He saw the truth in her eyes. She wasn't replacing Sara. No. In her way, Kelsey was joining Sara in loving him.

He kept whistling as he settled into a busy morning of briefings and contract negotiations with Murphy and Roy. It was noon when Mother rapped on his door. "Hey, Boss. You have a visitor."

Alex cocked an eyebrow at Mother's interruption. By the gleam in her blue eyes and the way she enunciated visitor, she looked more like the cat that ate the canary than his admin assistant. Without waiting for his answer, she opened the door wider and ushered Kelsey in. Automatically, Alex jumped to his feet, along with Murphy and Roy. He was at her side before Mother could wipe the smirky smile off her face.

Kelsey looked intimidated as she peeked around the room. She was dressed in nothing fancy, just her old faded jeans and a simple pale blue sweater. "I brought your cell phone," she said timidly.

Alex checked his suit pocket in surprise. He grinned. That proved he was head over heels in love. He had never even missed it. "How'd you get here?"

"I walked. It's not too far."

He pulled her against him. For a minute he deliberated taking the rest of the day off, but then common sense kicked in. He turned to his senior agents, well aware they had just witnessed a side of him they hadn't seen before.

"Kelsey Durrant. These gentlemen are my Senior Agents Murphy Finnegan and Roy Hudson. They run the show when I'm gone. Gentlemen, this is Kelsey Durrant, my houseguest." Alex smirked at his understated description of the woman he loved. So what was she, he wondered, girlfriend, lover, all of the above? *Wife* came to mind.

"Well, hello. I've been waiting a long time to meet you, little girl." Murphy took her hand in both of his. "The last time we talked, you kids were in a pretty bad way."

She nodded. "Oh, you're Mr. Finnegan. Thank you for answering the phone that day. We really needed your help."

"Well, you call us anytime." He leaned in toward her with a conspiratorial whisper. "We might not answer the phone for him, but we'll definitely answer when you call. So how do you like the east coast?"

"It's beautiful," Kelsey replied. "The trees are gorgeous."

"You're right. Fall is extra pretty this year. Moira and I will have to invite you and Alex over for dinner while you're in town."

"I'd love that." She shot a shy smile to Alex.

At that comment, Roy took over, his teeth bright against his dark skin. He bowed and kissed the back of her hand like a true southern gentleman. "It is very nice to meet you, Miss Kelsey. My goodness, you're as pretty as a Georgia peach. Where's this young man been hiding you?"

"Lift your feet." Murphy chuckled. "He's pouring it on thick."

"Like maple syrup on my Mama's homemade biscuits." Roy beamed with another flirtatious grin. "I'm just trying to make our lady friend here feel welcome. Besides, if you remember, this woman knows how to bake."

Her eyes lit up. "Oh, the chocolate chip cookies. Did you like them?"

Murphy harrumphed. "You didn't see any leftovers come back home, did you?"

"That was very considerate, young lady," Roy continued, a wicked gleam in his soft brown eyes. "Took us a while to figure out who brought 'em though. I think that was one for the history books, wasn't it, Murphy?"

"Knock it off," Alex growled, but he couldn't help noticing how relaxed she was with the friendly banter. She looked Murphy and Roy in the eye with confidence. Somehow, she had crossed a bridge and left part of her old self behind. She had blossomed right in front of his eyes.

Just then Zack sauntered into the office, a big grin on his face as well. "It's about time I get to meet you, Miss Kelsey. Man, the boss was fit to be tied when our operation got extended. I've never heard so many colorful ways of cursing in my life and I've been in the military. I've heard a few."

Kelsey offered her hand, but he brushed it aside and gave her a big hug that caught Alex by surprise as much as it did her. She looked so fragile in his big weight lifter's arms as he lifted her off her feet and hugged her tight.

"I've been dying to meet you," he said with a husky voice and his eyes closed. "You must be a very special lady to have won my boss's heart like you've done."

Alex scowled at Zack's very astute observation. What was it about this woman? Everyone seemed affected by her, and all she had done was show up.

He rescued her the minute her feet touched the floor. "This smart ass is Zack Lennox. He was with me in country the last two months."

Her eyes lit up in recognition. "You're the agent who's such a good shot."

Murphy and Roy chuckled at her kind remark, but Zack sputtered.

"I don't know about that." He nodded toward Alex. "He's the record holder. The rest of us are just wanna-bees. Ask him."

Alex deflected that comment as he nodded toward Mother. Until now she had stood waiting her turn to be introduced and still grinning like a Cheshire cat. "And this is Sasha Kennedy, the IT guru around here. We call her Mother because she's nosey."

Kelsey gasped at his mean introduction, but Mother did exactly what Alex was afraid she would do. She latched onto Kelsey's hand and pulled her away, her head bent into Kelsey's like she was about to share some of her motherly wisdom. "Now, don't you mind him. I never do. It's real nice to meet the woman who can put this man in his place."

Kelsey looked just as surprised at Mother's remark as she had been at Alex's introduction.

"Hey, listen. Why don't we plan a girl's night out or something? Ember's not here right now, but she would love to meet you. That will give us girls a chance to talk and get to know each other without the guys hanging around. Oh, the stories I could tell you."

Kelsey glanced over her shoulder at Alex. "That would be nice."

"How long are you staying in town?" Mother's bright eyes swept over Kelsey's plain clothes like a hawk as she steered her closer to the door.

"Mother." Alex interrupted his nosey techie. "Kelsey has plans today."

"Well, I just thought it would be nice to—"

"Another day," he said firmly.

Kelsey rescued the awkward moment. "It's nice to meet you. I am busy today, but I'd love to have lunch with you and Ember sometime."

Mother beamed, and Alex was once again surprised. Kelsey handled the situation much better than he had. Mother returned to her desk, Murphy muttered something about *that woman*, and Alex was enamored all over again.

Kelsey looked up at him expectantly and whispered, "I have plans?"

"There's someone else I'd like you to meet since you're here." He looked down into her pretty face, knowing full well his team still watched. "Come on. Let's go."

"It was nice to meet all of you," Kelsey said politely as Alex steered her to the elevator.

When the doors closed behind them, he hit the stop button. With his blood once again on fire, he pushed her against the wall, his mouth on hers and tasting what he hungered for. She arched against him, and that single reflexive movement kick-started every part of his body. His foolish male mind worked all the scenarios of what might be feasible in an elevator before logic re-engaged. *Not here. No sex in the elevator. I'm CEO, damn it.* He ended the kiss with a ragged sigh before he lost all control.

"Don't elevators have cameras?" Kelsey asked, her hands still roaming under his suit jacket and around his waist.

"My building." He blew out a ragged breath. "My elevator. No cameras."

"Well, in that case." Her fingers both went straight to his belt buckle.

"No." He caught her hands. "Not here. Not now."

"No?" She blinked up at him so wonderfully innocent and wickedly playful.

"If we keep this up, I'm going to need more time off."

Her eyes didn't break their connection. "I didn't know I had this kind of power," she said as she smoothed a hand over his chest, still studying him intently.

"Yeah, well," he growled. "You have no idea what you're doing to me right now, do you?"

"Me?" She shook her head, her gaze still pulling him in, and he was a lost lug bolt drawn relentlessly toward an industrial-strength magnet. His blood coursed, no, it drained from his brain to parts below. If she kept those brown eyes fastened on him the way they were, he was a goner. She would be half-naked in no time at all, and elevator sex with Kelsey would be damned good.

No. No. No. He hit the send button before he changed his mind.

"Well, okay then." She snuggled inside his jacket and under his arm. "I'm glad I got to meet your friends. I get the feeling Mother annoys you."

He nodded, glad for the change of subject. If anything could crash his libido, it was talking about Mother. "Don't get me wrong. I'd be lost without her. Just wish she would stay out of everyone's business."

Kelsey slid her fingers beneath the waistband to his slacks, her voice suggestively low. "Well, I'd like to get into your business."

Alex grinned and pulled her up to his mouth for another kiss. Her eyes were extra bright when the elevator doors opened to the on-site gym.

"David, I've got someone I want you to meet."

"Kelsey." Senior Agent David Tao took her hand and politely bowed to her. "I am so happy to meet you. Boss, she is beautiful."

And with a blush and a smile, Kelsey was introduced to the martial arts expert, an elegant, American-Chinese man. David was soft-spoken and polite to a fault.

"Would you care for a tour?"

For the next several minutes, he showed Kelsey around and explained how the other agents used the gym. He mentioned how Zack worked out for hours in the weight room and had the physique to prove it. Ember Davis liked to come down every morning for the yoga class. Murphy and Roy sparred with the other agents in friendly games of basketball, and Harley Mortimer, before he had disappeared off the face of the earth, used to do laps in the pool every afternoon. David and Alex had designed the gym to cover everyone's physical fitness needs.

"Unfortunately, I have yet to teach our boss to sit in the cross-legged meditation posture of the Buddha though." David winked mischievously to Kelsey.

"Not going to happen, Tao." Alex couldn't let that comment go. He sat patiently waiting for the tour to end.

"Agent Tao, do you only teach agents?" she asked curiously.

"I'd be most happy to teach you what little I know," David replied.

Once again Alex smiled. This was exactly why he had wanted Kelsey to meet David. This might be a good day, but there were still dark days ahead. She would need more internal tools to pull herself up and out of them.

She glanced at Alex as if asking for permission.

"Hey, don't look at me." Alex shrugged. "It's up to you. David can sure use the work."

"What I could use is a teachable student."

Alex waved his teasing comment aside. "Whatever." But then he turned to Kelsey. "So what are you interested in? Weights? Swimming? David teaches martial arts too and all that meditation stuff."

Her eyes light up when he had said martial arts.

"I'd like to know how to defend myself."

"Very wise decision," David said. "I teach the Chinese art of kungfu. You will learn conditioning exercises like stretching, stances, and meditation. You will learn about your Qi."

"Qi?"

"Yes. Qi is your inner life force. You must understand the energy within yourself as well as the energy in all things around you. Are you ready?" David cocked his head, his hand outstretched as if inviting Kelsey onto his gym floor right this moment.

"Yes." She scrunched her shoulders, and there was that little girl thing again. She was doing something that scared her, but she was doing it anyway. Her resilience amazed Alex. He remembered his own USMC martial arts classes. He used to believe in the things David taught. What happened? When did he stop?

When they left the gym, she turned to Alex. "Does everyone call you Boss?"

"To my face." He called the elevator. "Want to go to lunch?"

"No. You have work to do. Remember?"

He glanced at his watch. "I do, but I could cancel—"

She put a finger to his lips. "No. You've cancelled enough. I'll see you at home."

The way she said that last word made him smile. He kissed her tenderly at ground level. "By the way, don't be surprised if a couple deliveries come today."

"Oh?"

"Just show them where to put everything. You'll know where."

"You're not going to tell me what it is, are you?" she asked with a curious smile.

"You'll see."

Alex arrived home promptly at five PM, early for him. As usual, all the curtains in the front room were drawn, but for

some reason the kitchen was dark as well. That alone was odd
for Kelsey. She usually had dinner ready by now on the long
shot he would be home on time. If he wasn't, she warmed it
when he arrived. The tantalizing aroma of seafood still clung
to the air. Seafood and – what? Jasmine? He couldn't quite
detect the other fragrance filling his dark little house, but the
place was far too quiet.

He glanced out the back window. No. She wasn't out
walking the dogs. Both Whisper and Smoke lounged in their
kennel. Even that made him smile. It used to be they would
be sitting at attention the minute they would spot him in the
house. Now they only sat at attention for Kelsey. This woman
had already taken his heart. Was she taking his dogs, too? It
certainly looked like it.

Soft music reached his ears. *Ahhhh, so she is here.*
Quietly, he investigated his way to his bedroom. A glow
coming from under the door revealed the truth. He peered
through the barely open door.

There she stood in front of the floor-length mirror trying
on one of the three nightgowns he had bought for her today.
Already dressed in the red one with spaghetti straps, she
smoothed her hands down her sides and over her hips. He
gulped. She hadn't a seductive bone in her body, but the soft
swell of her breasts under the lacy bodice and the delicious
curve of her hips, especially as her hands slid down and over
her backside and – he gulped again. Combined with all that
silky brown hair flouncing off her shoulders and nearly to her
butt, yes, red was definitely her color. She looked—so—
damn—hot.

But she wasn't done yet. With a shimmy that about made
him choke, the red gown dropped to the floor. She kicked it

aside. And then he knew each gown he had chosen came with cute little boy short panties that barely covered the cheeks of her bottom. It was getting difficult to breath as he watched his fair lady put on the best strip tease show he had ever seen. Between those panties and her long hair, he was well on his way to total inebriation. Was it even possible to be drunk on the woman you love? Yes.

She dropped the panties to the floor along with the gown. He nearly swallowed his tongue.

Now for the blue. Another long gown, it was a glistening royal blue with black lace that trimmed the bra, the straps, and dropped in a ribbon to her feet. With a hitch and a wriggle, she snaked the matching panties up under the gown.

He smiled wickedly when he saw the back hem of the gown caught inside her panties. He wanted to offer assistance, but no. He stifled a chuckle and let the show continue. She made the necessary wardrobe adjustment when she twirled in front of the mirror. *Oh, Kelsey.*

With his grin about to crack his face, he noticed the new bed had also arrived. A comfortable queen-sized sleigh bed with a black and red comforter, it filled the modest room. He didn't care. The only thing he wanted to do was tear the blue gown off of this gorgeous woman like a little boy tears gift-wrap off his Christmas present. Alex wiped his face, his body responding to the view in more ways than one. This was better than Christmas. This was heaven.

The blue gown landed in the same heap as the red, and the blue panties right along with it. Kelsey stood naked in front of the mirror for a moment, studying her body with all its curves and flaws. She turned halfway around to view her back. From shoulder to shoulder and down her back, she still carried plenty of scars. Funny. He hadn't noticed them anymore.

She twisted herself around the other way and looked at her backside. Yes, harsh marks streaked there, too. She sighed, her hands on her hips, her lips pursed together in thought.

He stopped smiling, the joy of the moment gone.

Please see yourself as I see you. Please don't be sad. I love you just the way you are.

Alex faltered. He couldn't stand and watch anymore. Kelsey deserved more. This was her private moment, and here he stood like a stupid high school jock spying on the girl's shower. He was an ass, and she the most beautiful woman in the world. He reached for the doorknob to announce himself, but just as his fingers touched it, she twirled once, her hands around her shoulders. She smiled at her reflection in the mirror. "You'll do," she said.

His heart stuck in his throat. She spun around one more time and then scooped up the black panties. With another shimmy, she pulled them up and over her backside, or as much of it as they covered. Instantly, the scars disappeared. She examined herself in the mirror again, then slid the black gown over her shoulders until it draped elegantly to the floor. Only her toes showed. Happily, she picked the other gowns off the floor and stuffed them into the department store bag they had come in. He wished she had six-inch heels to finish that definite beauty queen look she had going for her, but it didn't matter. She was the most elegant woman on the planet, and heels or not, he was smitten. Hook, line and sinker.

With one last glance in the mirror, she smoothed the new duvet on the bed, and turned toward the door. He barely made it back to the kitchen before she did.

She startled when she saw him at the kitchen window, gazing intently at the dog kennel as if he had been there all along. "I didn't hear you come in."

He pulled her into his arms. Too choked up to speak, all he could do was bury his face in her hair and hold her tight.

"What's wrong? Tell me." She pulled back, her hand cupping his jaw in worry. "Did something happen at work today?"

"I'm just happy."

"Aw-w." She peered up at him. "I cry when I'm happy, too."

He nodded. Happy was such a small word.

She cocked her head. "Were you peeking at me?"

"Yes," he confessed as fast as he could. "I came home early. The lights were off and—"

She shushed him with a finger to his lips. Stepping away, she twirled once. "You like?"

He pulled her into his arms. "No. I love."

Months passed in their newly established rhythm. Alex diligently went out the door to work every morning at precisely five AM, a cup of black coffee in his hand, and contentment on his face. The TEAM prospered and became more successful than he had ever anticipated. He seemed to have a knack for hiring the best ex-snipers coming home from the armed forces. Good fortune smiled. His anger became a thing of the past.

Kelsey easily re-certified to teach kindergarten in the Virginia school system. She practiced kung fu at David's gym until she was nothing but lean muscle and a fairly decent martial arts student. Alex took her to the range and taught her to shoot. He had insisted she get her own concealed weapons permit, and they practiced religiously. David taught her the peaceful way, while Alex taught her what to do when all else fails.

When his schedule allowed, they took the dogs for long walks. Once they got home, they went to bed early. Not that they slept so much, but the sleigh bed became their ultimate form of communication where they talked about everything and anything. And they loved.

All things considered, life was just about perfect.

One night in early June, he came home late to find Kelsey sound asleep on the couch, her hair in one of those big clips she liked to use, her robe wrapped around her like a blanket. As he settled in his easy chair with a beer, Alex thought about the influence she had exerted on every facet of his life. All she had done was show up and his life was a thousand times better.

She yawned and stretched when she saw him across the room. "Hello there."

"Hello yourself," he replied wearily.

"Hard day?" She climbed onto his lap and snuggled against him, her arms around his neck.

"The usual. Briefings. Agents coming. Agents going. You know." He placed a kiss on her forehead as they relaxed together.

"I have to tell you something. It's important." Her voice turned serious.

He looked down into her brown eyes. They were barometers to her soul, and most of the time they sparkled. There was no sparkle tonight. Was she going to cry?

She pulled a long white envelope from her robe pocket. "I've wanted to do this for a long time. Louise helped me."

Kelsey put the envelope in his hand and looked away. She did have tears in her eyes. He was sure of it. Alex looked at the return address. It was an attorney's office. With one arm still around her, he pulled the papers out and smoothed them on his knee to read.

"Kelsey." He pulled her close, a huge knot caught in his throat. For a moment he had thought she might be leaving him. Instead, it was her divorce decree. "You scared me."

A tear slipped out of her eye. "I don't know why, but it was hard to do."

"I know." He tucked an errant strand of hair behind her ear. "But I'm glad you did it."

"I couldn't stand being married to him anymore."

Alex didn't want her to dwell on it. If he'd had his way, he would have put the child-killer in the ground. "I have to go to Seattle next week. I know you're busy, but—"

He didn't get another word out of his mouth.

Eighteen

Alex

"I brought the boys up here once. I was going to run away."

Kelsey pointed to the Washington State ferry dock where passengers and vehicles flooded off one of the huge ferries. "But I didn't have enough money. I was too scared to go through with it."

"You never stood a chance." Alex put an arm around her shoulder. This was part of her life he didn't know yet.

"That was a bad night." She shivered in his arms. "I used all the gas in my car."

He cringed at what probably happened next. "Sit with me awhile?"

She turned to him, the light back in her eyes as they made themselves comfortable on the wooden bench on the pier. As usual she was snug against him. "This is a better feeling."

"Look at this." He pulled a couple of photos from his inside coat pocket. "We need a new front door. Tell me what you think."

He waited while she looked at the pictures. The door was pretty enough and elegantly carved oak. Unlike the aged and weathered door they had now, this one had a floor length oval insert of clear glass surrounded with a border of two-by-two inch amber squares set in a stained glass motif. The second photo was a close up of the clear glass insert, and yes, it was a beautiful addition to the entryway. Kelsey was about to hand the photos back when she did a double take. He watched intently. Yes. She had seen what he intended her to see.

"How did you … when did you …?"

The cool breeze blowing off the sound made his eyes water. "What do you think?"

She turned into his arms with tears in her eyes. That's just the way she was, and it touched him. She cried when she was happy, sad, and anytime in between. Since he had met her, sometimes, he did, too.

"I love you so much," she whispered hoarsely. "I don't know what to say."

Alex held her tight and wiped his own face.

"I remember now," she said softly. "That day in my apartment, you had a black paint brush and some kind of powder."

"Finger print kit," he said. "It's a small thing."

"No," she cried, wiping her face on her coat sleeve. "It's not a small thing. It's them. It's my boy's fingerprints. It's—them."

He blinked rapidly.

"You've given me pieces of my boys back," she sobbed, the photos pressed to her chest. "My baby boys left these for me."

The anguish in her voice stabbed him. For a moment he thought he had ruined their evening.

"Thank you," she whispered tearfully. "It's the most perfect door I've ever seen."

"I hoped you'd like it," he said humbly.

He pulled her coat tightly around her and just held her. In the breadth of a heartbeat, he had done what he set out to do. He had changed her memory of this gray Seattle pier. The slate was wiped clean. Now she would recall this place by the two little boy's fingerprints on her front door.

A chilling drizzle settled in for the evening. The rest of the world hurried on in its normal, every day busyness that was downtown Seattle. Watercraft of all sizes lumbered across the gray waters of Elliot Bay, foamy wakes dissolving behind them as fast as they were made. Rush hour traffic on hectic Alaskan Way roared behind them while gulls overhead squawked in the fading evening light. He sat with his arms wrapped around the graceful woman at his side. One had only to look close to see the expression of utter love on her face.

For that single moment, the world revolved around Alex and Kelsey.

Tuesday arrived bright and clear. After a boring day with the realtor on Monday, Alex was ready to get out of town. He rented a truck just like the one he owned in Virginia so he could haul supplies and an ATV. This time, he planned a quicker trip into his cabin instead of a couple hours walk. They stopped at a home improvement store where he purchased a bundle of cedar shake shingles, paneling for the walls and linoleum flooring. They would only be there a week, but with Kelsey's help, he planned to transform the cabin into a fit place for a woman. He also bought a real toilet instead of the one he had improvised. The septic tank had been installed years ago. Now it was time to get civil.

They paid a somber visit to the cemetery before they left town. She laid two-dozen red roses on Tommy and Jackie's grave and stood there remembering.

"The headstone is nice." She leaned her back into Alex. They were both in jeans and Seattle Mariner matching T-shirts today. Kelsey sported a pink baseball cap, her hair corralled for now through the back hole of it.

"You chose well." He kissed the side of her head as he held her tight.

Alex glanced around the cemetery. He had bought the headstone. It was what Kelsey wanted. If her sister, Louise had her way, there would have been two little teddy bears and a flowery poem about snips and snails and puppy dog tails. Now the etched faces of Tommy and Jackie smiled up from the ground. The date of their birth and death was inscribed beneath a line from the Book of Isaiah.

"I hate leaving them. If there was any way possible, I'd take them home with us." Her tears started.

"Me, too." If only it were that simple.

A string of Canada geese strolled the edge of the road, pecking at the gravel pathway as they went. Three fuzzy goslings followed the two adult geese, honking in quiet conversation with each other.

"You've changed a lot." He rocked with his arms around her and his chin in her neck.

"It's been a long year."

"Yes, and you're ready to teach next year. I'd say you're healthier, too."

"I'm certainly fatter." She wiped her eyes.

"I like a woman I can get my hands on."

"I'm not the same person at all."

"You're everything I thought you were, sweetheart."

"You mean that nut case running around the forest?" She blinked hard, but the tears spilled over anyway.

"But a pretty nut case." He kissed her neck gently. "My nut case."

"I miss them. They're with me every single day."

"I know." Without thinking he patted his pocket that held a diamond ring. He had plans for Tommy and Jackie's pretty mother. Honorable plans. "Anymore I feel like I have all three of them with me. Abby, Tommy, and Jackie, too."

"Are they happy when you think of them?"

"Yes," he answered quickly. "I can see my little Abby talking your boys into tea parties and doll houses. She would be bossing them around, you know, being the typical big sister. Of course, I can also see them giving her a run for her money, teasing, maybe pulling her hair like brothers would do."

"That's a nice picture."

A cool Pacific breeze wafted across the shady lawn. Abby would have loved two little brothers. He could envision them playing together, a bossy little blonde chasing two brown-headed brothers as they played tag beneath the pines. It was a soothing thought that lingered in the back of his mind. He was lost in that reverie when Kelsey interrupted him with a tug at his arm.

"Guess we better get going."

"Yes." Alex pulled her into a hug so she wouldn't see the moisture in his eyes. The thought of those three children playing together was more than he could bear, especially on the day he was going to propose to Tommy and Jackie's pretty little mother. He couldn't help but think that if he had met her sooner, they would still be alive.

Alex and Kelsey climbed back into the truck and headed east. The beauty of spring abounded in the Northwest. Rhododendrons and azaleas blossomed everywhere, while yellow daffodils and all colors of tulips blossomed like weeds along the roadside. Blackberry bushes strangled hillsides and ditches with burgeoning mounds of white blossoms while wild pink and white foxglove spiked everywhere. Even the great trees of the forest glowed with the lime green of new growth.

He smiled at the carefree feeling between them. They looked like a couple of kids, and the country music filling the truck cab enhanced the moment. He tugged on the brim of her hat. She responded with her usual bright-eyed smile.

Yes. This was the perfect day to propose to the woman he loved.

Kelsey

The night air was full of music to Kelsey's ears, as crickets and frogs chirped in one continual chorus. After the drizzle of the night before, the insects and amphibians of the forest were in rare form. She couldn't imagine feeling any happier as she gazed across the crackling fire at Alex, his tan face awash with the orange glow. But he had a worried look tonight. He was like that a lot, always bringing work home from his office. She imagined he was still trying to figure out what happened to one of his best agents, Harley Mortimer. She knew it bothered Alex that the man had been missing over a year. Harley sounded like a nice person. She hoped she would get the chance to meet him some day.

But for now she studied Alex. He was an amazing man in her life, and yet, there was still so much to learn. When she stopped daydreaming, she saw that he watched her, too. He patted the ground next to him, and she was at his side in a second.

"Whatcha thinking?" he asked.

"Ha. I was just going to ask you the same thing. You look so serious."

Without another word, he placed a ring box in her palm. She gasped and with trembling fingers, pried the lid off. A diamond solitaire sparkled in the light of the crackling fire.

His voice choked as he took her hand. She noticed his hands shook. "Will you do me the honor of marrying me, Kelsey? Will you become Mrs. Alexander Stewart?"

She couldn't speak. Marriage was not something she wanted to repeat. The very word struck terror into her heart that only a moment ago had been carefree and full of joy. She knew she had a foolish deer in the headlights look, but so many bad memories accompanied his simple question. *Will you marry me? And then what? Will you hurt me?*

Her fear screamed loud and clear. *Been there. Done that. Got the T-shirt. No way.*

Just as quickly, courage spoke up with its usual too-quiet voice. *Look at him. See him.*

She looked at Alex. He sat holding his breath, her hand still snug in his. This intense man who could turn from hard and rugged to soft and gentle in a flash, sat staring back at her with hope in his eyes. He looked like a little boy, completely vulnerable with that big question asked but not yet answered.

With her next words, she could break his heart or make him smile. She held her breath. Her heart pounded with indecision. She wanted to make him smile, but—marriage?

Logic intervened. *This is Alex.*

She took a deep breath and looked skyward, her heart lodged in her throat. A million stars shimmered high beyond the giant pines. Drawing in a deep breath and closing her eyes, all her confidence plummeted. The future frightened her, but... *This is Alex. He's always taken care of me. And loved me.* She reached her hands to his face to caress his cheek. Blue eyes claimed her with their intensity. She smoothed the wrinkles at the corners of that piercing blue. *Oh yes. This is Alex.*

"You're killing me here," he said hoarsely.

She gulped. "Yes. I'll marry you. There isn't anything I want more."

With a relieved smile and a very big sigh, he pulled her into his lap and kissed her extra long and hard. He slid the ring over her knuckle, his eyes as misty as hers.

"I do love you." He kissed her again.

She snuggled under his chin as he stroked her hair. Yes, this was where she belonged, snug against him where she could hear his heart and listen to him breathe. This was all she needed. She huffed a big sigh of relief, shrugging the specter of her ex-husband off her shoulders and out of her life forever. Soon she wouldn't even share his name.

"Next question. Where do you want to live?"

"Ahh, with you?" Glancing up at him, she chuckled at what sounded like a very silly question. He looked so serious, like a man with a plan.

"I know that." He chuckled along with her, and she was happy. "Guess I didn't ask the right question. What I meant is that I'd like to build a house for you. Where would you like me to build it?"

She traced her fingers along the edge of his jaw. The one thing she knew for sure about Alex was that he always had to be busy. Even sitting around the campfire, he was planning something as huge as building a new home. Silly man. "Why do you want to move?"

"Because I know a woman wants her own things in her own house."

"But your home is a very nice little house and I like it."

"Come on. You'd like something new, wouldn't you?" He twirled a handful of her hair in his fingers as he looked down at her. She could not help the smile that covered her face. He was determined. She had to give him that much.

"But, it's *your* home." She straightened in his lap.

"And that's why I want to build. Then we'd live in *our home*."

"Yes, but I'm getting a new door and I'm really happy there." *And it's the first place I've felt safe in years, she thought. I don't want to move. I just got here.*

He sighed. "I guess we stay put then."

She saw the unwilling resignation in his eyes, and it made her smile. This man was too used to getting his own way.

"But think about it, okay?" His brow arched. "There is no need for you to live in another woman's house."

"I've always thought I was living in *your* house."

He pulled her close for another quick kiss. "You're something else, Kelsey Stewart."

"Mmm. Kelsey Stewart. I like the way that sounds." She smiled up at him, but Alex didn't respond as she had expected. His eyes were fixed at something behind her.

She turned around to peer into the dark. "What's going on?

This time he pulled her up off the ground and into his side, the magic of the moment gone.

"Let's go inside. Now."

Alex

Something or someone was out there watching. He was sure of it.

Once in the cabin, Alex went straight to his satellite phone. There hadn't been a signal since they had arrived. Kelsey stood at the bedroom door waiting. He had felt her eyes on him earlier. As much as he had tried to conceal his worry, his gut was screaming. Something was not right in the forest tonight. He pulled his backpack off the floor, and removed his pistol, the same make as Kelsey now used.

"What's going on?" she whispered.

"Did you bring my SIG like I asked?"

She nodded.

"Get it."

She pulled her gun case out of her backpack, unzipped it, and took hold of the gun. Automatically, she jammed one of the three magazines into place, flipped the safety off, and racked the slide. Pride flashed through him. She had changed so much. *Good girl.*

"Remember what I taught you? If you're ever forced to pull your weapon, always shoot to kill, right?" Alex looked deeply into her eyes. "I don't want to scare you, honey, but someone's been watching us tonight. I'm going back out front to talk with them. They might just be hunters or hikers."

"Or they might be lost," she whispered breathlessly. "Like I was."

He peered out the glass window on his front door. Shadows moved just beyond the light of the camp, the two-legged animal kind of shadows. Someone was definitely lurking too close for comfort. They were not lost. He spotted another. And another. They didn't move like hunters either. More like trouble.

"Listen. There's a trap door in the back room. It's at the bottom of the bed. You shouldn't have to use it, but you need to know it's there." He blew out a small breath through pursed lips. They had guns. Rifles. Bags slung over their shoulders.

He turned to Kelsey. "There are several people out there. I don't know what they think they're doing, but I'm going to put a stop to it. If anything goes wrong, you hightail it back to the gas station. It's dark so you won't get far, but you get far enough away from this cabin. You lay down, and stay out of sight until this is over. Got it?"

"But I don't want to leave you."

A jolt of déjà vu gripped him. Those were the exact words she had uttered a year ago, just before he had gotten shot. He pulled her close, his words hurried and edgy. "Promise me. I need to know you'll be safe."

"Yes," she answered so quietly he still didn't believe her.

"Listen. You must follow orders. Please? For me?"

She never got a chance to reply. A tear gas canister crashed through the side window, filling the small room with fumes in seconds. Alex pushed her into the back room and slammed the door behind them. Gunshots peppered the front of the cabin, sending shards of glass and splintered wood across the small room. Within seconds, they were both out the trap door, crouched beneath the cabin. Concealed by the dense underbrush, they listened.

He cocked his head to listen. The howling and shrieks from the front of the cabin sounded like a pack of deranged animals set loose in the forest. *Damn. What the hell is going on?*

Alex pushed her out from under the cabin and into the dark. He pointed into the dark as he shouldered his rifle and rounded the cover of the huge blackberry brush.

"Go now. Do it, Kelsey. Go!"

Nineteen

Kelsey

Kelsey didn't run.

Instead she crouched in the dark, listening, her heart pounding so hard she could barely breathe. Within seconds of Alex leaving, the cabin's roof burst into flames. She heard one gunshot and then another. Men's voices shrieked over the roar of the fire. Hugging the weapon to her breast, her knees shook so much she could barely stand.

A man's voice screamed, "Shooter. We got a shooter. Ain't no one even in that cabin."

Her heart dropped. *That voice. No. It couldn't be.*

Two more shots followed in quick succession, and then another familiar voice cackled, "I got him boys. I got that Stewart fella."

It couldn't be—them. Both of them?

She couldn't leave. She crept through the brush to the front of the burning cabin where she saw four men sprawled on the ground while another four stood over Alex's prone figure by the fire pit. Her heart sank. Nick Durrant stood in the clearing with two men she didn't recognize. One was a big man, bald with his arms covered in tattoos. The other was average size with a Mohawk, but the fourth wasn't a man at all. It was an older woman with a short, squatty body and gray stringy hair. Ethel Durrant, Nick's hateful mother. Kelsey cringed. Her two worst enemies were here, and they had Alex.

"I'll teach you," the bald man yelled down at Alex's unconscious form. "You go shooting my guys like that. Who do you think you are?" He tied Alex's hands and feet, then tossed a rope over the nearest tree branch. Within minutes, Alex was hanging by his arms. Kelsey stifled a cry. He looked unconscious, or dead.

The man turned to the trees. "Okay, sweetheart. I know you're out there watching. Why don't you come on in so we can get acquainted? We got your boyfriend. If you want him to live, you'll get your butt down here and you'll do it now." He stabbed a pointed finger to the ground at his feet. "You hearing me?"

She shivered. He had called to her like he knew right where she stood. She was a kindergarten teacher, not a marksman. The only things she had ever killed were paper targets at the range. That's all. She couldn't take her eyes off Alex. He hadn't moved.

Nick joined the taunting chorus. "Yeah, sweetheart. Look what I'm gonna do." With a quick slash of his hunting knife, he peeled the buttons off Alex's shirt and cut a single thin line across his chest. Droplets of blood ran from the wound.

No. Stop.

The bald man flashed a massive hunting knife over his head. "You see this little blade? I ain't never skinned a boyfriend before, but I'm gonna like doing this guy, 'specially since he just killed four of my boys."

She froze. Common sense screamed *RUN!* She didn't. She couldn't. They had Alex.

"Git your dumb ass down here," Nick bellowed. "It's time you get what's coming to you."

The bald man glared at Nick. "Thought you said she's mine."

"You stupid or what, Buck? I git her first. She's my ex." Nick jabbed his thumb into his chest.

Kelsey gulped in disbelief. Nick had bartered her away like chattel.

"Listen fool. I got four dead men. You get nothing." Buck drew his knife on Nick. "How about I kill this guy here and now, then start on you?"

Kelsey blew out a fast breath. Her heart pounded in her ears. There was no choice. She emerged from the dark, her pistol pointed at Nick. Both men shut up. Buck grunted as his eyes raked Kelsey up and down. She tried to hold the SIG steady. Now was not the time to miss. Alex needed her.

Nick squinted. "That you, Kelsey?"

"Let him down," she commanded, her voice wavering nearly as much as her hands.

Buck slapped his thigh. "This is your ex? You didn't say she was a looker."

"Yeah. She's my ex." The excitement was gone from Nick's voice as he eyed Kelsey's gun.

"Man, you and me gonna have us a good time, little girl. Maybe you're worth losing four men. What ya think?" Buck all but jumped up and down. He licked his lips, his eyes bright with anticipation.

"Whatever," Nick answered, more subdued than he had been all night. "She's got a gun."

"I said let him down," Kelsey repeated, licking her lips at the nightmare in front of her. Alex had not moved an inch.

"What you gonna do?" Buck taunted as he walked over to the rope that held Alex upright. With a jerk of his wrist, he unwound it, dropping Alex to the ground with a thud. Buck turned to Kelsey, his eyes bright and cruel. He closed his eyes and sniffed the air, his head tilted back as he took a deep breath. "I can smell you from here, little girl," he growled. "Oh, man. I can hardly wait."

Her knees turned weak. This man was an animal. She took one look at Alex and righted the shaky pistol in her hands. Everything was up to her now. She could do it.

Buck winked at her slyly, his nose still twitching. "Why don't you just put that thing down and come to daddy? Let's get this party started."

Kelsey racked the slide. She knew how to handle a gun now. A nine-millimeter cartridge slid into the chamber as her blood pressure spiked. There were four of them. Alex had killed four of their friends. It was up to her to kill the other four—or die trying. That's what Alex would do.

"You're as dumb as your old man," Buck muttered. "Say I let this guy stay down, little girl. Now what? Or maybe I don't want to." He turned to the guy with the Mohawk. "Stand him up, Jess. One. More. Time."

Jess grabbed the rope, jerking Alex back to his feet. His head rolled back. Blood trickled down his chin and neck.

"Stop it. You're hurting him," she yelped.

Ethel moved into the shadows to her left. Nick moved to her right. Four against one.

"That's the idea," Buck took a step toward her. Then another.

Kelsey bit her lip, gulping past the knot in her dry throat.

Jess jerked Alex off his feet and tied the rope, leaving him suspended, his boots barely touching the ground. Jess twirled the opposite end of the rope as if it were a lasso, grinning.

Buck took another step toward her. Closer. "Come to daddy."

Her gun wavered. She looked from Buck to Jess and back again. *Where are Ethel and Nick?*

Jess gave Alex a roundhouse kick that sent him spinning.

Buck crouched like he was ready to run.

A single shot blasted from the gun in her hand.

Jess dropped dead.

Alex

"Daddy!" Abby squealed with delight. Alex lifted his baby girl high over his head, her light golden hair spilling around his face as she squirmed in his hands. His only thought was how much he loved her.

"You're an airplane, baby girl." He twirled her around in a big circle so she could feel the breeze beneath her.

She laughed with that sweet voice, clinging to his hands on her waist, her golden hair nothing but ribbons of sunshine in the breeze. "I'm flying. I'm flying." She giggled down at him with smiling blue eyes. "Look at me, Daddy. I'm flying."

"Not for long. Now you're landing." He deposited his fairy princess aircraft on the soft grass at the park. Other kids played on the swing or the slide, but Abby wanted to play with her daddy. She wrestled, pretending he was a dinosaur come to life and she wanted to ride his back. And then he was her pony. Abby could get so rowdy. Alex smiled as he remembered. She was not always a dainty little princess.

"I'm a cowboy." Her laughter was sunshine to his heart.

"You mean, you're a cowgirl."

"No, Daddy. I'm a cow–boy." She bounced a little harder until Alex rolled over. Down she came, still bouncing and giggling. As he hugged her, Abby snuggled under his chin. She hugged him hard with all her strength, her soft baby hair spilling over his face. He loved the smell of baby shampoo. And then he felt them. Butterfly kisses. He relaxed, her warm tender body pressed against his heart while Abby blessed him with sweet, eyelash kisses on his cheek.

Too soon she jumped to her feet. With a giggle she was out of his arms, running away as she grinned over her shoulder. "Look at me, Daddy. I have to go. You have to stay."

He reached for her, but Abby faded right before his eyes. He touched nothing as he grasped after the tiny hand he had just felt around his neck. She disappeared. All he heard was her sweet voice in the air. "Look, Daddy. Find her, Daddy. Find her."

The grass and ground of the park disappeared beneath him into a gaping black hole. He was falling, falling...

Alex fell from heaven with a thud. The solid ground beneath him felt like the stings of a thousand cuts. A man's voice talked to him from very far away.

"Hey, boss, I've got you now. You're going to be okay."

Alex knew that voice. He just couldn't remember who it belonged to. Someone held a bottle to his lips. The cool water felt good running down his neck, but then that same someone held his head steady, and eased a trickle between his lips.

Drop by drop, it made its way down his parched throat. His head pounded so fiercely, he couldn't think with the smell of baby shampoo still in his nose.

"Abby," he croaked, barely loud enough to hear himself. "I want Abby."

Whoever helped him was thankfully persistent with the water. More water and finally, he swallowed enough to moisten his tongue and throat.

"Hey, Boss." Alex heard that familiar voice again. "I don't know about Abby. I only know about Kelsey."

Kelsey. Her name burst into his brain. Jerked back to reality, his heart screamed for her. *Kelsey*.

"Where is she?" He turned toward the familiar man, but he either didn't hear him or chose not to answer. Instead, gentle hands loosened the ropes that circled his wrists. They moved over his arms and shoulders, firmly feeling and diagnosing as they went. The man muttered quietly. His hand felt kind and gentle until—

"Sorry, Boss. This is gonna hurt." With a quick jerk, he pulled Alex's right arm down to the normal position at his side.

Sonofabitch. He shuddered at the pain. Black waves of unconsciousness threatened to take over. He had barely caught his breath when the same procedure was repeated with his other arm. Whoever'd just saved him was torturing him now. It took all the strength he had left not to black out.

Once again the man said, "Sorry about that, Boss."

A warm, wet tongue lapped Alex's face.

"Whisper. Off," the man said, and immediately, Whisper's tongue withdrew.

He groaned in as much confusion as pain. *What the hell? My dogs are here? What's going on? Where's Abby? Kelsey? Am I delirious? Dying maybe?*

More shuffling sounded around him, and the unknown man set something soft beneath his head. He gave Alex more water. Finally, he knew the voice.

"Harley?" He croaked the question. *I've lost my mind. I really am dying.*

"Yeah, Boss. It's me. You're coming around. I can hear you now. Good. You're gonna be okay." Harley patted his chest very carefully. "You're pretty beat up. Looks like someone cut you up a little, but I've got you now. You're going to be okay."

"You gotta get Kelsey."

"Working on it, Boss. You're gonna be okay. You need to hold still though. Help is on its way, but I'm trying to stop some of this bleeding." Harley's voice was calm. Too calm.

"Listen." Alex tried to command. "You tell me I'm gonna be okay one more time, and I'll—" A spasm of breath-stopping coughing intervened. He spat the blood out of his mouth, the taste sweet, salty, full of copper and bile.

Once again Harley did not hear or did not choose to listen. His hands on Alex's chest were too gentle and too kind. Taping. Pressing. Bandaging. "Hold still, Boss. I need you to stay still so I can bandage your back."

Alex lay heavy on the ground, laboring to suck in enough air just to talk. "You've got to find her."

"I will in a minute. Honest, I will. I promise." Despite his words, Harley continued bandaging with steady hands. "Can you tell me what happened?"

At that point Alex was angry. "Get me the hell up." He tried to rise, but pain skewered him into the ground. Another fit of coughing left him gasping for air and weaker still.

Harley wiped Alex's mouth and chin with a cloth. "Boss, I'm sorry, but you aren't going anywhere. I need you to lie still so you don't make things worse. Your bleeding to death isn't going to help anyone."

"Stop patting my sonofabitchin arm." Alex gasped, but he also heard the gentleness in Harley's voice. *Damn. I'm in bad shape.* "They mean to kill her," he huffed.

"Who, Boss? Who's got Kelsey?" Harley continued with his first aid as patiently as a parent with a demanding child. At least he listened this time.

"Durrant. Her ex. He's got a couple others with him." Alex looked toward Harley's voice. He thought of Kelsey. If they had done this to him, what were they doing to her?

"You need a lot more help, Boss. I need to finish what I'm doing here before you—"

"No. No." Alex writhed in frustration. "Save her. Not me."

Harley stopped what he was doing. "It's the middle of the night, Boss. She'll be hard to find. They've got ATVs and a head start. Hell, they burned your ATV. They could be in the next state by now. Even if I do find her—"

"Harley. Please." Alex couldn't see and he could barely talk. All he had left was heart. It must've been enough. Without a deep sigh, Harley stood. Alex thought maybe he had left, but the man returned with a blanket. He covered Alex and crouched alongside, his hand firm on Alex's shoulder.

"You've got an open bottle of water and your SIG at your right hand. I know you might not be able to reach it, but just in case."

Alex strained to listen.

"I'm leaving Smoke. He'll stay with you until search and rescue gets here."

"Go," Alex commanded hoarsely.

Harley sighed.

"Please go." Alex felt something warm trickle down his cheek. Blood or tears, they were all the same.

"Yep." Harley stood. "You stay put and wait for them, you hear me? Don't go dying on me."

Alex heard the pain in Harley's voice. This would be the last time they ever talked to each other. Harley had to understand.

"I love her," he whispered.

"I know," Harley replied gently. "Whisper. Come." This time he walked away.

Alex shuddered, the pain of all he stood to lose more than he could bear. Kelsey. Maybe Harley now, too. He had to know.

"Where … you been?" Alex shook beneath the blanket. He heard his voice—old, weak, and dying.

The quiet answer came from the edge of the trees. "Rehab, Boss."

Twenty

Kelsey

Kelsey opened her eyes. She was bound and gagged, tied to the back roll bar of Buck's ATV, and headed away from the cabin. Shooting Jess had surprised her as much as everyone else. She had gotten another shot off before Nick and Buck tackled her, but it went wild, and giving herself up didn't help Alex like she had hoped. They had kicked and cut him anyway, then slapped her around and tore her shirt off. Down to just her bra and jeans, she knew the worst was yet to come. She bit her lip, fighting the urge to cry. His words came back to her. *It's not the load that breaks you down. It's how you learn to carry it.*

The reality of the brutality she had just witnessed battled her last shred of hope. There was no way Alex could help her tonight, but he had rescued her so many times in the past year. She clung to irrational optimism. Somehow he would find a way. She knew it.

At last, the ATV stopped. Buck jerked her out off the back and dropped her against a tree like a bag of potatoes. With a few quick twists of a rope, he tied a noose around her neck and then to the tree. She wasn't going anywhere with her hands tied behind her back and her ankles tied, too. Kelsey didn't see it coming. He slapped her hard, the rings on his fingers sharp on her cheekbone. He had knocked the breath right out of her.

"You killed my brother." He hit her again, his face mean and hard in the ATV's headlights.

She shook. Nick had hit her before, but this felt different. The blood pouring from her nose and down her chest chilled her, but the hard look on Buck's face filled her with paralyzing fear. Nick was mean, but Buck was cruel. And she knew the difference. She gulped, prepared for another slap, but Nick charged up to the tree wild eyed and full of – concern?

"Knock it off, Buck. Let her be."

Kelsey stared dumbfounded at her ex-husband. *How odd that he came to my rescue.*

"You gonna make me, Durrant?" Buck whirled on Nick, his knife drawn and ready to fight. "You man enough to make me?"

Nick's hands went up in instant submission. "Just don't want you killing her too soon, that's all. We got what we wanted. Let her be."

"No, we didn't get what we wanted, you fool. I got five dead men back there and one of them was Jess." Buck gestured angrily back in the direction of the cabin. "Keep shooting your face off, and there'll be one more right here, right now."

Of course Nick backed right down. Kelsey blinked the sweat out of her eyes. Nick wasn't here to help her. No way.

"And you." This time Buck leveled an accusing finger at Ethel. "You can't torture a dead man, you ever think of that? I thought that was the plan, but no. You had to hit him so hard. You nearly took his head off, you dumb bitch."

Ethel glared at Buck without a word.

"We move at first light," Buck growled. "'Til then, stay the hell outta my way."

Kelsey lay against the tree trying to catch her breath and listening to the power struggle. When Buck was done threatening and bellowing, he stomped off into the trees. She knew exactly what would happen next. Nick had to prove he was a big man. She was right. Buck was no more than out of sight when Nick strutted toward her, kicking dirt as he came. She was already hurt, and he was only going to hurt her worse, but she wasn't the same foolish girl he had married. He was going to understand one thing before he killed her. Fear gripped her throat, but strength raised her eyes.

"You proud of yourself?" Nick leaned into her face. "Who do you think you are running around with that guy anyway?"

"I'm your ex-wife. Ex as in no longer married. Remember?" She glared back at him, like she wasn't the one tied to a tree. Every muscle trembled, but she didn't care.

"You think you can sass me? Do you, huh?" He was so close she could smell his cheap brand of beer breath.

"I don't belong to you. Never did." Even in her precarious position, it felt good standing up to him. That was one lesson she had learned from Alex when he had taught her how to shoot. *Never back down, Kelsey. You might take a beating, but you'll know you gave your best shot.*

"Shut your stinking mouth." Nick punched her in the chest like she knew he would, but she had anticipated his move. It still hurt, but she lifted her head and glared back at him. Again Alex's words reminded her. *Never lie down to a bully. They're nothing but cowards. You're not.*

"Coward," she gasped. "That's all you'll ever be."

Nick pulled his knife, and with a fancy little twirl of the weapon, pressed it under her chin. Kelsey felt the blade nick her skin, but she didn't lower her eyes. Inches away, she willed herself not to cry or blink. Instead, she pictured Alex. He had told her she already possessed what she needed to win deep inside. It was all about heart. *And you have the perfect heart, Kelsey.*

"What you looking at?" Nick sputtered.

Until now she had never realized Nick was so easily antagonized. For an instant, she was back at the shooting range, Alex's arm around her and his words soft and warm in her ear. *Never give up, Kelsey. Even when you're outnumbered and out gunned. Never give up. Help might be just around the corner.*

"A baby killer. That's—"

He slapped her before she could finish, knocking her head sideways with his open hand. She spit, caught another breath and turned to face him, her eyes stinging and her voice shaky. "It doesn't matter what you do to me. You can't hurt me anymore."

"We'll see about that." Nick tossed his knife to the ground. Kelsey knew what was coming. With a jerk, he snapped the belt off of his waist and wrapped the buckle around his fist. "I said I was gonna teach you a lesson, didn't I?"

She stiffened and waited. She had used to think she deserved this kind of treatment, but no more. Now she knew Nick Durrant was nothing but a cruel little man who preyed on babies. The strength and enlightenment that Alex had bolstered her with flooded her now. Just in time.

Nick took a half step forward, cocked his arm back like a baseball pitcher, and brought the belt down. Again and again, it bit into the tender skin of her arms, chest, stomach, and legs. She twisted to protect herself, but the ropes held tight.

Alex, she thought.

With each whip, Nick cursed everyone she loved, Tommy, Jackie, and Alex. At last he tired. Despite her resolve, she whimpered. Red welts crawled like fire across her tender skin. Some bled, but she hadn't given Nick what he wanted. She hadn't cried, and she hadn't begged him to stop. Not once.

He crouched beside her, yanking her hair back so she had to look at him. An odd expression flickered across his face, like maybe he was trying to figure her out. It didn't last. With an evil smirk, he stuck his index finger in the middle of her forehead. "Pow. Should've killed you last time. You remember that day, don't ya? The time I shot your boyfriend in the back?"

Kelsey gathered her wits and fired back, "You mean the time I let you live?"

"Why you." Nick jerked her off the ground by her neck, pulling against the ropes that now strangled her. She squeezed her eyes tight, knowing this was it. This was the end. Here she would die, strangled by the same man who had already killed everyone she loved.

"You don't know when to quit, do you?" he bellowed.

From out of nowhere, Ethel Durrant's hand was on her son's arm, restraining him. "No, Nicky. You can't kill her. You gotta stick to your deal."

"No, I don't, Ma." Nick spit into Kelsey's face he was so close. "Mind yer own damned business."

"I know just how you feel, Nicky, but Buck's not gonna take too kindly to us if you finish everything right here and now. Let him have his fun, okay?" Ethel's voice was slick and sweet as she wheedled and coaxed. She clutched his arm, her eyes black and hard on Kelsey. "Then it'll be your turn."

Nick was still plenty mad. He dropped Kelsey to the ground. In frustration, he circled the tree. Once. Twice. He stopped at her feet and glared. Kelsey still met his eyes. She pushed the pain away and thought of Alex. Nick kicked dirt as he fumed, cursed, and circled again.

Ethel sat watching the drama. "He ain't back yet. You still got time to play."

Kelsey turned to her ex mother-in-law. "What did I ever do to you?"

Ethel wrinkled her nose and shrugged. "You know what you did, running around on my boy like you did."

"I never—" Kelsey couldn't finish the sentence.

"Leave my Ma alone." Nick snarled.

She saw the hard look in his eye. He pulled his knife from the dirt, and this time Kelsey held her breath, prepared to die. The sweet faces of Tommy and Jackie flashed to her mind along with Alex's. Blue eyes shone with love. Her last thought was for him. She pushed her back into the tree trunk, steeled her resolve and faced Nick one last time.

Crouching at her side, he grabbed her hair, and wound it around his fist. Nick stuck his knee into her breastbone until she gasped for air. "That don't feel so good, does it?"

And then he began slashing her hair off, cutting her scalp as he pressed the knife too deep in his haste. Not once did she look away. With one final dig of his knee and slice of his knife, he was the one who looked away. He was done. She gulped in a lungful of air, thankful for the simple gift of breathing. *Alex. Alex. Alex.*

"Hey, Ma, lookee here. I'm an Indian brave." Nick swaggered back to where Ethel sat watching, the trophy held high in his hand. "You was right. She ain't so pretty now."

His heartless mother smiled with disturbing approval. One thing Kelsey knew for sure. Ethel never liked her.

"Wait a minute." Nick returned to Kelsey. This time he grabbed her off the ground by her bound hands. Face down to the dirt, she felt him twist Alex's ring off her finger. Nick dropped her to the ground. Staring up from where she had landed, Kelsey watched the gift giving with sadness. All she had left of Alex was his ring. Her last vestige of hope failed.

Nick tossed the ring to his mother. "Got you something, too."

Ethel pushed it halfway onto her fat pinky finger. "That's my boy."

Alex

The bear faded out of the mist and ambled over to Alex with feet the size of floppy couch cushions, twelve-inch nails clattering against the rocky ground. He smelled it's putrid breath, its slimy nose and drooling jowls slobbering across his bloody face as it sampled its prey. With a saliva-drenched slurp, it paused as if savoring the taste of human sweat and blood. Then it took another cleansing swipe with its washcloth tongue. In his delirium, he chuckled. He recalled the first rule when confronted with a bear. Play dead. *I can handle that.*

Another bear, smaller and with lighter fur appeared out of the same foggy mist. Of all things, a little girl in a gossamer pink gown walked beside it, her hand comfortable on the predator's wide forehead. Now Alex knew he was either hallucinating or already dead. Either way, it was better than being eaten alive.

The child walked over to him. He peered up at her. With blue eyes that looked vaguely familiar, she gazed down at him. Wings fluttered on her back, her voice crystal tinkling bells. "Are you still here?"

Alex blinked hard at her strange question and then remembered. He couldn't see. *Ah, so I am dreaming.* In the reasonable level of all dreams where logic remains partially at play, he thought dreaming was a pretty good thing. Or maybe he was dying. That might also be a good thing. Whatever. A strange sense of euphoria and a kind of weightlessness had replaced all his pains. He tried to make sense of it. Life had been good, but death felt pretty good, too.

The winged child peered down at him. "Daddy?"

Ah, so it's Abby come to take me home. Maybe she can explain the bears.

The sweet child sat next to him, her legs crossed, her feet wrapped in some kind of ballerina shoe. Or was it a fairy princess slipper? A father of a little girl should know such things. Again, he reminded himself that he couldn't really see. His head was bashed in and his eyes were blind. This was merely an illusion, the dream state between life and death.

Just like that, the dream rippled and changed. All at once he was teaching his little daughter to play baseball. The bears had turned into his goofball dogs, Whisper and Smoke. Abby wore little white shorts and a pink T-shirt with *Daddy's Girl* printed across the front. He remembered that shirt from so long ago. It used to make him smile.

She missed the first pitch and the second, so Alex threw the ball again. This time, with a little girl squeal of delight, Abby hit it high into the sky with her red plastic bat. Straight up. Fly ball. Anyone else would've been out. Not his little girl. As he caught it in his old White Sox catcher's mitt, a sense of overwhelming peace and contentment washed over him. He felt the score burn his heart with truth. She was— safe.

Even in this crazy dream, he sighed. Ah, this was truly heaven on earth. Playing baseball with his little girl on a summer evening, the smells of fresh mown lawn in the air, the light golden at this perfect time of day – could life get any better? But just when he wound up for another pitch, his arm pulled back, his knee raised toward his chest to let the ball go – the dream changed again.

Abby turned into a beautiful young woman. She was stunning to look at, her golden hair swept up in a braid and wrapped around her head in a mist of tiny green flowers and pink ribbons. He dropped his arm, the ball rolled to the ground, and his heart swelled with pride. This beautiful young woman was his daughter, all grown up. She looked mature and womanly, not the little girl he remembered at all. What's more, Abby seemed wise beyond her years. Her blue eyes looked right through him and he knew for a certainty – she still loved him. Even though he had not been there that day, even though he had been a couple thousand miles away the day she had died – she radiated a daughter's unconditional love. It felt warm, like a blanket of peace wrapped around him after all these years.

"Are you still here?" she asked, sweetly patting his arm in her motherly way. Somehow, she floated just beyond his reach, her feet not even close to touching the ground. Just as sweetly, she reached toward him. He lifted his arms for her embrace, but instead of the hug he fully expected, she stabbed him in the chest with a ten-inch hypodermic needle.

He gasped. She had changed again.

The Pierce County Search and Rescue team had arrived.

Twenty-One

Kelsey

The worst was yet to come.

Kelsey knew it. The power struggle between Buck and Nick turned brutal the minute Buck woke up. His eyes widened in rage when he looked at her. He looked twice, and all hell broke loose.

"You cut her hair. She's all bloody. What the—" He didn't finish. Instead he charged Nick, knocking him to the ground before Nick had a chance to close his surprised mouth. "You cheating, no good sonofabitch. You made her ugly."

Kelsey turned away. She wished she could close her ears to the sounds of fists making contact with Nick's face and body. There was no side to root for in this fierce battle between two brutish men. Both meant to do her harm. Their contest was only a momentary reprieve. The minute Buck was done with Nick, he would forget what he was mad about, and come after her. Kelsey shuddered. Her only hope lay in the slim possibility they killed each other. Not likely. There was still Ethel.

"She's mine," Nick sputtered, and Kelsey had no doubt his nose and mouth were bleeding by the wet sound of his words. *Good. Kill each other. Please.*

"No." Buck grunted as another blow landed. "She ain't. You lying pig. You beat her up and made her look like—that?"

It sounded like bones crunched. Kelsey grimaced, not wanting to hear anymore. Her night of purgatory had evolved into a morning of living hell that she wouldn't survive. Ethel's shrieks for Buck to leave her little Nicky alone went unheeded. Pinkish sunlight hinted at the edges of the gray-black sky. Birds clamored in the nearby trees. And the battle of murderers continued. By the sounds of it, Nick was losing. She cringed. Nick's brand of abuse she was used to. With him, she knew what to expect. But with Buck...

Boots crunched against gravel. More groaning. More punching. Ethel grumbled again. She screamed, demanding Buck leave her boy alone. Then another sound Kelsey couldn't recognize, some kind of a super sonic hummingbird zipping through the forest like a—

BLAM! The ATV on the opposite side of the lean-to exploded. The ground shook. She jerked her eyes to the sight of a burning ATV seat falling down from the sky in a lazy orange spiral. It landed nearly on top the fighting men.

"They found us!" Buck bellowed. "Git your guns."

Kelsey blinked, not understanding what had just happened. Nick scrambled off the ground. With blood running down his face, he ran to his mother. Ethel tossed his gun to him, and he caught it, whirling around like a crazy man, the rifle hard to his shoulder. Buck was just as quick. Kelsey cringed. Both men were coming for her.

"Whatever happens," Buck ordered. "Don't let 'em get her."

"I'll kill her first," Nick muttered, his eyes deadly, his rifle already aimed at her.

A small yelp escaped her mouth. She shook. This was it.

Alex. I love you. I'll always love you.

Another supersonic hummingbird zeroed into camp. Then another. Ethel shrieked. Kelsey opened one eye to see Nick kneeling maybe two yards away with his head tilted straight upwards, his mouth wide open to the sky. He collapsed like an accordion, all folded back on himself. All she could see of Buck were the soles of his huge boots.

"Nicky!" Ethel screamed, her hand to her mouth. "Not my Nicky!"

Kelsey still tried to make sense of what had happened. Buck and Nick were—dead? How? Who?

"You!" Ethel pointed at her, a look of pure hatred on her face. "You did this."

I did this? I wish I had. All Kelsey could do was blink back at her in dumb amazement. Ethel was out of her mind.

"You're nothing but a two-bit slut. I oughta..." Ethel took a step toward her, but then she must have thought better. Glancing nervously up the hillside, she changed her mind, turned and ran, leaving her jacket where she had been sitting before the mayhem broke loose, back when she was just there to watch the show.

Kelsey's heart stuck in her throat. Everyone around her had been used for rifle practice. Was she next? Was it even possible? Alex?

She heard him before she saw him. A whine in the early morning shadows turned into—Whisper?

"Ah." she cried, tears of relief washing her face. "Whisper. You're here."

The big dog ran to her, covering her face with kisses. He placed both front paws right in the middle of her lap while she laid her head against him, her tears in his fur.

"Whisper," she sobbed over and over as he licked her clean. His anxious whine told her someone else was coming, but the dog was not about to leave. He pushed against her, planting his big German Shepherd butt firmly onto her lap, and she was so happy, all she could do was lean into him and cry. Her guardian angel was here. That meant Alex. She didn't know how he had survived the beating, but she had no doubt. Alex was here. Her heart leapt to her throat for joy. He was here.

The trees parted. A man in a black polo and camouflage cargo pants stepped out, but—it wasn't him. Her heart stalled. This man looked grim, his rifle still in his hand as he nodded once to acknowledge her, then went to the lean-to and scouted the area. Whisper's bony butt jabbed into her legs, but Kelsey's eyes were intent on this stranger. He hadn't said a word, but she could tell by the way he moved he was ex-military. Maybe as tall as Alex, this guy didn't wear a hat. He had unruly sandy hair as if he had slept on it and forgot to comb it. He stood for a moment over Nick and Buck's bodies, his jaw set in a hard line. She thought he would kick the bodies he looked so angry, but he didn't. Instead, he turned to the lean-to, jerked the walls apart, and covered the dead men with the canvas. At last he walked to where she sat trembling with Whisper on her lap. That Whisper allowed him to approach told her plenty. If the dog thought he was safe, he must be.

She calmed her nerves as much as she could, but this guy was scary quiet. His dark countenance didn't change until he crouched at her feet.

"Ma'am?" he said softly. "Whisper and me have come to take you home. Would that be okay with you?"

She lost it right then and there. Her heart broke wide open with relief. Tears gushed and she knew she looked awful, but she was safe. She choked, ashamed her emotion spasmed out of her like it did.

"Hey." He leaned in quickly, the knife in his hand slicing through the rope at her neck, arms, and ankles. He untied her so fast, his hands moving smoothly over her as he diagnosed, but fear still ruled. The second she was freed she threw herself into his chest, shaking with sobs.

"Save me," she ground out. "Please. Don't let them—"

She glanced at the canvas-covered bodies. Nick and Buck were dead. They couldn't hurt her, but her mind was convinced there was danger. Ethel. Her wicked mother-in-law was out there.

He smothered her to his chest, one arm in a gentle circle around her and the other against the side of her head. "Come on now, darlin', please don't cry. I won't hurt you. They're not going to hurt you ever again. I promise."

"Where is she?" she asked, her head shaking so hard it bumped against his chin.

"Who, darlin'? Are you talking about that other guy?"

"No." Kelsey didn't know what other guy Harley was talking about. "Ethel. Where's Ethel?"

"Who's Ethel?"

"My m-mother-in-law," she whispered, still looking around. "She's still here. She ran, but she's still here."

"That was a woman?" He whistled out a big breath. "Damn. That's one ugly, twisted mother-in-law. I'm real sorry. She got away. You want me to send Whisper to find her?"

"No." She clutched Whisper's neck with her other arm, and the big dog obliged, licking the side of her face with adoring dog kisses, and then she calmed. She was safe. Whisper wouldn't let anyone near her. "I need my boy."

She couldn't speak. All she could do was hang on tight, so thankful for Whisper and the feel of this man's arms around her. But then she felt it. A tiny drop of moisture hit her bare shoulder, and it hadn't come from her. She hiccupped another sob as she leaned away enough to look at the man who had rescued her. Gentle eyes gazed down at her. Another tear fell.

"You're crying, too?" she stammered.

He wiped his face. "Yes, ma'am. Guess I am. Sorry," he said softly, his finger tracing a line over her shoulder. "They hurt you."

He shuddered. There was no reason to answer. She had nothing to hide. With her body exposed the way it was, he already knew what they had done to her. The very real knowledge of what Buck and Nick intended next overwhelmed her with another wave of panic. She clenched this man tight even as Alex's wise words whispered again. *Never give up. Help might be just around the corner.* And here was that help just like Alex had said. She collapsed, thankful beyond what words could express.

The man shrugged out of his jacket even as he held her, and wrapped it around her shoulders, pulling her head gently back into his shoulder. He seemed to be shaking as much as she was, his heart hammering just as hard. She stilled. This man was scared, too. He had killed to protect her, but it must have been a hard thing he had done.

"You're the second person I've rescued today, Kelsey girl," he murmured softly, his words soft and warm against her shorn head.

"Alex?"

"Yes, ma'am. The first person I bumped into last night was my boss, Alex Stewart."

"Is he..." She couldn't say it. *Alive?*

"Let's just say he was bossing me plenty the last time I seen him." She heard the right words, but she sensed there was more. Too tired to think beyond the moment, she took comfort in the fact that Alex was alive. The shock of the night caught up with her. Tremors hit her hard, and the more she tried to calm herself, the worse she got.

"Who are you?" she asked through chattering teeth.

"Harley, ma'am. My name's Harley Mortimer. Alex sent Whisper and me to bring you home." He tipped her chin up to see him. "You okay with that?"

"Yes," she answered. "I've always wanted to meet you."

His eyes widened. "Me?"

"You're a good guy. Alex says so."

A dubious smile shifted over his face before his eyes turned serious. "I need to ask you something. Are you going to be okay to travel?"

She nodded quickly.

"They didn't..." He bit his lip, his eyes scanning down to the open zipper of her jeans where her panties showed, and quickly back to her face.

She shook her head. Now she knew what he was really asking. "No. They didn't do that." She cringed. But they were going to. Kelsey bowed her forehead to Harley's chest as uncontrollable sobs racked her inside out. She couldn't stop. He pulled her close. Even Whisper whined anxiously, his paw on her shoulder.

"It's okay, Whisper." Harley comforted the dog while he rocked Kelsey. "She's just scared, but we've got her now. She'll be okay, won't she, boy?"

Whisper leaned against Kelsey's shaking back, and she was ashamed. She should be happy, instead of falling apart.

"Okay then." Harley eased her off his leg and settled her next to the tree again. "You stay here while I get us ready to travel. I'll be right back."

"Okay." She sighed. Whisper was all over her and his nearness helped. She buried her face in his fluffy mane, remembering all the other times he had loaned his strength. Sobs wrenched out of her, and once again, Whisper took it all in, staring off into the trees as if this was his lot in life, to protect, guard, and to forever be her four-legged warrior angel.

With one arm around him, she watched Harley rummage around camp, locate a gas can, and top off the ATV's fuel tank. He gathered up all the weapons he could find, and stashed the cell phones he found in his pants pocket. He seemed so efficient, as if he knew exactly what to do. Before long, he was back at her side.

"Are you sure you can ride?" he asked again, his hand outstretched to help her off the ground.

She nodded once she was on her feet, turning aside to zip her jeans, and to zip his jacket up to her neck. She had no more than accomplished those simple actions when a wave of nausea struck. The world spun. She felt his hand at her elbow, holding her steady while he eased her back to the ground.

"Easy now," he said gently. "Take a minute to catch your breath."

"Let's just go." She couldn't speak. A wave of darkness rolled over her. Harley and Whisper faded nearly away...

A gentle hand cupped her neck and water against her lips. Harley was muttering, and Whisper's fur brushed softly against her hand.

"Damn it, Mortimer. You're dumb as a box of rocks." He leaned over her, still coaxing water into her mouth. "You should've known she would be dying of thirst."

She licked her lips and drank from the bottled water he offered. The coolness of it trickled down her throat, bringing relief she hadn't realized she needed. He tipped her head forward so she could drink better. It tasted so good. Satisfied she'd had enough, Harley eased her back to the ground. She noticed Ethel's coat had been folded beneath her head for a pillow.

"You okay?" Harley peered down with such a serious face. He brushed something off her cheek.

"Yeah." She closed her eyes. The truth was she was barely hanging on to her emotions. She was sick, hurt, and the only thing that would truly help would be to feel the safety inside Alex's arms again. Gathering the last of her resolve, she struggled to her elbows, and then accepted Harley's hand up and off the ground one more time. She staggered to the ATV.

"I'm ready," she said wearily, her head still buzzing, but not wanting to admit it to Harley. He took the driver's seat, watching her out of the corner of his eye.

"You sure?" he asked.

She nodded, waving up hill. "Sure," she said softly. The blackness was back, creeping at the edges of her vision, a shadow she could almost feel. She focused on breathing, sure this awful feeling would pass. It didn't. Harley drove nearly to the crest of the small hill before he stopped the vehicle and let it idle.

"You're not feeling good, are you?"

"No, please. Keep going," she insisted, but when she turned to face him, the tenderness in his eyes was more than she could bear. He reached his hand to her arm, and she summoned all her strength to return his look without breaking down. "Please," she begged. "Let's just go."

"No, ma'am." He shook his head. "Listen, darlin'. I know men aren't your favorite creatures right now, but you need to ride over here where I can get a hold of you, okay? I can't have you falling off now that I found you, can I?"

The moment he put his arm around her, she broke down. The horror of the night swept over her with a vengeance. She needed Alex, but Harley was here. "Would you hold me?"

He did. Harley scooped her tight onto his lap and tucked her under his chin, his arms gentle, safe, and strong. She cried like she couldn't stop. He gave her a cloth from somewhere, and she drenched it in minutes, the flood unstoppable. Sunlight warmed her back and still she cried. It was all too much. She was tired and beat up. Her hair was gone and the few shreds of it left felt like an awful crew cut. What would Alex say when he saw her? She wasn't even a little bit pretty anymore. Her head hurt, and her heart, too. He might never want her after this. He might make her go home, and she would... Kelsey gulped. Love reminded her. Alex was never going to make her leave. He loved her, and she didn't have a clue why she was acting like this. The tears slowed. She sniffed while the weariness of the day took the last of her strength.

She listened, her head against his chest. His heart beat strong and true, a definite rhythm that never faltered. Not even once. He smoothed a hand over her shoulder and down her arm, patiently waiting for her to be ready to move again. Finally spent, she straightened in his lap.

"I'm sorry," she said softly.

"It's okay, Kelsey girl." He brushed her cheek tenderly. "You've been through hell. You're suffering right now, but you're gonna be okay. I promise."

She nodded, wanting to believe. Whisper sat at Harley's side of the ATV, watching.

"So, what brought you and Alex all the way out here to the not-so-great Northwest?"

"He asked me to marry him," she whispered, her voice small and breathless. "Is he really okay?"

"Don't you worry about Alex, ma'am. He's tough. You oughta know that by now."

"But they..." She groped for the right words.

"They beat him up a little, but he'll be okay. You'll see."

"They kicked him so much."

"Yep, they did, but search and rescue is taking good care of him right now. For all I know, he's in the hospital and getting fixed up already." He tucked her under his chin and kicked the clutch. "Come on. Let's get you some real help. Hang on tight."

She rested against him again as he maneuvered the ATV one-handed around boulders and logs. He didn't want to talk about Alex. That's why he had changed the subject and started driving. The hopelessness of the night stabbed her. Alex was hurt badly. She knew it.

"Whisper and I have you now, darlin', and that means you've got the best. The Boss sent us to find you, and you know how he is. He only sends the best," Harley rambled, and she knew what he was doing. He was giving her hope when there was none. He was stringing her along. "That oughta make you feel a little bit better now, doesn't it?"

She was silent.

"And you're safe. And by the looks of it, old Whisper kinda likes you, huh? I could tell. He thinks he belongs to you, doesn't he? Or maybe he thinks you belong to him the way he was kissing all over you. I mean, you know how dogs are. They kinda choose who they're gonna love, and I can tell that big old hound loves you, doesn't he?"

Kelsey slumped against him. The darkness was back. It was winning.

"Talk to me."

She mumbled something even she couldn't understand.

"Kelsey girl, I need you to talk to me." Harley brought the ATV to a halt as he tried to rouse her. "You've got to stay with me. Can you do that?"

She wanted to believe, but somehow, in the process of being rescued, all her resolve had fled.

"Come, on, Kelsey. Stay with me. We're almost there, and then you can rest, okay?" Harley was scared. She heard him talking, but his worried face kept fading in and out of focus. So much darkness. Too many shadows. They wavered close by, threatening and teasing her senses. She closed her eyes to make them stop.

"I don't know if you can hear me or not, but you and me are going to say some prayers. Can you do that for me?"

She sighed, not able to open her eyes this time.

"'The Lord is my shepherd.'"

She mumbled soft and low, trying to form the words he wanted her to say. Nothing made sense. Why was he trying to get her to pray in the middle of the forest anyway?

"Good, Kelsey girl. Good job. Okay. Next line. 'No want shall I know.'"

"No-o..." He thought she was trying to pray, but she wasn't. Not anymore. *I'm dying. Just let me go.*

"That's real good." Harley continued, jostling her in his arms as if to keep her awake. It wasn't working. "'He maketh me to lie down in green pastures.' Come on. Say it with me."

She huffed a sigh of resignation. *It doesn't matter. Alex is dead. Tommy and Jackie are dead. I want to be dead, too.*

Harley growled deep in his chest. She felt the rumble of that far away growl. The last thing she heard was his fervent prayer. "Jesus Christ, I need some freaking help down here!"

Twenty-Two

Kelsey

Flashing lights. Pine branches like lace against the blue morning sky. Kelsey blinked the fog away, dazed with the sounds of men's voices. Too close. The men were too—

"Ahh," she screamed, rolling away from Buck and Nick and—

"Kelsey." Harley's voice penetrated her panic. "I'm here. I'm right here."

"Don't let them get me." She latched onto his hand, pulling herself up and out of Buck and Nick's clutches. "Help me."

"You're okay." Harley was saying all the right words, but the hammering in her chest pushed her to fight or flight. Buck and Nick were still too close. She could hear them and...

Someone pressed her to the ground as the scene materialized. Two uniformed men moved around her, one tucking a blanket around her legs, the other holding her arm firm against his side as he waited to insert an IV. She gasped, at last understanding. Harley. Paramedics. Not Buck. Not Nick. But Harley. For sure—Harley.

"You're safe." He knelt at her side, one hand locked on hers as he smoothed the other over her cheek. "I'm not leaving. I promise."

She squeezed her eyes tight, fighting tears and gasping for air.

"These guys are going to transport you to the nearest hospital," he explained. "You'll be okay. Just relax."

She nodded, her heart beating out of control. For now, her only link with cold, hard reality was him, and he had said he wouldn't leave. She felt the prick of the IV in her arm, and squeezed his hand tighter.

He returned the squeeze, leaning over her. "You've got quite a grip for a woman," he teased. "Do you work out or something?"

"Kung fu," she whispered. "David..."

"David Tao's teaching you kung-fu?" He seemed surprised. "Damn. You're some catch."

She nodded, suddenly groggy. His face moved in and out of focus, and she knew what was happening. The drug in her system should have made her relax, but she fought it. Too soon. It was too soon to be restrained again, and she needed Alex. Only Alex was not here.

"No. Don't... don't leave me."

She felt his hand on her cheek, gently thumbing her tears away. He was lifeline and comfort rolled into one. She tried to hang on. He was her only link to Alex. But the drug was winning.

Harley bumped his forehead into hers. "Go to sleep. Me and Whisper will be right here when you wake up."

"Hey, Kelsey girl."

Harley knocked on her hospital door as he let himself in. "You in here?"

She looked up in surprise, her smile quickly replaced with uncertainty. She had been hospitalized, her lip stitched, and her numerous other wounds treated. Most of it was a groggy memory of the emergency room with fragments of Murphy's and Harley's soft voices nearby, and the odd notion that Whisper had slept under her bed all night. Of course he didn't, but the thought soothed Kelsey. If Harley noticed her nervousness, he didn't let on.

"I hear they're going to cut you loose tomorrow?"

"Ah, yes. I get to leave. I hope." Kelsey didn't want him to stay. She was embarrassed. Couldn't he understand? He was part of that whole horrible night, and even though he had saved her, she didn't expect to face him again so soon. Not now. Not today. Maybe not ever.

Dressed in blue denim jeans and a light blue checked western shirt, he stood awkwardly at her bedside like a little boy with nothing better to do. He pulled a gold chain out of his jeans pocket. At the end of it swung a gold locket, about the size of a fifty-cent piece. Delicate filigreed hearts and flowers were engraved on the shiny ornament. She turned away, afraid to look him in the eye.

"So, I was wondering what I could bring you, you know," he drawled with that lazy cowboy twang of his.

She remembered it now. That was part of the reason she had trusted him. His good ol' boy approach had calmed her to her core—then. But now—not so much.

"I thought I oughta bring you flowers or something, cuz you've been stuck in here the last couple of days, but then I figured flowers just die and chocolate gets eaten and anyway..."

He handed her the locket.

"You didn't have to do this." She took it unwillingly, still avoiding his eyes. She didn't need any more reminders of that night. "Thanks."

"Hey, its no big deal. Just needed to do something for my favorite girl." He stood there like he was waiting for something.

She fingered the locket, biting her lip as she waited for him to leave.

"Are you gonna open it?" he asked shyly.

"I was just going to..." She let her words trail away. She didn't want to open it. She just wanted to forget. With a quiet click of the locket, her worries evaporated.

Kelsey looked at the gift he had brought, and then she looked up at him. For the first time, she noticed those hazel eyes were flecked with green and gold. It wasn't something she remembered from their first meeting. Those hazel eyes also looked like they could be full of mischief if he would let them. Definite laugh lines crinkled at the corners, but right now all she saw was tenderness and concern. If she didn't know better, she might think those gentle eyes were full of love, and maybe they were. He had certainly brought the perfect gift. On each side of the locket was a picture of two of Kelsey's best friends. Whisper and Smoke.

"I thought you might like that instead of flowers," he said, nervously shifting his weight from one foot to the other. "You know, cuz flowers die and stuff, and I know you love those goofy dogs."

Kelsey's eyes brimmed with tears. Whisper's bright eyes stared back from the locket frame. He had been so heroic that morning while Smoke had stayed steadfast at Alex's side. They were her heroes. Harley, too. But she wasn't so thankful for her heroes that she wasn't also embarrassed. She cringed. The first thing Harley'd done out there was cover her nakedness and protect her modesty. Yes, he was there. He had seen her at one of the worst moments in her life, but he had also protected her. He had respected her.

"Thank you." She bit her lip, embarrassed to her core.

"Ah, it's nothing." He blushed. "It's a small thing."

"No, I mean for everything."

"Yeah, well, that was something, definitely something. I'm just glad I got there in time. Well, almost in time anyway." He wiped his hand across his face, and she remembered he had cried when he had found her.

"So, how are my boys?" Kelsey changed the subject. Harley looked as nervous as she felt. Even now the lines left by Nick's belt circled her neck and arms in bright red stripes. She couldn't hide them from Harley anymore than she could hide her humiliation.

"Whisper and Smoke? They're fat and lazy like me." He chuckled as he looked around the room. The awkwardness of Kelsey's rescue hung between them. His attempt at humor sounded hollow and trite among the serious sterile sheets and IV drip.

"I'll wear this locket forever. Would you help me put it on?" Kelsey changed the subject yet again. There had to be some way to bridge the gap between them.

"Yes, ma'am." Harley leaned over and latched the gold chain around her neck. "So check this out."

He wormed his cell phone out of his tight jeans pocket and brought up a couple pictures of the dogs. One showed Whisper nose to nose with a fluffy-tailed gray squirrel. A peanut lay between them on the ground and, although the squirrel had his teeth just about on the nut, it also had both eyes locked on the predator's flared nostrils inches away. Whisper's lazy ear made him look comical, but both black eyes were intently focused on that furry happy-meal in front of his vacuum cleaner nose. The silly dog's eyes looked like they were crossed.

Kelsey couldn't contain her smile. "How'd you get him to do that?"

And that broke the ice. As Harley talked about the dogs and showed her more pictures, she relaxed and laughed at their antics. Harley was a true dog handler. It seemed he could get Whisper and Smoke to do anything and everything. In another shot, Smoke sat up straight on his haunches with a can of beer balanced on his nose. In the next picture, it was two cans, one stacked on top of the other.

"See. Those cans are really empty," Harley explained, pointing at the shot, "but it's a cool picture, huh?"

"You have to teach me how to do that."

"What? Sit on your butt with a can on your nose?"

"No. I think I can already do that trick." Kelsey punched his arm good-naturedly. It felt like they had been friends for years.

He settled on the edge of her bed. "It's sure good to hear you laugh, darlin'. So how about I come by and show you how to teach these boys a couple more tricks when you're feeling better? Murphy tells me you're a pretty fair canine handler yourself. Is that right?"

"I don't know." She shrugged. "I just love them. They're my best friends. I'm glad they're staying with you right now."

"You know," he drawled mischievously. "I was gonna put a couple different pictures in that locket."

She raised her eyebrows. He was teasing; she could tell.

"But I figured pictures of me and Alex would be just plain scary."

She smiled again. There was nothing between her and this handsome man but trust and friendship. He might have been there that morning, but Kelsey knew he would never betray her. She had more than just two best friends.

"Harley?"

"Yes, ma'am?"

"Can I give you a hug?"

"Why sure, darlin'."

"Thank you for saving my life," she whispered into his ear. "If it couldn't be Alex, I'm so glad it was you."

He patted her back with a heartfelt sigh. "Anytime, Kelsey girl. Anytime."

Alex

Alex could be mean.

Hospitals didn't agree with him, and this time was no different. After surgery to remove one shattered kidney and another to repair his perforated spleen, he wanted to run from it all, but hell, he couldn't even walk. Worse, he could barely stay awake. If that wasn't bad enough, he had undergone rotor cuff repair on both shoulders. Brain swelling forced his doctors to induce coma therapy, then a shunt to reduce the fluid around his brain, and surgery to remove a portion of his skull. When he had finally stabilized, Murphy's calm blue eyes stared down at him.

"Kelsey," was the only word he could come up with, the only question still unanswered.

"She's safe," Murphy answered. "Harley got to her in time. Now you listen to the doctors, you hear?"

And Alex drifted away, floating between dreams of Sara and Abby, and memories of chocolate brown eyes that cried at the drop of a hat. Kelsey. He just wanted Kelsey.

The surgery on his skull seemed to do the trick. The next morning he woke to more control of his thoughts and a desire to eat. No such luck. His diet was reduced to steamed, pureed, and broth. He wanted steak and he wanted to feel good, neither of which were going to happen very soon. Frustration stoked his anger, and he had plenty of both. He barked at doctors and nurses alike—when he was conscious. He couldn't see, his hands were useless, and he had more tubes draining fluids and infections from more parts of his body than his damned truck had hoses.

Life sucked, and not even Murphy would talk about what happened with Kelsey. Alex had asked, but all Murphy would say was she was doing better. *Better than what?* When he had tried to pin Murphy down, all he got was the run around. *Kelsey will be in as soon as they let her. You just hold on. She'll tell you all about it, son. You just listen to your doctors and blah, blah, blah.*

And that was another thing. No one was allowed into intensive care but Murphy, and that set Alex off again. He slept too much. The pain meds didn't help. He wanted Kelsey. It was all too much.

Finally, one of the nurses told him they were moving him out of the ICU and into another room. That meant Kelsey could visit him. *About time.* He cursed, slept, and cursed some more. The last thing he remembered was the alarm on his monitor going off like a beeping siren. When he came to, it sounded like the whole hospital was in his room. The more they worked on him, the worse he felt. Being blind didn't help.

Muted voices chatted overhead like he wasn't even there, like he was already dead or dying. *Lucky if he lives... defib... intracranial hemorrhaging... angioplasty... mood swings... another stent... brain injury... may never see again... poor guy.*

A heavy hand pressed hard against his sternum, too hard this time. *Did I have another heart attack?* He couldn't move and he couldn't fight. They covered his face with a sheet. *Oh, hell. I'm dead.*

The room was quiet when he came to, the uproar over, everyone gone. Alex was alone, weary beyond belief, and surrounded by nothing but darkness, inside and out. The realization of all his brokenness crept in to lay with him. He ached for Kelsey, but was rewarded with despair, and despair told him this time was different. The pain was relentless. No matter what meds they had tried, he couldn't get ahead of it, and his heart was in trouble. Three attacks already. How many more could he survive?

Hopelessness took hold. *What's the use?*

Most discouraging of all, he couldn't see. His sharpshooter eyes were damaged, his one skill, his God-given talent, and his pride. The absence of light became an evil spirit that messed with his head.

Melancholy whispered dark thoughts. *You're blind, Stewart. Blind. Blind. Blind.*

With all the medicine pumped into him, he had lost his edge. Death sat at his bedside, biding its time. He knew it now. He wasn't going to make it.

The gloom of too many dark days lied to him. *You'll never see again, old man.*

He had counted on his anger when he first came to. It gave him energy. Direction. Motivation. But the circle of so much pain had turned into a noose that choked the life out of him. This time was different all right.

The downward spiral beckoned. *You're nothing but a beggar with a tin cup.*

He thought about Kelsey. As much as he had wanted her before, he dreaded her now. She would be better off if he were to die. He loved her so much, and he knew she loved him. That was the problem. She would stay until the end, no matter how bad things got. That's just how she was, but he didn't want her to watch him die. She had already lost so much.

Pessimism poisoned him. *You're an old man, Stewart. Let her go. Let her live.*

He counted his years. *We have our whole lives ahead of us.*

Just as quickly darkness rebutted. *A whole life of what? Wheelchair for you? Misery for her? Changing adult diapers, and old before her time? You call that life?*

He agonized. Sunlight would have helped. The scent of Kelsey would have helped more. But there was none. No light. No Kelsey. No hope.

At last he knew what had to be done. It was a hard decision, but he had made plenty of tough decisions before. If he loved her, it was the only way. She had been through enough. And he really loved her.

He had to let her go.

Alex stayed quiet when Kelsey entered his room the next morning.

"Good morning, sweetheart," she whispered in his ear. In her wonderful loving way, she rested her head on his chest, just breathing. Something prickled his chin. Her hair? His heart stalled. This was what he really craved, her sweet gift of joy in the middle of so many crappy days. All his first responders flickered to life. Even his heart felt better. He yearned to hold her, to feel her once more in his arms and in his bed. But that day was past. The crippled soul within held back. There was no sense lying.

She lifted away from him, and put something on the counter by his bed. His nose twitched at the scent of flowers. That was so like her to brighten his room even though he couldn't see. They smelled good, but she smelled better, of green apple shampoo and that soft perfume she liked. He listened, feigning sleep as she settled into the chair and fidgeted with something. Pages turned. She had brought something to read while she waited in her patient way for him to wake up. He steeled his resolve and turned his bandaged eyes toward her.

"Is that you?" He couldn't even speak her name. Even in his ears, his voice sounded old and feeble. Impotent. Yes. This was the best decision. She deserved a better life.

"Alex." She was at his side in an instant, her hands warm and gentle on his brow. "I've missed you so much." She laid her head on his chest again, and he choked, her touch unexpectedly sweeter than he had imagined. He had craved it for so long; he almost couldn't go on. How could he live without her? The truth was simple. He wasn't going to live. And if by some small miracle he did, what kind of man would he be to bind her forever to the decrepit excuse for a man he had become? He steeled his nerve. It was now or never.

"Why are you here?" His voice cracked.

She leaned in to kiss him, but he sensed her nearness and turned away. Her lips barely brushed his cheek.

"Are you okay?" She sounded worried. "Alex. What's wrong?"

He sighed, the knowledge of what he was about to do stabbing him with sharp, deep stiletto cuts. *Make it quick. Do it right. Let her go. Let her live.*

"You shouldn't be here," he croaked.

"But they said I could visit today, and I've missed you so—"

"No." He cut her short, trying to steel his voice. *Do it. It's for her good.* "I don't want you here."

Her breath caught. "What? Why?"

Even blind, he felt her pain-filled surprise. It was all he could do to repeat himself. "I don't want you here. Go."

"But Alex? Why don't you want me anymore?" Kelsey sat at the edge of his bed.

He heard the frightened little girl emerge in her voice, the child who forever thought she was unworthy of love. He hesitated. *Why am I doing this? Why am I being so cruel?*

Depression reminded him. *So she can live a life worth living. Let her go. Let her live.*

He took another deep breath. "You need to go."

She leaned into the side of his face. He felt her sweet breath on his ear – and her tear. "You're just sick, Alex. You don't mean it," she said kindly, instantly forgiving him. "I'll never leave you."

Oh, Kelsey. Always too good for me...

He had to make her understand, so he turned away from her sweet breath. "Just go."

"But I—"

"Go. Just go." Frustration added venom to his words even as his heart shuddered with a different kind of heart attack. He was hurting her. He knew it. There was no other way.

"If that's what you want, I'll… I'll… go then," she said timidly. "But I'll be back. I promise."

Slowly she gathered her things. She was frightened again. He could tell. He wanted so much to pull her into his worthless arms and tell her everything would be okay, and that's why he didn't. His arms were worthless. He was worthless. He couldn't even hold the woman he loved.

He sensed her at his side again—where she belonged. He cringed. Somehow, he had to be tough. *Didn't she get it? She had to go and she had to go now. One more minute of this charade and I'll have to hold her again. I'll have to kiss her and worse, I'll have to believe I can live.*

"Go." The one word cracked out of him. She didn't move. What did she want from him? A kiss? A pat on the butt? A good-bye hug? She had to leave, or she would have all those things and more. "I told you—take your flowers and leave. Get out. Go."

He heard her sharp intake of breath.

"I'm going, but..." she whispered meekly from the doorway.

"Get out of my life." Alex roared this time.

He held his breath, stilled and listened. The door clicked quietly on its hinge. He had gotten what he wanted, but there was no joy in it. Anguish strangled him instead.

"Just go, sweetheart. Live. Please live."

Only silence answered.

Kelsey was gone.

Twenty-Three

Alex

Week three began with another heart procedure called coronary angioplasty and another called stenting. Between the heart medicines and blood thinners, Alex felt wretched inside and out. The medications wrecked havoc on his energy as well as his already nasty disposition. The only bright spot in his days were Murphy's visits, and they were few and far between. He didn't blame Murphy. The man was managing the business alone from a hotel room across country.

Alex cursed his failure to heal as much as he cursed everything and everyone else. So it was a pleasant surprise when Harley showed up. He had been back to DC until Alex moved out of the intensive care unit, and Alex was glad for the company.

"Hey, Boss."

"Harley? That you? How've you been?" Alex tried to pull himself into a sitting position. It took a while with two arms in slings, so Harley gave him a hand.

"I'm doing well. Getting back in the saddle and keeping busy, you know how it is."

"Not really." Alex growled. "Seems all I do is sleep, and get something else stuck in me. So tell me. We looked for you for months, and all of a sudden you show up in the middle of nowhere. What's that all about?"

"Yeah, well." For a boy from New York, Harley had the best fake Texas drawl Alex had ever heard. He was drawling plenty. "Guess I sorta felt there weren't nothing else I could do. I'd hit rock bottom again, and I was just making excuses. You knew that."

He listened as Harley stretched his long legs. "I kinda had a come-to-Jesus moment when I woke up with two naked women, and I didn't even know their names. For that matter, I couldn't remember what I drank or stuck up my nose either. No sirree, Boss. That's when I thought of you, cuz I knew I didn't want to be like me anymore. So I got up, got dressed, and hightailed it outta there. Committed myself to a tough rehab in Texas."

"What were you using?"

"Blow. Booze. Women."

"Cocaine's a tough road."

"It is." Harley's voice mellowed with his true confessions. "I can tell you I'm sorry if that's what you want to hear."

Alex shook his head. "We tried everything to find you." He didn't mean it to sound accusing, but it did. He had known Harley needed help when he had hired him. He had just never expected Harley to run. It helped knowing now the kid had run for help instead of away from it.

"I figured you guys would come looking for me, and I didn't want to be found, you know, so did the only thing I could think of to keep off the grid."

Alex waited.

"I registered under your name." Harley said it so brightly that Alex couldn't help but chuckle. He should have known. Leave it to Harley. "Yep. Seemed like a good idea at the time, you know, since I wanted to be like you and all."

The silence in the room stifled Alex. Harley didn't know what he was asking for.

"So anyway, I went into the office as soon as I left Texas. I thought I'd go hang out for a couple days, get caught up on all the gossip, and see how that Lennox kid was working out. Man, he's good, isn't he?"

"He is." Alex was already exhausted. "We're keeping him a little too busy, but he doesn't mind the extra work."

"I'm looking forward to working with him..." Harley paused, "if you'll let me keep my job."

"You're still working for me last time I checked."

"Thanks." Harley blew out a huge sigh. "I sure appreciate that."

"I should be thanking you. You showed up just in time."

"That was a bad night." Harley scooted his chair closer. "What happened anyway?

"It's a long story. Kelsey's ex-husband was a real piece of work. I was stupid. That's all."

"I noticed you got five of them." Harley sounded pleased.

"No, only four."

"Well, there were five bodies at the cabin. Who got—"

Alex gasped. He knew exactly who took that fifth shot.

"Kelsey went down fighting." Harley was impressed. "Your woman's a trooper."

The revelation and Harley's choice of descriptors agitated Alex. "We shouldn't have been there in the first place."

"Things happen. So what'd they do? Ambush you two in the middle of the night or something?"

"She was supposed to run. I told her to run."

"Did she ever talk to you about that night?" Harley's voice softened.

Of course she never talked about that night. He didn't give her a chance.

"She needs to talk to you." Harley just said a mouthful.

"Why is this your damned business?"

"Because you asked me to save her, and I did. Only she's gone now, but you already know that, don't you?"

Alex clenched his sheet.

Harley continued patiently. "I went over to her hotel room this morning after I got in. Thought I'd check on her, you know, tell her what the dogs are up to. She loves those goofy dogs of yours."

Alex turned toward his words, a stab of guilt twisting his gut. His conscience pricked. *Whisper loved Kelsey from the second he found her. Whisper loved purely. So did Kelsey.*

"Only she's not there. By the time I tracked her down she was up at SEA-TAC, and headed to her sister's place in Oregon. So I asked her what's going on while we're waiting for her plane, only it was real hard to get her to talk. She was crying you know."

"I told her to go," Alex said quickly, a catch in his voice. The realization of what he had set in motion strangled him. *She's tenderhearted. I made her cry.*

"So I hear. Why'd you do that?" Harley's voice was still as gentle as could be. "Didn't she tell you what happened out there?"

Again, Alex didn't reply. He couldn't. The pounding in his chest was heart damage of a different kind. *What have I done?*

"Or didn't you ask?" Harley stood and pushed his chair back. "Well, you need to hear it from her, but I'll tell you this much. When I got to her that morning, you want to know the first thing she asked me? She wanted to know if *you* were okay. Here I'm holding this little lady of yours, and she's bloody and hurt, and all she wants to know is if *you're* hurt. Go figure. All she cared about was—*you*."

Alex paled. That was what he loved so much about her. She was the most genuine love of his life. *Of course they hurt her. What have I done?*

"You know, you're the toughest man I know." Harley didn't seem to be able to shut up. "I look up to you. We all do. I don't know why, but for some reason you're like this bigger-than-life super hero or something, and yeah, we know you're hurting. We get it. You're scared you might die this go round. Hell, *we're* scared you're gonna die this go round. I ain't the brightest bulb in the box, but it seems to me even a tough guy like you might want to die happy instead of telling the best thing in his life to take a hike."

Alex rallied as if he could justify what he had done. "She deserves a hell of a lot better than waiting around for me to—"

"To what? *Die?*" Harley leaned into Alex's ear, his voice a low growl of conviction. "You ain't gonna die, Boss. This might be the toughest battle you've ever fought, but you ain't gonna die. Not at Nick Durrant's hand, you're not. Not the Alex Stewart I know."

Alexfelt something tossed onto the bed by his legs.

"Here. I took this off that bastard ex-husband of hers. It's not for me to keep, and I'm sure she doesn't want it. Guess its yours now."

Alex didn't move.

"See you later, Boss."

Alex lay still until the quiet whoosh of the door told him Harley had left. Then he fumbled to reach what Harley'd left behind. It felt like a pouch with a drawstring, but it took a while to loosen the knot, his arms and fingers still so stiff and sore. The knotted trophy spilled into his hands. He choked, clenching Kelsey's silky hair against his nose. For the first time in his life, profanity offered no relief.

He wept.

He just didn't know Harley still stood inside the closed door doing what a sniper does best.

Watching.

Kelsey

Kelsey snapped the radio off, cutting Gene Autry short before she had to hear one more syllable of that stupid, old-fashioned love ballad. That was the last thing she needed right now. Besides, it was summer in the Rockies. She didn't need to be reminded of love and all its lies. Her sister, Louise, was headed to her job at the local nursing home and Phil, Louise's husband, was already out in the fields baling the second crop of grass hay for the year. They would be gone most of the day, and that meant she would be left to her own wiles again. As if she had wiles.

She had been in Oregon two weeks now. Somewhere in this dusty town she was supposed to locate a counselor.

That's what the emergency doctor told her to do once she was released. Find a counselor. Seek help. There's plenty to be found. She didn't. She thought of calling Harley instead, just to talk. He had been there. He would understand. She didn't do that either.

With all her heart, she missed Whisper and Smoke. They had been solace and comfort in the days after her sons' funeral. All those long walks in Alexandria came back to her now. She had been safe and loved unconditionally with them. She had seen it in their black eyes. Somehow Whisper and Smoke had become her new boys, and she had poured her heart into them. She missed Murphy, too. He had taken her under his wing like the grandfather she never had, and poor Harley. He had cried that morning when he had found her, and then again at the airport when she left. He was as softhearted as she was. That's why she knew she could trust him.

But she hurt for Alex. Her hands, her feet, and every muscle in between ached with a pain she couldn't escape. Every waking thought left her wanting his breath in her face, his hands on her body, and his heartbeat under her ear. The distance between them sucked the life out of her. There was no taste to food, no warmth in sunshine, and no strength in her bones. She wiped the endless stream of tears away. It seemed heartache was all she had to show for her pitiful life.

Tucked against the Blue Mountains in Northeastern Oregon, Pendleton had sprouted up in the middle of nowhere. Home of the famous Pendleton Roundup and Rodeo, it was a hot, dusty town in summer and a frozen-solid truck stop in winter. Wheat fields stretched as far as the eye could see, while formidable Dead Man's Pass loomed in the east like a wall at the end of creation. It was a farm town, a cow town, and an out of the way, I-can-hide-here-forever kind of town.

She stared at the immensity of nothing above her. The first thing she noticed when she had arrived in Pendleton was the scarcity of trees combined with the wide-open sky. Until now, she had lived a sad life sheltered beneath pines, but now, even that small comfort was stripped away. Cobwebs of jet contrails stretched from east to west over this forgotten corner of the world. The acid-washed sky loomed endlessly overhead, too wide and infinitely too big.

And Kelsey felt so small.

Alex

"Enough."

The nurse was barely quick enough with her escape before the closest thing he could reach hit the wall behind her. Alex tore the line from his arm, the other from the back of his hand. The drainage tube inserted in his abdomen offered the pain he was looking for. With a groan, he wrenched it from his gut, and flung it across the room in an arc of yellow fluid and pus. He'd had enough of hospital care and recuperation. The frustration of being dependent too long at last took its toll on him, and the whole place was on his hit list.

"I want my damned clothes," he bellowed as he staggered blindly across the room, bumping into the rolling bed table and chair as he went. He shoved them both out of his way. The closet was there somewhere. He just had to find it. Profanities flew until he heard the door open, but he was ready for the fight. *Bring it on.*

"Morning, Alex." That's all Murphy had to say to check Alex's temper. As usual he sounded patient and understanding. "What's going on, son?"

"I gotta get oughta here. I've got a business to run." Even as Alex said the words, he knew they were lies. Murphy took his arm, pulled a chair off the floor, and steered him to it. Alex grumbled, but he let Murphy take charge.

"Sure you do. You go rampaging like this again, and you'll tear all them stitches out. You know that, don't you?"

"I need to get back to work." Alex fumed. He knew he was making an ass of himself. He just couldn't stop.

"Uh, huh." Murphy patted his shoulder, and that set him off again.

"Don't patronize me. You of all people."

"Going back into hiding again?" Murphy muttered.

"What that mean?" Alex turned toward his second in command's voice.

"It means you bury your head in your work when life gets hard, you lash out at everyone, and you swear like a banshee. Just like you did when you lost Sara and Abby."

Alex ran a hand over his head in frustration. "What should I do? Work's all I've got."

"No, Alex. It's not."

Alex ignored the gentle rebuff.

"Besides, you're not going anywhere until they get that piece of skull bone back in your head."

"I'm not staying here one more day."

"You're staying here until they release you, son. That's all there is to it."

Alex snarled at the truth in Murphy's words. At times like this he wished Murphy'd fight back, fight dirty, just fight for hell's sake. But Murphy didn't. He was a rare man and a rarer friend.

"This doesn't have anything to do with Kelsey, does it?"

"No." Alex all but spit the word out of his mouth. *Of course it had to do with Kelsey. Every stinking minute of every crappy day had to do with Kelsey.*

"You know, that little gal would be back here in two seconds flat if you called her."

The calm truth of Murphy's words rang true, but Alex couldn't answer. Anger might be the fuel he ran on these days, but it didn't allow much room for humility, and he wasn't going to change now. He let Murphy guide him back to bed.

"Seems to me you've still got plenty of healing to do, young man. You got tubes and wires attached, or at least you did last time I was in here. What'd you do? Pull 'em all out? Damn it, Alex."

Alex didn't take the bait. He had lost the edge to his anger the minute Murphy stepped through the door. Murphy was right, as usual.

"Murph?"

"Yeah?" Murphy sighed.

"Send me the latest contracts. I want to get the next operations lined up and assigned."

"You want me to send them to you in Braille?" Murphy was more than a little sarcastic.

"No. In Mother. Send Mother. She can still read, can't she?" Alex clenched the hospital blanket Murphy'd just pulled over his legs. "She can help me get some work done while I'm laid up. Tell her to bring one of those fancy laptop computers she's always yapping about. At least I can get something done while I'm stuck here."

"You know Alex, you're a dumb ass when it comes to women. Just call her," Murphy suggested gently, but the mask was back on.

Alex was ready to bury himself under the cover of work and long hours once more. Within the day, Mother was on her way west to help her boss manage his business.

At least, that's what he thought.

Twenty-Four

Kelsey

Kelsey opened her bedroom window to let the fresh summer breeze in. Along with it came a myriad of country smells, the ever-present dust blown off crops and fields, the fresh cut grass hay Phil sold to neighboring ranchers, and roses, always roses. Louise had a thing for roses. The clapboard home she and Phil built years ago was fringed in rose bushes of every kind and color. Blessed with a green thumb, Louise could make anything grow. Kelsey thought cynically how all she could do was make everything die. She was nothing like her sister.

Once again the farmhouse was quiet as Louise and Phil went on with their daily routine. Since she was left to herself, Kelsey figured the least she could do was keep up with the housekeeping while Louise worked. This morning's self-assigned chore was laundry. She had stripped the beds of sheets and pillowcases. Kelsey decided to use the clothesline instead of the dryer. Not only did it give her an excuse to go outdoors, but linens always smelled better when dried by the sun. And she needed the sun in her life.

As she pulled the cotton bedding off the line, Kelsey held the last pillowcase against her face. Instantly, the fresh linen fragrance reminded her of Alex. He had always ironed his shirts and he always smelled so clean—so good. Her favorite fragrance in the world was him. She stood swaying in the heat of the summer sun, her eyes closed and her thoughts a couple hundred miles away. So lost in the sweet memory of the man she loved, she could feel his arms around her again. She stood remembering fierce blue eyes that could change to loving in a heartbeat, his breath against her neck in the morning before he headed to the shower, and the way he knew when she needed his arm around her, which was always now that she had time to think about it. Always. Until now.

Enough.

She snapped the sheet, folded it and laid it in the basket. Today's the day. By the time Louise and Phil returned this afternoon, she hoped to have an apartment lined up and maybe a deposit made on it, too. She couldn't stay in this old farmhouse any longer. Her sister drove her crazy with all her helpful suggestions and free advice. Kelsey had already checked with the Oregon state school board. Her credentials were acceptable. She could start teaching in August. Kelsey thought she would teach older kids from now on. Maybe she would get back to a boring life again. Like she did before Nick. Before Alex.

His name came like medicine and poison at the same time, like napalm and a lullaby, love and heartbreak all rolled into one. As much as she craved it, she hated it. The old saying 'love hurts' was the hardest lesson of all, because love hurt like hell. She dashed the foolish tears from her eyes and grabbed the laundry basket. She had to move on.

As she straightened, she saw a man walking up Louise and Phil's gravel driveway, which was very odd. They were so far out in the middle of nowhere. The driveway was more like a road; it was so long and winding. The man's profile looked familiar, but it couldn't be him. Not all the way down here. Harley? As he came closer she was sure of it. Dressed in his usual jeans and western shirt, his worn-out boots kicked up small puffs of dust as he walked. Kelsey set the laundry basket on the porch. He strolled up as casual as if he just happened to be passing through the neighborhood.

"You're certainly a long ways off the beaten trail, little lady," Harley drawled like the cowboy he wasn't.

"It's good to see you." She shielded her eyes from the sun. "What brings you all the way to Pendleton?"

He pushed his black cowboy hat back off his forehead and his sunglasses down over his nose. "Well, ma'am, I'm looking for a pretty little thing named Kelsey. You seen her?"

Kelsey ignored his flirtation and turned for the steps. "Come in. I'll make lemonade."

"Just a minute." Harley let out a shrill whistle. As quick as if they were chasing squirrels back home in Alexandria, Smoke and Whisper bolted up the driveway and full speed toward Kelsey. She knelt on the grass before they bowled her over. With tails thumping and those big mutt bodies wriggling, Whisper and Smoke whined and barked their excitement at seeing her again.

Kelsey grabbed Whisper in an especially tight hug, tears streaming down her face. "I've missed you boys so much."

"Looks like these fellows think they're your dogs," Harley observed quietly.

She wiped her nose. "I've missed them." She couldn't let Whisper go. With his usual German shepherd-speak, he growlingly let her know he enjoyed the extra long hug. When she stood, he stayed at her side while Smoke took a self-guided tour around the flowerbeds, lifting his leg and marking a few rose bushes as he went.

"Whisper and Smoke look good, Harley. I'm glad you brought them with you."

Harley filled a bucket from the garden hose for the dogs. "I reckon you could use a visit from a couple of friends."

Alex

I've ruined everything.

Alex sat thinking on the hospital patio. The orderly had moved him outside to sit in the sun and get some fresh air. Other patients chatted around him, but he didn't join in. He didn't need or want human companionship, but at least the sun felt good. Birds chirped overhead and the summer air felt cool. He knew the calm wouldn't last. Mother was probably looking for him by now. Too soon she would interrupt the quiet. That was Mother's way.

He was healing, able to stand and walk. That was a major accomplishment. Physical therapy helped, and soon he would know if the blindness was permanent. That was the real kick in the gut. He pushed the thought away. Like Murphy said, no need to borrow trouble.

But blind or not, his doctor wouldn't release him until the infection draining from his multiple surgeries cleared up, and that was the problem. Murphy was on their side. He wouldn't help Alex leave without that stupid permission, and he couldn't do it alone. He was his own worst enemy. He knew it.

Jed McCormack, his friend and financial backer, had called earlier just to talk. That was kind. Jed was as solid a friend as Murphy. For some reason Alex knew he would never be able to drive those two men away no matter how ignorant and rude he was. They saw through him like good friends do.

Jed and he had talked about how successful the business had become. In less than a year, Alex had repaid the multi-million dollar loan Jed had advanced him. The TEAM had barely operated in the red at all, and built a solid reputation in the process. By the world's standards Alex had it all, wealth, success, and the right kind of fame. Opportunity had smiled on him. He should be happy.

He wasn't. He knew what real happiness was, and it had nothing to do with success. No. Happiness was a sixty-watt light bulb shining on his front porch and a plate of homemade lasagna waiting in his microwave. It was chocolate-brown eyes that spilled love and light on him the minute he walked through his door at night. He had too much time to think and every thought turned to Kelsey. She hadn't made a single phone call or sent a letter, not that he expected any. He hadn't called her either, but what he wouldn't give to hear her laugh again or feel her light touch on his cheek. Her absence was the worst physical pain. Murphy was right. He was a dumb ass.

The hospital patio door swooshed open behind him, and right on schedule, Mother gushed like he had been missing a year. "So this is where you are. I've been looking all over for you."

He turned away. *She found me.*

"Well, that last contract's written just like you wanted. It's setting on your table, all ready for you to sign when you get back to bed. I put one of them sticky tabs on it so you can feel your way through it. Just be sure you sign right next to that tab, okay?" She pulled up a chair beside him. "Course I'll show you exactly where to sign if you need more help."

The fragrance of her expensive perfume wafted over him like a stifling sauna. He wondered if she bathed in it. Why use a drop when a pint will do? He wanted to move. *Where's that orderly?*

"I sure wish you'd tell me when you go gallivanting around the hospital though. I got better things to do than wander all over this place looking for your ornery butt." She chastised him like he didn't sign her paycheck.

Alex said nothing. Mother took too many liberties. He wished she would respect the line between employer and employee, but also knew why she didn't. Mother was a genius, pure and simple. She didn't need the job as much as he needed her. She knew it, too.

"Merciful heavens, I wish you'd let me do the negotiating the next time the Army comes calling. I'm sure I can get more bang for your buck, pardon the pun." Mother chuckled to herself. "I mean we are talking about covert surveillance and snipers and all, right?"

Alex didn't reply. No need. Mother was a veritable talking machine. All output.

"So what's next, Boss? You need me to run grab you a Starbuck's coffee or anything?"

"No thanks."

"How about a glass of water? You need a drink? You look kinda thirsty sitting out here in the sun like you are."

"No."

"Well, then do you want me to place any calls for you? You know, maybe to Harley or David back at the office? I hear Jed McCormack called this morning. So how'd that go?"

"Fine." He contemplated returning to his room. *Where's the orderly?*

"Come on now, Boss. Let me call someone. Talking with one of your friends is a whole lot better than sitting here feeling sorry for yourself, you know what I mean?"

"I'm fine, Mother."

"Well then, how about I ring up Kelsey's sister? I still got her number from the last time you wanted to talk to her, and—"

"Stop." Alex held up a hand to silence Mother. *If only.*

Her voice kicked into wheedling gear. "At least you could talk with her, Boss, and find out how Kelsey's doing. I mean, if you'd learn to listen sometimes, instead of always—"

"For hell's sake Mother, give it a rest." Alex snapped.

Mother was quiet only as long as it took her to take another breath. She sniffed as if offended, but Alex knew better. Mother was a master manipulator, and all that sniffing was just another tool in her vast arsenal of ways to get what she wanted and around people. "Well, I guess the important thing is *you're* feeling better, never mind how she feels. And just so you know, I'm flying back first thing in the morning. There's no sense in staying where I'm not wanted."

"Good." *Thank God and United Airlines.*

"I knew you'd be saying something rude like that. How long are you staying in the hospital? When are you coming home? Do you know yet?"

"Soon." *So freaking pushy.*

"And when you going to try that walker or that cane? You have to move on you know, you can't just sit in a wheelchair for the rest—"

"Mother. Sasha. Enough." Alex bellowed at the top of his voice. "Enough already."

"Well, I just—"

"This is the first day I've left the room. Give it a rest." He heard her huff and sniff. *Leave me alone.*

She sat drumming her fingertips on the armrest, no doubt as exasperated with him as he was with her. Their problem was always the same. He wanted to know what time it was, and she tended to tell him how to build the clock, how to set it, dust it, and where to put it on the mantle. He kept his personal life private while she was an open book, and an audio book at that. He didn't share, and she continually pried.

"So. Have you talked to Murphy lately?" She wouldn't give up.

"Every day." Alex sighed deeply.

"Well, okay then. I'm going."

It's about time.

Mother rose from the chair and gave him a gentle hug. "I'll stop by in the morning before I leave."

"I'll be here." He rolled his wheelchair backwards into the shade. Instantly, an orderly asked if he was ready to return to his room. Alex nodded in relief.

Twenty-Five

Kelsey

Good ol' Harley.

Kelsey brought a plate of homemade chocolate chip cookies along with the icy drinks to the living room. As she sat down on the couch, he drank a full glass and devoured several cookies. She smiled to see his appetite. Within minutes she refilled his glass and waited for him to talk. Sunburned and windblown, his hazel eyes sparkled from the white mask left by his sunglasses. He snagged another couple cookies.

"Well, you may not know this about me, Kelsey, but I'm a man of few words," he said with his mouth full.

"I don't know much about you at all, Harley, except I owe you my life. You're my friend," she said quietly. "But let's get to the point. Why are you here?"

"I'm on a mission, ma'am." He started again. "It's kind of a mission from God, if you know what I mean."

Kelsey leaned back into the sofa with her arms crossed. "What? Alex send you?"

Harley smirked. "Well, he does think he's God sometimes, doesn't he? But no, he doesn't have a clue I'm even in the country. I had Murphy tell him a story about me being on some operation in Turkey. Anyway, the boss isn't himself right now, so he fell for it." Harley watched from his side of the couch. "Which is really saying something because Alex doesn't fall for much."

Kelsey heard what Harley didn't say. *Not too long ago Alex had fallen for her. Did that make her special? She used to think so.*

"I'd like to think I'm here more as your friend than anything else."

"I'm worn out, Harley. I'm tired." Kelsey brushed a tear off her cheek and looked away. "I've had the year from hell. What do you want?" She had seen the tenderness in his eye, the last thing she needed.

"Okay, so here's the deal." He blurted it right out. "Alex is an idiot."

Leave it to Harley to make her laugh. She felt the quick rise of tears just the same.

"You know, I'd just got out of rehab. I didn't know anything about Alex and you 'til that night," he said quietly.

"You were in rehab all the time you were missing?" Kelsey leaned back into the couch cushions behind her. She would have never have guessed Harley for a rehab kind of a person. He looked like a big kid with his wide-open smile, sun-bleached streaks scattered through his brown hair, and sunglasses perched on the top of his head. Murphy had told her Harley was from up-state New York, but he could pass for a cowboy any day of the week. She wondered how he came to develop that alternate persona.

"Yes, ma'am, I was. I've been kind of a mess since I got home from Iraq. Done a lot of crap I ain't proud of. You know, when you get down so far you can't get up, well that's when you figure all you got left to do is to pull your head out of your ... ah... " He stuttered as he corrected his language. "I mean, then you pull yourself up by your boot straps and do something smart for a change."

She smiled at his bright eyes. It touched her that he tried not to cuss around her. Much. "Was rehab hard?"

"Yes and no. This one was tougher than others I have been in." Harley blew out a big sigh. "You've got to understand something about addicts, Kelsey. We're mean, thoughtless, selfish people. I didn't care who I hurt when I was using. Heck." He looked away, scrubbing a hand over his face before he continued. "My Mom and Dad won't have a thing to do with me anymore. I've put them through hell. I don't blame them."

She let him talk, but it was hard to see the man he had just described. He looked handsome, strong, and healthy sitting there on Louise's couch.

"I'm an addict. I won't lie to you. Right now I'm clean. I don't drink booze either. It's all the same crap, and I don't go near it. Any of it."

"What made you seek help?"

"It's crazy, but..." He scrubbed his face again. "I thought of my boss. Alex believed in me, and I threw his trust back in his face like it was nothing. But I woke up one day and I just didn't want to be me anymore. I wanted to be like him."

"The rehab helped?"

"Nope. Not right away, it didn't. You know, none of them places work unless you really want the help. This time I was lucky. I got a good counselor. Sonny served in Iraq, plus he's a recovering addict. It makes a difference when you're talking with someone who understands what you've been through."

Harley leaned back into the couch; every cookie long gone and his fingers licked clean.

Kelsey saw the honesty behind those boyish eyes. Harley wasn't complicated by a long shot. He just wanted to be in control of his life, to be free from the drugs. He wanted to live.

"I ain't gonna lie to you. That crap's still calling my name. Sometimes, it's all I can do not to go looking for my old friends. That's why I need to work. My job's real important right now."

"You tried to get me to pray that morning, didn't you?"

"Mostly I just wanted to keep you talking. You scared the hell out of me." He shook his head remembering.

"Me, too." Her words were soft. "What happened then?"

"So, anyway..." Harley went on about how he had dropped into his old office hoping he still had a job. He explained how the BOLO from Washington police, the Be on the Look Out warning, had alarmed The TEAM, and how he had taken Whisper and Smoke to Washington state the same afternoon on an Air Force C-130 transport into Joint Base Lewis-McChord. He told her how he had found Alex, but then left him with only a gun and Smoke, because Alex made Harley promise to find her. And lastly, Harley told her how scared he was when he found her, how he thought he had lost two of the most important people in his life.

"Now wait a minute." Kelsey stopped him with a hand to his arm. "You didn't even know me. How could I have been one of the most important people in your life?"

"Simple, Kelsey girl. You're the most important person in the world to him, and that's good enough for me." Harley winked. "That's how it works. I've got his back even when

he's the biggest idiot in the world, and I know he's got mine."
He paused for effect. "And Alex *is* the biggest idiot in the
world."

Harley made her smile. It felt good to talk with someone
who knew Alex.

"The man can't help it, darlin'. He's got this bigger-than-
life persona, this huge idea of how to live and make a
difference. He'll never be a nine-to-five kinda guy. Alex has
too much to give, too many people to save, too much..."
Harley took a deep breath, but Kelsey stopped him again.

"I get it Harley. He's an idiot. I get it."

She bit her lip and turned away before she broke down.
She would go back to Alex right this second, but his last
words still rang like curses in her ears. One thing she knew
for sure, she would not live another life of abuse.

Harley took her hand and wrapped her fingers around a
familiar object. He smiled that crooked smile. "I found this in
one of their jackets that morning."

She gasped. Once again Kelsey held the diamond
solitaire ring she thought she had lost forever. In a flash she
was back beside a crackling fire, looking into hopeful blue
eyes, listening to Alex's voice, husky with emotion. *"Will you
do me the honor of marrying me, Kelsey? Will you become
Mrs. Alexander Stewart?"*

The fire within the stone still sparkled, but so much had
happened since that night. It felt like forever ago. Kelsey
stared into the brilliant rock. She had felt like a lost treasure
in his arms, finally found and cherished, but she also
remembered his crushing last words. *"Get out of my life."*

Harley interrupted her reverie with a gentle hand on her
shoulder. "The thing is, me and Mother been talking since

you left. We think this started when the boss had that last heart attack. You know, Alex might be a tough ex-Marine and all, but I'll bet he thought he was gonna die. He was scared. I think the man just didn't want to put you through the pain of watching him die, too. You've already had more than your share, Kelsey girl."

She blinked back the tears that fell anyway. She had heard the telling single word. *Too.* Tommy, Jackie, and Alex—too. They were all part of the same heartache, the same wretched purgatory, and she had lost them all. Nick had stolen her boys, and Alex had sent her away as if distance between his life and love was a lesser pain. And she had gone. Like a fool she had gone.

Ah. Kelsey knew now she should've screamed her refusal to leave. She should have presented him with other more physical options. She should have told him to shut up and kiss her. Anything. She should have done anything, but leave. It was her choice, too. They were both idiots.

"The doctor's releasing Alex this week, and even that news didn't perk him up none. The man's a mess without you. He knows it. He just ain't smart enough to know how to fix it."

Kelsey knew Alex loved her. Even as she left him, she knew.

"Whatcha thinking, Kelsey girl?" Harley gave her shoulder a gentle squeeze. "Would you ever consider coming back with me and giving my idiot boss a good talking to? I've got a pretty fast truck and two hound dogs ready to travel to the ends of the earth, just for you."

And there it was – the real reason Harley was here. The cookies gone, the question asked, the perfect end to a tragic love story just waiting on her answer. She breathed out a big sigh and studied him again. Harley was an enigma, a highly qualified sniper who had killed men for his country, yet a simple man who had learned to rely on the Lord. It was obvious he idolized Alex, and she knew without a doubt Harley cared for her, too. Here he was again, come all the way to Pendleton, out in the middle of nowhere Oregon, trying to save the two most hopeless people ever.

"You make it sound so easy."

Harley didn't say a word.

"I'm getting my own place in town pretty soon, and then I'm going to start teaching again, and then..."

Harley held his breath.

"And I am so sick of crying." She jumped off the couch, stalked through the kitchen door, turned around, and came right back into the living room.

"I can't do this again!" she ranted. "You come down here like it's no big deal to ask me to go back to him. Back to what? Like I'm a ping-pong ball that just keeps bouncing back for more? Hit me again. Yeah, hit me again. Knock me down, just one more time. Punch me. Beat me. Scream at me. Well, I can't do it anymore, Harley. Do you hear me?"

With that outburst, she marched into the kitchen again only to turn on her heel and march right back to where poor Harley sat dumbfounded on the sofa. With her face drenched in tears, she knew she was making a fool of herself, but she couldn't stop. Her voice grew squeakier and squeakier as the torrent poured out.

"I think I deserve better. I mean, I buried my boys already and that's my fault, because I'm ... I was their mother. I should've protected them. I should've left Nick. I should've run."

Her tears fell like rain. Once more she stomped into the kitchen, so angry she only half knew what she was shouting about. This time she was only gone long enough to grab a dishtowel to mop her face. She came right back, a frenzied tigress taking her anger and frustration out on the only man standing. Poor Harley sat there and took it without batting an eye.

"I thought Alex loved me. For once in my whole stupid, messed up life – I thought I'd met the man of my dreams. I am so dumb." She outright wailed she was so upset and hurt and mad. "It's not like I was at the mall shopping that night. I know what they did to him."

Kelsey gulped back a suffocating sob as that night came back into focus. She stood in the dark again, her heart pounding in terror as Buck dragged Alex through the fire pit and tied him to the tree. The thought of that first cut took her breath away again.

"I was there," she said with sudden, eerie calmness. "I know they c-cut him, and k-kicked him, and he's hurt and..."

She stared. The knowledge of how much she ached to hold Alex stormed her foolish heart. Kelsey could almost feel him in her arms. He needed her. Despite the miles between them, she heard him whisper her name. Somewhere out there he was calling to her. The man was hurt to the point of death only because he had stood between her and danger. All the anger in the world could not deny the continuous cycle of strength and protection he had offered. Her screaming tirade ended with a sad whisper.

"I'm hurt, too. I've had enough."

This time when she went to the kitchen, she slammed the door behind her. The silence in the house was as deafening as her outburst. She leaned against the kitchen sink with the towel pressed hard against her face and sobbed. Somewhere in the world there had to be a safe place she could curl up and die. There had to be.

The kitchen door opened quietly, and she felt Harley snake an arm around her waist. She leaned into him with a shudder. "I'm sorry. I'm not mad at you. I shouldn't have said those awful things. I'm sorry."

"No, you're right. It's okay," he murmured. "You deserve better than Alex. You're too good for him. Anyone can see that."

She dropped the towel into the sink and stared out the window. "I don't have anything left to give."

"It's okay, darlin'." Harley gave her another squeeze as the storm subsided. "Murphy told me a story about Alex in the first Gulf War. You wanna hear it?"

Kelsey sighed. Harley seemed able to talk at the drop of a hat. She didn't know if she wanted to hear anymore.

"Anyway, Alex and his squad were working through one of them crowded Baghdad neighborhoods. Saddam was on the loose, and lots of insurgents were still active throughout the city." He paused to catch his breath. His hand felt strong and sure on her waist. For a moment, she relaxed into his shoulder and just listened. As angry as she was with Alex, her foolish heart craved to hear any story about him.

"Alex and another soldier got pinned down. The other guy was hurt pretty bad, so they hunkered down for a couple hours waiting for a medic. But you know how Alex is." He squeezed her tight. "He got sick and tired of waiting, and came out shooting like a madman. There were five of them insurgents, and all of a sudden, this maniac charges right up to them, guns blazing and screaming. I'd have given anything to have seen their faces. I think he just shocked the hell out of them guys. Alex killed all five of 'em. Never got a scratch. He saved the kid with him, too. I think his name was McCormack or something, but that's Alex for you."

His hand had moved to her shoulder where he massaged a small circle of comfort. She was glad he was there. He had just described Alex to a T. The man was always fierce, angry, but always saving someone. Even her.

"Yes, sir, he can be one mean sonofabitch, darlin', but I'll bet he thinks that's his one good quality. Don't ya think?"

Kelsey nodded, her thoughts still lost somewhere far away. "He's so serious. There's never enough time in the day. Work. Work. Work. That's all he knows how to do."

Her voice faded as another picture materialized in her mind. She could see Alex clearly at his kitchen table. He had made coffee, listened to her, and wiped her nose. Piercing blue eyes asked her once again, *"What is it you want, Kelsey?"*

Her heart cried out, "You. I want you."

"That's how he keeps one step ahead of remembering, darlin'. He's got a boatload of crap in his head he's still trying to forget. Kinda like me." Harley pulled her close. "Guess it comes with the job. You don't train a man to be a killer and end up with a regular guy now, do ya?"

"But he's not a killer. He's kind and thoughtful, he builds cradles every year for the kids at the cancer ward." She turned to face Harley. "Did you know that?"

"No, ma'am. I sure didn't."

"Everything he does is so important. I mean, it's not like he can just take a couple hours off work, you know. I've been to his office. He's important and his work's important, too."

"No, darlin', his job isn't like most jobs, that's for sure."

She shook the image of Alex from her mind. Why was she defending him? She stared out the window as the puzzle that was Alex confounded her all over again. The field of alfalfa beyond the manicured lawn rippled as a summer breeze carved its way over and through the purpling flowers, but all she could see was – him. He was hurt, and she had left him.

"Hey, listen. I was out of line showing up like I did." Harley gave her a final squeeze and stepped away. "I had no business asking you to go back to Alex. Me and the boys will just head back home and mind our own business like we should have done in the first place."

He whistled to the dogs, but her hand on his arm brought him right back around.

"Wait."

He turned to face her. "Whatcha need, darlin'?"

She clenched the edge of the sink. "I don't know. I do, but I don't. It's just that..."

Harley waited.

"It's just that I'm the stupidest woman on the face of the earth and..." The tears started again. "I love him."

"He loves you, too, Kelsey girl. I've seen it with my own eyes."

"Oh, hell, Harley. Hell. Hell. Hell." She stomped her foot with every cuss word.

He kept grinning.

"I don't know what to do."

"How about I hold him? You smack him?" He arched a devilish brow. "I could find you a big ol' two-by-four."

"That's actually a good idea." Kelsey smiled through her tears.

Harley grasped her shoulders and wiped her face gently with the kitchen towel. "Listen, darlin'." He tipped her chin up so she had to look at him. "I think you already know what you need to do. Trust yourself for a change. Don't stay with Alex if you know you shouldn't. Yeah, he isn't the easiest guy to live with, but you gotta trust him, too. He's packing a heap of grief all by himself, but one thing's for sure. He loves you. Anyone can see that." He tucked his hand under her chin. "Sounds to me like he's the one who needs a little saving this time around, doesn't he?"

A splash of summer breeze whipped past the kitchen curtain. For a moment, it swirled with cool respite around the two friends. Harley kissed her forehead with a heavy sigh. "Ya know, we keep meeting like this, and I'm gonna ask you to marry me. I'm not the brightest guy around, but I'm not as dumb as Alex. I could give that old man a run for his money."

He said it so seriously, Kelsey couldn't help but smile. If it had been anyone else, she had have felt awkward and shy, but Harley was her friend. With another squeeze, they walked back to the living room, her hand securely fastened over his arm.

"I never for one single minute thought you was a ping pong ball, darlin'." His phony Texas drawl was back in full force. "And you're a regular little Suzy homemaker. Why, you make the best chocolate chip cookies I ever tasted."

"Louise made them."

"What?" The Texas drawl disappeared along with the smirky smile. He held her at arm's length. "You mean you didn't make all those cookies I just ate?"

"You mean inhaled?" She watched the comic disbelief on his face. This guy had a definite knack for putting her at ease. "And no, I didn't make them. Louise has been trying to fatten me up since I got here. She made them."

"Come to think of it, they weren't so good. Arghhh." He choked like he was coughing up a hairball, and she smiled even more. He grinned. "I do love you, Kelsey girl. I do."

"And I'll always love you." She patted his arm affectionately. She knew what kind of love Harley meant. In the process of rescuing her, he had become the brother she never had.

"Then what say me and the dogs get you back to that dumb-assed boss of mine?"

"Yes. I do want to go back to Alex."

He stood at the door while she wrote a quick note to Louise and grabbed her purse. Leaving wasn't complicated. Louise and Phil would understand.

"Now you're sure you really want to go back to Alex?" he asked in his very best Texas twang. "I mean you've still got a pretty good offer on the table, little lady, even if I do say so myself."

"What? You or the cookies?"

"Well, I was kinda thinking both?"

Her arched brow must've told him everything.

"Okay. Okay. I'm getting the truck."

Twenty-Six

Alex

"Well, today's the big day." Dr. Jax clapped Alex gently on the shoulder. "Are you ready, young man?"

"Yeah. Ready."

Mother had cancelled her flight and was still in town. Supposedly she was excited for the bandages to come off. Alex didn't know why it was such a big deal. If blind, he would have to learn to deal with it. If his sight was restored, he would get back to work. It was a no brainer, but as usual, Mother fussed over everything. Alex wished she had gone back to Virginia. He didn't need the drama.

"Okay then, here we go." Dr. Jax snipped the tape and unwrapped the first layers of gauze. "I have the lights dimmed so you may not see much at first. Sometimes it takes a few minutes, maybe a few hours. Just take your time. Be patient." He pulled the last of the gauze away. "My nurse will remove the cotton packing and wash your eyes with a saline solution. It shouldn't hurt, but let me know if you feel anything painful."

"I don't know about you gentlemen, but I've sure got my fingers crossed," Mother gushed with her usual over-the-top excitement. "It'll be so good to get you back to normal, won't it, Boss?"

Alex didn't respond. He sat on the edge of the bed as the nurse pulled the cotton packing off both eyes, applied a cleansing ointment and wiped his face and eyes. Her touch was so light he didn't see how she could be cleaning anything. As his impatience escalated, he wanted to take the cloth and do it himself. The nurse dabbed more of the cleanser around his eyes with sterile cotton pads and then, just like the first time, she wiped the top and bottom of each eyelid as well as brows and cheeks with measured slowness. Alex had to admit, it did feel good to get the bandage off, and the skin beneath it cleaned. It had been too many weeks since he had felt fresh air on his face, but the nurse moved so slowly. She seemed nervous and timid. The simple process was taking forever.

With great gentleness, she tipped his head back, and filled each eye with a squirt of cool saline solution. Alex felt her soft breath on his cheek. At least she was quiet, but her silence was just as annoying as Mother's incessant chatter. Again, the sensation of cleansing was a welcome relief to eyes that had been sealed tight for weeks. Alex thought about all the complications from the brain swelling, the induced coma, the shunt, the removal of part of his skull, as well as the temporary blindness. He knew he was lucky to be alive. He should be happy.

I'm lucky all right—a stupid, lucky man.

One thought played relentlessly behind the others. *Kelsey.* He would be a lot happier if he didn't dread the moment he opened his eyes. Sight would confirm she was gone. Cynically, he thought blindness was all he deserved. Maybe that was his reward from karma, blindness in exchange for his cruelty to the woman karma had blessed him with. Kelsey had always believed their paths converged in that forest through an act of divine intervention, but he had hurled the blessing of her sweet love back into the face of God in a moment of despair and self-pity. He remembered the selfish thoughts he had when he had first found her at his cabin. For a smart man, he hadn't learned much since then.

I deserve to be blind.

The nurse's final act of drying his face brought him out of his reverie. She patted the soft cotton cloth against his nose and stepped away.

"Slowly open your eyes," Dr. Jax directed.

"I can hardly stand it. It's almost like Christmas, isn't it, Boss?" Mother clapped her hands like a little girl, an annoying little girl.

Alex didn't respond. He would have preferred sharing this moment with Kelsey, but it was Mother here instead. The dynamics of karma struck him. Mother was all he deserved. Not Kelsey. He cast his negative thoughts aside, and did as he was instructed, squinting as the light pierced his healing retinas. As dim as it was, it still felt like a laser pinging off the back of his skull.

"I'm seeing some light, but a lot of shadows, too." Alex peered through bleary eyes, the room full of more darkness than light. "A lot of shadows."

"Good, real good." Dr. Jax tipped Alex's head back and examined both eyes further.

"Man, that's bright," Alex complained, his eyes watering under the doctor's bright scope.

Dr. Jax continued his cursory exam. "Hmm. I like what I'm seeing and what I'm not seeing. We'll do a complete exam later, but for now, I'm satisfied with your progress. I'm confident your vision will be nearly one hundred percent restored."

"What's nearly supposed to mean?" Alex asked, his voice instantly edgy. Nearly one hundred percent was never an acceptable margin.

"You might still need a little more work, Alex. Nothing too serious considering how bad this could've gone. You must live a charmed life." Dr. Jax stepped back to look Alex in the eye. "So tell me, how does it feel to see again?"

"It'd help if there was a little more light in this room," Alex said sarcastically. Everything was veiled behind a murky curtain. He couldn't see Mother, which was fine, but the annoying nurse stood too close, still waiting for what he didn't know.

"This is good progress. I'm pleased. We'll talk about that procedure later if you'd like." Dr. Jax offered his hand. "Congratulations, young man. This is a lot like bringing old Lazarus back from the grave. Shall we call it a day and get some fresh bandages back on those eyes?"

The nurse reached for the instrument tray, but Alex wasn't having any of it. With a curse on his tongue, and his hand clamped on her slender wrist, he turned to Dr. Jax. "There's no sonofabitchin way I'm—"

Alex gasped. A burst of recognition flashed behind those tired blues. His head jerked back to the nurse. It happened so fast. He exploded off the bed and tackled her. She yelped. He misjudged the distance, but caught her roughly in his arms. The instrument tray clattered to the floor, but that sound was nothing compared to the groan from Alex.

"Kelsey?"

He didn't wait for an answer. He knew. Pulling her into his arms, he covered her mouth with his. With her slender body bent backwards over the counter, he kissed her harder than he had ever kissed her before. "You're here. I can't believe it. You're here. I'm sorry. Kelsey, I'm sorry." Tears flooded his eyes until he couldn't see anymore. "I'm so sorry."

He kissed her again, trying to pour all his love back into her as if he could make up for the pain he had caused. Choked with emotion, his hands searched her body for any sign of disgust or rejection. There was none. She arched into him as if she had never left. They clung together, sweet murmurs mixed with tears. At last, Alex pulled her onto the hospital bed and planted her firmly on his lap, his hands smoothing over her face and neck to prove she was here, that she had returned, that she really loved him.

"I see you kinda like my nurse," Dr. Jax said gently.

Alex wiped his face with the back of his hand, trying unsuccessfully to contain his emotions. Someone shoved a couple of tissues at him. It was Mother, who for once didn't say a word. Shading his eyes, he could just barely discern a familiar, tall, gangly figure leaning against the door. "Harley? Is that you?"

"How you doing, Boss?" It looked like Harley had the widest Cheshire cat smile plastered all over his face. He gave Kelsey the thumbs up sign and winked. "Looks like you two need a room. Oh, wait. This is your room."

"How's Turkey?" Alex asked between kisses to the side of Kelsey's head. He had what he wanted in his hands. It was time for everyone to leave.

"Don't know, but Pendleton's not too bad," Harley said. "You oughta try it sometime."

Alex buried his face in Kelsey's short-cropped hair instead of responding. Ah, just the scent of her filled his soul with hope he didn't deserve. She sat snuggled under his chin with one hand clasped tight in his like a lifeline, like she had never left at all, like he had never said those mean words in the first place.

"I love you," he whispered. He couldn't keep his eyes or hands off her. She felt so good, so soft and warm and—

"Ahem," Murphy coughed from the back of the dimly-lit room. That gentle reminder brought Alex back to the friends in his hospital room.

"Murphy?" Alex squinted into the shadows. "Is that Roy with you?"

"We're here," Roy drawled, his voice extra soft. "We've been waiting for this day."

Alex strained to separate his friends from shadows. Along with Harley and Mother, he could vaguely discern Murphy and Roy. Dr. Jax had already excused himself.

"Doesn't anyone work anymore?" Alex meant it to sound serious, but everyone laughed. He didn't care. The last thing on his mind was business. He buried his face against Kelsey again, hoping to hide his emotions.

"We're going to get breakfast to give you kids some time to yourselves," Murphy said. "Then we'll discuss all those young fellows you hired for the Seattle office, Alex, and—"

Alex held his hand up to silence his friend. "Get out of here."

Kelsey

The door closed quietly. Kelsey and Alex were left alone, and she had never felt happier. He pulled her with him back onto the bed.

"They hurt you," he declared angrily.

"They hurt you, too," she whispered.

He smothered her in his arms, one hand at the back of her head as he held her tight with his other. Sobs wrangled their way out of him in wretched gasps he fought to hide. Feeling his torment shudder through him, she couldn't bear one more moment of it.

"Alex?"

His only reply was to squeeze her tighter. She rested under his chin and against his proud heart. Even now it thumped much too fast for its own good, but for the first time in weeks, she felt at peace. This was all she had ever wanted. Closing her eyes, Kelsey absorbed the familiar sensation of his strength around her, the smell of him, the solid weight of his hands, and the strong emotions that tortured him. She knew it now. Alex would always be tortured simply because he did it to himself, and it was okay. He was a man of passion. He loved his country enough to die for it, but at the same time, he loved her enough to show her how to live.

"Do you want to know what I think?" She felt him nod. Kelsey smiled. Here he lay, the strongest man in her world, arrogant and tough when he needed to be, proclaimed by the business world as one of the top entrepreneurs of the year, and he wouldn't let her see him cry. "I'm happiest when I'm with you."

"Well I'm a helluva better man when I'm with you," he muttered hoarsely, wiping his face and quickly securing her in his arms again.

Kelsey let him. She hadn't returned to toss an ultimatum in his face. Neither did she come back to make demands or exact harsh expectations in exchange for his repentance. No. The moment he had recognized her, she had what she wanted. He was where she belonged. He was her safe place. Alex could build her a castle, or they could live in a trailer park; it was all the same to her. As long as they were together her life was complete.

"Do you know what else I think?"

His hand smoothed over her head, feeling through the short-cropped hair that she'd had trimmed extremely short in an attempt to look halfway normal. He shuddered when he fingered one of the scars, and she knew how deep his rage went, but she also knew he was as angry with himself as he was with the men who had done this to her. Again he didn't answer.

"The next time you tell me to leave. This will be my answer."

Kelsey moved to his chin, nibbling as she scooted up against him, and continued the gentle assault on his jaw and cheek until she ended at his mouth. He cupped her face between his hands, and kissed her as tenderly as he had never done before. Her breath caught. As his kiss deepened, she offered herself all over again. His hands skimmed gently over her shoulders and down her back until they came to rest possessively on her backside. His mouth and tongue became more demanding, and once again, she knew she would do whatever he asked, even here in his hospital bed. Right now.

"I've missed you," he murmured hotly against her lips, removing his hands from her backside only to wrap them around her ribs in a vise-like grip.

"You've helped me so much," she whispered.

"I've hurt you so much," he protested.

"But you love me so much," she countered, and again he nodded.

"I do," he said sorrowfully.

They lay side by side where he could no longer hide his emotion. She smoothed her thumb across his cheek to wipe that moisture away.

"I don't know why I ever thought you should leave. I'm the dumbest ass in the world."

"I shouldn't have left. I knew you loved me." She sighed. "When I'm with you, I feel beautiful and smart and—"

"You are beautiful and smart. You can do anything. You've proven it so many times." His eyes searched hers so piercingly that she thought again how he must be able to see into her soul. "You're the strong one. Not me. I've done so many things—"

"I've made mistakes, too," she gulped. "Mistakes I have to live with the rest of my life."

"No! You had no more choice than Jackie and Tommy!"

She stilled, wanting so much to believe his vehement declaration.

"Your only mistake was believing in a man who didn't deserve you." His voice caught. "I don't want you to make that mistake again because—I don't deserve you either."

Her heart melted. This kind, warm, wonderful man thought he was less than her? There was no way. Finally, he relaxed. His anger dissipated. They lay wrapped in each other's arms, and Kelsey knew there was no better place for either of them.

"Do you remember the first time we made love?" she asked.

He grunted like that was a silly question.

She smiled at his response. There was no way she could forget those wonderful days either. It was the honeymoon that wouldn't end. "Remember the evening it rained? You built a fire in the fireplace, and I was kneeling in front of the hearth. Do you remember?"

"And I covered you with a blanket –"

"Yes, but you only covered the front of me—"

"Because I had serious intentions for the back of you—"

She giggled softly. "Yes, and you kissed my neck and—"

"And then I kissed your shoulders—"

"And my back—"

"And your bottom."

She giggled softly. "Why did you do that?"

He blew out a big sigh. "Because I was making new memories on every part of you I could reach." He cupped her chin with his fingers, and she hoped he really could read her mind. "Do you need me to do that again, sweetheart?" he asked tenderly.

She nodded, too full of emotion to speak.

Leaning his forehead into hers, he softly assured her, "Look at us. Our heads are shaved, we're dented up pretty bad, and one of us might need bodywork. I know it's going to take awhile getting back to who we used to be, but I have to know. Would you still marry me?"

She lifted her left hand to his view. The diamond glowed brightly between them. "I've already given you my answer."

His smile lit up her eyes. Kissing her long and hard, once again she knew she would willingly submit to anything this handsome man had in mind. Anytime. Anywhere. Even now his hands prowled knowingly over her body, igniting her needs along with his. He owned her heart, body, and anything else he wanted to own. She was his.

Alex came to his senses with an aggravated sigh. "I want to go home. Tonight. I just want to go home."

She sighed happily. "I already am."

Epilogue

Alex

Alex and Kelsey stood at the Stewart family gravesite. It was a restful setting now, not colored with sorrow and loss so much as with acceptance and even a small measure of joy. The sprays of carnations and baby's breath filled the air with the fragrance of clove and cinnamon. He re-positioned the flower baskets one more time beneath the bronze statue and the engraved words of one of Kelsey's favorite authors.

The little bronze girl was exactly the way he remembered Abby in his dreams, the happy princess who loved to roughhouse and play. He could almost hear her giggle, the wind tossing her hair as she ran. A bronze butterfly sat on her shoulder. Now she chased after two bronze boys, their hair jostled, their faces split with wide smiles as they ran hand in hand, two little brothers in eternal mischief. At last Tommy and Jackie played in peace beneath the pines, within walking distance of the home where their fingerprints once more declared their childhood and their mother's undying love.

"This was a good idea, Mr. Stewart." Kelsey rested her head on Alex's broad shoulder. The re-interment of her sons to Alexandria had eased the tremendous hole in her heart. His, too. It was a small thing to do for the woman he loved. Sometimes he felt like George Bailey in the old-time movie,

It's a Wonderful Life. He would willingly lasso the moon if it made her smile.

"I believe you're right, Mrs. Stewart," he whispered into her hair, his arms securely around her.

After all these months, he agreed. It wasn't coincidence that had deposited her at his cabin all those months ago. No. The forest was too big, his cabin much too small for a coincidence of that magnitude. Neither was it coincidence the same woman he'd found and begrudgingly helped had loved him unconditionally and in spite of himself.

Something greater than luck was at work that day. And as far as him being the hero, yeah right. He knew better. He might have found Kelsey that day in the forest, but she was the one who had saved him.

And that was enough.

THE END

Thank you for reading Alex!

Be sure to check out the rest of the guys and gals of Irish Winters' series: *In the Company of Snipers*

Other Irish Winters' books:

King of Hearts, Deuces Wild Series, *#1*
Joker Joker, Deuces Wild Series, *#2*
Smoke, Hearts and Ashes Series, *#1*
Ash, Hearts and Ashes Series, *#2*

Coming soon!

Seth, In the Company of Snipers, #17
One-Eyed Jack, Deuces Wild Series, #3

YOU are the key to this book's success!

Please tell other readers why you liked Alex and Kelsey's story by leaving an honest review at the retail site where you purchased it. Recommend it to your friends. Lend it. Most of all, enjoy it!

The best way to keep up with my new releases, giveaways, and actionable intel is to sign up for my spam-free newsletter at IrishWinters.com.

About the Author

Irish Winters is an award winning, Amazon best-selling author who, when she isn't writing, dabbles in poetry, grandchildren, and rarely (as in extremely rarely) the kitchen. More prone to be outdoors than in, she grew up the quintessential tomboy on a dairy farm in rural Wisconsin, spent her teenage years in the Pacific Northwest, but calls the Wasatch Mountains of Northern Utah home. For now.

She believes in making every day count for something, and follows the wise admonition of her mother to, "Look out the window and see something!"

Connect with Irish!
On Facebook: https://www.facebook.com/author.irishwinters
On Twitter: https://twitter.com/irishwinters1
Or at www. IrishWinters.com

Lightning Source UK Ltd.
Milton Keynes UK
UKHW010654310321
381306UK00002B/295